Praise for Gene Wolfe and *The Urth of the New Sun*

"In this book as in the four preceding volumes, Wolfe is waging guerrilla warfare on appearances and challenging established conventions of narration. Wolfe does not so much answer questions raised previously as rephrase them by depicting them in four dimensions."

—American Book Review

"Another brilliantly inventive, dense, demanding, at times intellectually stunning effort."

—Kirkus Reviews

"This is another extraordinary Wolfe novel, in which his language and imagery reach back to the roots of modern fantasy, to Poe, to myths and Bible stories."

—Publishers Weekly

"If this book is less brilliant than its predecessor, the flaw is one that is hard to spot with the unaided eye."

—The Times (London)

"Wolfe's offbeat sense of humor and grotesque inventiveness enliven *The Urth of the New Sun* like monsters capering in the margins of a medieval manuscript."

—Locus

By Gene Wolfe from Tom Doherty Associates

Novels
The Fifth Head of Cerberus
The Devil in a Forest
Peace
Free Live Free
The Urth of the New Sun
Soldier of the Mist
Soldier of Arete
There Are Doors
Castleview
Pandora by Holly Hollander

Novellas
The Death of Doctor Island
Seven American Nights

Collections
Endangered Species
Storeys from the Old Hotel
Castle of Days
*The Island of Doctor Death and
Other Stories and
Other Stories*

The Book of the New Sun
Shadow and Claw
(comprising *The Shadow of the Torturer* and
The Claw of the Conciliator)
Sword and Citadel
(comprising *The Sword of the Lictor* and
The Citadel of the Autarch)

The Book of the Long Sun
Nightside the Long Sun
Lake of the Long Sun
Caldé of the Long Sun
Exodus from the Long Sun

Gene Wolfe

The Urth of the New Sun

A Tom Doherty Associates Book
New York

THE URTH OF THE NEW SUN

This book was originally published as a Tor hardcover in November
1987.

An Orb Edition
Published by Tom Doherty Associates, Inc.
175 Fifth Avenue
New York, NY 10010

Tor Books on the World Wide Web:
http://www.tor.com

Library of Congress Cataloging-in-Publication Data

Wolfe, Gene.
    The Urth of the new sun / Gene Wolfe.
      p. cm.
    "A Tom Doherty Associates book."
    ISBN 978-0-312-86394-4
    I. Title.
    PS3573.052U78   1997
    813'.54—dc21   97-22177
                               CIP

40 39 38 37 36 35 34 33

This book is dedicated to
Elliott and Barbara,
who know why.

Awake! for Morning in the Bowl of Night
Has flung the Stone that puts the Stars to Flight:
And Lo! the Hunter of the East has caught
The Sultan's Turret in a Noose of Light.

—FITZGERALD

The Urth of the New Sun

CHAPTER I

The Mainmast

HAVING CAST ONE MANUSCRIPT INTO THE SEAS OF TIME, I now begin again. Surely it is absurd; but I am not—I will not be—so absurd myself as to suppose that this will ever find a reader, even in me. Let me describe then, to no one and nothing, just who I am and what it is that I have done to Urth.

My true name is Severian. By my friends, of whom there were never very many, I was called Severian the Lame. By my soldiers, of whom I once commanded a great many, though never enough, Severian the Great. By my foes, who bred like flies, and like flies were spawned from the corpses that strewed my battlefields, Severian the Torturer. I was the last Autarch of our Commonwealth, and as such the only legitimate ruler of this world when we called it Urth.

But what a disease this writing business is! A few years ago (if time retains any meaning), I wrote in my cabin on the ship of Tzadkiel, re-creating from memory the book I had composed in a clerestory of the House Absolute. Sat driving my pen like any clerk, recopying a text I could without difficulty bring to mind, and feeling that I performed the final meaningful act—or rather, the final meaningless act—of my life.

So I wrote and slept, and rose to write again, ink flying across my paper, relived at last the moment at which I entered poor Valeria's tower and heard it and all the rest speak to me, felt the proud burden of manhood dropped upon my shoulders, and knew I was a youth no more. That

1

was ten years past, I thought. Ten years had gone by when I wrote of it in the House Absolute. Now the time is perhaps a century or more. Who can say?

I had brought aboard a narrow coffer of lead with a close-fitting lid. My manuscript filled it, as I knew it would. I closed the lid and locked it, adjusted my pistol to its lowest setting, and fused lid and coffer into a single mass with the beam.

To go on deck, one passes through strange gangways, often filled by an echoing voice that, though it cannot be distinctly heard, can always be understood. When one reaches a hatch, one must put on a cloak of air, an invisible atmosphere of one's own held by what appears to be no more than a shining necklace of linked cylinders. There is a hood of air for the head, gloves of air for the hands (these grow thin, however, when one grasps something, and the cold seeps in), boots of air, and so forth.

These ships that sail between the suns are not like the ships of Urth. In place of deck and hull, there is deck after deck, so that one goes over the railing of one and finds oneself walking on the next. The decks are of wood, which resists the deadly cold as metal will not; but metal and stone underlie them.

Masts sprout from every deck, a hundred times taller than the Flag Keep of the Citadel. Every part appears straight, yet when one looks along their length, which is like looking down some weary road that runs beyond the horizon, one sees that it bends ever so slightly, bowing to the wind from the suns.

There are masts beyond counting; every mast carries a thousand spars, and every spar spreads a sail of fuligin and silver. These fill the sky, so that if a man on deck desires to see the distant suns' blaze of citron, white, violet, and rose, he must labor to catch a glimpse of them between the sails, just as he might labor to glimpse them among the clouds of an autumn night.

As I was told by the steward, it sometimes happens that a sailor aloft will lose his hold. When that occurs on Urth, the unfortunate man generally strikes the deck and dies.

Here there is no such risk. Though the ship is so mighty, and filled with such treasures, and though we are so much nearer her center than those who walk upon Urth are to the center of Urth, yet her attraction is but slight. The careless sailor drifts among the shrouds and sails like thistledown, most injured by the derision of his workmates, whose voices, however, he cannot hear. (For the void hushes every voice except to the speaker himself, unless two come so near that their investitures of air become a single atmosphere.) And I have heard it said that if it were not thus, the roaring of the suns would deafen the universe.

Of all this I knew little when I went on deck. I had been told that I would have to wear a necklace, and that the hatches were so constructed that the inner must be shut before the outer can be opened—but hardly more. Imagine my surprise, then, when I stepped out, the leaden coffer beneath my arm.

Above me rose the black masts and their silver sails, tier upon tier, until it seemed they must push aside the very stars. The rigging might have been cobweb, were the spider as large as the ship—and the ship was larger than many an isle that boasts a hall and an armiger in it who thinks himself almost a monarch. The deck itself was extensive as a plain; merely to set foot on it required all my courage.

When I sat writing in my cabin, I had scarcely been aware that my weight had been reduced by seven-eighths. Now I seemed to myself like a ghost, or rather a man of paper, a fit husband for the paper women I had colored and paraded as a child. The force of the wind from the suns is less than the lightest zephyr of Urth; yet slight though it was, I felt it and feared I might be blown away. I seemed almost to float above the deck rather than to walk on it; and I know that it is so, because the power of the necklace kept outsoles of air between the planks and the soles of my boots.

I looked around for some sailor who might advise me of the best way to climb, thinking that the decks would hold many, as the decks of our ships did on Urth. There was no one; to keep their cloaks of air from growing foul, all hands remain below save when they are needed aloft, which is but seldom. Knowing no better, I called aloud. There was, of course, no answer.

A mast stood a few chains off, but as soon as I saw it I knew I had no hope of climbing it; it was thicker through than any tree that ever graced our forests, and as smooth as metal. I began to walk, fearing a hundred things that would never harm me and utterly ignorant of the real risks I ran.

The great decks are flat, so that a sailor on one part can signal to his mate some distance away; if they were curved, with surfaces everywhere equally distant from the hunger of the ship, separated hands would be concealed from each other's sight, as ships were hidden from one another under the horizons of Urth. But because they are flat, they seem always to slant, unless one stands at the center. Thus I felt, light though I was, that I climbed a ghostly hill.

Climb it I did for the space of many breaths, perhaps for half a watch. The silence seemed to crush my spirit, a hush more palpable than the ship. I heard the faint taps of my own uneven footfalls on the planks and occasionally a stirring or humming from beneath my feet. Other than these faint sounds, there was nothing. Ever since I sat under Master Malrubius's instruction as a child, I have known that the space between the suns is far from empty; many hundreds and perhaps many thousands of voyages are made there. As I learned later, there are other things too—the undine I twice encountered had told me that she sometimes swam the void, and the winged being I had glimpsed in Father Inire's book flew there.

Now I learned what I had never really known before: that all these ships and great beings are only a single handful of seed scattered over a desert, which remains when the sowing is done as empty as ever. I would have turned and limped back to my cabin, if I had not realized that when I reached it my pride would force me out again.

At last I approached the faint descending gossamers of the rigging, cables that sometimes caught the starlight, sometimes vanished in the darkness or against the towering bank of silver that was the top-hamper of the deck beyond. Small though they appeared, each cable was thicker than the great columns of our cathedral.

I had worn a cloak of wool as well as my cloak of air; now I knotted the hem about my waist, making a sort of bag or pack into which I put the coffer. Gathering all my strength into my good leg, I leaped.

Because I felt my whole being but a tissue of feathers, I had supposed I would rise slowly, floating upward as I had been told sailors floated in the rigging. It was not so. I leaped as swiftly and perhaps more swiftly than anyone here on Ushas, but I did not slow, as such a leaper begins to slow almost at once. The first speed of my leap endured unabated—up and up I shot, and the feeling was wonderful and terrifying.

Soon the terror grew because I could not hold myself as I wished; my feet lifted of their own accord until I leaped half sidewise, and at last spun through the emptiness like a sword tossed aloft in the moment of victory.

A shining cable flashed by, just outside my reach. I heard a strangled cry, and only afterward realized it had come from my own throat. A second cable shone ahead. Whether I willed it or not, I rushed at it as I might have rushed upon an enemy, caught it, and held it, though the effort nearly wrenched my arms out of their sockets, and the leaden coffer—which shot past my head—almost strangled me with my own cloak. Clamping my legs around the icy cable, I managed to catch my breath.

Many alouattes roamed the gardens of the House Absolute, and because the lower servants (ditchers, porters, and the like) occasionally trapped them for the pot, they were wary of men. I often watched and envied them as they ran up some trunk without falling—and, indeed, seemingly without knowledge of the aching hunger of Urth at all. Now I had myself become such an animal. The faintest tug from the ship told me that downward lay toward the spreading deck, but it was less than the memory of a memory: once, perhaps, I had fallen, somehow. I recalled recollecting that fall.

But the cable was a sort of pampas trail; to go up it was

as easy as to go down, and both were easy indeed. Its many
strands provided me with a thousand holds, and I scrambled up like a long-haunched little beast, a hare bounding
along a log.

Soon the cable reached a spar, the yard holding the lower
main topsail. I sprang from it to another, slimmer, cable;
and from it to a third. When I mounted to the spar that
held it, I found I was mounting no longer; the whisper of
down was silent, and the grayish-brown hull of the ship
simply drifted, somewhere near the limit of my vision.

Beyond my head, bank after bank of silver sails rose still,
apparently as endless as before I had mounted into the
rigging. To right and left, the masts of other decks diverged
like the tines of a birding arrow—or rather, like row upon
row of such arrows, for there were still more masts behind
those nearest me, masts separated by tens of leagues at
least. Like the fingers of the Increate they pointed to the
ends of the universe, their topmost starsails no more than
flecks of gleaming tinsel lost among the glittering stars.
From such a place I might have cast the coffer (as I had
thought to do) into the waste, to be found, perhaps, by
someone of another race, if the Increate willed it.

Two things restrained me, the first less a thought than a
memory, the memory of my first resolve, made when I
wrote and all speculations about the ships of the Hierodules were new to me, to wait until our vessel had
penetrated the fabric of time. I had already entrusted the
initial manuscript of my account to Master Ultan's library,
where it would endure no longer than our Urth herself.

This copy I had (at first) intended for another creation;
so that even if I failed the great trial that lay before me, I
would have succeeded in sending a part of our world—no
matter how trifling a part—beyond the pales of the universe.

Now I looked at the stars, at suns so remote that their
circling planets were invisible, though some might be
larger than Serenus; and at whole swirls of stars so remote
that their teeming billions appeared to be a single star. And
I marveled to recall that all this had seemed too small for

my ambition, and wondered whether it had grown (though the mystes declare it no longer grows) or I had.

The second was not truly of thought either, perhaps; only instinct and an overmastering desire: I wanted to mount to the top. To defend my resolution, I might say that I knew no such opportunity might come again, that it scarcely accorded with my office to settle for less than common seamen achieved whenever their duties demanded it, and so on.

All these would be rationalizations—the thing itself was glorious. For years I had known joy in nothing but victories, and now I felt myself a boy again. When I had wished to climb the Great Keep, it had never occurred to me that the Great Keep itself might wish to climb the sky; I knew better now. But this ship at least was climbing beyond the sky, and I wanted to climb with her.

The higher I mounted, the easier and the more dangerous my climb became. No fraction of weight remained to me. Again and again I leaped, caught some sheet or halyard, scrambled until I had my feet on it, and leaped once more.

After a dozen such ascents, it struck me that there was no reason to stop until I reached the highest point on the mast—that one jump would take me there, if only I did not prevent it. Then I rose like a Midsummer's Eve rocket; I could readily have imagined that I whistled as they did or trailed a plume of red and blue sparks.

Sails and cables flew past in an infinite procession. Once I seemed to see, suspended (as it appeared) in the space between two sails, an indistinct golden shape veined with crimson; insofar as I considered it at all, I supposed it to be an instrument positioned where it might be near the stars—or possibly only an object carelessly left on deck until some minor change in course had permitted it to float away.

And still I shot upward.

The maintop came into view. I reached for a halyard. They were hardly thicker than my finger now, though every sail would have covered ten score of meadows.

I had misjudged, and the halyard was just beyond my grasp. Another flashed by.

And another—three cubits out of reach at least.

I tried to twist like a swimmer but could do no more than lift my knee. The shining cables of the rigging had been widely separated even far below, where there were for this single mast more than a hundred. None now remained but the startop shroud. My fingers brushed it but could not grasp it.

CHAPTER II

The Fifth Sailor

THE END OF MY LIFE HAD COME, AND I KNEW IT. ABOARD the *Samru*, they had trailed a long rope from the stern as an aid to any sailor who might fall overboard. Whether our ship towed such a line, I did not know; but even if it did, it would have done me no good. My difficulty (my tragedy, I am tempted to write) was not that I had fallen from the rail and drifted aft of the rudder, but that I had risen above the entire forest of masts. And thus I continued to rise—or rather, to leave the ship, for I might as easily have been falling head downward—with the speed of my initial leap.

Below me, or at least in the direction of my feet, the ship seemed a dwindling continent of silver, her black masts and spars as slender as the horns of crickets. Around me, the stars burned unchecked, blazing with splendor never seen on Urth. For a moment, not because my wits were working but because they were not, I looked for her; she would be green, I thought, like green Lune, but tipped with white where the ice-fields closed upon our chilled lands. I could not find her, nor even the crimson-shot orange disk of the old sun.

Then I realized I had been looking in the wrong place. If Urth was visible at all, Urth would be astern. I looked there and saw, not our Urth, but a growing, spinning, swirling vortex of fuligin, the color that is darker than black. It was like some vast eddy or whirlpool of emptiness; but circling it was a circle of colored light, as though a billion billion stars were dancing.

9

Then I knew the miracle had passed without my notice, had passed as I copied out some stodgy sentence about Master Gurloes or the Ascian War. We had penetrated the fabric of time, and the fuligin vortex marked the end of the universe.

Or its beginning. If its beginning, then that shimmering ring of stars was the scattering of the young suns, and the only truly magical ring this universe would ever know. Hailing them, I shouted for joy, though no one heard my voice but the Increate and me.

I drew my cloak to me and pulled the leaden coffer from it; and I held the coffer above my head in both my hands; and I cast it, cheering as I cast it, out of my unseen cloak of air, out of the purlieu of the ship, out of the universe that the coffer and I had known, and into the new creation as final offering from the old.

At once my destiny seized me and flung me back. Not straight downward toward the part of the deck I had left, which might well have killed me, but down and forward, so that I saw the mastheads racing by me. I craned my neck to see the next; it was the last. Had I been an ell or two to the right, I might have been brained by the very tip of the mast. Instead I flashed between its final extension and the starsail yard, with the buntlines far out of reach. I had outraced the ship.

Enormously distant and at a different angle altogether, another of the uncountable masts appeared. Sails sprouted from it like the leaves on a tree; and they were not the now familiar rectangular sails, but triangular ones. For a time, it seemed I would outrace this mast too, and then that I would strike it. Frantically, I clutched at the flying jib stay.

Around it I swung like a flag in a changing wind. I clung to its stinging cold for a moment, panting, then threw myself down the length of the bowsprit—for this final mast was the bowsprit, of course—with all the strength of my arms. I think that if I had crashed into the bow, I would not have cared; I wanted nothing more, and nothing else, than to touch the hull, anywhere and in any way.

I struck a staysail instead, and went sliding along its

immense silver surface. Surface indeed it was, and seemed all surface, with less of body than a whisper, almost itself a thing of light. It turned me, spun me, and sent me rolling and tumbling like a wind-tossed leaf down to the deck.

Or rather, down to some deck, for I have never been certain that the deck to which I returned was that which I had left. I sprawled there trying to catch my breath, my lame leg an agony; held, but almost not held, by the ship's attraction.

My frantic panting never stopped or even slowed; and after a hundred such gasps, I realized my cloak of air was incapable of supporting my life much longer. I struggled to rise. Half-suffocated though I was, it was almost too easy—I nearly threw myself aloft again. A hatch was only a chain away. I staggered to it, flung it wide with the last of my strength, and shut it behind me. The inner door seemed to open almost of itself.

At once my air freshened, as though some noble young breeze had penetrated a fetid cell. To hasten the process, I took off my necklace as I stepped out into the gangway, then stood for a time breathing the cool, clean air, scarcely conscious of where I was—save for the blessed knowledge that I was inside the ship again, and not wandering wrack beyond her sails.

The gangway was narrow and bright, painfully lit by blue lights that crept slowly along its walls and ceiling, winking and seemingly peering into the gangway without being any part of it.

Nothing escapes my memory unless I am unconscious or nearly so; I recalled every passage between my cabin and the hatch that had let me out onto the deck, and this was none of them. Most of them had been furnished like the drawing rooms of châteaus, with pictures and polished floors. The brown wood of the deck had given way here to a green carpeting like grass that lifted minute teeth to grip the soles of my boots, so that I felt as though the little blue-green blades were blades indeed.

Thus I was faced with a decision, and one I did not relish. The hatch was behind me. I could go out again and search from deck to deck for my own part of the ship. Or I could proceed along this broad passage and search from inside. This alternative carried the immense disadvantage that I might easily become lost in the interior. Yet would that be worse than being lost among the rigging, as I had been? Or in the endless space between the suns, as I had nearly been?

I stood there vacillating until I heard the sound of voices. It reminded me that my cloak was still, ridiculously, knotted about my waist. I untied it, and had just finished doing so when the people whose voices I had heard came into view.

All were armed, but there all similarity ended. One seemed an ordinary enough man, such as might have been, seen any day around the docks of Nessus; one of a race I had never encountered in all my journeyings, tall as an exultant and having skin not of the pinkish brown we are pleased to call white, but truly white, as white as foam, and crowned by hair that was white as well. The third was a woman, only just shorter than I and thicker of limb than any woman I had ever seen. Behind these three, seeming almost to drive them before him, was a figure that might have been that of a massive man in armor complete.

They would have passed me without a word if I had allowed it, I think, but I stepped into the middle of the corridor, forced them to halt, and explained my predicament.

"I have reported it," the armored figure told me. "Someone will come for you, or I shall be sent with you. Meanwhile you must come with me."

"Where are you going?" I asked, but he turned away as I spoke, gesturing to the two men.

"Come on," the woman said, and kissed me. It was not a long kiss, but there seemed to be a rough passion in it. She took my arm in a grip that seemed as strong as a man's.

The ordinary sailor (who in fact did not look ordinary at all, having a cheerful and rather handsome face and the yellow hair of a southerner) said, "You'll have to come, or they won't know where to look for you—if they look at all.

It probably won't be too bad." He spoke over his shoulder as he walked, and the woman and I followed him.

The white-haired man said, "Perhaps you can help me."

I supposed that he had recognized me; and feeling in need of as many allies as I might enlist, I told him I would if I could.

"For the love of Danaides, be quiet," the woman said to him. And then to me, "Do you have a weapon?"

I showed her my pistol.

"You'll have to be careful with that in here. Can you turn it down?"

"I already have."

She and the rest bore calivers, arms much like fusils, but with somewhat shorter though thicker stocks and more slender barrels. There was a long dagger at her belt; both the men had bolos, short, heavy, broad-bladed jungle knives.

"I'm Purn," the blond man told me.

"Severian."

He held out his hand, and I took it—a sailor's hand, large, rough, and muscular.

"She's Gunnie—"

"Burgundofara," the woman said.

"We call her Gunnie. And he's Idas." He gestured toward the white-haired man.

The man in armor was looking down the corridor in back of us, but he snapped, "Be still!" I had never seen anyone who could turn his head so far. "What's his name?" I whispered to Purn.

Gunnie answered instead. "Sidero." Of the three, she seemed least in awe of him.

"Where is he taking us?"

Sidero loped past us and threw open a door. "Here. This is a good place. Our confidence is high. Separate widely. I will be in the center. Do no harm unless attacked. Signal vocally."

"In the name of the Increate," I asked, "what are we supposed to be doing?"

"Searching out apports," Gunnie muttered. "You don't

have to pay too much attention to Sidero. Shoot if they look dangerous."

While she spoke, she had been steering me toward the open door. Now Idas said, "Don't worry, there probably won't be any," and stepped so close behind us that I stepped through it almost automatically.

It was pitch dark, but I was immediately conscious that I no longer stood on solid flooring but on some sort of open and shaky grillwork, and that I was entering a place much larger than a common room.

Gunnie's hair brushed my shoulder as she peered past me into the blackness, bringing with it the mingled smells of perfume and sweat. "Turn on the lights, Sidero. We can't see a thing in here."

Lights blazed with a yellower hue than that of the corridor we had just left, a jaundiced radiance that seemed to suck the color from everything. We stood, the four of us crowded together in a compact mass, upon a floor of black bars no thicker than a man's smallest finger. There was no rail, and the space before us and below us (for the ceiling just above us must have supported the deck) would have held our Matachin Tower.

What it now held was an immense jumble of cargo: boxes, bails, barrels, and crates of all kinds; machinery and parts of machines; sacks, many of shimmering, translucent film; stacks of lumber.

"There!" Sidero snapped. He pointed to a spidery ladder descending the wall.

"You go first," I said.

There was no rushing toward me—we were not a span apart—and thus no time for me to draw my pistol. He seized me with a strength I found amazing, forced me back a step, and pushed me violently. For an instant I teetered at the edge of the platform, clawing air; then I fell.

Doubtless I would have broken my neck on Urth. On the ship, I might almost be said to have floated down. Yet the slowness of my fall did nothing to allay the terror I felt in falling. I saw ceiling and platform revolve above me. I was conscious that I would land on my back, with spine and skull bearing the shock, and yet I could not turn myself. I clutched for some support, and my imagination fervently, feverishly conjured up the flying jib stay. The four faces looking down at me—Sidero's armored visor, Idas's chalk-white cheeks, Purn's grin, Gunnie's beautiful, brutal features—seemed masks from a nightmare. And surely no waking unfortunate flung from the top of the Bell Tower had so long in which to contemplate his own destruction.

I struck with a jolt that knocked out my breath. For a hundred heartbeats or more I lay gasping, just as I had panted for air when I had at last regained the interior of the ship. Slowly I realized that though I had suffered a fall indeed, it had been no worse than I might have suffered in falling from my bed to the carpet in some evil dream of Typhon. Sitting up, I found no broken bones.

Bundles of papers had been my carpet, and I thought Sidero must have known they were there and that I would not be hurt. Then I saw beside me a crazily tilted mechanism, spiky with shafts and levers.

I got to my feet. Far above, the platform was empty, the door that led to the corridor closed. I looked for the spidery ladder, but all except the uppermost rungs were obscured by the mechanism. I edged around that, impeded by the unevenly stacked bundles (they had been tied with sisal, and some of the cords had broken, so that I slipped and slid over documents as I might have over snow), but greatly aided by the lightness of my body.

Because I was looking down to find my footing, I did not see the thing before me until I was actually peering into its blind face.

CHAPTER III

The Cabin

MY HAND WENT TO MY PISTOL—I HAD IT OUT AND LEVELED almost before I knew it. The shaggy creature seemed no different from the stooped figure of the salamander that had once nearly burned me alive in Thrax. I expected it to rear erect and reveal the blazing heart within.

It did not, and until too late I did not fire. For a moment we waited motionless; then it fled, bouncing and scrambling across the boxes and barrels like an awkward puppy in pursuit of the lively ball that was itself. With that vile instinct every man has to kill whatever may fear him, I fired. The beam—potentially deadly still, though I had reduced it to its lowest strength to seal the leaden coffer —split the air and set a solid-looking ingot to clanging like a gong. But the creature, whatever it was, was a dozen ells away at least, and in another moment it had disappeared behind a statue swathed in protective wrappings.

Someone shouted, and I thought I recognized Gunnie's husky contralto. There was a sound like a singing arrow, then a yell from another throat.

The shaggy creature came bounding back, but this time, having regained my senses, I did not shoot. Purn appeared and fired his caliver, swinging it like a fowling piece. Instead of the bolt I expected, it shot forth a cord, something flexible and swift that looked black in the strange light and flew with the singing I had heard a moment before.

This black cord struck the shaggy creature and wrapped

16

it with a loop or two, but seemed to produce no other result. Purn gave a shout and leaped like a grasshopper. It had not occurred to me before that in this vast place I could leap myself just as I had on deck, but I imitated him now (mostly because I did not wish to lose contact with Sidero before I had revenged myself) and nearly dashed out my brains against the ceiling.

While I was in the air, however, I had a magnificent view of the hold beneath me. There was the shaggy creature, which might have been fallow under Urth's sun, streaked with black yet still skipping with frantic energy; even as I saw him, Sidero's caliver blotched him more. There was Purn nearly upon him, and Idas and Gunnie, the latter firing even as she ran in great leaps, from high place to high place across the jumbled cargo.

I dropped near them, climbed unsteadily atop the tilted breach of a mountain carronade, and hardly saw the shaggy creature scrambling toward me until it had bounced almost into my arms. I say "almost" because I did not actually grasp it, and certainly it did not grasp me. Nevertheless, we remained together—the black cords adhered to my clothing as well as to the flat strips (neither fur nor feathers) of the shaggy creature.

A moment after we had tumbled from the carronade, I discovered another property of the cords: stretched, they contracted again to a length less than the first, and with great force. Struggling to free myself, I found myself more tightly bound than ever, a circumstance that Gunnie and Purn found highly amusing.

Sidero crisscrossed the shaggy creature with fresh cords, then told Gunnie to release me, which she did by cutting me free with her dagger.

"Thank you," I said.

"It happens all the time," she said. "I got stuck onto a basket like that once. Don't worry about it."

Led by Sidero, Purn and Idas were already carrying the creature away. I stood up. "I'm afraid I'm no longer accustomed to being laughed at."

"One time you were? You don't look it."

"As an apprentice. Everyone laughed at the younger apprentices, especially the older ones."

Gunnie shrugged. "Half the things a person does are funny, if you come to think of it. Like sleeping with your mouth open. If you're quartermaster, nobody laughs. But if you're not, your best friend will slip a dust ball into it. Don't try to pull those off."

The black cords had clung to the nap of my velvet shirt, and I had been plucking at them. "I should carry a knife," I said.

"You mean you don't?" She looked at me commiseratingly, her eyes as large, as dark, and as soft as any cow's. "But everybody ought to have a knife."

"I used to wear a sword," I said. "After a while I gave it up, except for ceremonies. When I left my cabin, I thought my pistol would be more than adequate."

"For fighting. But how much do you have to do, a man who looks like you do?" She took a backward step and pretended to evaluate my appearance. "I don't think many people would give you trouble."

The truth was that in her thick-soled sea boots she stood as tall as I did. In any place where men and women bore weight, she would have been as heavy too; there was real muscle on her bones, with a good deal of fat over it.

I laughed and admitted that a knife would have been useful when Sidero threw me off the platform.

"Oh, no," she told me. "A knife wouldn't have scratched him." She grinned. "That's what the whoremaster said when the sailor came." I laughed, and she linked her arm through mine. "Anyway, a knife's not mainly for fighting. It's for working, one way or another. How're you going to splice rope without a knife, or open ration boxes? You keep your eyes open as we go along. No telling what you'll find in one of these cargo bays."

"We're going in the wrong direction," I said.

"I know another way, and if we went out the way we came in, you'd never find anything. It's too short."

"What happens if Sidero turns out the lights?"

"He won't. Once you wake them up they stay bright until

there's nobody to watch. Ah, I see something. Look there."

I looked, suddenly certain she had noticed a knife during our hunt for the shaggy creature and was merely pretending to have found it now. Only a bone hilt was visible.

"Go ahead. Nobody'll mind if you take it."

"That wasn't what I was thinking about," I told her.

It was a hunting knife, with a narrowed point and a heavy saw-backed blade about two spans long. Just the thing, I thought, for rough work.

"Get the sheath too. You can't carry it in your hand all day."

That was of plain black leather, but it included a pocket that had once held some small tool and recalled the whetstone pocket on the manskin sheath of *Terminus Est*. I was beginning to like the knife already, and I liked it more when I saw that.

"Put it on your belt."

I did as I was told, positioning it on the left where it balanced the weight of my pistol. "I would have expected better stowage on a big vessel like this."

Gunnie shrugged. "This isn't really cargo. Just odds and ends. Do you know how the ship's built?"

"I haven't the least idea."

She laughed at that. "Neither does anyone else, I suppose. We have ideas we pass along to each other, but eventually we usually find out they're wrong. Partly wrong, anyway."

"I would have thought you'd know your ship."

"She's too big, and there are too many places where they never take us, and we can't find for ourselves, or get into. But she's got seven sides; that's so she'll carry more sail, you follow me?"

"I understand."

"Some of the decks—three, I think—have deep bays. That's where the main cargo is. They leave the other four with wedge-shaped spaces. Some's used for odds and ends, like this bay. Some's cabins and crew's quarters and what not. But speaking of quarters, we'd better get back."

She had led me to another ladder, another platform. I

said, "I imagined somehow that we would go through a secret panel, or perhaps only find that as we walked these odds and ends, as you call them, became a garden."

Gunnie shook her head, then grinned. "I see you've seen a bit of her already. You're a poet too, aren't you? And a good liar, I bet."

"I was the Autarch of Urth; that required a little lying, if you like. We called it diplomacy."

"Well, let me tell you that this is a working ship; it's just that she wasn't built by people like you and me. Autarch —does that mean you run the whole Urth?"

"No, I ran only a small part of it, although I was the legitimate head of the whole of it. And I've known ever since I began my journey that if I succeed, I won't come back as Autarch. You seem singularly unimpressed."

"There are so many worlds," she told me. Quite suddenly she crouched and leaped, rising into the air like a large blue bird. Even though I had made such leaps myself, it was strange to see a woman do it. Her ascent carried her a cubit or less above the platform, and she might honestly have been said to have floated down upon it.

Without thinking, I had supposed the crew's quarters would be a narrow room like the forecastle of the *Samru*. There was a warren of big cabins instead, many levels opening onto walkways around a common airshaft. Gunnie said she had to return to her duty, and suggested I look for an empty cabin.

It was on my tongue to remind her I had a cabin already, which I had left only a watch before; but something stopped me. I nodded and asked her what location was best—by which I meant, as she understood, which would be nearest hers. She indicated it to me, and we parted.

On Urth the older locks are charmed by words. My stateroom had a speaking lock, and though the hatches had needed no words at all and the door Sidero had flung open had required none, the olive doors of these crew compartments were equipped with locks of the same kind. The first two I approached informed me that the cabins they guarded were occupied. They must have been old mechanisms indeed; I noticed that their personalities had begun to differentiate.

The third invited me to enter, saying, "What a nice cabin!"

I asked how long it had been since the nice cabin had been inhabited.

"I don't know, master. Many voyages."

"Don't call me master," I told it. "I haven't decided to take your cabin yet."

There was no reply. No doubt such locks are of severely limited intelligence; otherwise they might be bribed, and they would surely go mad soon. After a moment the door swung open. I stepped inside.

It was not a nice cabin compared with the stateroom I had left. There were two narrow bunks, an armoire, and a chest; sanitary facilities in a corner. Dust covered everything to such a thickness that I could readily imagine it being blown from the ventilating grill in gray clouds, though the clouds would be seen only by a man who had some means of compressing time as the ship compressed it; if a man lived as a tree does, perhaps, for which each year is a day; or like Gyoll, running through the valley of Nessus for whole ages of the world.

While thinking of such things, which took me much longer to meditate upon than it has taken me just now to write about them, I had found a red rag in the armoire, moistened it at the laver, and begun to wipe away the dust. When I saw that I had already cleaned the top of the chest and the steel frame of one bunk, I knew that I had decided to stay, however unconsciously. I would locate my stateroom again, of course, and more often than not I would sleep there.

But I would have this cabin as well. When I grew bored, I would join the crew and thus learn more about the operation of the ship than I ever would as a passenger.

There was Gunnie too. I have had women enough in my arms to have no conceit about the number—one soon comes to realize that union cripples love when it does not enhance it—and poor Valeria was often in my thoughts; yet I hungered for Gunnie's affection. As Autarch I had few friends save for Father Inire, and Valeria was the only woman. Some quality in Gunnie's smile recalled my happy childhood with Thea (how I miss her still!) and the long trip to Thrax with Dorcas. It had been a journey I had counted mere exile at the time, so that each day I had hurried forward. Now I knew that in many ways it had been the summer of my life.

I rinsed the rag again, conscious that I had done so often, though I could not have told how often; when I looked about for another dusty surface to wipe, I found that I had wiped them all.

The mattress was not so easily dealt with, but it had to be cleaned in some fashion—it was as filthy as everything else had been, and we would surely want to lie upon it occasionally. I carried it onto the walkway overhanging the airshaft and beat it until it yielded no more dust.

When I had finished and was rolling it up to take back into the cabin, the wind from the airshaft brought a wild cry.

CHAPTER IV

The Citizens of the Sails

IT CAME FROM BELOW. I PEERED OVER THE TWIG-THIN railing and as I peered heard it again, filled with anguish and a loneliness that echoed and re-echoed among the metal catwalks, the metal tiers of metal cabins.

Hearing it, it seemed to me for a moment that it was my own cry, that something I had held deep inside me since that still-dark morning when I had walked the beach with the aquastor Master Malrubius and watched the aquastor Triskele dissolve in shimmering dust had freed itself and separated itself from me, and that it was below, howling in the faint, lost light.

I was tempted to leap over the rail, for then I did not know the depth of that shaft. As it was, I flung the mattress through the doorway of my new cabin and descended the narrow winding stair by jumping from one flight to the next.

From above, the abyss of the shaft had seemed opaque, the strange radiance of yellow lamps beating upon it without effect. I had supposed that this opacity would vanish when I reached the lower levels—but it solidified instead, until I was reminded of Baldanders's chamber of cloud, though it was really not so thick as that. The swirling air grew warmer too, and perhaps the mist that shrouded everything was only the result of warm, moist air from the bowels of the ship mixing with the cooler atmosphere of the upper levels. I was soon sweating in my velvet shirt.

Here the doors of many cabins stood ajar, but the cabins themselves were dark. Once, or so it seemed to me, the ship must have had a more numerous crew, or perhaps had been used to transport prisoners (the cabins would have done well as cells, if the locks were differently instructed) or soldiers.

The cry came again, and with it a noise like the ringing of a hammer on an anvil, though it held a note that told me it rang from no forge, but from a mouth of flesh. Heard by night, in a fastness of the mountains, they would have been more terrible than the howling of a dire-wolf, I think. What sadness, dread, and loneliness, what fear and agony were there!

I paused for breath and looked around me. Beasts, so it seemed, were confined in the cabins farther down. Or perhaps madmen, as we of the torturers had confined pain-crazed clients on the third level of the oubliette. Who could say that every door was shut? Might not some of these creatures be unconfined, kept from the upper levels by mere chance or their fear of man? I drew my pistol and made sure it was at its lowest setting and that it had a full charge.

My initial glimpse of the vivarium below confirmed my worst fears. Filmy trees waved at the edge of a glacier, a waterfall tumbled and sang, a dune lifted its sterile yellow crest, and two score creatures prowled among them. I watched them for a dozen breaths before I began to suspect that they were confined nonetheless, and for fifty more before I felt sure of it. But each had its own plot of ground, small or large, and they could no more mingle than could the beasts in the Bear Tower. What a strange group they made! If every swamp and forest on Urth were combed for oddities, I do not believe such a collection could be assembled. Some gibbered, some stared, most lay comatose.

I holstered my pistol and called, *"Who howled?"*

That was only a joke made to myself, yet a response came—a whimper from the rear of the vivarium; I threaded my way through the beasts, following a narrow and nearly invisible track made, as I soon afterward learned, by the sailors sent to feed them.

It was the shaggy creature I had helped catch in the cargo bay, and I beheld him with a certain warmth of recognition. I had been so much alone since the pinnace had carried me from the gardens of the House Absolute to this ship that to meet even so queer a being as he was seemed the second time almost a reunion with an old acquaintance.

Then too, I was interested in the creature himself, since I had assisted in his capture. When we had pursued him, he had appeared almost spherical; now I saw that he was in fact one of those short-limbed, short-bodied animals that generally live in burrows—something like a pika, in other words. There was a round head atop a neck so short that one had to take it on faith; a round body too, of which the head seemed a mere continuation; four short legs, each ending in four long, blunt claws and one short one; a covering of flattened, brownish-gray hairs. Two bright black eyes that stared at me.

"Poor thing," I said. "How did you ever get into that hold?"

He came to the limit of the invisible barrier that enclosed him, moving much more slowly now that he was no longer frightened.

"Poor thing," I said again.

He reared upon his hind legs as pikas sometimes do, forelegs nearly crossed over his white belly. Strands of black cord still streaked the white fur. They reminded me that the same cords had stuck to my shirt. I plucked at what remained of them and found them weak now, some crumbling under my fingers. The cords on the shaggy creature seemed to be falling away as well.

He whimpered softly; instinctively, I reached out to comfort him as I would have an anxious dog, then drew my hand away, fearful he might bite or claw me.

A moment later, I cursed myself for a coward. He had harmed no one in the hold, and when I had wrestled with him, there had been no indication that he was trying to do more than escape. I thrust a forefinger into the barrier (which proved no barrier to me) and scratched the side of his tiny mouth. He turned his head just as a dog would have, and I felt small ears beneath the fur.

Behind me, someone said, "Cute, ain't it?" and I turned to look. It was Purn, the grinning sailor.

I answered, "He seems harmless enough."

"Most are." Purn hesitated. "Only most die and drift off. We only see a few of 'em, that's what they say."

"Gunnie calls them apports," I remarked, "and I've been thinking about that. The sails bring them, don't they?"

Purn nodded absently and stretched a finger of his own through the barrier to tickle the shaggy creature.

"Adjacent sails must be like two large mirrors. They're curved, so somewhere—in fact, in various places—they must be parallel, and the starlight shines on them."

Purn nodded again. "That's what makes the ship go, as the skipper said when they asked about the wench."

"I once knew a man called Hethor who summoned deadly things to serve him. And I was told by one called Vodalus—Vodalus was not to be trusted, I'll admit—that Hethor used mirrors to bring them. I've a friend who works mirror spells too, though his are not evil. Hethor had been a hand on a ship like this."

That captured Purn's attention. He withdrew his finger and turned to face me. "You know her name?" he asked.

"The name of his ship? No, I don't think he ever mentioned it. Wait . . . He said he'd been on several. 'Long I signed on the silver-sailed ships, the hundred-masted whose masts reached out to touch the stars.'"

"Ah." Purn nodded. "Some say there's only one. That's something I wonder about, sometimes."

"Surely there must be many. Even when I was a boy, people told me of them, the ships of the cacogens putting into the Port of Lune."

"Where's that?"

"Lune? It's the moon of my world, the moon of Urth."

"That was small stuff, then," Purn told me. "Tenders

and launches and so forth. Nobody never said there wasn't a lot of little stuff shuttling around between the various worlds of the various suns. Only this ship here and the other ones like it, allowing that there's more than the one, they don't come in so close, generally. They can do it all right, but it's a tricky business. Then too, there's a good bit of rock whizzing around, close in to a sun, usually."

The white-haired Idas appeared carrying a collection of tools. *"Hello!"* he called, and I waved to him.

"I ought to get busy," Purn muttered. "Me and that one are supposed to be taking care of 'em. I was just looking around to be sure they were all right when I saw you, uh, uh . . ."

"Severian," I said. "I was the Autarch—the ruler—of the Commonwealth; now I'm the surrogate of Urth, and its ambassador. Do you come from Urth, Purn?"

"Don't think I've ever been, but maybe I have." He looked thoughtful. "Big white moon?"

"No, it's green. You were on Verthandi, perhaps; I've read that its moons are pale gray."

Purn shrugged. "I don't know."

Idas had come up to us by then, and he said, "It must be wonderful." I had no notion of what he meant. Purn moved away, looking at the beasts.

As if we were two conspirators Idas whispered, "Don't worry about him. He's afraid I'll report him for not working."

"Aren't you afraid I'll report *you*?" I asked. There was something about Idas that irritated me, though perhaps it was only his seeming weakness.

"Oh, do you know Sidero?"

"Who I know is my own affair, I believe."

"I don't think you know anyone," he said. And then, as if he had committed a merely social blunder, "But maybe you do. Or I could introduce you. I will, if you want me to."

"I do," I told him. "Introduce me to Sidero at the first opportunity. I demand to be returned to my stateroom."

Idas nodded. "I will. Perhaps you wouldn't mind if I

came there to talk with you sometime? You—I hope you'll excuse me for saying this—you know nothing about ships, and I know nothing about such places as, ah . . ."

"Urth?"

"Nothing of worlds. I've seen a few pictures, but other than that, all I know are these." He gestured vaguely toward the beasts. "And they are bad, always bad. But perhaps there are good things on the worlds too, that never live long enough to find their way to the decks."

"Surely they're not all evil."

"Oh, yes," he said. "Oh, yes they are. And I, who have to clean up after them, and feed them, and adjust the atmosphere for them if they need it, would rather kill them all; but Sidero and Zelezo would beat me if I did."

"I wouldn't be surprised if they killed you," I told him. I had no desire to see such a fascinating collection wiped out by this petty man's spite. "Which would be just, I think. You look as though you belong among them yourself."

"Oh, no," he said seriously. "It's you and Purn and the rest who do. I was born here on the ship."

Something in his manner told me he was trying to draw me into conversation and would gladly quarrel with me if only it would keep me talking. For my part, I had no desire to talk at all, much less quarrel. I felt tired enough to drop, and I was ravenously hungry. I said, "If I belong in this collection of exotic brutes, it's up to you to see I'm fed. Where is the galley?"

Idas hesitated for a moment, quite plainly debating some sort of exchange of information—he would direct me if I would first answer seven questions about Urth, or something of that sort. Then he realized I was ready to knock him down if he said anything of the kind, and he told me, though sullenly enough, how to get there.

One of the advantages of such a memory as mine, which stores everything and forgets nothing, is that it is as good as paper at such times. (Indeed, that may be its only advantage.) On this occasion, however, it did me no more good than it had when I had tried to follow the directions of that lochage of the peltasts whom I met upon the bridge of Gyoll. No doubt Idas had assumed I knew more of the ship than I did, and that I would not count doors and look for turnings with exactness.

Soon I realized I had gone wrong. Three corridors branched where there should have been only two, and a promised stair did not appear. I retraced my path, found the point at which (as I believed) I had become lost, and began again. Almost at once, I found myself treading a broad, straight passageway such as Idas had told me led to the galley. I assumed then that my wanderings had sent me wide of part of the prescribed route, and I strode along in high spirits.

By the standards of the ship, it was a wide and windy place indeed. No doubt it was one that received its atmosphere directly from the devices that circulated and purified it, for it smelled as a breeze from the south does on a rainy day in spring. The floor was neither of the strange grass I had seen before nor of the grillwork I had already come to hate, but polished wood deeply entombed in clear varnish. The walls, which had been of a dark and deathly gray in the crew's quarters, were white here, and once or twice I passed padded seats that stood with their backs toward the walls.

The passageway turned and turned again, and I felt that it was rising ever so slightly, though the weight I lifted with my steps was so slight I could not be certain. There were pictures on the walls, and some of these pictures moved —once a picture of our ship as it might have been limned by someone far distant; I could not help but stop to look, and I shuddered to think how near I had come to seeing it so.

Another turn—but one that proved not to be a turn, only the termination of the passageway in a circle of doors. I chose one at random and stepped into a narrow gangway so dark, after the white passage, that I could hardly see more than the lights overhead.

A few moments later, I realized that I had passed a hatch, the first I had seen since reentering the ship; still not wholly free from the fear that had gripped me when I saw that terrible and beautiful picture, I took out my necklace as I strode along and made certain it had not been damaged.

The gangway turned twice and divided, then twisted like a serpent.

A door swung open as I passed, releasing the aroma of roast meat. A voice, the thin and mechanical voice of the lock, said, "Welcome back, master."

I looked through the doorway and saw my own cabin. Not, of course, the cabin I had taken in the crew's quarters, but the stateroom I had left to launch the leaden coffer into the great light of the new universe aborning only a watch or two before.

CHAPTER V

The Hero and the Hierodules

THE STEWARD HAD BROUGHT MY MEAL AND, FINDING ME not in my stateroom, had left it on the table. The meat was still warm under its bell; I ate it ravenously, and with it new bread and salt butter, celeriac and salsify, and red wine. Afterward I undressed, washed myself, and slept.

He woke me, shaking me by my shoulder. It was odd, but when I—the Autarch of Urth—had boarded the ship, I had scarcely noticed him, though he brought my meals and willingly saw to various little wants; no doubt it was that very willingness which had unjustly wiped him from my attention. Now that I myself had been a member of the crew, it was as though he had turned to show another face.

It looked down at me now, blunt-featured yet intelligent, the eyes bright with suppressed excitement. "Someone wishes to see you, Autarch," he murmured.

I sat up. "Someone you felt you should wake me for?"

"Yes, Autarch."

"The captain, perhaps." Was I to be censured for going on deck? The necklace had been provided for emergency use, but it seemed unlikely.

"No, Autarch. Our captain's seen you, I'm sure. Three Hierodules, Autarch."

"Yes?" I fenced for time. "Is that the captain's voice I hear sometimes in the corridors? When did he see me? I don't recall seeing him."

"I've no idea, Autarch. But our captain's seen you, I'm sure. Often, probably. Our captain sees people."

31

"Indeed." I was pulling on a clean shirt as I digested the hint that there was a secret ship within this ship, just as the Secret House was within the House Absolute. "It must interfere with his other work."

"I don't believe it does, Autarch. They're waiting outside —could you hurry?"

I dressed more slowly after that, of course. To draw the belt from my dusty trousers, I had to remove my pistol and the knife that Gunnie had found for me. The steward told me I would not need them; so I wore them, feeling absurdly as though I were going to inspect a reconstituted formation of demilances. The knife was nearly long enough to be called a sword.

It had not occurred to me that the three might be Ossipago, Barbatus, and Famulimus. As far as I knew, I had left them far behind on Urth, and they had most certainly not been in the pinnace with me, though of course they possessed their own craft. Now here they were, disguised (and badly) as human beings, just as they had been at our first encounter in Baldanders's castle.

Ossipago bowed as stiffly as ever, Barbatus and Famulimus as gracefully. I returned their greetings as well I could and suggested that if they wished to speak to me, they were welcome in my stateroom, apologizing in advance for its disorder.

"We cannot come inside," Famulimus told me. "However much we would. The room to which we bring you is not too far away." Her voice, as always, was like the speaking of a lark.

Barbatus added, "Cabins like yours are not as safe as we might wish," in his masculine baritone.

"Then I will go wherever you lead me," I said. "Do you know, it's truly cheering to see you three again. Yours are faces from home, even if they are false faces."

"You know us, I see," Barbatus said as we started down the corridor. "But the faces beneath these are too horrible for you, I fear."

The corridor was too narrow for us to go four abreast; he and I walked side by side, Famulimus and Ossipago side by side behind us. It has taken me a long time to lose the despair that seized me at that moment. "This is the first time?" I asked. "You have not met me before?"

Famulimus trilled, "Though we do not know you, yet you know us, Severian. I saw how pleased you looked, when first you came into our sight. Often we have met, and we are friends."

"But we will not meet again," I said. "It's the first time for you, who will travel backward through time when you leave me. And so it's the last time for me. When we first met, you said, 'Welcome! There is no greater joy for us than greeting you, Severian,' and you were saddened at our parting. I remember it very well—I remember everything very well, as you had better know at once—how you leaned over the rail of your ship to wave to me as I stood upon the roof of Baldanders's tower in the rain."

"Only Ossipago here has memory like yours," Famulimus whispered. "But I shall not forget."

"So it's my turn to say welcome now, and mine to be sad because we're parting. I've known you three for more than ten years, and I know that the hideous faces beneath those masks are only masks themselves—Famulimus took hers off the first time we met, though I did not understand then that it was because she had done so often before. I know that Ossipago is a machine, although he is not so agile as Sidero, who I am beginning to believe must be a machine too."

"That name means iron," Ossipago said, speaking for the first time. "Though I do not know him."

"And yours means bone-grower. You took care of Barbatus and Famulimus when they were small, saw to it that they were fed and so on, and you've remained with them ever since. That's what Famulimus told me once."

Barbatus said, "We are come," and opened the door for me.

In childhood, one imagines that any door unopened may open upon a wonder, a place different from all the places one knows. That is because in childhood it has so often proved to be so; the child, knowing nothing of any place except his own, is astonished and delighted by novel sights that an adult would readily have anticipated. When I was only a boy, the doorway of a certain mausoleum had been a portal of wonder to me; and when I had crossed its threshold, I was not disappointed. On this ship I was a child again, knowing no more of the world around me than a child does.

The chamber into which Barbatus ushered me was as marvelous to Severian the man—to the Autarch Severian, who had Thecla's life, and the old Autarch's, and a hundred more to draw upon—as the mausoleum had been to the child. I am tempted to write that it appeared to be underwater, but it did not. Rather we seemed immersed in some fluid that was not water, but was to some other world what water was to Urth; or perhaps that we were underwater indeed, but water so cold it would have been frozen in any lake of the Commonwealth.

All this was merely an effect of the light, I believe—of the freezing wind that wandered, nearly stagnating, through the chamber, and of the colors, tintings of green shaded with blue and black: viridian, berylline, and aquamarine, with tarnished gold and yellowed ivory here and there shining sullenly.

The furnishings were not of furniture as we understand it. Mottled slabs of seeming stone that yielded to my touch leaned crookedly against two walls and were scattered across the floor. Tattered streamers hung suspended from the ceiling and, because they were so light and the attraction of our ship hardly felt, seemed in need of no suspension. So far as I could judge, the air was as dry here as in the corridor; yet the ghost of an icy spray beat against my face.

"Is this strange place your stateroom?" I asked Barbatus.

He nodded as he removed his masks, revealing a face that was at once handsome, inhuman, and familiar. "We have seen the chambers your kind makes. They are as disturbing to us as this must be to you, and since there are three of us—"

"Two," Ossipago said. "It does not matter to me."

"I'm not offended, I'm delighted! It's the greatest of privileges for me to see how you live when you live as you wish."

Famulimus's falsely human face was gone, revealing some huge-eyed horror with needle teeth; she pulled that away as well, and I saw (for one last time, as I then believed) the beauty of a goddess not born of woman. "How fast we learn, Barbatus, that these poor folk we'll meet, who hardly know what we know best, know courtesy as guests."

If I had attended to what she said, it would have made me smile. As it was, I was far too busy still in looking about that strange cabin. At last I said, "I know your race was formed by the Hierogrammates to resemble those who once formed them. Now I see, or think I see, that you were once inhabitants of lakes and pools, kelpies such as our country folk talk of."

"On our home, as on yours," Barbatus said, "life rose from the sea. But this chamber has no more received its impression from that dim beginning than your own have received theirs from the trees where your forebears capered."

Ossipago rumbled, "It is early to begin a quarrel." He had not removed his disguise, I suppose because it did not render him less comfortable; and in fact I have never seen him do so.

"Barbatus, he speaks well," Famulimus sang. Then to me, "You leave your world, Severian. Like you, we three leave ours. We climb the stream of time—you are swept down that stream. This ship thus bears us both. For you the years are gone, when we will counsel you. For us they now begin. We greet you now, Autarch, with counsel we have brought. To save your race's sun, one thing is needful only: that you must serve Tzadkiel."

"Who is that?" I asked. "And how do I serve him? I've never heard of him."

Barbatus snorted. "Which is less than surprising, since Famulimus was not supposed to give you that name. We will not use it again. But he—the person Famulimus mentioned—is the judge appointed to your case. He is a Hierogrammate, as is to be expected. What do you know of them?"

"Very little, beyond the fact that they are your masters."

"Then you know very little indeed; even that is wrong. You call us Hierodules, and that is your word and not ours, just as *Barbatus, Famulimus,* and *Ossipago* are your words, words we have chosen because they are not common and describe us better than your other words would. Do you know what *Hierodule* means, this word of your own tongue?"

"I know that you are creatures of this universe, shaped by those of the next to serve them here. And that the service they desire of you is the shaping of our race, of humanity, because we are the cognates of those who shaped them in the ages of the previous creation."

Famulimus trilled, "*Hierodule* is 'holy slave.' How could Hierodules be holy, did we not serve the Increate? Our master is he, and he only."

Barbatus added, "You've commanded armies, Severian. You're a king and a hero, or at least you were up until you left your world. Then too, you may rule again, should you fail. You must know that a soldier doesn't serve his officer, or at least, that he shouldn't. He serves his tribe, and receives instructions from his officer."

I nodded. "The Hierogrammates are your officers, then. I understand. I possess my predecessor's memories, as you perhaps do not yet realize; so I know that he was tried as I will be and that he failed. And it's always seemed to me that what was done to him, returning him unmanned to watch our Urth grow worse and worse, to take responsibility for everything, and yet know that he had failed in the one attempt that might have set everything right, was cruel indeed."

Famulimus's face was almost always serious; now it seemed more serious than ever. "His memories, Severian? Have you no more than memories?"

For the first time in many years, I felt the blood rise in my cheeks. "I lied," I said. "I am he, just as I am Thecla.

You three have been my friends when I had few, and I should not lie to you, though so often I must lie to myself."

Famulimus sang, "Then you must know that all are scourged alike. And yet the nearer to success, the worse the pain each feels. That is a law we cannot change."

Outside in the gangway, not far distant, someone screamed. I started toward the door, and the scream ended on the gurgling note that signals that the throat has filled with blood.

Barbatus snapped, "Wait, Severian!" and Ossipago moved to block the door.

Famulimus chanted urgently, "I have but one thing more to tell. Tzadkiel is just and kind. Though you may suffer much, remember so."

I turned on her; I could not help it. "I remember this—the old Autarch never saw his judge! I didn't recall the name because he had striven so to forget it; but we recall everything now, and it was *Tzadkiel*. He was a kinder man than Severian, a more just person than Thecla. What chance does Urth stand now?"

Though I do not know whose hand it was—Thecla's, perhaps, or one of the dim figures behind the old Autarch —a hand was on my pistol; no more do I know whom it would have shot, unless it was myself. It never left the holster, for Ossipago seized me from behind, pinning my arms in a grip of steel.

"It is Tzadkiel who will decide," Famulimus told me. "Urth stands such chance as you provide."

Somehow Ossipago opened the door without releasing me, or it may be that it opened itself at some command I did not hear. He whirled me around and thrust me out into the gangway.

CHAPTER VI

A Death and the Dark

IT WAS THE STEWARD. HE LAY FACE DOWN IN THE GANGWAY, the worn soles of his carefully polished boots not three cubits from my door. His neck had been nearly severed. A clasp knife, still closed, lay beside his right hand.

For ten years I had worn the black claw I had pulled from my arm beside Ocean. When first I ascended to the autarchy, I had often tried to use it, always without result; for the past eight years, I had scarcely given it a thought. Now I took it from the little leathern sack Dorcas had sewn for me in Thrax, touched the steward's forehead with it, and sought to do again whatever it had been that I had done for the girl in the jacal, the man-ape beside the falls, and the dead uhlan.

Although I have no wish to do so, I will try to describe what happened then: Once when I was a prisoner of Vodalus, I was bitten by a blood bat. There was very little pain, but a sensation of lassitude that grew more seductive every moment. When I moved my foot and startled the bat from its feast, the wind of its dark wings had seemed the very exhalation of Death. That was but the shadow, the foretaste, of what I felt then in the gangway. I was the core of the universe, as we always are to ourselves; and the universe tore like a client's rotten rags and fell in soft gray dust to nothing.

For a long time I lay trembling in the dark. Perhaps I was conscious. Surely I was not aware of it, nor of anything

38

except red pain everywhere and such weakness as the dead must feel. At last I saw a spark of light; it came to me that I must be blind, and yet if I saw that spark there was some hope, however slight. I sat up, though I was so shaken and weak that it was agony.

The spark appeared again, an infinitesimal flash, less than the gleam that sunlight summons from the point of a needle. It lay in my hand, but was extinct before I realized it, long gone before I could move my stiff fingers and discover them slippery with my blood.

It had come from the claw, that hard, sharp, black thorn that had pricked my arm so long ago. I must have clenched my fist; I had driven the claw into the second joint of the first finger until its point had pierced the skin a second time from within, impaling it like a fishhook. I jerked it out, hardly conscious of the pain, and pushed it back into its sack still wet with my blood.

By then I was sure again that I was blind. The smooth surface on which I lay seemed no more than the floor of the gangway; the paneled wall that my groping fingers discovered once I clambered to my feet might easily have been its wall. Yet the gangway had been well lit. Who would have carried me elsewhere, to this dark place, and made my whole body an agony to me? I heard the moaning of a human voice. It was my own, and I clamped my jaw to silence it.

In my youth, when I had traveled from Nessus to Thrax with Dorcas, and from Thrax to Orithyia largely alone, I had carried flint and steel to kindle fires. Now I had none. I searched my mind and my pockets for something that would give light, but I could hit on nothing better than my pistol. Drawing it, I drew breath too, to shout a warning; and only then thought to cry out for help.

There was no reply. I listened, but could hear no footfall. After making certain the pistol was still at its lowest setting, I resolved to use it.

I would fire a single shot. If I could not see its violet flame, I would know that I had lost my sight. I would consider then whether I wished to lose my life as well while

I retained the necessary desperation, or whether I would
seek out whatever treatment the ship might offer. (And yet
I knew even then that although I—although we—might
choose to perish, we could not. What other hope had
Urth?)

With my left hand, I touched the wall so that I might
align the barrel with the gangway. With the other, I raised
my pistol to shoulder height, as a marksman does who
shoots at a distance.

A pinprick of light shone before me, like red Verthandi
seen through clouds. The sight startled me so much that
though it was my injured finger that jerked back the trigger,
I was hardly aware of it.

Energy split the dark. In the violet glare, I saw the
steward's body, the half-open door of my stateroom beyond it, a writhing shape, and the flash of steel.

Darkness returned instantly, but I was not blind. Sick,
yes; aching in every limb—I felt I had been spun about by
a whirlwind and dashed against some pillar—but not
blind. Not blind!

Rather, the ship was plunged in darkness as if in night.
Again I heard the groan of a human voice, but this voice
was not my own. Someone had been in the corridor after
all; someone who had meant to take my life, since what I
had glimpsed had surely been the blade of some weapon.
The diminished beam had seared him as the diminished
beams of the Hierodules' pistols had once seared Baldanders. This had been no giant, I thought, but he still lived as
Baldanders had lived; and it might be that he was not
alone. Stooping, I groped with my free hand until I found
the body of the steward, climbed over it like a crippled
spider, and at last managed to creep through the door of
my stateroom and bolt it behind me.

The lamp by whose light I had recopied my manuscript
was as dark as the gangway lights, but as I fumbled the
escritoire to find it, I touched a stick of wax and remembered there was a golden candle too for melting the wax, a
candle that lit itself at the pressing of a stud. This ingen-
ious device had been stored with the wax in a pigeonhole,

so that to think of it should have been to lay my hand upon it. It was not there, but I soon found it among the litter on the writing board.

Its clear yellow flame shot up at once. By its light I saw the ruin of my stateroom. My clothes had been strewn across the floor, and every seam of every garment ripped out. A sharp blade had opened my mattress from end to end. The drawers of the escritoire had been turned out, my books strewn over the room, the very bags in which my belongings had been carried on board had been slashed.

My first thought was that all this had been mere vandalism; that someone who hated me (and on Urth there had been many such) had vented his fury at not finding me asleep. A little reflection convinced me the destruction had been too thorough for that. Almost at the instant I had left it, someone had entered the stateroom. Doubtless the Hierodules, whose time ran counter to the time we know, had foreseen his arrival and sent the steward for me largely to snatch me from him. Finding me gone, he had searched my belongings for something so small it might have been concealed in the collar of a shirt.

Whatever he had sought, I had possessed only one treasure: the letter Master Malrubius had given me, identifying me as the legitimate Autarch of Urth. Because I had not expected my stateroom to be robbed, I had not concealed it at all, merely putting it in a drawer with some other papers I had brought from Urth; of course it was gone now.

On leaving my stateroom, the searcher had met the steward, who must have stopped him and attempted to question him. That could not be tolerated, since the steward would have been able to describe him to me later. The searcher had drawn his weapon; the steward had tried to defend himself with a clasp knife, but had been too slow. I had heard his scream as I talked with the Hierodules, and Ossipago had prevented me from leaving so that I would not encounter the searcher. So much seemed clear.

But now came the strangest part of the whole affair. When I found the steward's body, I had tried to reanimate it, using the thorn in place of the true Claw of the Conciliator. I had failed; but then I had failed also on every previous occasion when I had sought to call upon whatever power I had commanded with the true Claw. (First, I believe, when I had touched the woman in our oubliette who had constructed the furnishings of her room from stolen children.)

Those failures, however, had been no more violent than the failure of a word that is not the word of power: one pronounces the word, but the door does not open. So had I touched with the thorn, but no cure or resuscitation had taken place.

This time had been quite different; I had been stunned in a fashion that had left me sick and weak still, and I had not the least notion what it was. Absurd though it may sound, that gave me hope. Something had happened, at least, though it had nearly cost me my life.

Whatever it had been, it had left me unconscious, and the darkness had come. Emboldened by it, the searcher had returned. Hearing my cry for help (which a well-intentioned person would have answered) he had advanced to kill me.

All these thoughts took much less time than I have taken to write about them. The wind is rising now, blowing our new land, grain by grain, to the sunken Commonwealth; but I will write for a little while more before I go to my bower to sleep: write that the only useful conclusion to which they carried me was that the searcher might be lying wounded in the gangway still. If so, I might induce him to reveal his motive and confederates, assuming that he had either. Snuffing the candle, I opened the door as silently as I could and slipped out, listened for a moment, then risked relighting it.

My enemy had gone, but nothing else had changed. The dead steward remained dead, his clasp knife by his hand. The gangway was empty as far as the wavering yellow light could probe it.

Fearing that I would exhaust the candle or it would

betray my location, I extinguished it again. At close quarters, the hunting knife Gunnie had found for me seemed likely to be more useful than a pistol. With the knife in one hand and the other brushing the wall, I went slowly down the gangway in search of the Hierodules' stateroom.

When Famulimus, Barbatus, Ossipago, and I had gone there, I had paid no heed to either the route or the distance; but I could recall each door we had passed, and almost every step I had taken. Though it took me so much longer to return than it had to go the first time, still I knew (or at least believed I knew) precisely when I had arrived.

I tapped on the door, but there was no response. Pressed to it, my ear detected no sounds from within. I knocked again, more loudly, but with no more result; and at last I pounded on it with the pommel of my knife.

When that too was without result, I crept through the dark to the doors on either side (though each was some distance off, and I was sure both were incorrect) and knocked at them as well. No one answered either.

To return to my stateroom would be to invite assassination, and I congratulated myself heartily on having already secured a second lodging. Unfortunately, to reach it by the only route I knew, I would have to pass the door to my stateroom. When I had studied the history of my predecessors and scanned the memories of those whose persons are merged in mine, I had been struck by the number who had lost their lives in a last repetition of some hazardous action—in leading the last charge of a victory, or by risking incognito a farewell visit to some mistress in the city. Recalling the route as I did, I felt I could guess in which part of the ship my new cabin lay; I decided to proceed down the gangway, turn from it when I could, and double back, and so come eventually to my goal.

I shall pass over my wanderings, which were wearying enough to me and need not weary you, my hypothetical reader. It should be enough to say that I found a stairway to a lower level and a gangway that seemed to run beneath the one I had left, but soon ended in another descending stair leading to a maze of walkways, ladders, and narrow passages as dark as the pit, where the floor moved beneath my feet and the air grew ever warmer and more humid.

At length this sweltering air carried to me an odor pungent and oddly familiar. I followed it as well as I could, I who have so often boasted of my memory now sniffing along for what seemed a league at least like a brachet and ready almost to yelp for joy at the thought of a place I knew, after so much emptiness, silence, and blackness.

Then I yelped indeed, because I saw far off the gleam of some faint light. My eyes had grown so used to the dark in those watches of wandering through the entrails of the ship that, faint though the gleam shone, I could see the renitent surface under my feet and the mossy walls about me; I sheathed my knife then, and ran.

A moment later circular habitats surrounded me, and a hundred strange beasts. I had returned to the menagerie where the apports were imprisoned—the gleam proceeded from one of their enclosures. I made my way to it and saw that the creature within was none other than the shaggy thing I had helped to capture. He stood upon his hind legs, with his forelegs braced against the invisible wall that contained him, and a phosphorescent glow rippled along his belly and shone strongly from his handlike forepaws. I spoke to him as I might have to some favorite cat upon returning from a journey, and he seemed to welcome me as a cat might, pressing his furry body to the unseen wall and mewing, regarding me with beseeching eyes.

An instant later his little mouth split in a snarl and his eyes glared like a demon's. I would have started back from him, but an arm circled my neck and a blade flashed toward my chest.

I caught the assassin's wrist and stopped the knife without a thumb's width to spare, then struggled to crouch and throw him over my head.

I have been called a strong man, but he was too strong for me. I could lift him readily enough—on that ship I could have lifted a dozen men—but his legs clamped my waist like the jaws of a trap; I bent to throw him, but I succeeded only in throwing us both to the ground. Frantically I twisted to get away from his knife.

Nearly in my ear, he screamed with pain.

Our fall had brought us inside the habitat, and the shaggy animal's teeth had fastened on his hand.

CHAPTER VII

A Death in the Light

BY THE TIME I HAD RECOVERED MYSELF ENOUGH TO RISE, the assassin was gone. A few bloodstains, nearly black in the light of the golden candle, remained in the circle ruled by my shaggy friend. He himself sat upon his haunches with his hind legs folded in an oddly human way beneath him, his light extinguished, licking his paws and smoothing the silky hair around his mouth with them. "Thank you," I said, and he cocked his head attentively at the sound.

The assassin's knife lay not far off, a big, broad-bladed, rather clumsy bolo with a worn handle of some dark wood. He had been a common sailor then, in all probability. I kicked it away and called to mind his hand as I had glimpsed it—a man's hand, large, strong, and rough, but with no identifying marks, so far as I had seen. A missing finger or two would have been convenient, but it was at least possible that he had those now: a sailor with a badly bitten hand.

Had he followed me so far through the dark, down so many stairs and ladders, along so many twisted passages? It seemed unlikely. He had come upon me here by accident then, seized his opportunity, and acted—a dangerous man. It seemed better to me to search for him at once than to wait until he had time to recover himself and concoct some tale to explain his injured hand. If I could discover his identity, I would make it known to the officers of the ship; and if there was not time for that or they would take no action, I would kill him myself.

Holding the golden candle high, I started up the stairs to the crew's quarters, knitting plans much faster than I walked. The officers—the captain the dead steward had mentioned—would refurnish my stateroom or assign another to me. I would have a guard posted outside, not so much to protect me (for I intended to stay there no more than I had to in order to keep up appearances) as to give my enemies something to strike at. Then I . . .

Between one breath and the next, every light in that part of the ship came on. I could see the unsupported metal stair on which I stood, and through the twining black metal of its treads the pale greens and yellows of the vivarium. To my right, radiance from indistinct lamps lost itself in nacreous mist; the distant wall at my left shone gray-black with damp, a dark tarn turned on edge. Above, there might have been no ship at all, but a clouded sky besieged by a circling sun.

It lasted no longer than a breath. I heard distant shouts as sailors here and there called the attention of their mates to what could not in any case be missed. Then a darkness fell that seemed more terrible than before. I climbed a hundred steps; light flickered as though every lamp were as tired as I, then went out again. A thousand steps, and the flame of the golden candle shrunk to a dot of blue. I extinguished it to save what little fuel remained and climbed on in the dark.

Perhaps it was only because I was leaving the depths of the ship and ascending toward that uppermost deck which confined our atmosphere, but I felt chilled. I tried to climb more quickly, to warm myself by the exertion, and found I was unable to do so. Haste only made me stumble, and the leg that had been laid open by some Ascian infantryman at the Third Battle of Orithyia drew the rest toward the grave.

For a time I was afraid I would not recognize the tier that held my cabin and Gunnie's, but I left the stair without thought, kindled the golden candle for an instant only, and heard the creaking of hinges as the door swung open.

I had shut the door and found the bunk before I sensed that I was not alone. I called out, and the voice of Idas, the white-haired sailor, answered me in a tone of mingled fear and interest.

I asked, "What are you doing here?"

"Waiting for you. I—I hoped you would come. I don't know why, but I thought you might. You weren't with the others down there."

When I said nothing, he added, "Working, I mean. So I slipped away myself and came here."

"To my cabin. The lock shouldn't have let you in."

"But you didn't tell it not to. I described you, and it knows me, you see. My own cabin's near here. I told it the truth, that I only wanted to wait for you."

I said, "I'll order it to admit no one but myself."

"It might be wise to make exceptions for your friends."

I told him I would consider it, actually thinking that he would certainly not be such an exception. Gunnie, perhaps.

"You have a light. Wouldn't it be nicer if you used it?"

"How do you know I've got one?"

"Because when the door opened, there was a light outside for a moment. It was something you were holding, wasn't it?"

I nodded, then realized he could not see me in the dark and said, "I prefer not to exhaust it."

"All right. I was surprised, though, when you didn't use it to find that bed."

"I remembered where it was well enough."

The fact was that I had refrained from lighting the golden candle as a matter of self-discipline. I was tempted to use it to see whether Idas had been burned or bitten. But reason told me the assassin who had been burned would be in no condition to make a second attempt on my life, and that the one who had been bitten could hardly have reached the iron stair in the airshaft far enough ahead of me to have climbed it unheard.

"Would you mind if I talked to you? When we met earlier and you spoke of your home world, I wanted to very much."

"I'd like to," I told him, "if you wouldn't mind answering a few questions." What I would really have liked was a chance to rest. I was still far from recovered, but an opportunity to gain information was not to be squandered.

"No," Idas said. "Not a bit—I'd very much enjoy answering your questions, if you'll answer mine."

Seeking an innocuous way to begin, I took off my boots and stretched myself upon the bunk, which complained of me softly. "Then what do you call the tongue we're speaking?" I began.

"The way we're talking now? Why, Ship, of course."

"Do you know any other languages, Idas?"

"No, not I. I was born on board, you see. That was one of the things I wanted to ask you about—how life is different for someone from a real world. I've heard a lot of stories from the crew, but they're just ignorant seamen. I can tell that you're a person who thinks."

"Thank you. Having been born here, you've had a lot of chances to visit real worlds. Have you found many where they spoke Ship?"

"To tell the truth, I haven't taken shore leave as often as I could have. My appearance . . . you've probably noticed—"

"Answer my question, please."

"They speak Ship on most worlds, I suppose." Idas's voice sounded a trifle nearer than it had, I thought.

"I see. On Urth, what you call Ship is spoken only in our Commonwealth. We hold it a more ancient tongue than the others, but up until now I've never been sure that was true." I decided to steer the talk to whatever had plunged everything in darkness: "This would be a great deal more satisfying if we could see each other, wouldn't it?"

"Oh, yes! Won't you use your light?"

"In a moment, perhaps. Do you think they'll get the ship's lights working again soon?"

"They're trying to fix it so the most important parts have lights now," Idas said. "But this isn't an important part."

"What went wrong?"

I could practically see his shrug. "Something conductive must have fallen across the terminals of one of the big cells, but no one can find out what it was. Anyway, the plates burned through. Some cables too, and that shouldn't have happened."

"And all the other sailors are working there?"

"Most of my gang."

I was certain he was nearer now, no more than an ell from the bunk.

"A few got off for other things. That was how I got away. Severian, your home world . . . is it beautiful there?"

"Very beautiful, but terrible too. Possibly the loveliest things of all are the ice isles that sail up like argosies from the south. They're white and pale green, and they sparkle like diamonds or emeralds when the sun strikes them. The sea around them looks black, but it's so clear you can see their hulls far down in the pelagic deeps—"

Idas's breath hissed ever so faintly. Hearing it, I drew my knife as quietly as I could.

"—and each rears like a mountain against a royal-blue sky dusted with stars. But nothing can live on those ice isles . . . nothing human. Idas, I'm getting sleepy. Perhaps you'd better go."

"I'd like to ask you much, much more."

"And so you will, another time."

"Severian, do men touch each other sometimes on your world? Clasp hands as a sign of friendship? They do that on a lot of worlds."

"And on mine, too," I said, and shifted the knife to my left hand.

"Let's clasp hands then, and I'll go."

"All right," I told him.

Our fingertips touched, and at that moment the cabin light came on.

He was holding a bolo, its blade below his hand. He drove it down with all his weight behind it. My right hand flew up. I could never have stopped that blow, but I managed to deflect it; the broad point went through my

shirt and plunged into the mattress so near my skin that I
felt the chill of the steel.

He tried to jerk the bolo back, but I got his wrist, and he
could not pull free of my grip. I could have killed him
easily, but I ran my blade through his forearm instead, to
make him let go of the hilt.

He screamed—not so much from pain, I think, as from
the sight of my blade thrusting from his flesh. I threw him
down, and a moment later had the point of my knife at his
throat.

"Quiet," I told him, "or I'll kill you on the spot. How
thick are these walls?"

"My arm—"

"Forget your arm. There'll be time enough to lick your
blood. Answer me!"

"Not thick at all. The walls and floors are just sheets of
metal."

"Good. That means there's no one about. I was listening
while I lay on the bunk, and I didn't hear a single step. You
may wail all you want. Now stand up."

The hunting knife had a good edge: I slit Idas's shirt
down the back and pulled it off, revealing the budding
breasts I had half suspected.

"Who put you on this ship, girl? Abaia?"

"You knew!" Idas stared at me, her pale eyes wide.

I shook my head and cut a strip from the shirt. "Here,
wind your arm with this."

"Thank you, but it doesn't matter. My life's over anyway."

"I said to wind it. When I go to work on you, I don't
want to get any more blood on these clothes than I have
already."

"There will be no need to torture me. Yes, I was a slave
of Abaia's."

"Sent to kill me so I wouldn't bring the New Sun?"

She nodded.

"Chosen because you were still small enough to pass as
human. Who are the others?"

"There aren't any others."

I would have seized her, but she held up her right hand. "I swear it by Lord Abaia! There may be others, but I don't know them."

"It was you who killed my steward?"

"Yes."

"And searched my stateroom?"

"Yes."

"But it wasn't you I burned with my pistol. Who was that?"

"Only a hand I hired for a chrisos; I was down the gangway when you fired. You see, I wanted to cast the body adrift, but I wasn't sure I could carry it without help and work the hatches too. Besides . . ." Her voice trailed away.

"Besides what?"

"Besides, he'd have had to help me with other things too, after that. Isn't that right? Now, how did you know? Please tell me."

"It wasn't you that attacked me at the apport pens, either. Who was that?"

Idas shook her head as though to clear it. "I didn't know you'd been attacked at all."

"How old are you, Idas?"

"I don't know."

"Ten? Thirteen?"

"We don't number the years." She shrugged. "But you said we weren't human, and we're as human as you. We're the Other People, the folk of the Great Lords who dwell in the sea and underground. Now, please, I've answered your questions, so answer mine. How did you know?"

I sat on the bunk. Soon I would begin the excruciation of this lanky child; it had been a long while—perhaps before she was born—since I had been the Journeyman Severian, and I would not relish the task. I was half hoping she would bolt for the door.

"In the first place, you didn't talk like a sailor. I once had a friend who did, so I notice when others do, though that's much too long a tale to tell now. My troubles—the murder of my steward and so on—started soon after I met you and the others. You told me at once that you'd been born on this ship, but the others talked like seamen, except for Sidero, and you didn't."

"Purn and Gunnie are from Urth."

"Then too, you misdirected me when I asked the way to the galley. You meant to follow me and kill me when you could, but I found my stateroom, and that must have seemed better to you. You could wait until I was asleep and talk your way past the lock. That wouldn't have been hard, I suppose, since you're a member of the crew."

Idas nodded. "I brought tools, and I told your lock I'd been sent to mend a drawer."

"But I wasn't there. The steward stopped you as you were leaving. What were you looking for?"

"Your letter, the one that the aquastors of Urth gave you for the Hierogrammate. I found it and burned it there in your own stateroom." Her voice held a note of triumph now.

"You would have found that easily enough. You were looking for something else too, something you expected to be hidden. In a moment or two I'm going to hurt you very badly unless you tell me what that was."

She shook her head. "Is it all right if I sit down?"

I nodded, expecting her to sit on the chest or the spare bunk, but she sank to the floor, looking like a real child at last despite her height.

"A moment ago," I continued, "you kept asking me to kindle my light. After the second, it wasn't hard to guess you wanted to be certain your thrust would be a clean kill. So I used the words *argosy* and *pelagic*, because Abaia's slaves employ them as passwords; long ago someone who thought for a moment I might be one of you showed me a card saying he was to be found on Argosy Street, and Vodalus—you may have heard of him—once told me to give a message to one who should say to me, 'The pelagic argosy sights—'"

I never finished my quotation. On the ship, where heavy

things were so light, the child fell forward very slowly; and yet it was fast enough for a soft tap when her forehead struck the floor. I am sure she must have been dead almost from the beginning of my vainglorious little speech.

CHAPTER VIII

The Empty Sleeve

WHEN IT WAS TOO LATE I MOVED VERY SWIFTLY, TURNING Idas upon her back, feeling for a pulse, pounding her chest to shock her heart into renewed life, all of it perfectly useless. I found no pulse, and the reek of poison in her mouth.

It must have been hidden on her person. Not in her shirt, unless she had already slipped the pellet to her lips in the darkness, to be crushed and swallowed should she fail. In her hair, perhaps (though that seemed too short to have concealed anything), or in the waistband of her trousers. From either place she might easily have conveyed it unseen to her mouth as she staunched the blood from her arm.

Recalling what had occurred when I tried to reanimate the steward, I did not dare try to revive her. I searched her body, but found almost nothing beyond nine chrisos of gold, which I put into the pocket in the sheath. She had said that she had given a hand a chrisos to assist her; it seemed reasonable to suppose that Abaia (or whichever of his ministers had sent her out) had provided her with ten. When I cut away her boots, I found that the toes they had concealed were long and webbed. I sliced the boots to bits, searching them just as she had searched my own belongings a couple of watches earlier, but found no more than she had.

As I sat on my bunk and contemplated her body, I thought it strange that I had been deceived, though certainly I had been at first, deceived not so much by Idas as by

55

my recollection of the undine who had freed me from the nenuphars of Gyoll and accosted me at the ford. She had been a giantess; thus I had seen Idas as a gangling youth and not as a giant child, though Baldanders had kept a somewhat similar child—a boy, and much younger—in his tower.

The undine's hair had been green, not white; perhaps that had done most of all. I should have realized that such a true and vivid green is not found in men or beasts with hair or fur, and when it seems to occur is the effect of algae, like that in the blood of the green man at Saltus. A rope left hanging in a pond will soon enough be green; what a fool I had been.

Idas's death would have to be reported. My first thought was to speak to the captain, ensuring a favorable hearing for myself by contacting him through Barbatus or Famulimus.

I had no more than shut the door behind me when I realized that such an introduction was impossible. Our conversation in their stateroom had been their first encounter with me; it had therefore been my last with them. I would have to reach the captain in some other way, establish my identity, and report what had occurred. Idas had said that the repairs were being carried out below, and surely there would be an officer in charge of them. Once more I descended the windswept steps, this time continuing beyond the caged apports into an atmosphere warmer and damper still.

Absurd though it seemed, I somehow felt that my weight, which had been only slight on the tier of my cabin, diminished further as I descended. Earlier, when I had climbed the rigging, I had noticed that it dwindled as I ascended; it therefore followed that it should increase as I moved down from level to level in the bowels of the ship. I can only say that it was not so, or at least that it did not seem so to me, but the very reverse of that.

Soon I heard footsteps on the stair below me. If I had learned anything during the past few watches, it was that any chance-met stranger might be bent upon my death. I halted to listen, and drew my pistol.

The faint clanging of metal stopped with me, then sounded again, rapid and irregular, the noises of a climber who stumbled as he ran. Once there was a clatter, as of a sword or helmet dropped, and another pause before the faltering footsteps came again. I was descending toward something that some other fled; there seemed no doubt of that. Common sense told me I should flee too, and yet I lingered, too proud and too foolish to retreat until I knew the danger.

I did not have to linger long. After a moment I glimpsed a man in armor below me, climbing with fevered haste. In a moment more, only a landing intervened, and I could see him well; his right arm was gone, and indeed appeared to have been torn away, for tattered remnants still dangled and bled from the polished brassard.

There seemed little reason to fear that this wounded and terrified man would attack me, and much more to think that he might fly if I appeared dangerous. I holstered my pistol and called to him, asking what was wrong and whether I could help him.

He stopped and lifted his visored face to look at me. It was Sidero, and he was trembling. "Are you loyal?" he shouted.

"To what, friend? I intend you no harm, if that's what you mean."

"To the ship!"

It seemed pointless to promise loyalty to what was no more than an artifact of the Hierodules, however large; but this was clearly no time to debate abstractions. "Of course!" I called. "True to the death, if need be." In my heart I begged Master Malrubius, who had once tried to teach me something of loyalties, to forgive me.

Sidero began to climb the steps again, a little more slowly and calmly this time, yet stumbling still. Now that I could see him better, I realized that the dark oozing fluid I had supposed human blood was far too viscid, and a blackish green rather than crimson. The tatters I had thought shredded flesh were wires mingled with something like cotton.

Sidero was an android, then, an automaton in human form such as my friend Jonas had once been. I upbraided myself for not having realized it sooner, and yet it came as a relief; I had seen blood enough in the cabin above.

By this time, Sidero was mounting the last steps to the landing where I stood. When he reached me, he halted, swaying. In that gruff, demanding way one unconsciously assumes in the hope of inspiring confidence, I told him to let me see his arm. He did, and I recoiled in amazement.

If I merely write that it was hollow, that will sound, I fear, as if it were hollow as a bone is said to be. Rather, it was empty. The tiny wires and wisps of fiber soaked with dark liquid had escaped from its steely circumference. There was nothing—nothing at all—within.

"How can I help you?" I asked. "I've had no experience in treating such wounds."

He seemed to hesitate. I would have said that his visored face was incapable of expressing emotion; and yet it contrived to do so by its motions, the angles at which he held it, and the play of shadow created by its features.

"You must do exactly as I instruct. You will do that?"

"Of course," I said. "I confess I swore not long ago that I'd someday cast you from a height as you cast me. But I won't avenge myself upon an injured man." I remembered then how much poor Jonas had wanted to be thought a man, as indeed I and many others had thought him, and to be a man in fact.

"I must trust you," he said.

He stepped back, and his chest—his entire torso —opened like a great blossom of steel. And it opened upon emptiness, revealing nothing.

"I don't understand," I told him. "How may I help you?"

"Look." With his remaining hand, he pointed to the inner surface of one of the petallike plates that had made up that empty chest. "Do you see writing?"

"Lines and symbols, yes, in many colors. But I can't read them."

Then he described a certain complex symbol and the symbols surrounding it, and after some searching I discovered it.

"Insert sharp metal there," he said. "Twist to the right, one quarter turn and no more."

The slot was very narrow, but my hunting knife had a needle point, which I had wiped clean on Idas's shirt. Now I wedged this point into the place Sidero had indicated and twisted it as he had told me. The seeping of the dark liquid slowed.

He described a second symbol on another plate; and while I hunted for it, I ventured to tell him I had never heard or read of any such being as he.

"Hadid or Hierro could explain us to you better. I perform my duties. I do not think of such things. Not often."

"I understand," I said.

"You complain that I pushed you off. I did it because you did not attend to my instructions. I have learned that men like you are a hazard to the ship. If they are injured, it is no more than they would do to me. How many times do you think such men have tried to destroy me?"

"I've no idea," I said, still scanning the plate for the symbol he had described.

"Nor do I. We sail in and out of Time, then back again. There is only one ship, the captain says. All the ships we hail between the galaxies or the suns are this ship. How can I know how often they have tried, or how often they have succeeded?"

He was growing irrational, I thought, and then I found the symbol. When I had fitted the point of my hunting knife into the slot and turned it, the seepage of fluid dropped almost to nothing.

"Thank you," Sidero said. "I have been losing a great deal of pressure."

I asked whether he would not have to drink new fluid to replace that he had lost.

"Eventually. But now I have my strength again, and I will have full strength when you make the last adjustment." He told me where it was and what to do.

"You asked how we came to be. Do you know how your own race came to be?"

"Only that we were animals who lived in trees. That is what the mystes say. Not the monkeys, since the monkeys are there still. Perhaps something like the zoanthropes, though smaller. The zoanthropes always make for the mountains, I've noticed, and they climb trees in the high jungle there. At any rate, these animals communicated with one another, as even cattle do, and wolves, by certain cries and motions. Eventually, through the will of the Increate, it came to be that those who communicated best survived while those who did so poorly perished."

"Is there no more?"

I shook my head. "When they communicated well enough that they could be said to speak, they were men and women. Such are we still. Our hands were made to cling to branches, our eyes to see the next branch as we move from tree to tree, our mouths to speak, and to chew fruit and fledglings. So are they still. But what of your own kind?"

"Much like yours. If the story is true, the mates wanted shelter from the void, from destructive rays, the weapons of hostiles, and other things. They built hard coverings for themselves. They wanted to be stronger too, for war and work on deck. Then they put the liquid you saw into us so that our arms and legs would move as they wanted, but with greater force. Into our genators, I ought to have said. They needed to communicate, so they added talk circuits. Then more circuits so we could do one thing as they did another. Controllers so we could speak and act even when they could not. Until at last we spoke in storage and acted without a mate inside. Are you unable to find it?"

"I'll have it in a moment," I told him. The truth was that I had found it some time before, but I had wanted to keep him talking. "Do you mean the officers of this ship wear you like clothing?"

"Not often now. The mark is like a star, with a straight mark beside it."

"I know," I said, debating what I might do and judging the cavity inside him. My belt, with the knife and my pistol in its holster, would never fit, I thought; but without those I might go in well enough.

I told Sidero, "Wait a moment. I'm having to work in a half crouch to find this thing. These are digging into me." I slipped my belt free and laid it down, with the sheath and holstered pistol beside it. "This would be easier if you'd lie down."

He did so, and more quickly and gracefully than I would have thought possible, now that he was no longer bleeding so much. "Be quick. I have no time to waste."

"Listen," I told him, "if somebody were after you, he'd have been here by now, and I can't even hear anyone." While I pretended to dawdle, I was thinking furiously; it seemed a mad idea, yet it would give protection and a disguise, if it succeeded. I had worn armor often. Why not better armor?

"Do you think I fled them?"

I heard what Sidero said, but I paid little attention to it. I had spoken a moment before of listening; now there was something to listen to, and after listening I recognized it for what it was: the slow beating of great wings.

CHAPTER IX

The Empty Air

MY KNIFE POINT HAD ALREADY FOUND THE SLOT. I TWISTED it as I snatched off my cloak and rolled into Sidero's open body. I did not so much as try to see what creature those wings bore until I had thrust my head, with some pain, into his and could look out through his visor.

Even then I saw nothing, or almost nothing. The airshaft, which had been fairly clear at this depth earlier, now seemed filled with mist; something had carried the cool upper air lower, mixing it with the warm, moist, reeking air we breathed. Something that roiled that mist now, as though a thousand ghosts searched there.

I could no longer hear the wings, or anything else. I might as well have had my head locked in a dusty strongbox, peeping through the keyhole. Then Sidero's voice sounded—but not in my ear.

I do not know just how to describe it. I know well what it is to have another's thoughts in my mind: Thecla's came there, and the old Autarch's, before I grew one with them. This was not that. And yet it was not hearing, either, as I had known it. I can come no nearer to it than to say that there is something more that hears, behind the ear; and that Sidero's voice was there, without having passed through the ear to reach it.

"I can kill you."

"After I repaired you? I have known ingratitude, but never such depths as that." His chest had closed tightly,

62

and I struggled to get my legs into his, pushing with hands braced against the hollows of his shoulders. If I had been able to take a moment more outside, I would have removed my boots; then it would have been easy. As it was, I felt I had already fractured both ankles.

"You have no right in me!"

"I have every right. You were made to protect men, and I was a man in need of protection. Didn't you hear the wings? You can't make me believe there is supposed to be a creature like that loose in this ship."

"They have freed the apports."

"Who has?" My sound leg had at last straightened itself. My lame leg ought to have been easier, because its muscles had shrunk; but I could not summon strength enough to force it down.

"The jibers."

I felt myself bent forward, as one sometimes is in wrestling; Sidero was sitting up. He stood, and in standing shifted my position just enough for my lame leg to straighten. It was easy then to thrust my left arm into his. My right entered what had been his own right arm equally easily, but emerged from the damaged brassard, protected only at the shoulder.

"That's better," I said. "Wait a moment."

He sprang up the stairs instead, able now to take three at a stride.

I halted, turned, and descended again.

"I will kill you for this."

"For going back for my knife and pistol? I don't think you should; we may need them." I stooped and picked them up, the knife with my right hand, the pistol with my left, inside Sidero's. My belt had half fallen through the grillwork floor; but I retrieved it without difficulty, threaded sheath and holster on it, and buckled it around Sidero's waist without a thumb's width to spare.

"Get out!"

I fastened my cloak about his shoulders. "Sidero, I've had people inside me too, though you may not believe it. It can be pleasant and useful. Because I'm where I am, we have a right arm. You said you were loyal to the ship. So am I. Are we going to—"

Something pale dropped from the pale mist. Its wings were translucent as the wings of insects, but more flexible than the wings of bats. And they were huge, so wide they wrapped the landing where we stood like the curtains of a catafalque.

Suddenly I could hear again. Sidero had activated the circuits that conveyed sound from his ears to mine; or perhaps he was only too distracted to prevent their functioning. However that might be, I heard the wind that roared around us from those great and ghostly wings, a hiss like the quenching of a thousand blades.

My pistol was in my hand, though I was not aware of having drawn it. I looked frantically for something, head or claws, at which to fire. There was nothing, and yet something gripped my legs, lifting me and Sidero too as a child lifts a doll. I fired at random. A rent—but, oh, how small a rent—appeared in the titanic wings, its edges just defined by a narrow band burned black.

The railing struck my knees. As it did, I fired again and smelled smoke.

It seemed that it was my own arm that burned. I cried out. Sidero was struggling with the winged creature without my volition. He had drawn the hunting knife, and I feared for a moment he had slashed my arm, that the burning pain I felt was that which we feel when sweat is carried to a wound. I thought of turning my pistol on him, then realized that my own hand was in his.

The horror of the Revolutionary gripped me once more; I fought to destroy myself, and I no longer knew whether I was Severian or Sidero, Thecla to live or Thecla to die. We spun, head downward.

We fell.

The terror of it was indescribable. Intellectually, I knew we could fall but slowly in the ship; I was even half-aware that we fell no faster at the lower levels. And yet we were falling, air whistling by faster and faster, the side of the airshaft a dark blur.

All of it had been a dream. How strange it seemed. I had boarded a great ship with decks upon every side, climbed into a metal man. Now I was awake at last, lying on the icy slope of the mountain beyond Thrax, seeing two stars and imagining, half in dream, that they were eyes.

My right arm had shifted too near the fire, but there was no fire. It was the cold, then, that made it burn so. Valeria moved me to softer ground.

The deepest bell in the Bell Tower was ringing. The Bell Tower had risen by night on a column of flame, settling at dawn beside Acis. The iron throat of the great bell shouted to the rocks, and they reverberated with its echoing sound.

Dorcas had played the recording "Deep Bells Offstage." Had I delivered my final lines? "*In future times, so it has long been said, the death of the old sun will destroy Urth. But from its grave will rise monsters, a new people, and the New Sun. Old Urth will flower as a butterfly from its dry husk, and the New Urth shall be called Ushas.*" What fanfaron! Exit Prophet.

The winged woman of Father Inire's book awaited me in the wings. Her hands she clapped once, formally, as a great lady summons her maid. As they parted there appeared between them a point of white light, hot and flaming. It seemed to me that it was my own face, and my face a mask that stared into it.

The old Autarch, who lived in my mind but seldom spoke, muttered through my swollen lips. "*Find another. . . .*"

A dozen panting breaths had passed before I understood what he had told us: that it was time to surrender this body to death, time for us—time for Severian and Thecla, time for himself and all the rest who stood in his shadow—to take a step toward the shadows ourselves. Time for us to find someone else.

* * *

He lay between two great machines, already splattered with some dark lubricant. I bent, nearly falling, to explain what he must do.

But he was dead, his scarred cheek cold to my touch, his withered leg broken, the white bone thrusting through the skin. With my fingers I closed his eyes.

Someone came with hastening steps. Before they reached me, someone else was already at my shoulder, a hand behind my head. I saw the light of his eyes, smelled the musk of his hairy face. He held a cup to my lips.

I tasted, hoping for wine. It was water; but cold, pure water that tasted better than any wine to me.

A throaty female voice called, "Severian!" and a big sailor crouched at my side. It was not until she spoke again that I realized the voice had been hers. "You're all right. We were— I was afraid—" She had no words and kissed me instead; as she did, the hairy face kissed us both. Its kiss was quick, but hers went on and on.

It left me breathless. "Gunnie," I said when she released me at last.

"Now how are you feeling? We were afraid you were going to die."

"So am I." I was sitting up now, though it was all I could do to do so. Every joint ached, my head ached worst of all, and my right arm seemed to have been thrust into a fire. The sleeve of my velvet shirt hung in rags, and the skin had been coated with a yellow ointment. "What happened to me?"

"You must have fallen down the spiracle—that's where we found you. Or anyway, Zak did. He came and got me." Gunnie jerked her head toward the hairy dwarf who had held the water cup for me. "Before that, I guess you were flashed."

"Flashed?"

"Burned by an arc when something shorted out. Same thing happened to me. Look." She was wearing a gray workshirt; now she pulled it down far enough for me to see that the skin between her breasts had been seared an angry red and was smeared with the same ointment. "I was working in the powerhouse. When I got burned, they sent me to the infirmary. They put this stuff on and gave me a tube to use later—I guess that's why Zak picked me. You're not up to hearing all this, are you?"

"I suppose not." The oddly angled walls had begun to turn, circling with a slow dignity like the skulls that had swung about me once.

"Lie down again while I get you something to eat. Zak will keep a watch for jibers. There don't seem to be any down this far anyway."

I felt I should ask her a hundred questions. Much more, I wanted to lie down, to sleep if the pain allowed it; and I was lying down and half-asleep before I had time to do more than think about it.

Then Gunnie had returned with a bowl and a spoon. "Atole," she said. "Eat it." It tasted like stale bread boiled in milk, but it was warm and filling. I believe I ate most of it before I slept again.

When I woke next, I was no longer so near to agony, though I was yet in pain. My missing teeth were missing still, my mouth and jaw still sore; there was a knot the size of a pigeon's egg on the side of my head, and the skin of my right arm was beginning to crack despite the ointment. It had been ten years and more since Master Gurloes or one of the journeymen had thrashed me, and I found I was no longer so skilled at dismissing pain as once I had been.

I tried to distract myself with an examination of my surroundings. The place where I lay appeared not so much a cabin as a crevice in some great mechanism, the kind of place where one finds objects that appear to have come from nowhere—but such a place magnified many times. The ceiling was ten ells high at least, and slanted. No door preserved privacy or repelled intruders; an unobstructed passage led from a corner.

I lay on a heap of clean rags near the corner diagonally opposite. When I sat up to look around me, the hairy dwarf

Gunnie. called Zak appeared from the shadows and crouched beside me. He did not speak, but his posture expressed a concern for my well-being. I said, "I'm all right, don't worry," and at that he seemed to relax a bit.

The only light in the chamber came through the door; I used it to examine my nurse as well as I could. He seemed to me not so much a dwarf as a small man—that is to say, there was no marked disproportion between his torso and limbs. His face was not fundamentally different from any other man's except in being overshadowed by bushy hair and having a luxuriant brown beard and an even more luxuriant mustache, neither of which appeared ever to have been touched by scissors. His forehead was low, his nose somewhat flat, and his chin (so far as it could be guessed at) less than prominent; but many men have such features. He was indeed a man, I should add, and then a completely naked one save for a thick crop of bodily hair; but when he saw me glance at his crotch, he pulled a rag from the pile and knotted it about his waist like an apron.

With some difficulty, I got to my feet and hobbled across the room. He outraced me and planted himself in the doorway. There every line of his body reminded me of a servant I had once watched restraining a drunken exultant; it pleaded with me not to do as I intended, and simultaneously announced its owner's readiness to restrain me by force if I tried.

I was unfit for force of any sort, and as far as possible from those reckless high spirits in which we are ready to fight our friends when there are no enemies at hand. I hesitated. He pointed down the passage, drawing a finger across his throat in an unmistakable gesture.

"Danger there?" I asked. "You're probably right. This ship would make some battlefields I've seen look like public gardens. All right, I won't go out."

My bruised lips made it difficult to talk, but he appeared to have understood me, and after a moment he smiled.

"Zak?" I asked, pointed to him.

He smiled again and nodded.

I touched my chest. "Severian."

"Severian!" He grinned, showing small, sharp teeth, and performed a little dance of joy. Still joyful, he took my left arm and led me back to the pile of rags.

Though his hand was brown, it seemed faintly luminous in the shadows.

CHAPTER X

Interlude

"YOU HAD A GOOD RAP ON THE HEAD," GUNNIE SAID. SHE was sitting beside me watching me eat stew.

"I know."

"I ought to have taken you to the infirmary, but it's dangerous out there. You don't want to be anywhere other people know about."

I nodded. "Especially me. Two people have tried to kill me. Perhaps three. Possibly four."

She looked at me as if she suspected the fall had unsettled my wits.

"I'm quite serious. One was your friend Idas. She's dead now."

"Here, have some water. Are you saying Idas was a woman?"

"A girl, yes."

"And I didn't know it?" Gunnie hesitated. "You're not just making it up?"

"It isn't important. The important thing is that she tried to kill me."

"And you killed him."

"No, Idas killed herself. But there is at least one other and perhaps more than one. You weren't talking about them, though, Gunnie. I think you meant the people Sidero mentioned, the jibers. Who are they?"

She rubbed the skin at the corners of her eyes with her forefingers, the woman's equivalent of male head scratching. "I don't know how to explain it. I don't even know if I understand them myself."

I said, "Try, Gunnie, please. It may be important."

Hearing the urgency in my voice, Zak abandoned his self-assigned task of watching for intruders long enough for a concerned glance.

"You know how this ship sails?" Gunnie asked. "Into and out of Time, and sometimes to the end of the universe and farther."

I nodded, scraping the bowl.

"There are I don't know how many of us in the crew. It may sound funny to you, but I just don't. It's so big, you see. The captain never calls us all together. It would take too long, days of walking just for all of us to get to the same place, and then there'd be nobody doing the work while we were going there and getting back."

"I understand," I told her.

"We sign on and they take us to one part or another. And that's where we stay. We get to know the others who are already there, but there's lots of others we never see. The forecastle up from here where my cabin is, that's not the only one. There's lots of others. Hundreds and maybe thousands."

"I asked about the jibers," I said.

"I'm trying to tell you. It's possible for somebody, anybody, to lose himself on the ship forever. And I mean Forever, because the ship goes there, and it comes back, and that makes strange things happen to time. Some people get old on the ship and die, but some work a long time and never get any older and make a load of money, until finally the ship makes port on their home, and they see it's almost the same time there now as when they got on, and they get off, and they're rich. Some get older for a while, then get younger." She hesitated, afraid for a moment to speak more; then she said, "That's what's happened to me."

"You're not old, Gunnie," I told her. It was the truth.

"Here," she said, and taking my left hand, she laid it on her forehead. "Here I'm old, Severian. So much has happened to me that I want to forget. Not just to forget, I want to be young there again. When you drink or drug, you forget. But what those things did to you is still there, in the way you think. You know what I'm saying?"

"Very well," I told her. I took my hand from her forehead and held one of hers instead.

"But you see, because those things happen, and sailors know it and talk about it even if most longshore people won't believe them, the ship gets people who aren't really sailors and don't want to work. Or maybe a sailor will fight with an officer and get written up for punishment. Then he'll go off and join the jibers. We call them that because it's what you say a boat does when she makes a turn you don't want—she jibes."

"I understand," I said again.

"Some just stay in one place, I think, like we're staying here. Some travel around looking for money or a fight. Maybe just one comes to your mess, and he has some story. Sometimes so many come nobody wants to give them trouble, so you pretend they're crew, and they eat, and if you're lucky they go away."

"You're saying that they're only common seamen, then, who've rebelled against the captain." I brought in the captain because I wanted to ask her about him later.

"No." She shook her head. "Not always. The crew comes from different worlds, from other star-milks, even, and maybe from other universes. I don't know about that for sure. But what's a common seaman to you and me might be somebody pretty strange to somebody else. You're from Urth, aren't you?"

"Yes, I am."

"So am I, and so are most of the others here. They put us together because we talk the same and think the same. But if we went to another fo'c'sle, everything might be different."

"I thought I'd traveled a great deal," I told her, laughing inwardly at myself. "Now I see I haven't gone quite as far as I believed."

"It would take you days just to get out of the part of the ship where most of the sailors are more or less like you and me. But the jibers who move around get mixed up. Sometimes they fight each other; but sometimes they join together until there are three or four different kinds in one gang. Sometimes they pair up, and the woman has children, like Idas. Usually the children can't have children, though. That's what I've heard."

She glanced significantly toward Zak, and I whispered, "He's one?"

"I think he must be. He found you and came and got me, so I thought it would be all right to leave you with him while I went for food. He can't talk, but he hasn't hurt you, has he?"

"No," I told her. "He's been fine. In ancient times, Gunnie, the peoples of Urth journeyed among the suns. Many came home at last, but many others stayed on that world or this. The hetrochthnous worlds must by this time have reshaped humanity to conform to their own spheres. On Urth, the mystes know that each continent has its own pattern for mankind, so that if people from one shift their abode to another, they will in a short time—fifty generations or so—come to resemble the original inhabitants. The patterns of other worlds must be yet more distinct; and yet the human race would remain human still, I think."

"Don't say, 'By this time,'" Gunnie told me. "You don't know what the time would be if we were to stop at some sun. Severian, we've talked a lot and you look tired. Don't you want to lie down now?"

"Only if you will lie down too," I said. "You are as tired as I, or more. You've been going around collecting food and medicine for me. Rest now, and tell me more about the jibers." The truth was that I was sufficiently better to wish to put my arm about a woman and even to bury myself in a woman; and with many women, of whom, I think, Gunnie was one, there is no better way to attain intimacy than to permit them to talk, and to listen to them.

She stretched herself beside me. "I've already told you about everything I know. Most are sailors gone bad. Some are their children, born on the ship and hidden till they're old enough to fight. Then too, do you remember how we caught the apport?"

"Of course," I said.

"Not all the apports are animals, though there's a lot more of those than anything else. Sometimes they're people, and sometimes they live long enough to get inside the ship where there's air." She paused, then giggled. "You know, the others on their home worlds must wonder where they went when they were apported. Especially when it's somebody important."

It seemed strange to hear so massive a woman giggle, and I who seldom smile, smiled myself.

"Some people say too that some jibers are taken on board with the cargo, that they're criminals who want to get away from their home worlds and have stowed aboard that way. Or that they're only animals on their worlds and have been shipped as live cargo, though they're people like us. We'd only be animals on those worlds—that's what I think."

Her hair, near my face now, was piercingly fragrant; and it occurred to me that it could hardly be thus always, that she had perfumed herself for me before returning to our cranny.

"Some people call them muties because so many can't talk. Maybe they have some language of their own; but they can't talk to us, and if we catch one he has to talk by signs. But Sidero said one time that *mutist* means a rebel."

I said, "Speaking of Sidero, was he around when Zak took you to the bottom of the airshaft?"

"No, there was nobody there but you."

"Did you see my pistol, or the knife you gave me when we first met?"

"No, there wasn't anything there. Did you have them on when you fell?"

"Sidero had them. I was hoping he'd been honest enough to return them, but at least he didn't kill me."

Gunnie shook her head by rolling it back and forth on the rags, a process that brought one round and blooming cheek into contact with mine. "He wouldn't. He can play rough sometimes, but I never heard that he killed anybody."

"I think he must have struck me while I was unconscious. I don't think I could have hurt my mouth in the fall. I was inside him, did I tell you that?"

She drew away to stare at me. "Really? Can you do that?"

"Yes. He didn't like it, but I think that something in the way he's built kept him from trying to expel me as long as I was conscious. After we fell, he must have opened up and pulled me out with his good arm. I'm lucky he didn't break both my legs. When he got me out, he must have struck me. I will kill him for that, when we meet again."

"He's only a machine," Gunnie said softly. She slipped her hand inside my ruined shirt.

"I'm surprised you know that," I told her. "I would have thought you'd think him a person."

"My father was a fisherman, so I grew up on boats. You give a boat a name and eyes, and a lot of times it acts like a person and even tells you things. But it isn't a person, not really. Fishermen are funny sometimes, but my father used to say that you could tell when a man was really crazy, because if he didn't like his boat he'd sink it instead of selling it. A boat has a spirit, but it takes more than a spirit to make a person."

I asked, "Did your father approve of your signing on this ship?"

She said, "He drowned first. All fishermen drown. It killed my mother. I've got back to Urth pretty often, but it was never when they were alive."

"Who was Autarch when you were a child, Gunnie?"

"I don't know," she said. "It wasn't the kind of thing we cared about."

She wept a little. I tried to comfort her, and from that we might have slipped very quickly and naturally into making love; but her burn covered most of her chest and abdomen, and though I fondled her, and she me, the memory of Valeria came between us as well.

At last she said, "That didn't hurt you, did it?"

"No," I told her. "I'm only sorry I hurt you as much as I did."

"You didn't. Not at all."

"But I did, Gunnie. It was I who burned you in the gangway outside my stateroom, as we both know."

Her hand sought her dagger, but she had discarded it when she undressed. It lay beneath her other clothing and well out of her reach.

"Idas told me she'd hired a sailor to help her dispose of the corpse of my steward. She called that sailor 'he,' but she hesitated before she said the word. You were one of her workmates, and even though you didn't know she was female, it would have been quite natural for her to seek the help of a woman, if she had no male lover."

"How long have you known?" Gunnie whispered. She had not begun to sob again, but in the corner of one eye I could see a tear, large and rounded as Gunnie herself.

"From the first, when you brought me that gruel. Because it had been exposed, my arm had been burned by the digestive juices of the flying creature; it was the only part of me that hadn't been protected by Sidero's metal hide, and of course I thought of that at once when I regained consciousness. You said you'd been seared by a flash of energy, but such things don't discriminate. Your face and forearms, which had been exposed, were unburned. Your burns were in places that would surely have been protected by a shirt and trousers."

I waited for her to speak, but she did not.

"In the dark, I called out for help, but no one answered. Then I fired my pistol with the beam set low, to give me light. I held it at eye level when I fired, but I couldn't see the sights, and the beam was angled down a bit. It must have hit you at the waist. When I slept, you went looking for Idas, I suppose, so you could sell me to her for another chrisos. You didn't find her, of course. She's dead, and her body's locked in my cabin."

"I wanted to answer when you called," Gunnie said. "But we were supposed to be doing something secret. All I knew was that you were lost in the dark, and I thought the lights would come on again soon. Then Idas put his knife—her knife, you say, but I didn't know that—against my neck. He was right behind me, so close he didn't even get hurt when you shot me."

I said, "However that may be, I want you to know that Idas had nine chrisos on her when I searched her body. I put them in the pocket of the sheath on that knife you found. Sidero has my knife and pistol; if you'll return them to me, you may keep the gold and welcome."

Gunnie did not want to talk after that. I feigned sleep, though in fact I watched from beneath my lids to see if she would try to stab me.

Instead she rose and dressed, then crept out of the chamber, stepping over the sleeping Zak. I waited for a long time, but she did not return, and at last I slept myself.

CHAPTER XI

Skirmish

I LAY IN THE NOTHINGNESS OF SLEEP, AND YET SOME PART OF me remained awake, floating in the gulf of unconsciousness, which contains the unborn and so many of the dead.

"Do you know who I am?"

I did, though I could not have said how. "You are the captain."

"I am. Who am I?"

"Master," I said, for it seemed I was an apprentice once more. "Master, I do not understand."

"Who captains the ship?"

"Master, I do not know."

"I am your judge. This blossoming universe has been given to my guardianship. My name is Tzadkiel."

"Master," I said, "is this my trial?"

"No. And it is my own trial that grows near, not yours. You have been a warrior king, Severian. Will you fight for me? Fight willingly?"

"Gladly, master."

My own voice seemed to echo in the dream: "Master . . . master . . . master . . ." There was no reply beyond a booming reverberation. The sun was dead, and I was alone in the freezing dark.

"Master! Master!"

Zak was shaking my shoulder.

I sat up, thinking for a moment that he had more speech than I had supposed. "Hush, I'm awake," I said.

He parroted me: *"Hush!"*

"Was I talking in my sleep, Zak? I must have been, for you to hear that word. I remember—"

I fell silent because he had cupped a hand to his ear. I listened too and heard yells and scuffling. Someone called my name.

Zak was out the door before me, not so much running as launching himself in a flat leap. I was not far behind him, and after bruising my hands on the first wall, I learned to twist myself and strike them with my feet first as he did.

A corner and another, and we caught sight of a knot of struggling men. Another leap shot us among them, I not knowing which side was ours, or even if we had one.

A sailor with a knife in his left hand sprang at me. I caught him as Master Gurloes had once taught me and threw him against a wall, only then seeing that he was Purn.

There was no time for apology or question. The dagger of an indigo giant thrust for my lungs. I struck his thick wrist with both arms, and too late saw a second dagger, its blade held beneath his other hand. It flashed up. I tried to writhe away; a struggling pair pushed me back, and I beheld the steel-hearted blue nenuphar of death.

As if the laws of nature had been suspended for me, it did not descend. The giant's backward motion never stopped, fist and blade continuing backward until he himself was bent backward too, and I heard his shoulder snap, and the wild scream he gave when the jagged bones tore him from within.

Big though his hand was, the pommel of his dagger protruded from it. I got it in one hand and a quillon in the other, and wrenched the weapon free—then drove it up into his rib cage. He fell backward as a tree falls, slowly at first, his legs always stiff beneath him. Zak, hanging from his uplifted arm, tore the other dagger from him, much as I had the one I held.

Each was large enough for a short sword, and we did some damage with them. I would have done more if I had not had to step between Zak and some sailor who thought him a jiber.

Such fights end as suddenly as they begin. One runs, then another, and then all the rest must, being too few to fight. So it was with us. A wild-haired jiber with the teeth of an atrox tried to beat down my blade with a mace of pipe. I half severed his wrist, stabbed him in the throat—and realized that save for Zak I had no comrades left. A sailor dashed past, clutching his bleeding arm. I followed him, shouting for Zak.

If we were pursued, it was with little zeal. We fled down a twisting gangway and through an echoing chamber full of silent machinery, along a second gangway (tracking those we followed by fresh blood on the floors and bulkheads, and once by the body of a sailor) and into a smaller chamber where there were tools and workbenches, and five sailors, full of sighs and curses as they bandaged one another's wounds.

"Who are you?" one asked. He menaced me with his dirk.

Purn said, "I know him. He's a passenger." His right hand had been wrapped in bloodstained gauze and taped.

"And this?" The sailor with the dirk pointed toward Zak.

I said, "Touch him and I'll kill you."

"He's no passenger," the sailor said doubtfully.

"I owe you no explanation and give none. If you doubt that the two of us can kill all of you, try us."

A sailor who had not spoken before said, "Enough, Modan. If the sieur vouches for him . . ."

"I will. I do."

"That's enough, then. I saw you killing the jibers, and your hairy friend the same. How can we help you?"

"You can tell me why the jibers were killing you, if you know. I've been told there are always some on the ship. They can't always be that aggressive."

The sailor's face, which had been open and friendly, closed—though it seemed nothing in his expression had changed. "I've heard tell, sieur, that there's somebody aboard this voyage that they've been told to do for, only they can't find him. I don't know no more than that. If you do, you know more than me, like the hog told the butcher."

"Who gives them their orders?"

He had turned away. I looked around at the rest, and at last Purn said, "We don't know. If there's a captain of the jibers, we've never heard of him till now."

"I see. I'd like to speak to an officer—not just a petty officer like Sidero, but a mate."

The sailor called Modan said, "Well, bless you, sieur, so'd we. You think we jumped all them jibers, without no leader nor proper weapons? We was a work gang, nine hands, and they jumped us. Now we're not goin' to work no more without we have pikes, and marines posted."

The others nodded their agreement.

I said, "Surely you can tell me where I'd be likely to find a mate."

Modan shrugged. "For'ard or aft, sieur. That's all I can say. Mostly they're in one place or the other, those bein' the best for navigation and observations, the instruments not bein' blocked off so much by her sails. One or t'other."

I recalled seizing the bowsprit rigging during my wild career among the sails. "Aren't we pretty far forward here?"

"That's so, sieur."

"Then how can I get farther forward?"

"That way." He gestured. "And foller your nose. That's what the monkey told the elephant."

"But you can't tell me precisely how I should go?"

"I could, sieur, but it wouldn't be mannerly. Can I give you some advice, sieur?"

"That's what I've been asking for."

"Stay with us till we get someplace safer. You want a mate. We'll turn you over to the right one, when we can. You go off on your own and the jibers will kill you sure."

Purn said, "Right when you come out that door, then straight along till you come to the companionway. Up, and take the widest passage. Keep going."

"Thank you," I said. "Come on, Zak."

The hairy man nodded, and when we were outside jerked his head and announced, "Bad man."

"I know, Zak. We have to find a place to hide. Do you understand? You look on this side of the corridor, and I'll look on that one. Keep quiet."

He stared at me quizzically for a moment, but it was plain he understood. I had gone no more than a chain down the corridor when he pulled at my sound arm to show me a little storeroom. Although most of its space was taken up by drums and crates, there was room enough for us. I positioned the door so that a hairline crack remained for us to look through, and he and I sat down on two boxes.

I had been sure the sailors would leave the chamber in which we had found them soon, since there was nothing there for them once they had treated one another's wounds and caught their breath. In the event, they stayed so long that I was almost convinced we had missed them—that they had gone back to the scene of the fight, or down some branching passage that we had overlooked. No doubt they had disputed long before setting out.

However it had been, they appeared at last. I touched a finger to my lips to warn Zak, though I do not think that was necessary. When all five had passed and seemed likely to be fifty ells or more ahead, we crept out.

I had no way of knowing how long we would have to follow them before Purn would be last among them, or if he would ever be last; in the worst case, I was prepared to pin our hopes on our courage and their fears, and take him from their midst.

Fortune was with us—Purn soon lagged a few steps behind. Since succeeding to the autarchy, I have often led charges in the north. I feigned to lead such a charge now, shouting for pandours who consisted exclusively of Zak to follow. We rushed upon the sailors as though at the head of an army, flourishing our weapons; and they turned and fled as one man.

I had hoped to take Purn from behind, sparing my burned arm as much as I could. Zak saved me the trouble with a long flying leap that sent him crashing into Purn's knees. I needed only to hold the point of my dagger at his throat. He looked terrified, as well he should: I expected to kill him when I had wrung as much information from him as I could.

For the space of a breath or two we remained listening to the retreating feet of the four who had fled. Zak had snatched Purn's knife from its sheath, and now waited with a weapon in either hand, glaring at the fallen seaman from beneath beetling brows.

"You'll die at once if you try to run," I whispered to Purn. "Answer me and you may live awhile. Your right hand's bandaged. How was it hurt?"

Although he lay flat on his back, with my dagger against his throat, his eyes defied me. It was a look I knew well, an attitude I had seen broken again and again.

"I haven't enough time to waste any on you," I told him, and I prodded him with the point just enough to draw blood. "If you won't answer, say so plainly; and I'll kill you and be done with it."

"Fighting the jibers. You were there. You saw it. I tried to get you, sure, that's true enough. I thought you were one of them. With that jiber—" His eyes flickered toward Zak. "With him with you, anybody would have. You weren't hurt, and no harm done."

"'As the viper told the sow.' So a man called Jonas used to say. He was a sailor too, Purn, but as quick to lie as you are. That hand was wrapped in bandages already when Zak and I joined the fight. Take the bandages off."

He did so, reluctantly. The wound had been treated by a skillful leech, no doubt at the infirmary Gunnie had mentioned; the tear in his flesh was sutured now, yet it was clear enough what sort of wound it had been.

And as I bent to look at it, Zak, bending too, drew his lips back from his teeth as I have sometimes seen tame apes do. I knew then that the wild conjecture I had been trying to dismiss was the simple truth: Zak had been the shaggy, bounding apport we had hunted in the hold.

CHAPTER XII

The Semblance

TO HIDE MY CONFUSION, I PLANTED MY FOOT ON PURN'S chest and barked, "Why did you try to kill me?"

For some men, there comes a moment when they accept the certainty of death, and so are no longer afraid. That moment came for Purn, a change as unmistakable as the opening of an eye. "Because I know you, Autarch."

"You're one of my own people, then. You boarded the ship when I did."

He nodded.

"And Gunnie boarded with you?"

"No, Gunnie's an old hand. She's not your enemy, Autarch, if that's what you're thinking."

To my amazement, Zak looked at me and nodded. I said, "I know more of that than you do, Purn."

As if he had not heard me, he said, "I'd been hoping she'd kiss me. You don't even know the way they do it here."

"She kissed me," I told him, "when we met."

"I saw it, and I saw you didn't know what she meant. On this ship, every new hand's supposed to have an old one for a lover, to teach him ship's ways. The kiss is the sign."

"Women have been known to kiss and kill."

"Not Gunnie," Purn insisted. "Or anyhow, I don't think so."

"But you'd have killed me for that? For her love?"

"I signed to kill you, Autarch. Everybody knew where you were going, and that you meant to bring back the New

84

Sun if you could, turn Urth upside down and kill everybody."

So stunned was I, not just by what he said but by his very
evident sincerity, that I took a step backward. He was up in
a trice. Zak lunged for him. But though Zak's long blade
gashed his arm, it did not go deep; he was off like a hare.

He would have had Zak after him like a hound if I had
not called him back. "I'll kill him if he tries to kill me
again," I said. "And you may do the same. But I won't
hunt him down for doing what he believes is right. We're
both trying to save Urth, it seems."

Zak stared at me for a moment, then lifted his shoulders.

"Now I want to know about you. You worry me a great
deal more than Purn. You can speak."

He nodded vigorously. "Zak talk!"

"And you understand what I say."

He nodded again, though more dubiously.

"Then tell me the truth. Wasn't it you I helped Gunnie
and Purn and the others capture?"

Zak stared, then shook his head and looked to one side
in a fashion that showed very plainly he did not wish to
continue the conversation.

"It was I, actually, who caught you; and I didn't kill you.
I think perhaps you feel grateful for that. When Purn tried
to kill me— Zak! Come back!"

He had bolted, as I should have guessed he would, and
with my crippled leg I had no hope of overtaking him. By
some freak of the ship, he remained visible for a long time,
appearing from one direction only to vanish in another,
the soft slapping of his bare feet still audible even when
Zak himself was out of sight. I was vividly reminded of a
dream in which I had seen the orphan boy with the same
name as my own, wearing the clothes I had worn as an
apprentice, fleeing down corridors of glass; and it seemed
to me that just as little Severian the orphan had in some
sense been playing my part in that dream, so Zak's face
had taken on something of the long proportions of my
own.

Yet this was no dream. I was wide awake and not

drugged, merely lost somewhere in the innumerable windings of the ship. What sort of creature was Zak? Not an evil one, I thought; but then how many of the millions of species on Urth can be called evil in any real sense? The alzabo, certainly, and the blood bats and scorpions, perhaps; the snake called "yellow beard" and other poisonous snakes, and a few more. A dozen or two all told out of millions. I remembered Zak as he had been when I had seen him first in the hold: fallow-hued, with a shaggy coat that was not of hair or feathers; four-limbed and tailless, and surely headless as well. When I had seen him next in his cage, he had been covered with hair and had possessed a blunt-featured head; I had supposed my original impression mistaken without ever calling it clearly to mind.

On Urth there are lizards that take on the coloration of the things about them—green if they are among leaves, gray among stones, and so on. They do this not in order to capture their prey, as one might think, but to escape the eyes of birds. Might it not be, I thought, that on some other world there had come into being an animal that assumed the shape of others? Its original shape (if it could be said to possess one) might have been even stranger than the four-legged, nearly spherical thing I had first seen in the hold. Predators do not prey on their own kind, as a rule. What greater assurance of safety could the prey have than the appearance of a predator?

Human beings must have presented it with some severe problems: intelligence, speech, and even the distinction between hair on the head and clothing on the body. Quite possibly, the shaggy, ribbonlike covering had been a first attempt at clothing, made when Zak had believed it to be an organic part of his pursuers. He had soon learned differently; and if he had not been released by the mutists with the rest, we would eventually have discovered a naked man in his enclosure. Now he was a man for practical purposes, and at large. But it was no wonder he had run from me—to escape a member of the imitated species who probed his masquerade must have been one of his deepest instincts.

Pondering all this, I had been walking down the passage in which Zak had left me. It soon split into three, and I halted there for a moment, uncertain which to follow. There seemed to be no reason to prefer one to another, and I chose the left at random.

I had not gone far before I noticed I was having difficulty in walking. My first thought was that I was ill, my second that I had been drugged. Yet I felt no worse than I had upon leaving the cranny where Gunnie had hidden me. I was not dizzy, and did not sense that I might fall; nor did I experience any difficulty in maintaining my balance.

And yet I had begun to fall even as these thoughts crossed my mind. It was not that I had failed to recognize that I had lost my equilibrium, but simply that I was unable to take a step quickly enough to catch my weight, although I fell very slowly indeed. My legs seemed bound by some incomprehensible force, and when I tried to stretch my arms before me, they were bound too; I could not lift them from my sides.

Thus I hung in the air, unsupported and subject to the very slight attraction of the holds of the ship, but not falling. Or rather, falling so slowly that it seemed I should never come to rest on the dingy brown walkway of the passage. Somewhere in a more distant part of the ship, a bell tolled.

All this persisted without change for a long time, or at least for a time that seemed very long to me.

At last I heard footsteps. They were behind me; I could not turn my head to see. Fingers reached for the long dagger. I could not move it, but I clenched my fist on the grip and resisted. There was a jolt, and rushing blackness.

It seemed to me that I had fallen from my warm bed of rags. I groped for it, but found only a cold floor. The floor was not uncomfortable—I lay too lightly for that. Almost, I floated. Yet it was chill, so chill I might have floated in one of the shallow pools that form sometimes upon the ice of Gyoll, when there is a brief season of warmth, sometimes even in midwinter.

I wished to lie upon my rags. If I failed to find them again, Gunnie would not find me. I groped for them, but they were not there.

Seeking them, I stretched my mind. I cannot explain how; it seemed to take no effort at all to fill the whole ship with my mind. I knew the holds around which we crept as rats in a house creep through the walls encompassing its rooms, and they were mighty caverns crammed with strange goods. The mine of the man-apes had held silver bars, and gold; but every hold of the ship (and there were many more than seven) was mightier by far, and the least of their treasures were of distant stars.

I knew the ship, its strange mechanisms and those stranger still that were not in truth mechanisms, or living creatures, or anything for which we have words. In it were many human beings and many more that were not human —all sleeping, loving, working, fighting. I knew them all, but there were some I recognized and many I did not.

I knew the masts, taller by a hundred times than the thickness through the hull; the great sails spread like seas, objects huge in two dimensions that scarcely existed in the third. Once a picture of the ship had frightened me. Now I knew her through some sense better than sight, and I surrounded her as she surrounded me. I found my bed of rags, yet I could not reach it.

Pain brought me to myself. Perhaps that is what pain is for, or perhaps it is only the chain forged to bind us to the eternal present, forged in a smithy we can but guess at, by a smith we do not know. However that may be, I felt my consciousness falling in upon itself as the matter does in the heart of a star, as a building does when stone comes to stone again as they were deep in Urth in the beginning, as an urn does that is broken. Ragged figures leaned above me, many of them human.

The largest of all was the raggedest of all, and that seemed strange to me until I realized that he might be unable to obtain clothing to fit him, and so continued to wear what he had worn aboard, having it patched and patched again.

He seized me and pulled me erect, aided by some others, though he in no way required their help. It was the height of folly to struggle with him—they were ten at least, and all armed. And yet I did so, striking and being struck in a brawl I could not win. Since I had cast my manuscript into the void, it seemed that I have been chivied from place to place, never my own master for more than a few moments at a time. Now I was ready to strike at whoever sought to govern me, and if it were my fate that governed me, I would strike at that too.

But it was useless. I hurt the leader, I believe, about as much as the frantic warfare of a boy of ten would have hurt me. He pinned my arms behind me, and another tied them there with wire and prodded me to walk. So driven, I staggered along, and at last was pushed into a narrow room where there stood the Autarch Severian, by his courtiers surnamed the Great, royally attired in his yellow robe and gem-rich cape, the bacculus of power in his hand.

CHAPTER XIII

The Battles

IT WAS ONLY AN IMAGE, YET SO REAL AN IMAGE THAT FOR AN instant I was ready to believe it was a second self who stood there. As I watched, he wheeled, waved with preposterous grandeur toward a vacant corner of the room, and took two strides. With the third he vanished; but he had no sooner done so than he reappeared at the spot where he had first been. For a long breath he remained there, then he turned, waved once more, and strode forward.

The barrel-chested leader croaked an order in a tongue I did not understand, and someone loosed the wire that bound my hands.

Again my semblance stepped forward. Having relieved myself of something of the contempt I felt for him, I was able to note his dragging foot and the arrogant angle at which he poised his head. The leader spoke again, and a little man with dirty gray hair like Hethor's told me, "He desires you to do likewise. If you do not, we will kill you."

I scarcely heard him. I recalled the finery and gestures now, and without the least desire to return in memory to that time, I was captured by it as by the devouring wings in the air shaft. The pinnace (which I had not then known was merely the tender of this great ship) reared before me, its pont extended like a cobweb of silver. My Praetorians, shoulder to shoulder for more than a league, formed an avenue at once dazzling and nearly invisible.

"Get him!"

Ragged men and women swirled around me. For an

instant I supposed I was to be killed because I would not walk and raise my arm; I tried to call to them to wait, but there was no time for that or anything.

Someone seized my collar and jerked me backward, choking. It was an error; when I reeled against him, I was too near for him to use his mace, and I drove my thumbs into his eyes.

Violet light stabbed at the frenzied crowd; half a dozen died. A dozen more with half-ruined faces and missing limbs screamed. The air was full of the sweet smoke of burning flesh. I wrested his mace from the man I had blinded and laid about me. It was foolish—yet the jibers, who bolted from the room as rats fly a ferret, fared worse than I; I saw them reaped like grain.

More wisely, the barrel-chested leader had thrown himself to the floor at the first shot, an ell or so from my feet. Now he sprang for me. The mace head was a gear wheel; it struck him where the shoulder joins the neck, with every ounce of strength I possessed behind it.

I might as effectively have clubbed an arsinoither. Still conscious and still strong, he struck me as that animal strikes a dire-wolf. The mace flew from my hands, and his weight crushed the breath from my body.

There was a blinding flash. I saw his seven-fingered hands upraised, but there was between them only the stump of a neck that smoldered as stumps do where a forest has burned. He charged again—not at me but at the wall, crashed into it, and charged once more, wildly, blindly.

A second shot nearly cleaved him in two.

I tried to rise and found my hands slippery with his blood. An arm, immensely strong, circled my waist and lifted me. A familiar voice asked, "Can you stand?"

It was Sidero, and quite suddenly he seemed an old friend. "I think so," I said. "Thank you."

"You fought them."

"Not successfully." I recalled my days of generalship. "Not well."

"But you fought."

"If you like," I said. Sailors boiled around us now, some flourishing fusils, some bloody knives.

"Will you fight them again? Wait!" He moved his own fusil in a gesture meant to silence me. "I kept the knife and the pistol. Take them now." He was still wearing my belt, with my weapons on it. Clamping the fusil under what remained of his right arm, he released the buckle and handed the whole to me.

"Thank you," I repeated. I did not know what else to say; and I wondered whether he had indeed struck me unconscious, as I had supposed.

The metal vizard that was his face provided no clues to his feelings, his harsh voice hardly more. "Rest now. Eat, and we will talk later. We must fight again later." He turned to face the milling hands. *"Rest! Eat!"*

I felt like doing both. I had no intention of fighting for Sidero, but the thought of a meal shared with comrades who would guard me while I slept was irresistible. It would be easy (so I supposed) to slip off afterward.

The hands had carried rations, and we soon turned up more, the stores of the jibers whom we had killed. In a short time, we were sitting down to a fragrant dinner of lentils boiled with pork and accompanied by fiery herbs, bread, and wine.

Perhaps there were beds or hammocks nearby, as well as the food and the stove, but I for one was too exhausted to look for them. Though my right arm still pained me, I knew it could not do so severely enough to keep me awake; my aching head had been soothed by the wine I had drunk. I was about to stretch myself where I sat—though I wished that Sidero had preserved my cloak too—when a strongly built sailor squatted beside me.

"Remember me, Severian?"

"I should," I said, "since you know my name." The fact was that I did not, though there was something familiar in his face.

"You used to call me Zak."

I stared. The light was dim, but even after allowance had been made for that, I could hardly believe him the Zak I had known. At last I said, "Without mentioning a matter neither of us wishes to discuss, I cannot help but remark that you appear to have changed a great deal."

"It's the clothes—I took them from a dead man. I've shaved my face too. And Gunnie has scissors. She cut off some of my hair."

"Gunnie's here?"

Zak indicated the direction with a motion of his head. "You want to talk to her. She'd like to talk too, I think."

"No," I said. "Tell her I'll talk with her in the morning." I tried to think of something more to say, but all I could manage was, "Tell her what she did for me more than repaid any harm."

Zak nodded and moved away.

Mention of Gunnie had reminded me of Idas's chrisos. I opened the pocket of the sheath and glanced inside to establish that they were still there, then lay down and slept.

When I woke—I hesitate to call it morning because there was no true morning—most of the hands were already up and eating such food as remained after the feast of the night before. Sidero had been joined by two slender automatons, such creatures as I believe Jonas must once have been. The three stood some distance apart from the rest of us, talking in tones too low for me to overhear.

I could not be sure if these volitional mechanisms were nearer the captain and the upper officers than Sidero, and as I was debating whether to approach them and identify myself, they left us, disappearing at once in the maze of passages. As if he had read my thoughts, Sidero walked over to me.

"We can talk now," he said.

I nodded and explained that I had been about to tell him and the others who I was.

"It would do no good. I called when first we met. You are not what you say. The Autarch is secure."

I began to expostulate with him, but he held up his hand to silence me. "Let us not quarrel now. I know what I was told. Let me explain before we argue again. I hurt you. It is my right and duty to correct and chastise. Then I had joy of it."

I asked him if he referred to his striking me when I lay unconscious, and he nodded. "I must not." He seemed about to speak further, but did not. After a moment he said, "I cannot explain."

"We know what moral considerations are," I told him.

"Not as we. You believe you do. We know, and yet often make mistakes. We may sacrifice men to save our own existence. We may transmit and originate instructions to men. We may correct and chastise. But we may not become as you are. That is what I did. I must repay."

I told him he had already, that he had repaid me in full when he saved me from the jibers.

"No. You fought and I fought. This is my payment. We go to a greater fight, perhaps the last. The jibers stole before. Now they rise to kill, to take the ship. The captain tolerated jibers for too long."

I sensed how hard it was for him to speak critically of his captain, and how much he wished to turn away.

"I excuse you," he said. "That is my payment to you."

I asked, "You mean I don't have to join you and your seamen in the battle unless I want to?"

Sidero nodded. "We will fight soon. Get away quickly."

That was, of course, what I had intended, but I could not do so now. To escape by my own cunning, in the face of danger and by my own will, was one thing—to be ordered away from the battle like a spado was quite another.

In a few moments, our metal leader commanded us to fall in. When we did, the sight of my assembled comrades entirely failed to fill me with confidence; Guasacht's irregulars had been crack troops by comparison. A few had fusils like Sidero's, and a few bore calivers like those we had used to capture Zak. (It amused me to see Zak himself so armed now.) A sprinkling of others had pikes or spears; most, including Gunnie, who stood some distance from me and would not look toward me, had only their knives.

And yet all of them marched forward readily enough and gave the impression they would fight, though I knew that as

likely as not half or all would run at the first shot. I sought
and got a position well in the rear of their straggling
column, so that I could better judge the number of desert-
ers. There seemed to be none, and most of these sailors
turned warriors appeared to find the prospect of a pitched
battle a welcome change from their usual drudging.

As always in every sort of war I have known, there was
delay in place of the expected fight. For a watch or more,
we trooped through the bewildering interior of the ship,
once entering a vast, echoing space that must have been an
empty hold, once halting for an unexplained and unneces-
sary rest, twice joined by smaller parties of sailors who
appeared human, or nearly so.

To one who had directed armies, as I have, or taken part
in battles in which whole legions withered like grass cast
into a furnace—again, as I have—it was a great temptation to look on our marchings and our halts with amusement. I write "temptation" because it was one in the
formal sense of being wrong because false. The most trivial
skirmish is not trivial to those who die in it, and so should
not be trivial in any ultimate sense to us.

Let me confess, however, that I surrendered to that
temptation, as I have surrendered to many another. I was
amused, and still more amused when Sidero (plainly
hoping to put me in a position of safety) created a rear
guard and ordered me to take charge of it.

The sailors assigned to me were obviously those he felt
least able to bear themselves with credit when our ragtag
force went into action. Of ten, six were women, and all of
them women far smaller and less muscular than Gunnie.
Three of the four men were undersized and, if not actually
old, at least well past the zenith of their strength; I was the
fourth, and only I had a weapon more formidable than a
work knife or a steel crowbar. On Sidero's orders, we
walked—I cannot say marched—ten chains to the rear of
the main body.

Could I have done so, I would have led my nine hands,
for I was eager that any of the poor creatures who wished to
desert should do it. I could not; the shifting colors and

shapes, the floating light of the ship's interior, still bewildered me. I would have lost all track of Sidero and the main body at once. As the best available alternative, I put the most nearly able-bodied seaman ahead of me, told him what distance to maintain, and let the rest trail along behind us if they would. I admit to speculating on whether we would so much as be aware of it, should those ahead make contact with the enemy.

They did not, and we were aware of it at once.

Looking past my guide, I saw something leap into view, hurl a spinning, many-pointed knife, and spring at us with the heavy-shouldered bounds of a thylacosmil.

Though I do not remember feeling it, the pain of my burn may have slowed my hand. By the time I had my pistol clear of the holster, the jiber was hurtling over the unlucky seaman's body. I had not increased the pistol's setting, but Sidero must have; the gout of energy that struck the jiber blew him apart, pieces of his dismembered body flying by my head in a paroxysmal flock.

There was no time to glory in victory, even less to aid our guide, who lay at my feet drenching the jiber's hydra-knife with blood. I had no more than stooped to look at his wound than two score jibers surged from a gallery. I fired five times as fast as I could press the trigger.

A bolt of flame from some contus or war spear roared like a furnace, splashing blue fire across the bulkhead in back of me, and I turned and ran as fast as my bad leg would permit for half a hundred ells, driving the remaining sailors before me. As we fled, we could hear the jibers engaging the rear of the main body.

Three pursued us. I shot them down and distributed their weapons—two spears and a voulge—to sailors who declared they knew how to use them. We pressed forward past a dozen or more dead, some of them jibers, some Sidero's.

A whistling wind sprang up behind us, nearly snatching the tattered shirt from my back.

CHAPTER XIV

The End of the Universe

THE SAILORS WERE WISER THAN I, PUTTING ON THEIR necklaces at once. I did not understand what had taken place until I saw them.

Not far from us, the explosion of some dreadful weapon had opened the gangways to the void, and the air that had been held in this part of the ship was rushing out. As I got my necklace on, I heard the slamming of great doors, a slow, hollow booming, like the war drums of titans.

No sooner did I snap the catch of my necklace than the wind seemed to vanish, though I could still hear its song and see mad swirls of dust storming off like skyrockets. Around me, only a tempered breeze danced.

Creeping forward—for we expected at any moment to come upon more jibers—we reached the spot. Here if anywhere (I thought) I would be able to see enough of the structure of the ship to learn something of its design. I did not. Shattered wood, tortured metal, and broken stone mingled with substances unknown to Urth, as smooth as ivory or jade but of outlandish colors or no color. Others suggested linen, cotton, or the rough hair of nameless animals.

Beyond this layered ruin waited the silent stars.

We had lost contact with the main body, but it seemed clear the breach in the ship's hull would have to be closed as soon as possible. I signaled the eight remaining hands of what had been the rear guard to follow me, hoping that by

97

the time we arrived on deck we would find a repair gang at work.

Had we been on Urth, the climb up the ruined levels would have been impossible; here it was easy. One leaped cautiously, caught some twisted beam or stanchion, and leaped again, the best method being to cross the gap with each leap, which would have been madness elsewhere.

We achieved the deck, though it seemed at first that we had achieved nothing; it was as unpeopled as the plain of ice I had once surveyed from the highest windows of the Last House. Huge cables snaked across it; a few more trailed upward like columns, still mooring, far aloft, the wreckage of a mast.

One of the women waved, then pointed to another mast, whole leagues away. I looked, but for a moment could see nothing but a mighty maze of sail, yard, and line. Then came a faint violet spark, wan among the stars—and from another mast, an answering spark.

And then something so strange that for a moment I thought my eyes had deceived me, or that I dreamed it. The tiniest fleck of silver, leagues overhead, seemed to bow to us, then, very slowly, to grow. It was falling, of course; but falling through no atmosphere at all so that it did not flutter, and falling under an attraction so weak that to fall was to float.

Hitherto, I had led my sailors. Now they led me, swarming up the rigging of both masts while I stood on deck, entranced by that incredible spot of silver. In a moment I was alone, watching the men and women of the command that had been mine flying like arrows from cable to cable, and sometimes firing their weapons as they flew. Still I hesitated.

One mast, I thought, must surely be held by the mutists, the other by the crew. To mount the wrong one would be to die.

A second fleck of silver joined the first.

The shooting away of a single sail might be an accident, but to shoot away two, one after the other, could only be intentional. If enough sails, enough masts, were destroyed, the ship would never reach its destination, and there could be only one side that wished it should not. I leaped for the rigging of the mast from which the sails fell.

I have already written that the deck recalled Master Ash's plain of ice. Now in midleap, I saw it better. Air still rushed through the great rent in the hull where a mast had sprouted; as it hastened forth, it grew visible, a titan's ghost, sparkling with a million million tiny lights. These lights fell like snow—floating down slowly indeed, though not more slowly than a man might—leaving that mighty deck white and gleaming with frost.

Then I stood again before Master Ash's window and heard his voice: "What you see is the last glaciation. The surface of the sun is dull now; soon it will grow bright with heat, but the sun itself will shrink, giving less energy to its worlds. Eventually, should anyone come and stand upon the ice, he will see it only as a bright star. The ice he stands upon will not be that which you see, but the atmosphere of this world. And so it will remain for a very long time. Perhaps until the close of the universal day."

It seemed to me that he was beside me again. Even when the nearness of rigging brought me to myself once more, it seemed he flew with me, his words reechoing in my ears. He had vanished that morning as we walked down a gorge in Orithyia, when I would have taken him to Mannea of the Pelerines; on the ship I learned whence he had fled me.

I learned too that I had chosen the wrong mast; if the ship foundered between the stars, it would matter very little whether Severian, once a journeyman torturer, once an Autarch, lived or died. Instead of clinging to the rigging when I reached it, I spun myself around and leaped again, this time for the mast the jibers held.

No matter how often I seek to describe those leaps, I will never paint the wonder and terror of them. One jumps as on Urth—but the first instant is extended to a dozen breaths, as it is for a ball children throw; glorying in it, one knows that should one miss every line and spar, it is destruction—as if the ball should be thrown into the sea and lost forever. Leaping, I felt all this even with the vision

of the plain of ice still before my eyes. And yet my arms
were stretched before me, my legs behind, and I felt myself
not so much a ball as a magical diver in some old story,
who dove where he would.

Without sound or warning, a new cable appeared before
me in the space between the masts where no cable should
be—a cable of fire. Another crossed it, and another; and
then all vanished as I streaked across the void where they
had been. The jibers had recognized me then, and were
firing from their mast.

It is seldom wise to permit an enemy mere target
practice. I jerked my pistol from its holster and took aim at
the point from which the last bolt had come.

Much earlier I told how, when I stood in the dark
corridor outside my stateroom with the dead steward at
my feet, the tiny charge light at the breech of my pistol had
frightened me. Now it frightened me again, for I glimpsed
it just as I pulled the trigger, and there was no spark there.

Nor was there any bolt of violet energy a moment
afterward. If I had been as wise as I have sometimes
pretended to be, I would have cast the pistol from me then,
I think. As it was, I thrust it back into its holster out of
habit and hardly noticed another bolt of fire, the nearest of
all, until it was past.

Then no time remained for shooting or being shot at.
The cables of the rigging rose on every side, and because I
was yet in its lower parts, they were like the trunks of great
trees. Ahead I saw the cable I would have to hold, and on it
a jiber who ran along it to reach the place. At first I thought
him a man like myself, though an uncommonly large and
powerful one; then—all this in much less time than is
needed to write of it—I saw that he was not, for he was
able to grip the cable in some way with his feet.

He extended his hands toward me as a wrestler does who
prepares to receive his opponent, and the long claws on
those hands shone in the starlight.

He had reasoned, I feel sure, that I would have to catch
the cable or die, and that as I caught it he would make an
end to me. I did not catch it, but dove straight at him and

stopped my leap by burying my knife in his chest.

I said I stopped my leap, but the truth is I nearly failed to. For a moment or two we swung about, he like a moored boat, I like a second tied to it. Blood, the same crimson, I thought, as human blood, welled up from around the blade and formed spheres like carbuncles, which simultaneously boiled, froze, and withered as they drifted outside his mantle of air.

For a moment, I feared I would lose my grip on the knife. Then I tugged at it, and as I hoped, his ribs provided resistance enough for me to pull myself to the cable. Of course, I should have mounted higher at once, but I paused for a moment to look at him, with some vague notion that the claws I had seen might be artificial, like the steel claws of the magicians or the *lucivee* with which Agia had torn my cheek, and if artificial, they might be of some use to me.

They were not, I thought. Rather they seemed the result of some hideous surgery performed while he was a child, as are the mutilations of the men in certain tribes among the autochthons. The claws of an arctother had been shaped from his fingers—ugly and innocent, incapable of holding any other weapon.

Before I could turn aside, my attention was caught by the humanity of his face. I had stabbed him as I had killed so many others, without our ever exchanging a word. It had been a rule among the torturers that one should not speak to a client, nor understand anything a client chanced to say. That all men are torturers was one of my earliest insights; here it was confirmed for me by the bear-man's agony that I remained a torturer still. He had been a jiber, true; but who could say he had chosen that allegiance freely? Or perhaps he had felt that his reasons for fighting for the jibers were as good as I had felt mine to be when I fought for Sidero and a captain I did not know. With a foot braced on his chest, I bent and wrenched my knife free.

His eyes opened, and he roared, though foaming blood flew from his mouth. For an instant, it seemed stranger to me that I should hear him in that infinite silence than that he, who had appeared dead, should live again; but we were so near that our atmospheres joined, and I could hear the very gushing of his wound.

I stabbed at his face. By ill luck, the point struck the thick frontal bones of the skull; with no purchase for my feet, the thrust lacked force enough to penetrate and drove me back, backward into the emptiness that surrounded us.

He lunged for me, his claws tearing my arm, so that we floated furiously together with the knife hanging between us, its polished, bloody blade gleaming in the starlight. I tried to snatch it, but his claws batted it whirling into the void.

My fingers caught his necklace of cylinders and jerked it free. He should have clung to me then, but perhaps he could not, with those hands. He struck me instead, and I watched him gasp for air and die as I spun away.

Any triumph I might have felt was lost in remorse and the certainty that I must soon follow him in death. Remorse because I regretted his death with all the easy sincerity the mind calls up when there is no danger it will be put to the test; certainty because it was clear from my course and the angles of the masts that I would never come nearer than I was now to any strand of rigging. I had only the vaguest idea how long the air bound by the necklaces would last: a watch or more, I thought. I had a double supply—say, three watches at most. At the end of that time, I would die slowly, gasping faster and faster as more and more of the life principle in my atmosphere became locked in the form that only trees and flowers may breathe.

I remembered then how I had cast the leaden coffer that had held my manuscript into the void, and so been saved; and I tried to think of what I might cast now. To discard the necklaces was to die. I thought of my boots, but I had sacrificed boots once before, when I had stood for the first time in my life beside this all-devouring sea. I had cast the ruins of *Terminus Est* into Lake Diurturna; that suggested the hunting knife that had served me so ill. But it was already gone.

My belt remained, on it the black leather sheath with

nine chrisos in the sheath's small compartment, and my empty pistol in its holster. I pocketed the chrisos, took off belt, sheath, pistol, and holster, whispered a prayer, and flung them away.

At once I began to move faster, but not (as I had hoped I would) toward the deck or any strand of rigging. Already I was level with the top-hamper of the masts to either side. Looking toward the rapidly receding deck, I saw a single bolt of violet flash between masts. Then there were no more, only the uncanny silence of the void.

Soon, and with that intensity which signals our desire to escape all thoughts of death, I began to wonder why no one had shot at me, as they had when I leaped for the mast, and why no one was firing now.

I rose above the top of the sternward mast, and at once all such petty puzzles were swept aside.

Rising over the topmost sail as the New Sun of Urth might someday rise above the Wall of Nessus (yet far, far larger and more beautiful than even the New Sun can ever be, just as that smallest and uppermost sail was an entire continent of silver, compared to which the mighty Wall of Nessus, a few leagues in height and a few thousand long, might have been the tumbledown fence of a sheepfold), was such a sun as no one with his feet set upon grass will ever see—the birth of a new universe, the primal explosion containing every sun because from it all suns will come, the first sun, that was the father of all the suns. How long I watched it in awe I cannot say; but when I looked again at the masts below, they and the ship seemed very far away.

And then I wondered, for I recalled that when my little band of sailors had reached the rent in the hull and looked upward there, I had seen the stars.

I turned my head, and looked the other way. There the stars swarmed still, but it seemed to me they formed a great disk in the sky, and when I looked at the edges of that disk, I saw they were streaked and old. Since that time I have often pondered on that sight, here beside the all-devouring sea. It is said that so great a thing is the universe that no one can see it as it is, but only as it was, just as I,

when I was Autarch, could not know the present condition
of our Commonwealth, but only its conditions as they were
when the reports I read were written. If that is so, then it
may be that the stars I saw were no longer there—that the
reports of my eyes were like those reports I found when we
opened the suite that had once been the Autarchs' in the
Great Keep.

In the middle of this disk of stars, as it at first appeared
to me, shone a single blue star larger and brighter than all
the rest. It waxed even as I watched it, so that I soon
understood that it could not be as remote as I had
supposed. The ship, driven by light, outraced light, even as
the ships upon the uneasy seas of Urth, driven by the wind,
had once outraced that wind, close-hauled. Yet even so, the
blue star could be no remote object; and if it were a star of
any sort, we were doomed, for we steered for its heart.

Larger it grew and larger, and across its center there
appeared a single, curving line of black, a line like the
Claw—the Claw of the Conciliator as it had appeared
when I had seen it first, when I had drawn it forth from my
sabretache, and Dorcas and I had held it up to the night
sky, astonished at its blue radiance.

Though the blue star waxed, as I have said, that curving
line of black waxed faster, until it nearly blotted out the
disk (for by this time it was a disk) of blue. At last I saw it
for what it was—a single cable still linking the mast that
the mutists had blown away to our ship. I caught it, and
from that vantage point saw our universe, which is called
Briah, fade until it vanished like a dream.

CHAPTER XV

Yesod

BY ALL LOGIC, I OUGHT TO HAVE CLIMBED DOWN THAT cable to the ship, but I did not. I had caught it at a point near enough to the ship that the jibsails somewhat blocked my view, and I (whether thinking myself indestructible or already destroyed, I cannot say) climbed instead until I reached the detached mast itself, and then out upon a tilted yard to the end; and there I clung and watched.

What I saw cannot truly be described, though I will attempt it. The blue star was already a disk of clear azure. I have said it was not so distant as the ghost stars. But it was truly there, as they were not; so who is to say which was farthest? As I stared at it, I became more aware of their falsity—not merely that they were not where they appeared to be, but that they did not exist at all, that they were not merely phantoms, but, like most phantoms, lies. The azure disk widened until at last I saw it streaked with wisps of cloud. Then I laughed to myself, and in laughing was suddenly aware of my danger, aware that I might perish at any moment for having done as I had done. Yet I remained where I was for some time more.

Into the center of that disk we plunged, so that for a moment there was a ring of ebony set with ghostly stars all around our ship, the Diadem of Briah.

Then we were through and seemed suspended in azure light; behind us, where once I had seen the corona lucis of the young suns, I now saw our universe, a circle no larger than an ebon moon in the sky of Yesod, a moon that soon shrank to a solitary mote, then vanished.

If you who may someday read this retain the least respect for me despite the manifold follies I have recounted, you must lose it now, for I am about to tell you how I started as a baby does to see a turnip ghost. When Jonas and I rode to the House Absolute, we were attacked by Hethor's notules, mirror-fetched creatures that fly like so many scraps of scorched parchment up a chimney, but for all their insubstantiality can kill. Now I, looking aft toward the vanishing of Briah, thought to see such creatures again, but of silver, not fuligin as the notules were.

And I was struck by terror and sought to hide myself behind the yard. A moment later I realized what they were, as you have no doubt realized already—mere tatters torn from the gossamer burden of the ruined mast and whipped to frenzy by a wind. Yet that meant there was an atmosphere here, however thin, and not the void. I looked at the ship and saw it in all its vastness bare, all its sails vanished, ten thousand masts and a hundred thousand spars standing like a wood in winter.

How strange it was to cling there, breathing my own already outworn atmosphere, knowing but never feeling the mighty tempest that raged around me. I pulled both necklaces from my neck, and at once I was nearly torn from my perch, my ears filled with the roaring of a hurricane.

And I drank in that air! Words cannot do it justice save by saying that it was the air of Yesod, icy cold and golden with life. Never before had I tasted such air, and yet I seemed to know it.

It stripped my torn shirt from my back and sent it flapping off to join the scraps of the ruined sails, and in that instant I knew it indeed. On the evening I departed the Old Citadel for exile, I walked the Water Way, seeing the argosies and carracks that plied the wide river-road of Gyoll, and a wind had sprung up that sent my guild cloak billowing behind me and told me of the north; now that wind blew again, chanting loud of new years and singing all the songs of a new world.

But where? Beneath our ship, I saw nothing but an azure bowl and such wisps of cloud as I had beheld while we were yet in the old and soiled universe standing before this. After a moment or two (for it was an agony to remain inactive in that air) I gave up the puzzle and began the climb down to the ship.

And then I saw it—not below, where I had looked, but over my head, a vast and noble curve stretching away to either side, with white cloud flying between ourselves and it, a world all speckled over with blue and green like the egg of a wild bird.

And I saw a thing stranger still—the coming of Night to that new world. Like a brother of the guild, she wore a cloak of fuligin, spreading it over all that fair world as I watched, so that I recalled she had been the mother of Noctua in the tale I had once read Jonas from the brown book, that dire-wolves had frisked about her heels like puppies, and she had passed behind Hesperus and Sirus; and I wondered what made the ship fly on as it did, outracing the night, when its sails were furled and no light could urge it forward.

In the air of Urth, the ships of the Hierodules went where they would, and even the ship that had carried me (with Idas and Purn, though I had not known it) to this ship had initially made use of other means. Clearly this ship commanded them too, but it seemed strange her captain urged her straight on in such a way. As I climbed down, I considered these things—finding it easier to consider them than to come to any conclusion.

Before I reached the deck, the ship herself was plunged in darkness. The wind blew unabated, as though to sweep me away. It seemed to me that I should now feel the attraction of Yesod, but there was only the slight pull of the holds, as it had been in the void. At last I was so foolish as to try a short leap. The hurricane breath of Yesod caught me like a windblown leaf, and my leap sent me tumbling down the deck like a gymnast; I was fortunate that it did not send me crashing into a mast.

Bruised and bewildered, I groped along the deck in

search of a hatch. I found none, and I had reconciled
myself to waiting for day when day came, as sudden as the
voice of a trumpet. The sun of Yesod was of purest
white-hot gold, and it lifted itself above a dark horizon as
sharply curved as the top of a buckler.

For an instant it seemed to me that I heard the voices of
the Gandharvas, the singers before the throne of the
Pancreator. Then I saw far ahead of the ship (for my
wanderings in search of a hatch had taken me nearly to the
bow) the far-spreading wings of a great bird. We rushed
toward it like an avalanche, but it saw us, and with a single
beat of those mighty wings rose above us, singing still. Its
wings were white, its breast like frost; and if a lark of Urth
may be likened to a flute, the voice of this bird of Yesod
was an orchestra, for it seemed to have many voices that
sang all together, some high and piercingly sweet, some
deeper than any drum.

Cold though I was—and I felt nearly frozen—I could
not but stop and listen to it; and when it was astern and out
of hearing, and I could see it no longer because of the
thronging masts, I looked forward again for another.

There was none, but the sky was not empty. A ship of a
kind new to me sailed there on wings wider than the bird's
and as slender as sword blades. We passed beneath it as we
had passed beneath the bird; when we did, it folded its long
wings and dove at us, so that I thought for a moment it
must crash into us and perish, for it had not a thousandth
part of our bulk.

It passed above the top of the masts as a dart flies over
the spears of an army, drew ahead of us once more, and
settled on our bowsprit until it lay there as a pard stretches
itself upon some slender branch to watch a trail for deer, or
to bask in the sun.

I waited for the crew of the smaller ship to appear, but
they did not. After a moment, it seemed their ship held
ours more closely than I had supposed; and after a moment
more, as I watched wondering—that I had been mistaken
to think it a ship at all and surely wrong to believe I had
seen it hanging alone, argent against that cerulean world,

or soaring above the forest of our masts. Rather it seemed
a part of our own ship, of the ship on which I had now
sailed (as it seemed to me) for so long, an oddly thickened
bowsprit or beakhead, its wings no more than flying braces
to hold it the more firmly to the bow.

Soon I recalled that when the old Autarch had been
brought to Yesod, just such a ship had come for him.
Glorying, I raced over the deck searching for a hatch; and
it was good to run in that cold and in that air, though every
limping stride stung my feet; and at last I leaped up, and
the wind took me again as I had known it would and bore
me far down that immense hull before I could seize
hold of a backstay that nearly tore my arms from their
sockets.

It was enough. In my wild flight I had caught sight of the
rent through which my little command had climbed to the
deck. I ran to it and plunged into the familiar warmth and
errant gleams of the interior.

That voice which could never be distinctly heard and yet
could always be understood thundered in every corridor,
calling for the Epitome of Urth; and I ran on, happy for the
warmth, feeling the pure air of Yesod penetrate even here,
sure that my time of testing was at last at hand, or nearly
so.

Parties of sailors were searching the ship, but for a long
while I could not make contact with them, though I could
hear them all about me, and sometimes catch a glimpse of
one. At last, opening a shadowy door, I stepped through
onto a grillwork platform and saw in the dim radiance
from overhead a vast plain of jumbled lumber and machinery, where papers spilled like banks of dirty snow
and scented dust lay in pools like water. If it were not
the spot from which Sidero had thrown me, it was very
like it.

Toward me across this space moved a small procession,
and after a moment I realized it was a triumphal one.
Many of the sailors carried lights, and slashed the dimness
with their beams to create fantastic patterns, while others
capered or danced. Some were singing:

Away, mate, away! We'll dig no more today!
For we're signed aboard on a long, long trip,
To the end of the sky on a big, big ship,
And we won't come back till her sails rip!
No, we won't come back at all!

And so on.

Not all those in this procession were sailors, however. I saw several beings of polished metal, and indeed after a moment I realized that one was Sidero himself, easily identified because his arm had not been repaired.

A little separated from all these were three figures new to me, a man and two women in cloaks; and ahead of them, leading the column as it seemed, a naked man taller than any of the rest, who walked with his head bowed and his long, fair hair falling over his face. At first I believed him deep in thought, for his hands seemed clasped at his back, and I had often walked so myself, pondering the manifold difficulties that beset our Commonwealth; then I saw that his wrists were bound behind him.

CHAPTER XVI

The Epitome

NO LONGER SO UNLEARNED AS I HAD BEEN, I LEAPED OFF the platform and, after a long, slow fall rather pleasant than otherwise, met the procession halfway.

The prisoner did not so much as glance up. Though I could not see his face well, I saw enough to make me certain I had not seen it before. He was of the height of an exultant at least, and I would judge half a head taller than most. His chest and shoulders were magnificently developed, as were his arms, from what I could see of them. As he trudged along, great muscles in his thighs slipped like anacondas beneath skin translucently pale. His golden hair held no trace of gray; and from it and the slenderness of his waist, I judged him no more than twenty-five, and perhaps younger.

The three who followed this extraordinary prisoner could not have appeared more commonplace. All were of average height and seemed to have reached middle age. The man wore tunic and hose under his cloak; the two women had loose gowns that ended just below the knee. None were armed.

As they approached, I stepped well to one side; but only the sailors paid any attention to me. Several (though there were none I recognized) motioned for me to join them, their faces those of revelers who in their excess of joy summon every bystander to their celebration.

I hurried over, and before I knew it Purn had seized me by the hand. I felt a thrill of fear—he was near enough to have stabbed me twice over—but his expression held only welcome. He shouted something I could not quite hear, and slapped my back. In a moment, Gunnie had pushed him to one side and kissed me as soundly as at our first meeting.

"You wormy guiser," she said, and kissed me again, not so roughly this time, but longer.

It was no use trying to question them in that uproar; and in truth if they were willing to make peace, I (with no friend on board except Sidero) was more than glad they should.

Our procession wound out a doorway and down a long, swooping passage that led to a part of the ship like nothing I had seen before. Its walls were insubstantial, not because they were in any way dreamlike, but because they somehow suggested that they were thinner than tissue and might be burst in an instant, so that I was reminded of the trumpery booths and pavilions of the fair at Saltus, where I had killed Morwenna and met the green man. And for a moment or two I stood amid the hubbub, trying to understand why it should be so.

One of the cloaked women mounted a seat and clapped her hands for quiet. Because the sailors' high spirits had not been fueled with wine, she was soon obeyed, and my riddle answered: through the thin walls I could hear, however faintly, the rush of the icy air of Yesod. No doubt I had heard it before without being conscious of it.

"Dear friends," the woman began. "We thank you for your welcome and your help, and for all the many kindnesses all of you have shown us on board your vessel."

Various sailors spoke or shouted replies, some merely good-natured, others glowing with that rustic politeness which makes the manners of courtiers seem so cheap.

"Many of you are yourselves from Urth, I know. Perhaps it would be well to determine how many. May I see a show of hands? Raise one hand, please, if you were born upon the world called Urth."

Nearly everyone present raised his hand.

"You know that we have condemned the peoples of

Urth, and why. They now feel they have earned our forgiveness, and the chance to resume the places they held of old—"

Most of the sailors booed and jeered, including Purn, but not (as I noted) Gunnie.

"And they have dispatched their Epitome to claim it for them. That he lost heart and concealed himself from us should not be counted against him or them. Rather we consider that the sense of his world's guilt so manifested should be reckoned in their favor. As you see, we are about to take him to Yesod for his assize. Even as he will represent Urth in the dock, so must others represent it on the gradins. None of you need come, but we have your captain's permission to take from among you those who wish to come. They will be returned to this ship before it sails again. Those who do not should leave us now."

A few hands slipped from the back of the crowd.

The woman said, "We ask also that all those not born upon Urth leave us."

A few more departed. Many of those who remained appeared hardly human to me.

"All the rest of you will come with us?"

There was a chorus of assent.

I called, "Wait!" and sought to push my way to the front, where I would be heard. "If—"

Three things happened at once: Gunnie clapped her hand over my mouth; Purn pinned my arms behind me; and what I had believed only some strange chamber of our ship fell from under me.

It fell sidelong, tumbling the crowd of sailors and us into a single struggling mass, and its fall was not in the least like the leaps I had made in the rigging. The hunger of a world drew us at once; and though I do not think it was as great as that of Urth, after so many days in the weak pull of the holds it seemed great indeed.

A monstrous wind shouted outside the bulkheads, and in the wink of an eye the bulkheads themselves vanished. Something, we could not tell what, kept out that wind. Something kept us from tumbling out of the little flier like so many beetles swept from a bench—yet we were in the midst of the sky of Yesod, with only the narrow floor beneath our feet.

That floor tilted and leaped like a destrier in the wildest charge of the most desperate battle ever fought. No teratornis ever slipped down a mountain of air so swiftly as we, and at its bottom we shot upward like a skyrocket, spinning like a shaft in flight.

A moment later, and we were skimming the mastheads of the ship like a swallow, then like a swallow indeed we dove among them and darted between mast and mast, between cable and spar.

Because so many sailors had fallen or half fallen, I could see the faces of the three from Yesod who had led us into the flier, and I was able for the first time to see the full face of their prisoner too. Theirs were calm and amused; his ennobled by the most resolute courage. I knew my own reflected my fear, and felt much as I had when the Ascian pentadactyls had whirled over Guasacht's schiavoni. I felt something more as well, of which I shall write in a moment.

Those who have never fought suppose that the deserter who flies the field is consumed by shame. He is not, or he would not desert; with only trifling exceptions, battles are fought by cowards afraid to run. And it was just so with me. Ashamed to reveal my terror to Purn and Gunnie, I forced my features into an expression that no doubt resembled real resolution about as much as his death mask resembles the smiling countenance of an old friend. I lifted Gunnie then, muttering some nonsense to the effect that I hoped she had not been hurt. She answered, "It was the poor boy I fell on who caught it," and I realized she was ashamed just as I was and, just as I was, determined to stand firm though her bowels had turned to milk.

As we spoke, the flier rose above the masts again, leveled its flight, and spread its wings, so that we felt we stood upon the back of some great bird.

The woman who had addressed us before said, "Now you have an adventure to recount to your shipmates when you return to your ship. There is no cause for alarm. There will be no more tricks, and you cannot fall from this craft."

Gunnie whispered, "I knew what you were going to tell her, but can't you see they've found the real one?"

"I am what you call the real one," I said, "and I don't know what's happening. Have I told you—no, I haven't. I carry the memories of my predecessors, and indeed you may say I am the predecessors themselves as well as myself. The old Autarch who gave me his throne went to Yesod too. Went as I'm going—or rather, as I thought I was going."

Gunnie shook her head; I could see she pitied me. "You think you remember all that?"

"I do remember it. I can recall each step of his journey; I feel the pain of the knife that unmanned him. It wasn't like this at all; he was taken from the ship with the proper respect. He endured long testing on Yesod, and at last was judged to have failed, as he judged himself to have failed." I looked to where the woman and her companions stood, hoping I had attracted their attention.

Purn was beside us again. "Then you still claim you're really the Autarch?"

"I was," I told him. "And yes, I will bring the New Sun if I can. Will you still stab me for that?"

"Not here," he said. "Probably not at all. I'm a simple man, see? I believed you. Only when they caught the real one, I knew you'd been yarning me up. Or maybe your wits are mixed. I've never killed anybody, and I wouldn't want to kill a man for yarning. Killing a Port o' Lune man's worse—sure bad luck." He spoke to Gunnie as though I were not there. "You think he really believes it?"

"I'm positive he does," she said. After a moment she added, "It might even be the truth. Listen to me, Severian, because I've been on board a long time. This is my second voyage to Yesod, so I guess I was in the crew when they took your old Autarch, though I never saw him and didn't get to come down till later. You know this ship moves in and out of Time like a darning needle, don't you? Don't you know that by now?"

I said, "Yes, I'm coming to understand so."

"Then let me ask you. Isn't it possible we've been carrying two Autarchs? You and one of *your* successors? Suppose you were to go back to Urth. You'd have to choose a successor sooner or later. Mightn't he be the one? Or the one he chose? And if he is, what's the use of your going through with it, and losing some things you don't want to lose when it's over?"

"You mean that what I do can make no difference to the future."

"Not when the future's already up at the front of this tender."

We had talked as though the other sailors were not present, but it is never wholly safe to do that—one does it only with the sufferance of the ignored. One of the sailors to whom I had paid no heed grasped me by the shoulder and pulled me half a step toward him so that I could see better through the hyaline sides of our flier.

"Look!" he said. "Look at that, will you!" But for a beat of my heart I looked at him instead, suddenly aware that he who had been nothing to me was everything to himself, and I only a supernumerary to him, a lay figure permitting him, by sharing his joy, to double it.

Then I looked, because it would have seemed a species of betrayal not to; and I saw that we were turning, slowing, in a wide, wide, circle, above an isle set in an endless sea of blue, translucent water. The isle was clearly a single hilltop that rose above the waves, and it was dressed in the green of gardens and the white of marble, and it wore a fringe of little boats.

There was nothing to be seen so impressive as the Wall of Nessus, or even the Great Keep. Yet in its way, the isle was more impressive, because everything about it was beautiful, without exception, and there was a joy there that towered higher than the Wall, as high as a thunderhead.

It came to me then, seeing that isle and the stupid and brutal faces of the men and women all about me, that there was something more I did not see. A memory rose, sent by one of those dim figures who stand, for me, behind the old

Autarch, those predecessors whom I cannot see clearly and often cannot see at all. It was the figure of a lovely virgin, clothed in silks of many hues and dewed with pearls. She sang in the avenues of Nessus and lingered by its fountains until night. No one dared to molest her, for though her protector was invisible, his shadow fell all around her, rendering her inviolate.

CHAPTER XVII

The Isle

IF I WERE TO SAY TO YOU, WHO WERE BORN UPON URTH AND have drawn your every breath there, that the flier landed like a huge waterbird, you would imagine a comic splashing. It did, and yet it was not so; for on Yesod, as I saw from the sides of the flier a moment or two after we were down, the water birds have learned to drop onto the waves so gently and gracefully one might think the water only a cooler air to them, as it is to those little birds we see beside waterfalls, who hop into the falls to catch minnows and are as much at home there as another bird could be in a bush.

So we did, settling onto the sea and folding our immense wings even as we touched it, gently rocking while it seemed we still flew. Some of the sailors talked among themselves; and perhaps Gunnie or Purn would have talked to me, if I had given them the opportunity. I did not, because I desired to absorb all the wonders I might, and because I sensed that I could not speak without feeling still more keenly my duty to tell those who held another prisoner that it was myself they sought.

Thus I stared out (as I believed) through the sides of our flier, and tasted the wind, that glorious wind of Yesod that carries the fresh purity of its saltless sea and the perfume of all its glorious gardens, and life with them, and found that the sides, which earlier could not be seen, could not now be felt, so that we rode as though on a narrow raft, with our wings for a canopy overhead. And I saw much.

As was to be expected, one of the sailors pushed her

companion into the water; but others farther down our long hull drew her out again; and though she complained loudly of the cold, the water was not so cold as to harm her, as I found by stooping and dabbing my hands in it.

Then I cupped them and drew up so much as they would hold and drank of it, of the water of Yesod; and though it was chill, I was glad when some ran down my chest. For I recalled an old tale in the brown book I once carried in memory of Thecla, and how it told of a certain man who, crossing a wasteland late one night, saw other men and women dancing and joined them; and how when the dance was through he went with them and bathed his face in a spring never seen by day, and drank of its water.

And how his wife, counseled by a certain wise device, went to the same place a year later to the day, and there heard wild music and her husband's voice singing alone, and the sound of many dancing feet—yet saw no one. And how when she questioned that device concerning those things, she was told her husband had drunk of the waters of another world and washed in them, and would return to her no more.

Nor did he.

I held myself apart from the sailors as we trooped up the white street that led from the mooring to the building at the top of the hill, doing so by walking nearer the three and their prisoner than any of them dared to. Yet I myself did not dare to tell the three who I was, though I began to do so a hundred times at least, without making a sound. At last I spoke, but it was only to ask whether the trial would be held that day or the next.

The woman who had addressed us glanced back at me, smiling. "Are you so eager to see his blood?" she asked. "You will not. The Hierogrammate Tzadkiel does not sit in his Seat of Justice today, so we will have the preliminary examination only. That can be carried out in his absence, if need be."

I shook my head. "I have seen much blood; believe me, my lady, I've no itch to see more."

"Then why did you come?" she inquired, still smiling.

I told her the truth, though it was not the whole truth. "Because I felt it was my duty. But tell me, suppose Tzadkiel is not in his seat tomorrow, either. Will we be permitted to wait here for him? And are all of you not Hierogrammates too? And do all of you speak our tongue? I was surprised to hear it on your lips."

I had been walking a half step behind her; and she, as a consequence, had spoken to me more or less across her shoulder. Now with her smile grown wider, she dropped behind the others to link her arm in mine. "So many questions. How am I to remember them all, much less to answer them?"

I was ashamed and tried to mumble some apology; but I was so unnerved by the touch of her hand, warm and seeking as it slipped into my own, that I could only stammer.

"Nevertheless, for your sake I will try. Tzadkiel will be here tomorrow. Were you afraid you would be unable to return to your mopping and carrying soon enough?"

"No, my lady," I managed. "I would remain forever, if I could."

Her smile faded at that. "You will remain on this isle for less than a day all told. You—we, if you wish it—must do what we can with that."

"I do wish it," I told her, and in fact I did. I have said she was an ordinary-looking woman of middle age, and so she was: not tall, a few wrinkles apparent at her eyes and mouth, her hair touched at the temples with frost. Yet there was something I could not resist. Perhaps it was only the aura of the isle—so some common men find all exultant women attractive. Perhaps it was her eyes, which were large and luminous and of the deep, deep blue of her sea, unfaded by age. Perhaps it was some third thing, sensed unconsciously; but I felt again as I had when, so much younger, I had encountered Agia—a desire so strong that it seemed more spiritual than any faith, its flesh burned away in the heat of its own yearning.

". . . after the preliminary examination," she said.

"Of course," I answered. "Of course. I am my lady's slave." I hardly knew to what I had agreed.

A wide flight of white stone steps flanked by fountains rose before us with the airy lightness of a cloud bank. She looked up with a bantering smile I found infinitely attractive. "If you were truly my slave, I would have you carry me up this stair, halt leg or none."

"I will do it gladly," I said, and I stooped as though to pick her up.

"No, no." She had begun to climb, and as lightly as any girl. "What would your shipmates think?"

"That I had been signally honored, my lady."

Still smiling, she whispered, "Not that you had deserted Urth for us? But we have a moment before we reach the court, and I will answer your questions as well as I can. We are not all Hierogrammates. On Urth, are the children of sannyasins holy men and women themselves? I do not speak with your tongue, nor do any of us. Neither do you speak as we do."

"My lady . . ."

"You do not understand."

"No." I sought for something more to say, but what she had told me seemed so absurd that no reply was possible.

"I will explain after the examination. But now I must require a small service of you."

"Anything, my lady."

"Thank you. Then you will lead the Epitome into the dock for us."

I looked at her in bewilderment.

"We try him—we will examine him now—with the consent of the peoples of Urth, who have sent him to Yesod in their stead. To show it, a man or woman of Urth, who will represent his world just as he does though in a less significant way, must conduct him."

I nodded. "I'll do it for you, my lady, if you'll show me where I must take him."

"Good." She turned to the man and the other woman,

saying, "We have a custodian." They nodded, and she took
the prisoner by the arm and pulled him over (although he
could easily have resisted her) to where I waited. "We will
bring your shipmates into the Hall of Justice, where I will
explain what is to take place. I doubt that you need that.
You—what is your name?"

I hesitated, wondering whether she knew what the
Epitome's name ought to be.

"Come, is it so great a secret?"

Soon I should have to confess in any case, although I had
hoped I would be able to hear the preliminary examination
first, so that I would better equipped to succeed when my
own turn came. As we paused at the portico I said, "It's
Severian, my lady. Is it permitted that I ask yours?"

Her smile was as irresistible as when I had first seen it.
"We have no need of such things among ourselves, but now
that I am known to someone who does, I will be called
Apheta." She saw my doubt and added, "Never fear, those
to whom you say my name will know of whom you speak."

"Thank you, my lady."

"Now take him. The arch is to your right." She pointed.
"Go through there. You will find a long, elliptical corridor
from which you cannot stray, since it is without doors to
either side. Convey him to the end, then out and into the
Examination Chamber. Look at his hands; do you see how
they are fettered?"

"Yes, my lady."

"In the Chamber you will see the ring to which his fetter
is to be fastened. Lead him there and chain him—there is
a sliding link, you will understand it at once—and take
your place among the witnesses. When the examination is
complete, wait for me. I will show you all the wonders of
our isle."

Her tone made clear what she meant. I bowed and said,
"My lady, I'm wholly unworthy."

"Of that I shall judge. Go now. Do as I told you, and you
shall have your reward."

Bowing again, I turned and took the giant's arm. I have

said already that he was taller than any exultant, and so he was, nearly as tall as Baldanders. He was not so heavy, but young and vigorous (as young as I had been, I thought, on the day when I had left the Citadel through the Corpse Door bearing *Terminus Est*). He had to stoop to pass beneath the arch, but he followed me as one sees a yearling ram in the market follow the shepherd boy who has made a pet of him and now means to sell him to some family who will wether him to fatten for a feast.

The corridor was of the shape of the egg conjurors stand on end upon the table, having a high, almost pointed arch overhead, widely curved sides, and a flattened walkway. The lady Apheta had said that no doors opened from it, and she had been correct, but there were windows on both sides. These puzzled me, because I had supposed it to wind about a courtroom in the center of the building.

I looked out of them to right and left as we walked, at first with some curiosity about the Isle of Yesod, then with wonder to see it so like Urth, and at last with astonishment. For snow-capped mountains and level pampas gave way to strange interiors, as though I looked from each window into a different structure. There was a wide, empty hall lined with mirrors, another even wider where standing shelves held disordered books, a narrow cell with a high, barred window and a straw-strewn floor, and a dark and narrow corridor lined with metal doors.

Turning to the client, I said, "They were expecting me, that seems clear enough. I see Agilus's cell, the oubliette under the Matachin Tower, and so on. But they think you're me, Zak."

As though my speaking of his name had broken a spell, he whirled on me, tossing his long hair back to reveal his blazing eyes. The muscles of his arms stood out as though they would burst the skin as he strained against his manacles. Almost automatically, I stepped past his leg and threw him across my hip as Master Gurloes had taught me so long ago.

He fell to the white stone as a bull falls in the arena, and the crash seemed to shake that solid building; but he was on his feet again in a moment, manacled or not, and running down the corridor.

CHAPTER XVIII

The Examination

I RAN AFTER HIM, AND SOON SAW THAT, THOUGH LONG, HIS strides were clumsy—Baldanders had run better—and he was handicapped by having his arms pinioned at his back.

His was not the only handicap. My lame leg seemed to have a weight tied to its ankle, and I am sure our race gave me more pain than his fall had given him. The windows —charmed, perhaps, or perhaps merely cunning—crept by as I hobbled along. A few I looked through consciously, most I did not; yet they remain with me still, hidden in the dusty chamber that lies behind, or perhaps beneath, my mind. The scaffold where I once branded and decapitated a woman was there, a dark river bank, and the roof of a certain tomb.

I would have laughed at those windows, if I had not been laughing at myself already so that I would not weep. These Hierogrammates who ruled the universe and what lay beyond had not merely mistaken another for me, but now sought to remind me, who could forget nothing, of the scenes of my life; and did so (so it seemed to me) less skillfully than my own memories could have. For though every detail was present, there was something subtly mistaken about each view.

I could not stop, or at least I felt I could not; but at last I turned my head as I limped past one of these windows and truly studied it as I had not any of the others. It opened into the summerhouse on Abdiesus's pleasure grounds where I had questioned and at last freed Cyriaca; and in that single, long glance I understood at last that I saw these places not as I had seen them and remembered them, but as Cyriaca, Jolenta, Agia, and so on had perceived them. I was aware, for example, when I looked into the summerhouse, of a horrible yet benign presence just beyond the view framed by the window—myself.

That was the final window. The shadowy corridor had ended, and a second arch, brilliant with sunlight, rose in front of me. Seeing it, I knew with a sickening certainty only another who had grown up in the guild could understand, that I had lost my client.

I bolted through it and saw him standing bewildered in the portico of the Hall of Justice, surrounded by a surging crowd. At the same instant, he saw me and sought to push through them toward the principal entrance.

I called out for someone to stop him, but the crowd moved aside for him and seemed purposely to obstruct me. I felt as though I were in one of the nightmares I had suffered as Lictor of Thrax, and that I would wake in a moment gasping for breath, with the Claw pressing my chest.

A little woman dashed from the crowd and caught Zak by one arm, and he shook himself as a bull shakes to dislodge the darts in its hide. She fell, but grasped his ankle.

It was enough. I laid hold of him, and though I was lame once more here, where the greedy pull of Yesod was Urth's or nearly, I was still strong and he still manacled. With an arm at his throat I bent him back like a bow. At once he relaxed; and I knew, in the mysterious way we sense another's intent at times by a touch, that he would resist me no longer. I released him.

"Won't fight," he said. "No more run."

"All right," I told him, and stooped to raise the woman who had helped me. I recognized her then, and without much thought glanced down at her leg. It was perfectly normal, which is to say perfectly healed.

"Thank you," I muttered. "Thank you, Hunna."

She was staring. "I thought you were my mistress. I don't know why."

Often I have to make an effort to prevent Thecla's voice from issuing from my lips. Now I permitted it. We said, "Thank you," again, adding, "You were not mistaken," and smiling at her confusion.

Shaking her head, she backed into the crowd, and I caught sight of a tall woman with dark, curling hair entering the arch through which I had taken Zak. Even after so many years, there could be no doubt, no doubt at all. We tried to call her name. It remained in our throat, leaving us sick and silent.

"Don't cry," Zak said, his deep voice somehow childlike. "Please don't. I think it will be all right."

I turned to tell him I was not, and realized I was. If I had ever wept before, it was when I was so small I can scarcely remember it—apprentices learn not to, and those who do not are tormented by the rest until death takes them. Thecla had cried at times, and had wept often in her cell; but I had just seen Thecla.

I said, "I'm crying because I want so much to follow her, and we must go inside."

He nodded, and at once I took him by the arm and brought him into the Examination Chamber. The corridor along which the lady Apheta had sent me merely circled it, and I led Zak down a wide aisle, while the sailors watched from the banked benches on either side. There were many more places on the benches than sailors, however, so that the sailors occupied only the ones nearest the aisle.

Before us was the Seat of Justice, a seat far grander and more austere than any judge I had ever seen had occupied upon Urth. The Phoenix Throne was—or is, if it yet exists beneath the waters—a great gilt armchair upon whose back is displayed an image of that bird, the symbol of immortality, worked in gold, jade, carnelian, and lapis lazuli; upon its seat (which would have been murderously uncomfortable without it) was a cushion of velvet, with golden tassels.

This Seat of Justice of the Hierogrammate Tzadkiel was

as different as could be imagined, and indeed was hardly a
chair at all, but only a colossal boulder of white stone,
shaped by time and chancé to resemble one about as much
as the clouds in which we profess to see a lover's face or the
head of some paladin resemble the persons themselves.

Apheta had told me only that I would find a ring in the
chamber, and for a moment or two, while Zak and I
walked slowly down that long aisle, I searched for it with
my eyes. It was what I had at first supposed to be the sole
decoration of the Seat of Justice: a wrought circle of iron
held by a great iron staple driven into the stone at the
termination of one armrest. I looked then for the sliding
link she had mentioned; there was none, but I led Zak
toward the ring anyway, certain that when we reached it
someone would step forward to assist me.

No one did, but when I looked at the manacle I understood as Apheta had said I would. The link was there; when
I opened it, it seemed to me it slipped back so easily that
Zak himself might have loosed it with a finger. It united
loops of chain that held each wrist, so that when I removed
it the whole affair dropped from him. I picked it up, put
the chains about my own wrists, lifted my arms above my
head so that I could put the ring into the link, and awaited
my examination.

None took place. The sailors sat gaping at me. I had
supposed that someone would take Zak, or he would flee.
No one approached him. He seated himself on the floor at
my feet, not cross-legged (as I would have sat in his place)
but squatting in a way that reminded me at first of a dog,
then of an atrox or some other great cat.

"I am the Epitome of Urth and all her peoples," I told
the sailors. It was the same speech the old Autarch had
made, as I realized only after I had begun it, though his
examination had been so different. "I am here because I
hold them in me—men, women, and children too, poor
and rich, old and young, those who would save our world if
they could, and those who would rape its last life for gain."

Unbidden, the words rose to the surface of my mind. "I
am here also because I am by right the ruler of Urth. We

have many nations, some larger than our Commonwealth and stronger; but we Autarchs, and we alone, think not merely of our own lands, but know our winds blow every tree and our tides wash every shore. This I have proved, because I stand here. And because I stand here, I prove it is my right."

The sailors listened in silence to all this; but even as I spoke I looked past them for the others, for the lady Apheta and her companions, at least. They were not to be seen.

Yet there were other hearers. The crowd from the portico now stood in the doorway through which Zak and I had come; when I had finished they filed slowly into the Examination Chamber, coming not down the central aisle as we had, and as the sailors doubtless had, but dividing their column, left and right, into two that crept between the benches and the walls.

I caught my breath then, for Thecla was among them, and in her eyes I saw such pity and such sorrow as wrung my heart. I have not often been afraid, but I knew the pity and sorrow were for me, and I was frightened by the depth of them.

At last she turned from me, and I from her. That was when I saw Agilus in the crowd, and Morwenna, with her black hair and branded cheeks.

With them were a hundred more, prisoners from our oubliette and the Vincula of Thrax, felons I had scourged for provincial magistrates and murderers I had killed for them. And a hundred more besides: Ascians, tall Idas, and grim-mouthed Casdoe with little Severian in her arms; Guasacht and Erblon with our green battle flag.

I bent my head, staring at the floor while I awaited the first question.

No questions came. Not for a very long time—if I were to write here how long that time seemed to me, or even how long it actually was, I would not be believed. Before anyone spoke, the sun was low in the bright sky of Yesod, and Night had put long, dark fingers across the isle.

With Night came another. I heard the scrabble of its

claws on the stone floor, then a child's voice: *"Can't we go now?"* The alzabo had come, and its eyes burned in the blackness that had entered through the doorway of the Examination Chamber.

"Are you held here?" I asked. "It is not I who hold you."

Hundreds of voices cried out, saying, *"Yes, we are held!"*

I knew then that they were not to question me, but I to question them. Still I hoped it might not be so. I said, "Then go." But not one moved.

"What is it I must ask you?" I asked. There was no reply.

Night came indeed. Because that building was all of white stone, with an aperture at the summit of its soaring dome, I had scarcely realized it was unlit. As the horizon rose higher than the sun, the Examination Chamber grew as dark as those rooms the Increate builds beneath the boughs of great trees. The faces blurred and went out, like the flames of candles; only the eyes of the alzabo caught the fading light and shone like two red embers.

I heard the sailors whispering among themselves with fear in their voices, and the soft sighing of knife blades clearing well-oiled sheaths. I called to them that there was no reason to be afraid, that these were my ghosts, and not theirs.

The voice of the child Severa cried, *"We're not ghosts!"* with childish scorn. The red eyes came closer, and again there was the scrape of terrible claws on the stone floor. All the rest fidgeted in their places, so that the chamber echoed with the rustlings of their garments.

I wrenched futilely at the manacles, then fumbled for the sliding link and shouted to Zak not to try to stop the alzabo without a weapon.

Gunnie called (for I recognized her voice), "She's only a child, Severian."

I answered, "She's dead! The beast speaks through her."

"She's riding on its back. They're here by me."

My numb fingers had found the link, but I did not open it, knowing with a sudden certainty that could not be denied that if I were to free myself now and hide among the sailors, as I had planned, I would surely have failed.

"Justice!" I shouted to them. "I tried to act justly, and you know that! You may hate me, but can you say I harmed you without cause?"

A dark figure sprang up. Steel gleamed like the alzabo's eyes. Zak sprang too, and I heard the clatter of the weapon as it struck the stone floor.

CHAPTER XIX

Silence

IN THE CONFUSION I COULD NOT TELL AT FIRST WHO HAD freed me. I only knew that they were two, one to either side, and that they took my arms when I was free and led me quickly around the Seat of Justice and down a narrow stair. Behind us was pandemonium, the sailors shouting and scuffling, the alzabo baying.

The stair was long and steep, but it had been constructed in line with the aperture at the apex of the dome; faint light spilled down it, the final glimmer of a twilight yet reflected from a scattering of cloud, though Yesod's sun would appear no more until morning.

At the bottom we emerged into darkness so intense that I did not realize we were outdoors until I felt grass beneath my feet and wind on my cheek.

"Thank you," I said. "But who are you?"

A few paces away, Apheta answered, "They are my friends. You saw them on the craft that brought you here from your ship."

As she spoke, the two released me. I am tempted to write that they vanished at once, because that is how it seemed to me; but I do not think they did. Rather, perhaps, they walked away into the night without a word.

Apheta slipped her hand into mine as she had before. "I pledged myself to show you wonders."

I drew her farther from the building. "I'm not ready to see wonders. Yours, or any other woman's."

She laughed. Nothing is more frequently false in women

132

than their laughter, a merely social sound like the belching of autochthons at a feast; but it seemed to me that this laughter held real merriment.

"I mean what I say." The aftermath of fear had left me weak and sweating, but the wild bewilderment I felt had little or nothing to do with that; and if I knew anything at all (though I was not certain I did), it was that I did not want to begin some casual amour.

"Then we will walk—away from this place you wish so much to leave—and talk together. This afternoon you had a great many questions."

"I have none now," I told her. "I must think."

"Why, so must we all," she said sweetly. "All the time, or nearly."

We went down a long, white street that meandered like a river, so that its slope was never steep. Mansions of pale stone stood beside it like ghosts. Most were silent, but from some there came the sounds of revelry, the clink of glasses, strains of music, and the slap of dancing feet; never a human voice.

When we had passed several I said, "Your people don't speak as we do. We would say they don't speak at all."

"Is that a question?"

"No, it's an answer, an observation. When we were going into the Examination Chamber, you said you didn't speak our tongue, nor I yours. No one speaks yours."

"It was meant metaphorically," she told me. "We have a means of communication. You do not use it, and we do not use the one you use."

"You weave paradoxes to warn me," I said, though my thoughts were elsewhere.

"Not at all. You communicate by sound, we by silence."

"By gestures, you mean."

"No, by silence. You make a sound with your larynx and shape it by the action of your palate and lips. You have been doing that for so long that you have almost forgotten you do it; but when you were very young you had to learn to do it, as each child born to your race must. We could do it too, if we wished. Listen."

I listened and heard a soft gurgling that seemed to proceed not from her, but from the air beside her. It was as though some unseen mute had come to join us, and now made a croaking in his throat. "What was that?" I asked.

"Ah, you see, you have questions after all. What you heard was my voice. We call so, occasionally, when we are injured or in need of help."

"I don't understand," I said. "Nor do I wish to. I must be alone with my thoughts."

Between the mansions were many fountains and many trees, trees that seemed to me tall, strange, and lovely even in the darkness. The waters of the fountains were not perfumed as so many of ours were in the gardens of the House Absolute, but the scent of the pure water of Yesod was sweeter than any perfume.

Flowers grew there too, as I had seen when we had left the flier and as I was to see again in the morning. Most had now folded their hearts in the bowers of their petals, and only a pale moonvine blossomed, though there was no moon.

At last the street ended at the cool sea. There the little boats of Yesod were moored, just as I had seen them from above. Many men and women were there too, men and women who went to and fro among the boats, and between the boats and the shore. Sometimes a boat put out into the dark, lapping water; and at times some new boat appeared, with sails of many colors I could scarcely make out. Only rarely was there a light.

I said, "Once I was so foolish as to believe Thecla alive. It was a trick to draw me to the mine of the man-apes. Agia did it, but I saw her dead brother tonight."

"You do not comprehend what happened to you," Apheta told me. She sounded shamed. "That is why I am here—to explain it to you. But I will not explain until you are ready, until you ask me."

"And if I never ask?"

"Then I will never explain. It may be better, though, for you to know, especially if you are the New Sun."

"Is Urth really so important to you?"

She shook her head.

"Then why bother with it or me?"

"Because your race is important to us. It would be far less laborious if we could deal with it all at once, but you are sown over tens of thousands of worlds, and we cannot."

I said nothing.

"The worlds are very far apart. If one of our ships goes from one to another as fast as the starlight, the voyage takes many centuries. It does not seem so to those on the ship, but it does. If the ship goes even faster, tacking in the wind from the suns, time runs backward so that the ship arrives before it sails."

"That must be very inconvenient for you," I said. I was staring out over the water.

"For us, not for me personally. If you are thinking that I am in some fashion the queen or guardian of your Urth, dismiss the thought. I am not. But yes, imagine that we desire to play *shah mat* upon a board whose squares are rafts on that sea. We move, yet even as we move the rafts stir and slip into some new combination; and to move, we must paddle from one raft to the next, which takes so long."

"Against whom do you play?" I asked.

"Entropy."

I looked around at her. "It is said that game is always lost."

"We know."

"Is Thecla really alive? Alive outside myself?"

"Here? Yes."

"If I took her to Urth, would she be alive there?"

"That will not be permitted."

"Then I will not ask whether I can stay here with her. You have already answered that. Less than a day all told, you said."

"Would you stay here with her if it were possible?"

I thought about that for a moment. "Leaving Urth to freeze in the dark? No. Thecla was not a good woman, but . . ."

"Not good by whose measure?" Apheta asked. When I did not reply, she said, "I am truly inquiring. You may believe there is nothing unknown to me, but it is not so."

"By her own. What I was going to say, if I could find the words, was that she—that all the exultants except a very few—felt a certain responsibility. It used to astonish me that she who had so much learning cared so little about it. That was when we used to talk together in her cell. A long time afterward, when I had been Autarch for several years, I realized it was because she knew of something better, something she had been learning all her life. It was a rough ethology, but I find I can't say exactly what I mean."

"Try, please. I would like to hear it."

"Thecla would defend to the death anyone who could not help being dependent on her. That was why Hunna held Zak for me this afternoon. Hunna saw something of Thecla in me, though she must have known I was not really Thecla."

"Yet you said Thecla was not good."

"Goodness is so much more than that. She knew that too."

I paused, watching the white flashes the waves made in the darkness beyond the boats while I tried to collect my thoughts. "What I was trying to say was that I learned it from her—that responsibility—or rather I absorbed it when I absorbed her. If I were to betray Urth for her now, I would be worse than she, not better. She wants me to be better, as every lover wants his lover to be better than he."

Apheta said, "Go on."

"I wanted Thecla because she was so much better than I, socially and morally, and she wanted me because I was so much better than she and her friends, just because I did something necessary. Most exultants don't, on Urth. They have a great deal of power, and they pretend they're important; they tell the Autarch that they're ruling their peons, and they tell their peons they're ruling the Commonwealth. But they don't really do anything, and in their hearts they know it. They're afraid to use their power, or at least the best of them are, knowing they can't use it wisely."

A few sea birds, pale birds with huge eyes and bills like swords, wheeled overhead; after a time I saw a fish jump. "What was I talking about?" I asked.

"Why you could not leave your world to freeze in the dark."

I had remembered something else. "You said you didn't speak my language."

"I think I said I do not speak any tongue, that we have no tongues. Look."

She opened her mouth and held it up to me, but it was too dark for me to see whether she had deceived me. "How is it I hear you?" I asked. Then I understood what it was she wished, and kissed her; that kiss made me certain she was a woman of my own race.

"Do you know our story?" she whispered as we parted.

I told her what the aquastor Malrubius had told me upon another night upon another beach: that in a previous manvantara, the men of that cycle had shaped companions for themselves from other races, and that at the destruction of their universe these had escaped here to Yesod; that they ruled our universe through the Hierodules, whom they themselves had shaped.

Apheta shook her head when I had finished. "There is much more than that."

I said I had never supposed there was not, but that what I had just recited was all I knew. I added, "You said that you are the children of the Hierogrammates. Who are they, and who are you?"

"They are those of whom you spoke, those who were made in your image by a race cognate to your own. As for us, we are what I have told you we are."

She ceased to speak, and when some time had passed I said, "Go on."

"Severian, do you know the meaning of that word you used? Of Hierogrammate?"

I told her that someone had once told me it designated

those who recorded the rescripts of the Increate.

"So much is correct." She paused again. "Possibly we are too much in awe. Those whom we do not name, the cognates I spoke of, evoke such feelings still, though of all their works only the Hierogrammates remain. You say they desired companions. How could they shape companions for themselves, who were themselves ever reaching higher and higher?"

I confessed I did not know; and when she seemed disinclined to tell me more, I described the winged being I had seen in the pages of Father Inire's book and asked whether it had not been a Hierogrammate.

She said it was. "But I will speak no more of them. You asked about us; we are their larvae. Do you know what larvae are?"

"Why, yes," I answered. "Masked spirits."

Apheta nodded. "We carry their spirit, and even as you say, until we attain to their high state we must go masked —not with an actual mask such as those our Hierodules wear, but with the appearance of your own race, the race that our parents, the Hierogrammates, first set forth to follow. Yet we are not yet Hierogrammates, nor are we truly like you. You have listened to my voice for a long while now, Autarch. Listen to this world of Yesod instead and tell me what you hear, other than my words, when I speak to you. Listen! What do you hear?"

I did not understand. I said, "Nothing. But you are a human woman."

"You hear nothing because we speak with silence, even as you with sound. Whatever noises we find we shape, canceling those which are unneeded, voicing our thoughts in the remainder. That is why I led you here, where the waves murmur always; and why we have so many fountains, and trees to stir their leaves in the wind from our sea."

I hardly heard her. Something vast and bright—a moon, a sun—was rising, madly shaped and drenched with light. It was as though some golden seed soared in the atmosphere of this strange world, borne aloft upon a billion black filaments. It was the ship; and the sun called Yesod, though the horizon was above it, struck that vast hull full and was reflected with a light that seemed like day.

"Look!" I called to Apheta.

And she cried back, "Look! Look!" pointing to her mouth. I looked and saw that what I had taken for her tongue when we had kissed was but a lump of tissue protruding from her palate.

CHAPTER XX

The Coiled Room

I CANNOT SAY HOW LONG THE SHIP HUNG SO IN THE SKY. IT was less than a watch, surely, and it seemed no longer than a breath. While it was there, I had eyes for nothing else; what Apheta did then, I have no notion. When it was gone, I found her sitting on a rock near the water and looking at me.

"I've so many questions," I said. "Seeing Thecla again put them out of my mind, but now they're there again; and there are questions about her too."

Apheta said, "But you are exhausted."

I nodded to that.

"Tomorrow you must face Tzadkiel, and tomorrow is not far off. Our little world spins more quickly than your own; its days and night must seem short to you. Will you come with me?"

"Gladly, my lady."

"You think me a queen, or something of the sort. Will it amaze you to discover I live in a single room? Look there."

I looked and saw an archway concealed among trees, only a dozen paces from the water.

"Is there no tide here?" I asked.

"No. I know what that means because I have studied the ways of your world—thus I was chosen to bring the shipmen, and later to speak with you. But Yesod, having no companion, has no tides."

"You knew from the first that I was Autarch, didn't you?

If you have studied Urth, you surely knew. Putting manacles on Zak was only a stratagem."

She did not reply, even after we had reached the dark arch. Set in a white stone wall, it seemed the entrance to a tomb; but the air within was as fresh and sweet as all the air of Yesod.

"You must lead me, my lady," I said. "I cannot see in this blackness."

I had no sooner spoken than there was light, a dim light like a flame reflected from tarnished silver. It came from Apheta herself, and pulsed like the beating of a heart.

We stood in a wide room, hung on every side with muslin curtains. Padded seats and divans were scattered upon a gray carpet. One after another, the curtains were twitched aside, and behind each I saw the silent, somber face of a man; when he had looked at us for a moment, each man let his curtain fall.

"You're well guarded, my lady," I told her. "But you've nothing to fear from me."

She smiled, and it was odd to see that smile lit by its own light. "You would cut my throat in an instant, if it would save your Urth. We both know that. Or cut your own, I think."

"Yes. At least I hope so."

"But these are not protectors. My light means that I am ready to mate."

"And if I am not?"

"I will choose another while you sleep. There will be no difficulty, as you see."

She thrust aside a curtain, and we entered a wide corridor that bent to the left. Scattered about were seats such as I had seen outside, and many other objects as mysterious to me as the appliances in Baldanders's castle, though they were lovely and not terrible. Apheta took one of the divans.

"Does this not lead us to your chamber, my lady?"

"This is mine. It is a spiral; many of our rooms are, because we like that shape. If you follow it, you will come to a place where you may wash, and be alone for a time."

"Thank you. Have you a candle to lend me?"

She shook her head, but told me it would not be entirely dark.

I left her and followed the spiral. Her light went with me, growing fainter and fainter but reflected by the curving wall. At the end, which I was not long in reaching, a breath of wind suggested that what Gunnie had called a spiracle stretched from the roof to this place. As my eyes grew accustomed to the dark, I saw it as a circle of darkness less intense. Standing below it, I beheld the spangled sky of Yesod.

I thought about it while I relieved myself and washed, and when I returned to Apheta, who lay on one of the divans with her naked loveliness pulsing through a thin sheet, I kissed her and asked, "Are there no other worlds, my lady?"

"There are very many," she murmured. She had unbound her dark hair, which floated about her shining face, so that she seemed herself some eerie star, wrapped in night.

"Here in Yesod. On Urth we see myriad suns, dim by day, bright by night. Your day sky is empty, but your night sky is brighter than ours."

"When we require them, the Hierogrammates will build more—worlds as fair as this, or more fair. Suns for them too, should we require more suns. Thus for us they are there already. Time runs as we ask here, and we like their light."

"Time does not run as I ask." I seated myself on her divan, my aching leg stretched before me.

"Not yet," she said. And then, "You are lame, Autarch."

"Surely you've noticed that before."

"Yes, but I am seeking a way to tell you that for you time will run as for us. You are lame now, but if you bring the New Sun to your Urth, you shall not always be so."

"You Hierarchs are magicians. You're more powerful than those I once met, but magicians still. You talk of this

wonder and that, but though your curses may blast, I feel
your rewards are false gold that will turn to dust in the
hand."

"You misunderstand us," she told me. "And though we
know so much more than you, our gold is true gold, got as
true gold is, often at the cost of our lives."

"Then you're lost in your own labyrinth, and no wonder.
Once I had the power to cure such things—sometimes, at
least." And I told her of the sick girl in the jacal in Thrax,
and of the Uhlan on the green road, and of Triskele; and
last of all, I told her how I had found the steward dead at
my door.

"If I try to unravel this for you, will you understand that
I do not, no more than you yourself, know all the secrets of
your Briah, although they have been my study? They are
without end."

"I understand," I said. "But on the ship I thought we
had come to the end of Briah when we came here."

"So you did, but though you may walk into a house at
one door and walk out at the other, you do not know all the
secrets of that house."

I nodded, watching her naked beauty pulse beneath the
fabric and wishing, if the truth be known, that it lacked so
strong a hold on me.

"You saw our sea. Did you notice the waves there? What
would you say to someone who told you that you saw not
waves, but only water?"

"That I've learned not to argue with fools. One smiles
and walks away."

"What you call time is made up of such waves, and as
the waves you saw existed in the water, so time exists in
matter. The waves march toward the beach, but if you were
to cast a pebble into the water, new waves, a hundredth or
a thousandth the strength of the old, would run out to sea,
and the waves there would feel them."

"I understand."

"So do future things make themselves known in the past.
A child who will someday be wise is a wise child; and many

who will be doomed carry their dooms in their faces, so that those who can see even a short way into the future find it there and turn away their eyes."

"Aren't we all doomed?"

"No, but that is another matter. You may master a New Sun. Should you, its energy will be yours to draw upon, though it will not exist unless you—and your Urth —triumph here. But as the boy foreshadows the man, something of that faculty has reached you through the Corridors of Time. I cannot say whence you drew when you were on Urth. Partly from yourself, no doubt. But not all or even most can have come from you, or you would have perished. Perhaps from your world, or from its old sun. When you were on the ship there was no world and no sun near enough, so you took what could be drawn from the ship itself, and nearly wrecked it. But even that was not sufficient."

"And had the Claw of the Conciliator no power at all?"

"Let me see it." She held out a shining hand.

"It was destroyed long ago by the weapons of the Ascians," I told her.

She made no answer, but only stared at me; and when a heartbeat had passed, I saw that she was looking at my chest, where I carried the thorn in the little pouch Dorcas had sewn for me.

I looked myself, and saw a light—fainter far than hers, yet steady. I took out the thorn, and its golden radiance shone from wall to wall before it died away. "It has become the Claw," I said. "So I saw it when I drew it from the rocks."

I held it out to her; she did not look at it, but at the half-healed wound it had made. "It was saturated with your blood," she said, "and your blood contains your living cells. I doubt that it was powerless. Nor do I wonder that the Pelerines revered it."

I left her then, and groping, found my way to the beach once more, and for a long time I walked up and down the sand. But the thoughts I had there have no place here.

* * *

When I returned, Apheta was waiting for me still, her silver pulsing more importunate than before. "Can you?" she asked, and I told her she was very beautiful.

"But can you?" she asked again.

"We must talk first. I would be betraying my kind if I did not question you."

"Then ask," she whispered. "Though I warn you that nothing I say will help your race in the test to come."

"How is it you speak? What sound is there here?"

"You must listen to my voice," she told me, "and not to my words. What do you hear?"

I did as she had instructed me, and heard the silken sliding of the sheet, the whisper of our bodies, the breaking of the little waves, and the beating of my own heart.

A hundred questions I had been ready to ask, and it had seemed to me that each of the hundred might bring the New Sun. Her lips brushed mine, and every question vanished, banished from my consciousness as if it had never been. Her hands, her lips, her eyes, the breasts I pressed—all wondrous; but there was more, perhaps the perfume of her hair. I felt that I breathed an endless night. . . .

Lying upon my back, I entered Yesod. Or say, rather, Yesod closed about me. It was only then that I knew I had never been there. Stars in their billions spurted from me, fountains of suns, so that for an instant I felt I knew how universes are born. All folly.

Reality displaced it, the kindling of the torch that whips shadows to their corners, and with them all the winged fays of fancy. There was something born between Yesod and Briah when I met with Apheta upon that divan in that circling room, something tiny yet immense that burned like a coal conveyed to the tongue by tongs.

That something was myself.

I slept; and because I slept without a dream, did not know I slept.

When I woke, Apheta was gone. The sun of Yesod had come through the spiracle at the narrow end of the spiral chamber. Ever fainter, its illumination was directed to me by the white walls, so that I woke in a gilded twilight. I rose and dressed, wondering where Apheta might be; but as I pulled on my boots, she entered with a tray. I was embarrassed to have so great a lady serve me, and I told her so.

"Surely the noble concubines of your court have waited upon you, Autarch."

"What are they compared with you?"

She shrugged. "I am not a great lady. Or at least, only to you, and only today. Our status is decided by our closeness to the Hierogrammates, and I am not very near."

She set her tray down and sat beside it. It held small cakes, a carafe of cool water, and cups of some steaming liquid that looked like milk and yet was not milk.

"I cannot believe you are far from the Hierogrammates, my lady."

"That is merely because you think yourself and your Urth so important, imagining that what I say to you and what we do now will decide her fate. It isn't so, none of it. What we will do now will have no effect, and you and your world are of importance to no one here."

I waited for her to say more, and at last she said, "Except to me," and took a bite from one of the cakes.

"Thank you, my lady."

"And that only since you have come. Though I cannot but dislike you and your Urth, you care so much for her."

"My lady . . ."

"I know, you thought I desired you. It is only now that I like you enough to tell you I do not. You are a hero, Autarch, and heroes are always monsters, come to give us news we would sooner not hear. But you are a particularly monstrous monster. Tell me, as you walked the circular hall around the Examination Chamber, did you study the pictures there?"

"Only a few," I said. "There was the cell where Agia had been confined, and I noticed one or two others."

"And how do you suppose they came to be there?"

I took a cake myself, and a sip from the cup nearest me.

"I've no idea, my lady. I've seen so many wonders here that I've ceased to wonder about any save Thecla."

"But you could not ask much about her—even Thecla—last night for fear of what I might say or do. Although you were ready to do so a hundred times."

"Would you have liked me better, my lady, if I'd questioned you about an old love while I lay with you? Yours is a strange race indeed. But since you've brought her up yourself, tell me about her." A drop of the white beverage, which I had swallowed without tasting, ran down the side of the cup. I looked around for something with which to blot it, but there was nothing.

"Your hands shake."

"So they do, my lady." I put down the cup, and it rattled against the tray.

"Did you love her so much?"

"Yes, my lady, and hate her too. I'm Thecla and the man who loved Thecla."

"Then I will tell you nothing about her—what could I tell you? Perhaps she will tell you herself after the Presentation."

"If I succeed, you mean."

"Would your Thecla punish you if you failed?" Apheta asked, and a great joy entered my heart. "But eat, then we must go. I told you last night that our days are short here, and you have already slept away the first part of this one."

I swallowed the cake and drained the cup. "What of Urth," I said, "if I fail?"

She stood. "Tzadkiel is just. He would not make Urth worse than she is, no worse than she would have been had you not come."

"That is the future of ice," I said. "But if I succeed, the New Sun will come." As though the cup had been drugged, I seemed to stand infinitely far from myself, to watch myself as a man watches a mote, to hear my own voice as a hawk hears the squeaking of a meadow mouse.

Apheta had pushed aside the curtain. I followed her out into the stoa. Through its open arch shone the fresh sea of

Yesod, a sapphire flecked with white. "Yes," she said. "And your Urth will be destroyed."

"My lady—"

"Enough. Come with me."

"Purn was right, then. He wanted to kill me, and I should have let him." The avenue we took was steeper than that we had descended the night before, going straight up the hillside toward the Hall of Justice, which loomed above us like a cloud.

"It was not you who prevented him," Apheta said.

"Earlier, in the ship, my lady. It was he, then, last night in the dark. Someone stopped him then, or I should have died. I couldn't free myself."

"Tzadkiel," she said.

Though my legs were longer than hers, I had to hurry to keep up with her. "You said he wasn't there, my lady."

"No. I said he did not sit in his Seat of Justice that day. Autarch, look about you." She halted, and I with her. "Is this not a fair town?"

"The fairest I've ever seen, my lady. Surely a hundred times more fair than any on Urth."

"Remember it; you may not see it again. Your world might be as fair as this, if all of you wished it so."

We climbed until we stood at the entrance to the Hall of Justice. I had imagined pushing throngs, such as we had at our public trials, but the hilltop was wrapped in morning silence.

Apheta turned again and pointed toward the sea. "Look," she said again. "Can you see the isles?"

I did. They were scattered—endlessly as it seemed —across the water, just as I had beheld them from the ship.

"Do you know what a galaxy is, Autarch? A whorl of stars, uncountable, remote from all others?"

I nodded.

"This isle on which we stand judges the worlds of your galaxy. Each isle you see judges another. I hope knowing that will aid you, because it is all the aid I can give you. If you do not see me again, remember that I shall see you, nonetheless."

CHAPTER XXI

Tzadkiel

ON THE PREVIOUS DAY, THE SAILORS HAD BEEN SEATED IN the front of the Examination Chamber. The first thing I noticed when I entered it again was that they were not there. Those who had those places were wrapped in a darkness that seemed to emanate from them, and the sailors were by the door and toward the sides of the room.

Looking past the dark figures and down the long aisle that led to Tzadkiel's Seat of Justice, I saw Zak. He was seated upon that throne. Over the walls of white stone on each side of it, there spread what seemed tapestries of the finest tissue, worked in a pattern of eyes in gorgeous colors. It was not until they moved that I realized they were his wings.

Apheta had left me at the foot of the steps, and from that time I had been unguarded; as I stood staring at Zak, two sailors appeared to take my arms and lead me to him.

They left me, and I stood before him with head bowed. No speech of the old Autarch's came unbidden to my mind this time; there was only confusion. At last I stammered, "Zak, I've come to plead for Urth."

"I know," he said. "Welcome." His voice was deep and clear, like the blowing of a golden horn far away, so that I recalled a certain foolish tale of Gabriel, who wore the war horn of Heaven across his back, suspended on the rainbow. It suggested Thecla's book, in which I had read it; and that, in turn, the great volume of pavonine leather the old Autarch had shown me when I had asked him the way to

150

the garden, when he, having been told of me, supposed that I had arrived to replace him and would go to plead for Urth at once.

I knew then that I had seen Tzadkiel before I helped Sidero and the rest catch him as Zak, and that the male form I saw was no more true (though no less) than the winged woman whose glance had stunned me then, and that neither was more true, or less, than the animal shape that had saved me when Purn had tried to kill me outside his cage.

And I said, "Sieur—Zak—Tzadkiel, mighty Hierogrammate—I don't understand."

"Do you mean that you do not understand me? And why should you? I do not understand myself, Severian, or you. Yet I am as I am, your own race having made us so before the apocatastasis. Were you not told that they had shaped us in their image?"

I tried to speak, but I could not. At last I nodded.

"The form you have now was their first, the shape they bore when they were newly sprung from the beasts. All races change, shaped by time. Are you aware of it?"

I recalled the man-apes of the mine, and said, "Not always for the better."

"Indeed. But the Hieros grasped their own shaping, and that we might follow them, ours as well."

"Sieur—"

"Ask. Your final trial comes soon, and it cannot be just. Whatever reparation we can make, we will make. Now or after."

My heart froze at those words; behind me all those who sat upon the benches whispered, so that I heard their voices like the soughing of leaves in a forest, though I did not know who they were.

When I could speak again, I said, "Sieur, it is a foolish question. But once I heard two tales of shape-changers, and in one an angel—and I think that you, sieur, are such an angel—tore open his breast and gave the power he had to change his shape to a barnyard goose. And the goose used it at once, becoming a swift salt goose forever. Last night, the lady Apheta said I might not go lame always. Sieur, was he—was Melito—instructed to tell me that story?"

A little smile played at the corners of Tzadkiel's lips, recalling the way Zak used to grin at me. "Who can say? Not by me. You must understand that when a truth is known, as that has been known by so many for so many aeons, it spreads abroad and changes its own shape, taking many forms. But if you are asking that I give my ability to you, I cannot. If we could bestow it at will, we would give it to our children. You have met them, and they are imprisoned still in the form you wear now. Have you another question before we proceed?"

"Yes, sieur. A thousand. But if I am permitted only one, why did you come aboard the ship as you did?"

"Because I wished to know you. When you were a boy on your own world, did you never bend the knee to the Conciliator?"

"On Holy Katharine's Day, sieur."

"And did you believe in him? Did you believe with all your being?"

"No, sieur." I felt I was about to be punished for my unbelief, and to this day I cannot say whether I was or not.

"Suppose you had. Did you never know of one of your own age who did?"

"The acolytes, sieur. Or at least, so it was said among us, who were the torturers' apprentices."

"Would they not have wished to walk with him, if they could? Stand beside him when he was in danger? Care for him, perhaps, when he was ill? I have been such an acolyte, in a creation now vanished. In that too there was a Conciliator and a New Sun, though we did not use those names.

"But now we must talk of something else, and quickly. I have many duties, some more demanding than this. Let me say plainly that we have tricked you, Severian. You have come to stand our examination, and thus we have talked of it to you, and even told you this building is our Hall of

Justice. None of it is so."

I could only stare at him.

"Or if you wish it put in another way, you have already passed our testing, which was an examination of the future you will create. You are the New Sun. You will be returned to your Urth, and the White Fountain will go with you. The death agonies of the world you know will be offered to the Increate. And they will be indescribable—continents will founder, as has been said. Much that is beautiful will perish, and with it most of your race; but your home will be reborn."

Although I can, as I do, write the words he used, I cannot convey his tone or even hint at the conviction it carried. His thoughts seemed to thunder forth, raising pictures in the mind more real than any reality, so that while I imagined I saw the continents perish, I heard the crashing of great buildings and smelled Urth's bitter sea wind.

An angry murmur rose behind me.

"Sieur," I said, "I can remember the examination of my predecessor." I felt as I had when I was the youngest of our apprentices.

Tzadkiel nodded. "It was necessary that you recall it; it was for that reason he was examined."

"And unmanned?" The old Autarch trembled in me, and I felt my own hands shake.

"Yes. Otherwise a child would have stood between you and the throne, and your Urth would have perished forever. The alternative was the death of the child. Would that have been better?"

I could not speak, but his dark eyes seemed to bore into every heart that beat in mine, and at last I shook my head.

"Now I must go. My son will see that you are returned to Briah and Urth, which will be destroyed at your order."

His gaze left me, and I followed it to the aisle behind me, where I saw the man who had brought us from the ship. The sailors were rising and drawing their knives, yet I scarcely noticed them. The center places that had been theirs the day before held others now, figures no longer shadowed. Sweat sprang from my forehead as blood had when I had first seen Tzadkiel, and I turned to cry out to him.

He was gone.

Lame leg or not I ran, hobbling as swiftly as I could around the Seat of Justice in search of the stair by which I had been led away the night before. I think it only fair to myself to say that I fled not so much from the sailors as from the faces of the others I had seen in the Chamber.

However that may be, the stair was gone too; I found only a smooth floor of stone slabs there, one of which was, no doubt, raised by some concealed mechanism.

Now another such mechanism acted. Swiftly and smoothly, Tzadkiel's throne sank, as a whale that has surfaced to bask in the sun sinks back into the ice-choked Southern Sea. At one moment the great stone seat stood between me and the larger part of the Chamber, as solid as a wall; at the next the floor was closing over its back, and a fantastic battle spread before me.

The Hierarch whom Tzadkiel had called his son lay sprawled in the aisle. Over him surged the sailors, their knives flashing and many bloodied. Against them stood a score or so who seemed at first as weak as children—and indeed I saw at least one child among them—but held their ground like heroes and, when they had only their hands to fight with, fought weaponless. Because their backs were toward me, I told myself I did not know them; but I knew it for a lie.

With a roar that echoed from the walls, the alzabo burst from this encircled band. The sailors fell back, and in an instant it was crushing a man in its jaws. I saw Agia with her poisoned sword, and Agilus too, swinging a crimsoned avern like a mace, and Baldanders, unarmed until he seized a sailor and smashed another to the floor with her.

And Dorcas, Morwenna, Cyriaca, and Casdoe. Thecla, already down, the blood that trickled from her throat stanched by a ragged apprentice. Guasacht and Erblon slashed with their spathae as though they fought from the saddle. Daria wielded a slender saber in either hand.

Somehow chained again, Pia throttled a sailor with her chain.

I dashed past Merryn and found myself between Gunnie and Dr. Talos, whose flickering blade felled a man at my feet. A raging sailor charged me, and I—I swear it —welcomed him for his weapon, seizing his wrist, breaking his arm, and wrenching his knife away all in a single motion. I had no time to wonder at the ease of it before I saw that Gunnie had stabbed him in the neck.

It seemed that I had no sooner joined the battle than it was over. A few sailors fled from the Chamber; twenty or thirty bodies lay upon the floor or over the benches. Most of the women were dead, though I saw one of the women-cats licking blood from her stubby fingers. Old Winnoc leaned wearily on one of the scimitars used by the Peler-ines' slaves. Dr. Talos cut a dead man's robe to wipe the blade of his cane sword, and I saw that the dead man was Master Ash.

"Who are they?" Gunnie asked.

I shook my head, feeling I scarcely knew myself. Dr. Talos seized her hand and brushed its fingers with his lips. "Allow me. I am Talos, physician, playwright, and impresario. I'm—"

I no longer listened. Triskele had bounded up to me with blood-smeared flews, hindquarters quivering with joy. Master Malrubius, resplendent in the fur-trimmed cloak of the guild, followed him. When I saw Master Malrubius I knew, and he, seeing me, knew I did.

At once he—with Triskele, Dr. Talos, the dead Master Ash, Dorcas, and the rest—fell to silver shards of nothingness, just as he had that night on the beach after he had rescued me from the dying jungle of the north. Gunnie and I were left alone with the bodies of the sailors.

Not all were corpses. One stirred and groaned. We tried to bind the wound in his chest (it was from the doctor's narrow blade, I think) with rags ripped from the dead, though blood bubbled from his mouth. After a time the Hierarchs came with medicine and proper bandages, and took him away.

The lady Apheta had come with them, but she remained with us.

"You said that I would not see you again," I reminded her.

"I said that you might not," she corrected me. "Had things fallen out otherwise here, you would not have."

In the stillness of that chamber of death, her voice was scarcely a whisper.

CHAPTER XXII

Descent

"THERE MUST BE MANY QUESTIONS YOU WANT TO ASK," Apheta whispered. "Let us go out into the portico, and I will answer them all."

I shook my head, for I heard the water-music of rain through the open doorway.

Gunnie touched my arm. "Is somebody spying on us?"

"No," Apheta told her. "But let us go out. It should be pleasant there, and we have only a short time now, we three."

"I can understand you well enough," I told her. "I'll stay here. Perhaps some others among these many dead will begin to moan. That would make a fit voice for you."

She nodded. "It would indeed." I had seated myself where Tzadkiel had crouched on the first day; she sat down beside me, no doubt so that I might hear her better.

In a moment Gunnie sat too and sheathed her dagger, having cleaned the blade on her thigh. "I'm sorry," Gunnie said.

"Sorry for what? Because you fought for me? I don't blame you."

"Sorry the others didn't, that the magic people had to defend you against us. Against all of us but me. Who were they? Did you whistle them up?"

"No," I said. Apheta, "Yes."

"They were people I'd known, that's all. Some were women I'd loved. Many are dead—Thecla, Agilus, Casdoe

157

... Perhaps they're all dead now, all ghosts, though I didn't know it."

"They are unborn. Surely you know that time runs backward when the ship sails swiftly. I told you myself. They are unborn, as you are."

She spoke to Gunnie. "I said he had called them because it was from his mind that we drew them, seeking those who hated him, or at least had reason to. The giant you saw might have mastered the Commonwealth, had Severian not defeated him. The blond woman could not forgive him for bringing her back from death."

I said, "I can't stop you from explaining all this, but do it elsewhere. Or let me go where I need not hear it."

Apheta asked, "It gave you no joy?"

"To see them all again, tricked into defending me? No. Why should it?"

"Because they were not tricked, no more than Master Malrubius was on any of the occasions when you saw him after his death. We found them among your memories and let them judge. Everyone in this Chamber, save yourself, saw the same things. Has it not struck you as odd that I can scarcely speak here?"

I turned to stare at her, feeling I had been away and come back to hear her talk when it was of some other matter.

"Our rooms are always filled with the sound of water and the sighing of the wind. This was built for you and your kind."

Gunnie said, "Before you came in, he—Zak—showed us that Urth had two futures. It could die and be born new. Or it could go on living for a long time before it died forever."

"I've known that since I was a boy."

She nodded to herself, and for a moment I seemed to see the child she had been instead of the woman she had become. "But we haven't. We hadn't." Her gaze left my face, and I saw her looking from corpse to corpse. "In religion, but sailors never pay much attention to that."

For want of something better to say, I said, "I suppose not."

"My mother did, and it was like she was crazy, someplace in a corner of her mind. You know what I mean? And I think that was all it was."

I turned to Apheta and began, "What I want to know—"

But Gunnie caught me by the shoulder, her hand large and strong for a woman's, and drew me back to her. "We thought it wouldn't be for a long while yet, a long while after we were dead."

Apheta whispered, "When you sign aboard that ship, you sail from the Beginning to the End. All sailors know that."

"We didn't think about it. Not until you made us. He made us see it. Zak."

I asked, "And you knew it was Zak?"

Gunnie nodded. "I was with him when they caught him. I don't think I would have known otherwise. Or maybe I would. He'd changed a lot, so I knew already he wasn't what we thought at first. He's—I don't know."

Apheta whispered, "May I tell you? He is a reflection, an imitation, of what you will be."

I asked, "You mean if the New Sun comes?"

"No. I mean that it is coming. That your trial is over. You have been obsessed with it for so long, I know, and it must be difficult for you to realize that it is truly over. You have succeeded. You have saved your future."

"You have succeeded too," I said.

Apheta nodded. "You understand that now."

Gunnie said, "I don't. What are you talking about?"

"Don't you see? The Hierarchs and their Hierodules —and the Hierogrammates too—have been trying to let us become what we were. What we can be. Isn't that right, my lady? That's their justice, their whole reason for being. They bring us through the pain we brought them through. And—" I could not complete the thought. The words had become iron on my lips.

Apheta said, "You in turn will make us go through what you did. I think you understand. But you"—she looked to Gunnie—"do not. Your race and ours are, perhaps, no more than each other's reproductive mechanisms. You are a woman, and so you say you produce your ovum so that there will someday be another woman. But your ovum would say it produces that woman so that someday there will be another ovum. We have wanted the New Sun to succeed as badly as he has wanted to himself. More urgently, in all truth. In saving your race he has saved ours; as we have saved ours of the future by saving yours."

Apheta turned back to me. "I told you that you had brought unwelcome news. The news was that we might indeed lose the game you and I spoke of."

I said, "I have three questions, my lady. Let me ask them and I'll go, if you'll let me."

She nodded.

"How is it that Tzadkiel could say my examination was over, when the aquastors had to fight and die to save me?"

"The aquastors did not die," Apheta told me. "They live in you. As for Tzadkiel, he spoke as he did because it was the truth. He had examined the future and found the chance high that you would bring a fresh sun to your Urth, and thus save that strand of your race, so that it might produce ours in your Briahtic universe. It was on that examination that everything hinged; it was over, and the result favorable to you."

Gunnie looked from Apheta to me and seemed about to speak, but she said nothing.

"My second question. Tzadkiel said also that my trial could not be just, and that he would make what reparation he could. You have said that he is truthful. Did my trial differ from my examination? How was it unjust?"

Apheta's voice seemed no more than a sigh. "It is easy for those who need not judge, or judging need not toil for justice, to complain of inequity and talk of impartiality. When one must actually judge, as Tzadkiel does, he finds he cannot be just to one without being unjust to another. In fairness to those on Urth who will die, and especially to the poor and ignorant people who will never understand what it is they die for, he summoned their representatives—"

"Us, you mean!" Gunnie exclaimed.

"Yes, you shipmen. And he gave you, Autarch, those who had reason to hate you for your defenders. That was just to the shipmen, but not to you."

"I have deserved punishment often before, and not received it."

Apheta nodded. "For that reason certain of the scenes you saw, or at least might have seen had you troubled to look, were made to appear in the narrow passage that rings this room. Some recalled your duty. Others were meant to show you that you yourself had often meted out the harshest justice. Do you see now why you were chosen?"

"A torturer, to save the world? Yes."

"Take your head out of your hands. It is enough that you and this poor woman can scarcely hear me. At least permit me to hear you. You have asked the three questions you spoke of. Have you more?"

"Many. I saw Daria. And Guasacht and Erblon. Had they reason to hate me?"

"I do not know," Apheta whispered. "You must ask Tzadkiel, or those who assisted him. Or ask yourself."

"I suppose they had. I would have displaced Erblon if I could. As Autarch, I could have promoted Guasacht, but I did not; and I never tried to find Daria after the battle. There were so many other things—so many important things—to do. I see why you called me a monster."

Gunnie exclaimed, "You're no monster, she is!"

I shrugged. "Yet all of them fought for Urth, and so did Gunnie. That was wonderful."

"Not for the Urth you have known," Apheta whispered. "For a New Urth many will never see, except through your eyes and the eyes of others who recall them. Have you more questions?"

Gunnie said, "I've got one. Where are my shipmates? The ones who ran and saved their lives?"

I sensed that she was ashamed for them. I said, "Their running saved ours too, very likely."

"They will be returned to the ship," Apheta told her.

"What about Severian and me?"

I said, "They'll try to kill us on the voyage home, Gunnie; or perhaps not. If they do, we'll have to deal with them."

Apheta shook her head. "You will be returned to the ship indeed, but by a different way. Believe me, the problem will not arise."

Dark-robed Hierarchs came down the aisle with travails, gathering the dead. "They will be interred in the grounds of this building," Apheta whispered. "Have we reached your last question, Autarch?"

"Nearly. But look there. One of those bodies belongs to one of your own people, to Tzadkiel's son."

"He will lie here as well, with those who fell with him."

"But was it intended so? Did his father plan that too?"

"That he should die? No. But that he should risk death. What right would we have to risk your life and the lives of so many others if we would bear no risk ourselves? Tzadkiel risked death with you on the ship. Venant here."

"He knew what would happen?"

"Do you mean Tzadkiel or Venant? Venant surely did not know what would happen, yet he knew what might happen, and he went forth to save our race, as others have gone forth to save theirs. For Tzadkiel I cannot speak."

"You told me each of the isles judges a galaxy. Are we—is Urth—important to you after all?"

Apheta rose, smoothing her white gown. Her floating hair, which had seemed uncanny to me when I had seen it first, was familiar now; I felt sure that such a dark aureole was depicted somewhere in old Rudesind's illimitable gallery, though I could not quite call the proper painting to mind. She said, "We have watched with the dead. Now they go, and it is time that we went also. It may be that from your ancient Urth, reborn, the Hieros will come. I believe it to be so. But I am only one woman, and of no high position. I said what I did so that you would not die despairing."

Gunnie started to speak, but Apheta motioned her to silence, saying, "Now follow me."

We did, but she walked only a step or two to the spot

where Tzadkiel's Seat of Justice had stood. "Severian, take her hand," she told me. She herself took my free hand, and Gunnie's.

The stone on which we stood sank under us. In an instant the floor of the Chamber of Examination closed above our heads. We dropped, or so it seemed, into a vast pit filled with harsh yellow light, a pit a thousand times wider than the square of stone. Its sides were mighty mechanisms of green and silver metals, before which men and women hovered and darted like so many flies, and across which titanic scarabs of blue and gold clambered like ants.

CHAPTER XXIII

The Ship

WHILE WE FELL I COULD NOT SPEAK. I GRIPPED GUNNIE'S hand and Apheta's, not because I feared they might be lost, but because I feared I might; and there was no room left in my mind for any thought but that.

At last we slowed—or rather, we seemed to be dropping no more rapidly. I recalled my leaps among the rigging, for it seemed that here too the insensate hunger for matter had been abated. I saw my own expression of relief upon Gunnie's face when she turned to Apheta to ask where we were.

"In our world—our ship, if you are more comfortable calling it so, though it only circles our sun and requires no sails."

A door had opened in the wall of the well, and though it seemed we fell still, we did not leave this door behind. Apheta drew us there, into a dark and narrow corridor I blessed when I felt its firm floor beneath my feet. Gunnie managed to say, "On our ship, we don't have water on deck."

"Where do you have it?" Apheta asked absently. It was not until I noticed how much stronger her voice was here that I was aware of the noise, a humming like the song of bees (how well I remembered it!) and distant clatterings and clickings, as though destriers galloped down a plank road while locusts trilled unseen in trees that surely could not flourish in this place.

"Inside," Gunnie told Apheta. "In tanks."

"It must be terrible to go to the surface of such a world. Here it is something we look forward to very much."

A woman who looked rather like Apheta was striding toward us. She traveled a great deal faster than her walk should have carried her, so that she rushed past in an instant. I turned to stare after her, suddenly reminded of the way the green man had vanished down the Corridors of Time. When she had passed from sight, I said, "You do not come to the surface often, do you? I should have guessed; all of you are so pale."

"It is a reward for us, for working long and hard. On your Urth, women who look as I do, do no work at all—or so I have heard."

Gunnie said, "Some do."

The corridor divided, and divided again. We too rushed along, and it seemed to me that our path swung in a long curve, counterclockwise and descending. Apheta had said her people loved the spiral; perhaps they favor the helix as well.

Just as a wave rises abruptly before the bow of a storm-tossed carrack, double doors of tarnished argent rose before us. We halted in a way that made it seem we had never moved save at a walk. Apheta motioned toward the doors, which groaned like clients but would not swing back until I helped her push them.

Gunnie looked up at the lintel and, as though she read the words there, recited, *"No hope for those who enter here."*

"No, no," Apheta murmured. "Every hope." The hum and the clickings had been left behind.

I asked, "Is this where I will be taught to bring the New Sun?"

"You will not have to be taught," she told me. "You are gravid with the knowledge, and it will be born as soon as you approach the White Fountain sufficiently for you to be aware of it."

I would have laughed at her figure of speech, had not the utter emptiness of the chamber to which we had come stilled all amusement. It was wider than the Chamber of

Examination, with silver walls that rose to a great arch in that curve one sees traced by a stone hurled into the air; but it was empty, utterly empty save for us, who whispered in its doorway.

Gunnie repeated, "No hope," and I realized she had been too frightened to pay heed to Apheta or me. I put an arm around her shoulders (though the gesture seemed strange directed toward a woman who was as tall as I) and tried to comfort her, thinking all the while what a fool she would be to accept the comfort when it was clear I could do no more here than she herself.

She continued, "We used to have a sailor who said that. She was always hoping to go home, but we never landed in her time again, and after a while she died."

I asked Apheta how I came to carry such knowledge without being aware of it.

"Tzadkiel gave it to you as you slept," she said.

"You mean he came to your chamber last night?" I had spoken before I realized it would give Gunnie pain. I felt her muscles tighten as she shrugged my arm away.

"No," Apheta told me. "On the ship, I believe. I cannot tell you the precise moment."

I recalled then how Zak had bent over me in that hidden corner Gunnie had found for us—Tzadkiel become the savage that we, his paradigms, had once been.

"Come now," Apheta was saying. She led us forward. I had been wrong in thinking there was nothing in the chamber; there was a wide area of black upon the floor. Some of the flaking silver of the arched ceiling had fallen there, where it was most visible.

"You have, both of you, those necklaces sailors carry?"

In some astonishment, I felt for mine and nodded. Gunnie did the same.

"Put them on. You will be without air soon."

Only then did I realize what that sparkling darkness was. I drew out the necklace, wondering, I confess, whether each of its linked prisms functioned still, put it on, and went forward to look. My cloak of air came with me, so that I was conscious of no wind; but I saw Gunnie's hair tossed by a gale I could not feel, streaming before her until she had her own necklace in place, and Apheta's strange hair, which did not flutter as a human woman's does, but stood out like a banner.

That blackness was the void; yet as I walked, it rose as though it sensed my approach, and before I reached it, it had become a sphere.

I tried to stop.

In a moment Gunnie was beside me, struggling too and grasping my arm. The sphere was like a wall. At its center, just as I had seen it pictured on board, was the ship.

I have written that I sought to stop. It was difficult, and soon I could not resist. It may be that the void held some attraction like that of a world. Or perhaps it was only that the pressure of the wind on the air held static around me was so strong that I was driven forward.

Or perhaps the ship had some hold upon us both. If I dared, I would say that my destiny drew me, yet Gunnie cannot have been drawn by the same destiny, though perhaps her quite different fate drew her toward the same place. For if it were merely the wind, or the insensate hunger of matter for matter, why was Apheta not drawn with us?

I will leave it to you to explain these things. Drawn I was, and Gunnie too; I saw her flying through the void behind me, twisting and whirling as the universe twisted and whirled, saw her just as one leaf twirling in a spring storm might see another. Somewhere behind or before us, above us or below us, was a wide circle of light, spinning, frantically spinning, a thing like Lune, if such a thing as a moon of the most brilliant white can be imagined. Gunnie fluttered across it once or twice before she was lost in the diamond-decked blackness. (And once it seemed to me—and still seems when I call that frantic memory forth—that I saw Apheta's face as she leaned from that moon.)

With the next wild spin, it was not Gunnie who was lost but that spot of shining white, lost somewhere among the billions of staring suns. Gunnie was not far off, and I saw her turn her head to look at me.

Nor was the ship lost; it was indeed so near that I could see a sailor here and there in the rigging. Perhaps we were still falling. Surely we must have been traveling with great velocity, because the ship herself must have been hurtling from world to world. Yet all such speed was invisible, as the wind vanishes when a swift xebec scuds before a tempest on the Ocean of Urth. We drifted so lazily that if I had not had faith in Apheta and the Hierarchs, I would have feared we would never reach the ship at all and be lost forever in that endless night.

It was not so. A sailor sighted us, and we watched him leap from one to another of his comrades, waving and pointing until he was close enough for their cloaks of air to touch, so that he could speak.

Then one who carried a burden climbed a mast near us, rising in practiced leaps, until standing upon the topmost spar he took a bow and an arrow from his bundle, drew the bow, and sent the arrow hurtling toward us, trailing an interminable line of silver no thicker than a pack thread.

The arrow passed between Gunnie and me, and I despaired of catching the line; but Gunnie was more fortunate, and when she held it and had been pulled toward the ship some distance by the burly sailor, she cracked it as a drover snaps his whip, so that a long wave ran from her to me like a live thing and brought the line near enough for me to snatch.

I had not loved the ship when I had been a passenger and a seaman aboard her, but now the mere thought of returning to her filled me with pleasure. Consciously I knew, as I was reeled toward the mast, that my task was far from complete, that the New Sun would not come unless I brought it, and that in bringing it I would be responsible for the destruction it would cause as well as the renewal of Urth. Thus every common man who brings a son into the world must feel himself responsible for his woman's labor and perhaps for her death, and with reason fears that the world will in the end condemn him with a million tongues. Yet though I knew all this, my heart thought it was not so: that I, who had desired so desperately to succeed and had bent every effort toward success, had failed; and that I would now be permitted to reclaim the Phoenix Throne, as I had in the person of my predecessor—to reclaim it and enjoy all the authority and luxury it would bring, and most of all that pleasure in dealing justice and rewarding worth that is the final delight of power. All this while freed at last from the unquenchable desire for the flesh of women that has brought so much suffering to me and to them.

Thus my heart was wild with joy, and I descended to that titanic forest of masts and spars, those continents of silver sail, as any shipwrecked mariner would have clambered from the sea to some flower-decked coast with friendly hands helping him ashore, and, standing with Gunnie on the spar at last, embraced the sailor as I might Roche or Drotte, grinning I am sure like any fool, and leaped down from halyard to stay with him and his mates no more circumspectly than they, but as though all the wild elation I felt were centered not in my heart, but in my arms and legs.

It was only when my final leap carried me to the deck that I discovered such thoughts were no idle metaphors. My crippled leg, which had pained me so much when I had descended from the mast after casting away the leaden coffer that held the record of my earlier life, did not pain me at all but seemed as strong as the other. I ran my hands from thigh to knee (so that Gunnie and the sailors who had gathered around us believed I had injured it) and found the muscle there as abundant and firm as that of the other.

I leaped for joy then, and leaping left the deck and the others far below, and spun myself a dozen times as a gambler spins a coin. But I returned to the deck sobered, for as I spun I had beheld a star brighter than all the rest.

CHAPTER XXIV

The Captain

WE WERE SOON TAKEN BELOW. TO TELL THE TRUTH, I WAS happy enough to go. It is difficult to explain—so much so that I am tempted to omit it altogether. Yet I think it would be easy if only you were as young as once you were.

An infant in its crib does not at first know that there is a distinction between its body and the wood that surrounds it or the rags upon which it lies. Or rather, its body seems as alien as all the rest. It discovers a foot and marvels to find so odd a thing a part of itself.

So with me. I had seen the star; and seeing it —immensely remote though it was—had known it a region of myself, absurd as the baby's foot, mysterious as his genius is to one who has only just discovered it. I do not mean that my consciousness, or any consciousness, rested in the star; at that time, at least, it did not. Yet I was aware of existence at two points, like a man who stands waist deep in the sea, so that wave and wind are alike to him in that both are something less than the whole, the totality of his environment.

Thus I walked with Gunnie and the sailors cheerfully enough and held my head high. But I did not speak, or remember to take off my necklace until I observed that Gunnie and the sailors had removed theirs.

What a sad shock I felt then! The air of Yesod, to which I had in a day become accustomed, left me; and an atmosphere like—and yet unlike and inferior to—the atmosphere of Urth rushed to fill my lungs. The first fire must

170

have been kindled in an age now inconceivably remote. At that instant, I felt as some ancient must toward the end of his lifetime, when none save the eldest recalled the pure winds of bygone mornings. I looked at Gunnie and saw that she was looking at me. Each knew what the other felt, though we did not speak of it, then or subsequently.

How far we threaded the ship's mazed passages I cannot say. I was too wrapped in my own thoughts to count my strides; and it seemed to me that though time as it existed on that ship was not other than time as it existed upon Urth, yet time upon Yesod had been otherwise, stretched to the frontier of Forever yet over in a wink. Musing on that and the star, and a hundred further wonders, I plodded forward, knowing nothing of where I had been until I noticed that most of the sailors had gone, replaced by Hierodules masked as men. I had been so far lost amid chimeric speculations that for a while I supposed that those whom I had thought sailors had always been masked Hierodules, and had been recognized as such by Gunnie from the beginning; but when I cast back my mind to the moment we first stood upon the deck again, I found it was not so, though so charming a thought. In our mean universe of Briah, extravagance is but a weak recommendation of truth. The sailors had merely slipped away unnoticed by me, and the Hierodules—taller and far more formally arrayed—had taken their places.

I had only begun to study them when we halted before great doors of a shape recalling those through which Gunnie and I had passed with Apheta a watch before on Yesod. These, however, did not require my shoulder, but swung slowly and ponderously open of themselves, revealing a long vista of marmoreal arches—each at least a hundred cubits high—down which played such light as was never seen upon any world that circled a star, light silver, gold, and berylline by turns, flashing as though the air itself held splintered treasures.

Gunnie and the remaining hands recoiled in fear at all this and had to be driven through the doorway by the Hierodules with orders and even with blows; but I stepped inside readily enough, believing that from my years on the Phoenix Throne I recognized the pomps and wonders with which we sovereigns cow poor, ignorant people.

The doors shut behind us with a crash. I drew Gunnie to me, telling her as well as I could that there was nothing to fear, or at least that I thought there was nothing or little, and that if some danger arose, I would do anything I could to protect her. Overhearing me, the sailor who had shot the line to us (one of the few who remained with us) remarked, "Most that come here don't come back. This is the skipper's quarters."

He himself did not seem much frightened, and I told him so.

"I run with the tide. A man has to recollect that most is sent here for punishment. Once or twice she's commended a man here, instead of in front of his mates. They've come back, I believe. Not having nothing he wants hid does more to make a man brave than burnt wine, you'll find. That way he can run with the tide."

I said, "You have a good philosophy."

"It's the only one I know, which makes it easy to stick with."

"I'm Severian." I put out my hand.

"Grimkeld."

I have big hands, but the hand that clasped mine was bigger, and as hard as wood. For a moment we matched strength.

While we walked the tramping of our feet had grown to a solemn music, joined by instruments that were not trumpets nor ophicleides nor any others known to me. As our hands parted the strange music reached a crescendo, the golden voices of unseen throats calling all about us, one to another.

In an instant everyone fell silent. The winged figure of a giantess appeared, as sudden as the shadow of a bird but towering like the green pines of the necropolis.

All the Hierodules bowed at once, and a moment later so did Gunnie and I. The sailors who had come with us made their obeisance as well, pulling off their caps, bending their heads and knuckling their foreheads, or bowing less gracefully but even more abjectly.

If Grimkeld's philosophy had protected him from fear, my memory had protected me. Tzadkiel, I felt certain, had been the captain of this ship when I had sailed upon her previously. Tzadkiel, I felt certain, was her captain now; and on Yesod I had learned not to fear him. But at that instant I looked in Tzadkiel's eyes and saw the eyes that spangled her wings, and knew myself for a fool.

"There is a great one among you," she said, and her voice was like the playing of a hundred citharae, or the purr of the smilodon, the cat that slew our bulls as wolves kill sheep. "Let him step forward."

It was as difficult as anything I have done in all my lives, but I strode to the front as she had asked. She took me up as a woman lifts a puppy, holding me cupped between her hands. Her breath was the wind of Yesod, which I had thought never to feel again.

"Whence does so much power come?" It was but a whisper, yet it seemed to me that such a whisper must shake the whole fabric of the ship.

"From you, Tzadkiel," I said. "I have been your slave in another time."

"Tell me."

I tried to do so, and found, I do not know how, that each word of mine now carried the meaning of ten thousand, so that when I said *Urth*, the continents came with it, and the sea and all the islands, and the indigo sky wrapped in the glory of the old sun reigning amid his ring of stars. After a hundred such words, she knew more of our history than I had known I knew; and I had reached the moment when Father Inire and I had embraced, and I had mounted the pont to the ship of the Hierodules, which was to take me to this ship, the ship of the Hierogrammate, the ship of Tzadkiel, though I did not know it. A hundred words more, and all that had befallen me on the ship and in Yesod stood shining in the air between us.

"You have undergone trials," she said. "If you wish, I can give you that which will make you forget them all. Though only by instinct, you will still bring a young sun to your world."

I shook my head. "I don't want to forget, Tzadkiel. I've boasted too often that I forget nothing, and forgetting —which I have known once or twice—seems to me a kind of death."

"Say instead that death is a remembering. But even death can be kind, as you learned upon the lake. Would you rather I set you down?"

"I am your slave, as I've said. Your will is mine."

"And if it were my will to drop you?"

"Then your slave would seek to live still, so that Urth might live too."

She smiled and opened her hands. "You have forgotten already what a slight thing it is to fall here."

I had indeed, and felt a momentary terror; but to have fallen from a bed on Urth would have been a more serious matter. I settled to the floor of Tzadkiel's quarters as lightly as thistledown.

Even so, it was a moment or two before I collected my thoughts sufficiently to note that the others were gone and I stood alone. Tzadkiel, who must have seen my look, whispered, "I have sent them away. The man who rescued you will be rewarded, as will the woman who fought for you when the rest would have slain you. But it is not likely you will see either again."

She moved her right hand toward me until the tips of its fingers rested on the floor before me. "It is expedient," she said, "that my crew think me large, and not guess how often I move among them. But you know too much about me to be deceived in that way, and you deserve too much to be deceived in any. It would be more convenient for us now if we were of similar size."

I scarcely heard the last word. Something so astounding was taking place that all my attention was seized by it. The uppermost knuckle of her index finger was shaping itself into a face, and it was the face of Tzadkiel. The nail divided and redivided, then the whole of the first and second joints too, so that the lowest knuckle became her knees. The finger stepped away from the hand and put out arms and hands of its own, and eye-spangled wings; and the giantess behind it vanished like a flame blown out.

"I will take you to your stateroom," Tzadkiel said. She was not so tall as I.

I would have knelt, but she lifted me up.

"Come. You are fatigued—more than you know, and no wonder. There is a good bed for you there. Food will be brought to you whenever you wish it."

I managed to say, "But if you are seen . . ."

"We will not be seen. There are passages here that are used only by me."

Even as she spoke, a pilaster swung away from the wall. She led me through the opening it revealed and down a shadowy corridor. I remembered then that Apheta had told me her people could see in such darkness; but Tzadkiel did not pulse with light as Apheta had, and I was not so foolish as to suppose we would share the bed she had mentioned. After what seemed a long walk, dawn came —low hills dropping below the old sun—and it seemed we were not in a corridor at all. A fresh wind stirred the grass. As the sky grew lighter, I saw a dark box set in the ground before us. "That is your stateroom," Tzadkiel told me. "Be careful. We must step down into it."

We did so, onto something soft. Then we stepped down again, and at last onto a floor. Light flooded the room, which was much larger than my old stateroom and oddly shaped. The morning meadow from which we had come was no more than a picture on the wall behind us, the steps the back and seat of a long settee. I went to the picture and tried to thrust my hand into it, but met solid resistance.

"We have such things in the House Absolute," I said. "I see whence Father Inire took his model, though ours are not so well contrived."

"Mount that seat confidently, and you may go through,"

Tzadkiel told me. "It is the pressure of a foot upon the back that dissolves the illusion. Now I must go, and you must rest."

"Wait," I said. "I won't be able to sleep unless you tell me . . ."

"Yes?"

"I have no words. You were a finger of Tzadkiel's. And now you are Tzadkiel."

"You know our power to change shape; your younger self encountered me in the future, as you told me only a few moments ago. The cells of our bodies shift, like those of certain sea creatures on your Urth, which can be pressed through a screen yet reunite. What then prevents me from shaping a miniature and constricting the connection until it parts? I am such an atomy; when we reunite, my greater self will know all I have learned."

"Your great self held me in her hands, then vanished like any dream."

"Yours is a race of pawns," Tzadkiel told me. "You move forward only, unless we move you back to begin the game again. But not all the pieces on the board are pawns."

CHAPTER XXV

Passion and the Passageway

EXHAUSTION OPERATES STRANGELY UPON THE MIND. LEFT alone in my stateroom, I could only think that my door was unguarded now. Throughout my time as Autarch, there had always been sentries at my door, usually Praetorians. I wandered through several rooms searching for it merely to verify that there were none now; but when I opened it at last, half-human brutes in grotesque helmets sprang to attention.

I closed it again, wondering whether they were meant to keep others out, or myself inside; and I wasted a few moments more searching for some means of extinguishing the light. I was too spent, however, to keep that up for long. Dropping my clothing to the floor, I stretched myself across the wide bed. As my thoughts drifted toward that misty state we call dreaming, the light dimmed and went out.

I seemed to hear footsteps, and for what seemed a long time I struggled to sit up. Sleep pressed me to my mattress, holding me as securely as any drug. At last, the walker sat beside me and brushed back the hair from my forehead. Breathing her perfume, I drew her to me.

Curls brushed my cheek as our lips met.

When I woke, I knew I had been with Thecla. Though she had not spoken and I had not seen her face, there was no question in my mind. Odd, impossible, wonderful, I called it to myself; yet it was so. No one in this universe or

177

any other could have deceived me so long through so much intimacy. But it was not, surely not, impossible at all. Tzadkiel's children, the mere infants she brooded upon her world in Yesod, had brought Thecla back with the rest to fight the sailors. Surely it was not impossible for Tzadkiel herself to bring her again.

I leaped up, then turned to see if there were not some trace—a hair or a crushed blossom left upon the pillow. I would (as I told myself) have treasured such a token always. The unfamiliar pelt with which I had covered myself was smoothly spread. No impression of a second body showed next to the one left by my own.

Somewhere in those laborious writings I assembled in the clerestory of the House Absolute and even more laboriously will repeat aboard this ship at an unknown date in the future that has become my past, I have said that I have seldom felt myself alone, though I must have seemed so to the reader. In fairness to you, then, should you ever come across these writings as well, allow me to say that I did feel alone then, that I knew myself alone, though I was, as my predecessor had trained his equerries to call him, Legion.

I was that predecessor, and alone, and his predecessors; each as solitary as every ruler must be until better times —or rather, better men and women—shall come to Urth. I was Thecla too, Thecla thinking of a mother and half sister never to be seen again, and of the young torturer who had wept for her when she no longer had tears left for herself. Most of all was I Severian, and horribly lonely, as the last man on some derelict ship knows loneliness when he dreams of friends and wakes to find himself as solitary as ever, and goes on deck, perhaps, to stare at the peopled stars and the tattered sails that will never bear him to any of them.

That fear gripped me, even while I sought to laugh it away. I was alone in the great suite Tzadkiel had called my stateroom. I could hear no one; and it seemed possible, as all the delirious things we dream seem possible in the moment of waking, that there was no one to hear, that

Tzadkiel, for her own unfathomable reasons, had emptied the ship while I slept.

I bathed in the balneary, and scraped the disturbingly unscarred face that watched me from the glass, all the while listening for a voice or a footfall. My clothes were torn, and so dirty I hesitated to put them on again. The closets held clothing of many colors and many kinds, and particularly, so it seemed to me, of those kinds that can be readily adapted to masculine or feminine wear, and to any frame, all of them of the richest materials. I selected a pair of loose, dark trousers bound at the waist with a russet sash, a tunic with an open neck and large pockets, and a cloak of the true fuligin of that guild of which I am still officially a master, lined with particolored brocade. So arrayed I stepped at last from my door and was saluted as before by my monstrous ostlaries.

I had not been abandoned, and indeed by the time I had dressed myself the fear of it had largely left me; yet as I walked the grand and empty gangway beyond my suite, my mind dwelt upon the thought; and from the dreamed Thecla who had delighted and deserted me, it passed to Dorcas and Agia, to Valeria, and at last to Gunnie, whom I had been glad enough to take as my lover when she could be of service to me and I had no other, and from whom I had allowed myself to be separated without a word of protest when Tzadkiel told me she had sent the sailors away.

Throughout my life, I have been far too ready to abandon women who have had a claim on my loyalty—Thecla, of course, until it was too late to do more than ease her death; and after Thecla, Dorcas, Pia, and Daria, and at last Valeria. On this vast ship, I seemed about to cast aside another, and I resolved not to do so. I would seek out Gunnie, wherever she might be, and bring her to stay with me in my stateroom until we reached Urth and she could return, if she wished, to her fishing village and her own people.

So determined I strode along, and my newly mended leg permitted me to walk at least as rapidly as when I had set off up the Water Way that runs with Gyoll; but my thoughts were not wholly of Gunnie. I was conscious of the need to take note of my surroundings and the direction in which I walked, for nothing would have been easier than to lose myself aboard this vast ship, as I had done more than once on the voyage to Yesod. I was conscious too of something else, a bright point of light that seemed infinitely far, yet immediate.

Allow me to confess here that I confused it even then with that globe of darkness which was to become a disk of light when Gunnie and I passed through it. Certainly it is impossible that the White Fountain which has saved and destroyed Urth, the roaring geyser spewing raw gasses from nowhere, is the portal through which we passed.

That is to say, I have always found it impossible when I was busy in the daylit world, the world that would have perished without a New Sun; but sometimes I wonder. May it not be that Yesod, seen from our universe, is as different from Yesod seen from within as a man seen from without is from the image he sees of himself? I know myself often foolish and sometimes weak—lonely and frightened, too much inclined to passive good nature and all too ready, as I have said, to desert my closest friends in pursuit of some ideal. Yet I have terrified millions.

May it not be that the White Fountain is a window to Yesod after all?

The gangway twisted and twisted again; and as I had before, I observed that although it seemed, if not commonplace, at least nearly so in the part I occupied, yet the length that stretched ahead of me and the length I had left behind grew stranger and stranger as my eyes traversed them, full of mists and uncanny lights.

It occurred to me at last that the ship shaped herself for me as I passed and returned herself to herself for her own uses once I was gone, just as a mother devotes herself to her child when that child is present, speaking in the simplest words and playing babyish games—but pens an epic or entertains a lover at other times.

Was the ship in fact a living entity? That such a thing was possible, I did not doubt; but I had seen little to suggest it, and if it were so, why should she require a crew? The thing might have been done more easily, and what Tzadkiel had said the night before (reckoning the time in which I had slept to have been night) suggested a simpler mechanism. If the picture could be penetrated when the weight of my foot was on the back of the settee, might it not be that the light in my stateroom gradually extinguished itself when the weight of my feet left the floor, and that these protean gangways reshaped themselves to my footfalls? I resolved to use my mended leg to defeat them.

On Urth I could not have done so—but then on Urth that whole great ship would have crumbled to ruin beneath its own weight; and here on board, where I had been able to run and even to leap before, I could now outrace the wind. I dashed along; when I reached the next turning, I leaped and kicked the wall, sending myself hurtling down the gangway even as I had leaped through the rigging.

In an instant, I had left the passage I knew behind, and found myself among eerie angles and ghostly mechanisms, where blue-green lights flew like comets and the walkway writhed like a worm's gut. My feet struck its surface, but not in a fresh stride; they were numb, and my legs like the loose limbs of a marionette when the curtain has fallen. I went tumbling down the gangway, which shrank to a painfully bright but diminishing dot in a field of utter darkness.

CHAPTER XXVI

Gunnie and Burgundofara

AT FIRST I THOUGHT MY VISION BLURRED. I BLINKED, AND blinked again; but the faces, so much alike, would not become one. I tried to speak.

"It's all right," Gunnie told me. The younger woman, who seemed not so much a twin now as a younger sister, slipped her hand under my head and put a cup to my lips.

My mouth was filled with the dust of death. I sucked the water eagerly, moving it from cheek to cheek before I swallowed, feeling the tissues revive.

"What happened?" Gunnie asked.

"The ship changes herself," I said.

Both nodded without comprehension.

"She changes to suit us, wherever we are. I ran too fast—or failed to touch the floor enough." I tried to sit up, and to my own astonishment succeeded. "I got to a part where there wasn't any air—where there was only a gas that wasn't air, I think. Perhaps it was meant for people from some other world, or for no one at all. I don't know."

"Can you stand?" Gunnie asked.

I nodded; but if we had been on Urth, I would have fallen when I tried. Even on the ship, where one fell so slowly, the two women had to catch me and prop me as though I were sodden drunk. They were of the same height (which is to say each was nearly as tall as I) with wide dark eyes and broad, pleasant faces dotted with freckles and framed in dark hair.

"You're Gunnie," I muttered to Gunnie.

"We both are," the younger woman told me. "I signed on last voyage. She's been here for a long time, I believe."

"For a lot of those voyages," Gunnie agreed. "In time, it's forever, but less than nothing. The time here isn't the time you grew up with on Urth, Burgundofara."

"Wait," I protested. "I must think. Isn't there any place here where we can rest?"

The younger woman pointed to a shadowy archway. "That's where we were." Through it I glimpsed falling water and many padded seats.

Gunnie hesitated, then helped me in.

The high walls were adorned with large masks. Watery tears dripped slowly from their eyes to splash into quiet basins, and cups like the one the younger woman had filled for me stood upon the rims. There was an angled hatch in the farther wall of the chamber; from its design, I knew it opened onto a deck.

When the women had seated themselves on either side of me, I told them, "You two are the same person—so you say, and so I believe."

Both nodded.

"But I can't call you by the same name. What shall I call you?"

Gunnie said, "When I was her age and I left my village to ship on here, I didn't want to be Burgundofara anymore; so I got my mates to call me Gunnie. I've been sorry I did, but they wouldn't have changed it back if I'd asked them to—just made a joke of it. So call me Gunnie, because that's who I am." She paused to take a deep breath. "And call the girl I used to be by my old name, if you will. She's not going to change it now."

"All right," I said. "Perhaps there's some better way to explain what bothers me, but I'm still weak, and I can't think clearly enough to find it. Once I saw a certain man raised from the dead."

They only stared at me. I heard Burgundofara's indrawn breath.

"His name was Apu-Punchau. There was someone else there too, a man called Hildegrin; and this Hildegrin wanted to stop Apu-Punchau from returning to his tomb."

Burgundofara whispered, "Was he a ghost?"

"Not quite, or at least I don't think so. Or maybe it only depends on what you mean when you say 'ghost.' I think perhaps he was someone whose roots in time went so deep that he couldn't be wholly dead in our time, perhaps not in any. However that may be, I wanted to help Hildegrin because he was serving someone who was trying to cure one of my friends. . . ." My thoughts, still bewildered by the deathly atmosphere of the gangway, stuck on that point of friendship. Had Jolenta indeed been a friend? Might she have become one if she had recovered?

"Go on," Burgundofara urged me.

"I ran up to them—to Apu-Punchau and Hildegrin. There was something I can't really call an explosion, but it was more like that, or like lightning striking, than anything else I can think of. Apu-Punchau was gone, and there were two Hildegrins."

"Like us."

"No, the same Hildegrin twice. One who wrestled an invisible spirit and another who wrestled me. Then the lightning struck, or whatever it was. But before that, before I had even seen the two Hildegrins, I saw Apu-Punchau's face; and it was mine. Older, but mine."

Gunnie said, "You were right to want to stop somewhere. You have to tell us."

"This morning— Tzadkiel, the captain, gave me a very nice cabin. Before I went out I washed, and I shaved with a razor I found there. The face I saw in the mirror troubled me, but I know now whose it was."

Burgundofara said, "Apu-Punchau's?" and Gunnie, "Your own."

"There's something more I didn't tell you. Hildegrin was killed by the flash. I thought I understood that, later, and I still do. There were two of me, and because there were, two Hildegrins also; but the Hildegrins had been created by division, and a man cannot be divided so and live. Or perhaps it was only that once divided he could not reunite, when there was only one Severian again."

Burgundofara nodded. "Gunnie told me your name. It's a beautiful name, like a sword blade." Gunnie motioned her to silence.

"Now here I am, with both of you. There's only one of me, as far as I can tell. Do you see two?"

Burgundofara said, "No. But don't you see that it wouldn't matter if we did? If you haven't been Apu-Punchau yet, you can't die!"

I told her, "Even I know more of time than that. I was the future Apu-Punchau of what is now a decade past. The present can always change its future."

Gunnie shook her head. "I think I know more about time than you do, even if you're going to bring a New Sun and change the world. This man Hildegrin didn't die ten years ago, not to us here. When you get to Urth again, you may find it was a thousand years ago or who knows how many years ahead. Here it's not one nor the other. We're between the suns and the years too, so there can be two Gunnies with no danger to anybody. Or a dozen."

She paused. Gunnie had always spoken slowly, but now her words crept from her as those who still live creep from the hulk of a wreck. "Yes, I can see two Severians, even if they're just what I can remember. One's the Severian I grabbed one time and kissed. He's gone, but he was a handsome man in spite of his scarred face and lameness, and the gray in his hair."

"He remembered your kiss," I said. "He'd kissed many women, but he'd not often been kissed himself."

"And the other one's the Severian who was my lover, when I was a girl and newly signed. It was for his sake I kissed you then and fought for you later, the only real person fighting for you among the phantoms. I stabbed my old mates for him, even though I knew you didn't remember me." She rose. "You don't know where we are, neither of you."

Burgundofara said, "It seems to be a waiting room, but nobody's using it but us."

"I meant where the ship is. We're outside the circle of Dis."

I said, "Once I was told by a man who knew much of the future that a woman I sought was aboveground. I thought he meant merely that she was still alive. The ship's always been outside the circle of Dis."

"You know what I mean. When I came on board with you, I thought we had a long voyage ahead of us. But why should they—Apheta and Zak—have done that? The ship's leaving eternity now, slowing down so the tender can find her. Until she slows down, she isn't really a ship at all, did you know? We're like a wave, or a shout going through the universe."

"No," I told her. "I didn't. And I can hardly believe it."

"What you believe makes a difference sometimes," Gunnie said. "But not every time. That's something I've learned here. Severian, I told you one time why I kept on sailing. Do you remember?"

I glanced at Burgundofara. "I thought perhaps . . ."

Gunnie shook her head. "To be what I was again, but myself. You must remember yourself when you really were her age. Are you the same person now?"

As clearly as if he were in that chamber of tears with us, I saw the young journeyman striding along, his fuligin cloak billowing behind him and the dark cross of *Terminus Est* rising above his left shoulder. "No," I admitted. "I became another long ago, and another after that."

She nodded. "So I'm going to stay here. Maybe here, when there's only one of me, it'll happen. You and Burgundofara are going back to Urth."

She turned and left us. I tried to rise, but Burgundofara pulled me down again, and I was too weak to resist. "Let Gunnie go," she said. "It's already happened to you. Let her have her chance." The door swung shut.

"She's you," I gasped.

"Then let me have mine. I've seen what I'll be later. Is it still wrong, when you do that, to feel sorry for yourself?" There were tears in her eyes.

I shook my head. "If you don't weep for her, who will?"

"You are."

"But not for that reason. She was a true friend, and I haven't had many."

Burgundofara said, "I see now why all the faces cry. This is a hall made for crying."

A new voice murmured, "For those who come and go."

I turned to see two masked Hierodules, and because I was not expecting them, it took me a moment to recognize Barbatus and Famulimus. It was Famulimus who had spoken, and I shouted for joy. "My friends! Are you coming with us?"

Famulimus said, "We only came to bring you here. Tzadkiel sent us for you, but you were gone, Severian. Tell me if you will see us more."

"Many times," I told her. "Good-bye, Famulimus."

"You know our nature, that is plain. We greet you then, and say farewell."

Barbatus added, "The hatches will open when Ossipago dogs down the door. You both have amulets of air?"

I took mine from my pocket and put it on. Burgundofara produced a similar necklace.

"Then, like Famulimus, I greet you," Barbatus said, and stepped backward through the doorway, which closed after him.

The paired doors at the end of the room opened almost at once; the tears of the masks vanished as they fell, then dried altogether. Beyond the open doors shone the black curtain of night, hung from star to star.

"We have to go," I said to Burgundofara, then realized she could not hear and moved near enough to take her hand, at which there was no longer any need for speech. Together we left the ship, and it was only when I paused at the threshold and turned to look back that it struck me I had never known her true name, if she had one, and that three of the masks were the faces of Zak, Tzadkiel, and her captain.

The tender waiting for us was far bigger than the little craft that had brought me to the surface of Yesod, as large as that which had carried me to the ship from Urth. And indeed, I think it likely that it was the same vessel.

"Sometimes they bring the big one in a good bit closer than this," the hand detailed to guide us confided as we came aboard. "Only they can't help getting between somebody's eyes and a few stars when they do. So you'll be about a day with us."

I asked her to point out Urth's sun to me, and she obliged. He was a mere dot of crimson over the rail, and all his worlds, even Dis, were invisible save as specks that darkened when they crossed his sullen face.

I tried to indicate the faint white star that was a part of me; but the hand could not make it out, and Burgundofara looked frightened. Soon we walked through the portal of the tender and into the deckhouse.

CHAPTER XXVII

The Return to Urth

I HAD NOT BEEN CERTAIN BURGUNDOFARA AND I WOULD BE lovers; but we were assigned a single cabin (one perhaps a tenth the size of the stateroom I had occupied on my final night aboard the ship), and when I embraced and disrobed her she did not object. I found her less skillful far than Gunnie, though of course no virgin. How strange to think that Gunnie and I had lain together only once.

Her younger self told me afterward that no man had treated her gently before, kissed me for it, and fell asleep in my arms. I had never thought myself a temperate lover; I lay awake for some time, meditating upon it and listening, as once I had promised myself I would, to the centuries dashed against the hull.

Or perhaps they were merely years, the years of my life. I had thought at first, when I felt my mended leg beneath me, and later when I had shaved my strange new face in the stateroom, that they had somehow been lifted from me, as Gunnie had hoped hers would be lifted from her. Now I understood that it was not so.

It was only that the damage done by some nameless Ascian's spear, by Agia's palmed claws and the blood bat's teeth, had been undone; I was the man I would have been without those (and perhaps other) wounds, and thus it was that my face was the face of that strange being—for what being can be stranger than oneself, or act more inexplicably? I was Apu-Punchau, whom I had seen resurrected in the stone town. To me it had seemed youth, and it left me

189

mourning for the years I might have had. Perhaps someday I will board Tzadkiel's ship once more, to search for true youth as Gunnie has; but if I am carried to Yesod again, I will remain there if I am suffered to do so. In centuries, perhaps, that air might wash the years from me.

As I contemplated them and the few that came before them, it seemed to me that my acts toward women had depended not upon my will, but upon their attitude toward me. I had been brutal enough with the khaibit Thecla of the House Azure, then as mild and clumsy as any untouched boy with the real Thecla in her cell; fevered at first with Dorcas, quick and clumsy with Jolenta (whom I might have been said to have raped, though I believed then and believe still that she wished it). Of Valeria I have said too much already.

Yet it cannot be thus for all men, since many act in the same way toward all women; and it may not even be so for me.

I dozed, thinking of all these things—and woke to find myself upon my other side and Burgundofara no longer in my arms, dozed again, woke again, and rose, unable to sleep more and longing, though I could not have said why, for a glimpse of the White Fountain. As quietly as I could, I put on the necklace and made my way on deck.

The endless night of the void was almost vanquished. The shadows of the masts, and my own shadow too, seemed drawn upon the planks in the blackest paint, and the Old Sun had grown from a faint star to a disk as large as Lune. His light made the White Fountain appear farther and weaker than ever. Urth had ceased to streak across his crimson face, but hung just beyond the bowsprit, spinning like a top.

The officer of the watch came to speak to me, telling me I had better go below. Not, I think, because I was in any actual danger, but because it made him uneasy to have someone on deck who was not under his command. I told him I would, but that I wanted an interview with the captain of this vessel, and that my companion and I were hungry.

Burgundofara appeared while we were talking, saying that she had felt the same urge as I, though I think in her case it was in fact no more than a desire to look about and see the ship again before she left all such ships forever. She sprang up a mast, which so distracted the officer that I thought he might actually do her some harm. Had he not been a Hierodule, I would have laid hands on him; and as it was, I was forced to stand between them when a party of sailors had brought her down.

We argued with him until our air grew foul, mostly for the sport of it on my part (and hers too, I think), then went below docilely enough, found the galley, and ate like two children, laughing and recounting our adventures.

The captain—not another masked Hierodule, but a man who appeared to be an ordinary human being—visited us in our cabin a watch or so afterward. I told him I had talked to no one in authority since Tzadkiel had left me, and that I hoped to get instructions from him.

He shook his head. "I've none to give you. I feel sure Tzadkiel will have arranged for you to know all you need to."

Burgundofara interjected, "He's got to bring the New Sun!" adding when I glanced at her, "Gunnie told me."

"Can you?" the captain asked.

I tried to explain that I did not know, that I could feel the White Fountain as if it were a part of me, and that I had been trying to bring it closer; but that it did not seem to move.

"What is it?" he asked. Then, seeing my expression, "No, I really don't know. I was told nothing except that I was to take you and this woman to Urth and land you safely north of the ice."

"It's a star, I think, or something like one."

"Then it's too massive to move the way we do. When you're on Urth, you'll no longer be moving in the uranic sense. Perhaps then it will come for you."

Burgundofara asked, "Won't it take a long time for a star to get to Urth?"

He nodded. "Centuries at least. But I really understand

nothing about it—a great deal less than your friend here must. If it's part of him, he must feel it, as he tells us he does."

"I do. I feel its distance." As I spoke, I seemed to be standing again before the windows of Master Ash, looking out at the endless plains of ice; possibly in some sense I had never left them. I said, "Could it be that the New Sun will come only after our race is gone? Would Tzadkiel play such a trick on us?"

"No. Tzadkiel doesn't play tricks, though she may seem to. Tricks are for solipsists, who think everything will pass away." He stood. "You wanted to ask me questions. I don't blame you, but I've no answers. Would you like to go on deck and watch us land? It's the only real gift I can give you."

Burgundofara looked bewildered and asked, "So soon?" I confess I felt so myself.

"Yes, pretty soon now. I've got a few supplies for you, mostly food. Will you want weapons besides your knives? I can give them to you, if you need them."

I asked, "Do you advise it?"

"I don't advise anything. You know what you have to do. I don't."

"Then I'll take none," I said. "Burgundofara may decide for herself."

"No," she said. "Neither will I."

"Then come," the captain told us, and this time it was a command and not an invitation. We put on the necklaces and followed him out onto the deck.

Our ship skimmed high above the clouds, which appeared to boil beneath us, yet I felt that we had arrived. Urth flashed from blue to black, then blue again. The rail was ice cold in my hands, and I searched for Urth's ice caps; but we were too near, already too close for them to be visible. There was only the azure of her seas, glimpsed through the rents in her surging clouds, and occasionally a flash of land, brown or green.

"It is a lovely world," I said. "Not as lovely as Yesod, perhaps, but beautiful nonetheless."

The captain shrugged. "We could make it as good as Yesod if we wanted to."

"We will," I told him. I had not known I believed that until I said it. "We will when enough of us have left it and come back."

The clouds grew calmer, as though some mage had whispered a spell or a woman had bared her breast to them. Our sails were furled already; the watch swarmed aloft, making certain all our hamper was secure and as well braced as it could be.

As they leaped down again, the first thin winds of Urth struck us, impalpable, but bringing back (like the single motion of a coryphaeus's hand) the whole world of sound. The masts shrilled like rebecs while every strand of rigging sang.

A moment more, and the ship herself yawed, pitched, and went down at the stern until the sunlit clouds of Urth rose behind her quarterdeck and Burgundofara and I were left clinging to the railposts.

The captain, standing at ease with one hand on a halyard, grinned at us and shouted, "Why, I thought the girl was a sailor, anyway. Lift him up there, darling, or we'll send you to help the cook."

I would have aided Burgundofara if I could, and she tried to assist me as the captain had directed her; thus by clinging to each other we managed to stay erect on the deck (now steeper than many stairs, though it seemed as smooth as a dancing floor) and even to take a few cautious steps toward him.

"You've got to ship on a little 'un before you're a sailor," he told us. "It's a pity I've got to land you now. I might make proper seamen of you."

I managed to say that our arrival on Yesod had not been so violent.

He turned serious. "You didn't have much potential to lose there, you see. You'd used it up reaching the higher plane. We've come in without a rag to brake us, like we were falling into the star. Stay away from the railing for a bit. The wind there will broil the skin right off your arm."

"Wouldn't our necklaces preserve us from it?"

"They've got a good field; without them you'd fry like a crackling. But they can only put out so much, like any other device, and that wind . . . well, it's too thin to breathe, but if the keel weren't taking the brunt, we'd be blown away."

For a time the apostis glowed like a forge; gradually it dimmed and went out, and our ship resumed a more conventional position, though the wind still screamed in the rigging and the clouds scudded under us like flecks of foam in a mill race.

The captain climbed to his quarterdeck, and I went with him to ask whether we might not remove our necklaces. He shook his head and pointed at the rigging, which was now rimmed with ice, saying we could not stay on deck long without them and asking if I had not noticed my air freshening.

I admitted I had, but explained that I had thought myself deceived.

"There's some mixing," he told me. "When there's no air, the amulet draws back any that gets to the edge of the field. But it can't tell the difference between air it brought up from below and wind that's penetrated its pressure zone."

How the tender could have a wake above the clouds, I do not understand; but it left one, long and white, stretched across the sky behind us. I merely report what I saw.

Burgundofara said, "I wish I'd been on deck when we left Urth. Even when we got to the big ship, they made us stay below until we had some training."

"You'd only have been in the way," the captain told her. "We set all sail as soon as we're free of the atmosphere, so that's a busy time. Was it this vessel?"

"I think so."

"And now you're coming back somebody important, mentioned by name in Tzadkiel's orders. Congratulations!"

Burgundofara shook her head, and I noticed that enough wind was penetrating now to make her dark ringlets dance.

"I don't even know how she came to know it."

I said, "One usually doesn't, with her," reflecting that just as I was many in a single body, Tzadkiel was many bodies in a single person.

The captain pointed over the taffrail, where the sea of cloud seemed almost to wash the planking of the tender's hull. "We're about to go down into that. When we get under it, you can take off your amulets without freezing."

For a time we were trapped in mist. In a brown book I took from Thecla's cell, I have read that a region of mist separates the living from the dead, and that the forms we call ghosts are nothing more than the remnants of this barrier of mist clinging to their faces and their garments.

Whether that is true, I cannot say; but certainly Urth is separated from the void by such a region, and that seems strange to me. Possibly the four realms are but two, and we entered the void and left it at last just as specters visit the country of the living.

CHAPTER XXVIII

The Village Beside the Stream

I RECALL THINKING, AS I LEANED OVER THE RAILING AND watched dots of red and gold turn to woodlots, and brown smudges to fields of tangled stalks, how strange we should have looked had there been anyone to watch us, a trim pinnace—just such a vessel as might have lain alongside some wharf in Nessus—floating silently down out of the sky. I felt sure there was no one. It was earliest morning, when even small trees cast long shadows and scarlet foxes trot denward through the dew like flecks of fire.

"Where are we?" I asked the captain. "Which way does the city lie?"

"North by northeast," he said, pointing.

The supplies he was giving us were in long sarcins of about the bigness of a demicannon's barrel lashed to the base of the bonaventure. He showed us how to carry them, the strap over the left shoulder and fastened at the hip. He shook our hands, and seemed, so far as I could judge, to wish us well sincerely.

A silver pont slid from the seam where the deck met the tender's side. Burgundofara and I went down it and stood once more upon the soil of Urth.

We turned—as I believe no one could have helped turning—and watched the tender rise, righting herself as soon as her keel was free of the soil, bobbing in a gentle swell none but she could feel and lifting like a kite. We had come to Urth through clouds, as I have said; but the tender found an opening in them (I cannot but think it was so we might watch her) and rose through it, higher and higher, until hull and masts were no more than a pinprick of golden light. At length we saw her blossom to a shining speck, like the steel that falls from a file; then we knew that her crew had freed her sails, all of silver metal and each bigger than many an isle, and sheeted them home, and that we would not see her again. I looked away so that Burgundofara would not notice the tears in my eyes. When I looked back to tell her we should be going, I found that she had been weeping too.

Nessus lay north by northeast, so the captain had said; with the horizon still so near the sun, it was not hard to keep our course. We crossed frost-killed fields for half a league or more, entered a little wood, and soon reached a stream with a path meandering along its bank.

Burgundofara had not spoken until then, and neither had I; but when we saw the water, she went to it and scooped up as much as her hands would hold. When she had drunk it, she said, "Now I know we've really come home. I've heard that for landsmen it's eating bread and salt."

I told her that was so, though I had nearly forgotten it.

"For us it's drinking the water of a place. There's usually bread and salt enough on the boats, but water goes bad or leaks away. When we come to a new landing we drink its water, if it's good water. If it isn't, we put our curse on it. Do you think this runs to Gyoll?"

"I'm sure it must, or to some larger stream that does. Do you want to return to your village?"

She nodded. "Will you come with me, Severian?"

I remembered Dorcas, and how she had begged me to come with her down Gyoll to find an old man and a house fallen to ruin. "I will if I can," I told her. "I don't think I'll be able to stay."

"Then maybe I'll leave when you do, but I'd like to see Liti again first. I'll kiss my father and all my relations when I get there, and probably stab them when I go. Just the same, I have to see it again."

"I understand."

"I hoped you would. Gunnie said you were that kind of man—that you understood a lot of things."

I had been examining the path as she spoke. Now I motioned her to silence, and we stood listening for perhaps a hundred breaths. A fresh wind stirred the treetops; birds called here and there, though most had already flown north. The stream chuckled to itself.

"What is it?" Burgundofara whispered at last.

"Someone's run ahead of us. See his tracks? A boy, I think. He may have circled to watch us, or fetched others."

"A lot of people must use this path."

I crouched beside the footprint to explain to her. "He was here this morning, when we came. See how dark a mark he made? He'd come across the fields just as we did, and his feet were wet with dew. It will dry soon. His foot's small for a man's, but he runs with long strides—a boy that's nearly a man."

"You're deep. Gunnie said you were. I wouldn't have seen that."

"You know a thousand times more about ships than I do, though I've spent some time on both kinds. I was a mounted scout for a while. This is the sort of thing we did."

"Maybe we should go the other way."

I shook my head. "These are the people I've come to save. I won't save them by running from them."

As we walked on, Burgundofara said, "We haven't done anything wrong."

"You mean anything they know of. Everyone has done something wrong, and I a hundred such things—or rather, ten thousand."

Because the wood was so hushed and I had not smelled smoke, I had supposed that the place to which the boy had run was a league away at least. The path turned sharply, and a silent village of a dozen huts stood before us.

"Can't we just walk through?" Burgundofara asked. "They must be asleep."

"They're awake," I told her. "They're watching us

through their doorways, standing to the rear so we won't see them."

"You've got good eyes."

"No. But I know something of villagers, and the boy got here before us. If we walk through, we may get pitchforks in our backs."

I looked from hut to hut and raised my voice: *"People of this village! We're harmless travelers. We have no money. We ask only the use of your path."*

There seemed a slight stirring in the silence. I walked forward and motioned for Burgundofara to follow.

A man of fifty stepped from one of the doorways; his brown beard was streaked with gray, and he carried a flail.

"You're the hetman of this village," I said. "We thank you for your hospitality. As I told you, we come in peace."

He stared at me, reminding me of a certain mason I had once encountered. "Herena says you came from a ship that fell from the sky."

"What does it matter where we came from? We're peaceful travelers. We ask nothing more than that you let us pass."

"It matters to me. Herena is my daughter. If she lies, I must know of it."

I told Burgundofara, "You see, I don't know everything." She smiled, though I could see she was frightened.

"Hetman, if you would trust a stranger's word and not your daughter's, you're a fool." By then the girl had edged near enough the door for me to see her eyes. "Come out, Herena," I said. "We won't hurt you."

She stepped forward, a tall girl of fifteen with long brown hair and a withered arm no larger than an infant's.

"Why were you spying on us, Herena?"

She spoke, but I could not hear her.

"She wasn't spying," her father said. "She was gathering nuts. She's a good girl."

Sometimes, though only rarely, a man looks at something he has seen a score of times and sees it in a new way. When I, sulky Thecla, used to set up my easel beside some cataract, my teacher always told me to see it new; I never understood what he meant and soon convinced myself he meant nothing. Now I saw Herena's withered arm not as a permanent deformity (as I had always seen such things before), but as an error to be righted with a few strokes of the brush.

Burgundofara ventured, "It must be hard . . ." Realizing she might give offense, she concluded, "Going out so early."

I said, "I'll correct your daughter's arm, if you wish it."

The hetman opened his lips to speak, then shut them again. Nothing in his face seemed to have changed, but there was fear there.

"Do you wish it?" I asked.

"Yes, yes, of course."

His eyes, and the unseen stares of all the other villagers, oppressed me. I said, "She must come with me. We won't go far, and it won't take long."

He nodded slowly. "Herena, you must go with the sieur." (I suddenly realized how rich the clothes I had taken from the stateroom must have looked to these people.) "Be a good girl, and remember that your mother and I will always . . ." He turned away.

She walked before me, back along the path until the village was out of sight. The place where her withered arm joined her shoulder was concealed under her tattered smock. I told her to take it off; she did so, drawing it over her head.

I was conscious of the crimson-and-gold leaves, the pink-tinged brown of her skin, as I might have been of the jeweled colors of some microcosm at which I peered through an aperture. Birdsong and water-music were as remote and as sweet as the tinkling of an orchestrion in a courtyard far below.

I touched Herena's shoulder, and reality itself was clay to be smoothed and stretched. With a pass or two I molded her a new arm, the mirror image of the other. A tear that struck my fingers as I worked felt hot enough to scald them; the girl trembled.

"I'm finished," I said. "Put on your smock." I was in the microcosm again, and again it seemed the world to me.

She turned to face me. She was smiling, though her cheeks were streaked with tears. "I love you, my lord," she said, and at once knelt and kissed the toe of my boot.

I asked, "May I see your hands?" I myself could no longer believe what I had done.

She held them out. "They'll take me now to be a slave far away. I don't care. No, they won't—I'll go to the mountains and hide."

I was looking at her hands, which seemed perfect to me in every detail, even when I pressed them together. It is rare for a person to have hands as precisely the same size, the hand used most being always the largest; yet hers were. I muttered, "Who'll take you, Herena? Is your village raided by cultellarii?"

"The assessors, of course."

"Just because you have two good arms now?"

"Because I haven't anything wrong now." She stopped, stricken by a new possibility, eyes wide. "I don't, do I?"

It was no time for philosophy. "No, you're perfect—a very attractive young woman."

"Then they'll take me. Are you all right?"

"A little weak, that's all. I'll be better in a moment." I used the hem of my cloak to wipe my forehead, just as I had when I was a torturer.

"You don't look all right."

"It was mostly Urth's energies that corrected your arm, I think. But they had to come through me. I suppose they must have carried off some of my own with them."

"You know my name, my lord. What's yours?"

"Severian."

"I'll get you food at my father's house, Lord Severian. There's still some left."

A wind sprang up that sent the brightly colored leaves swirling about our faces as we walked back.

CHAPTER XXIX

Among the Villagers

MY LIFE HAS HELD MANY SORROWS AND TRIUMPHS, BUT FEW pleasures outside the simple ones of love and sleep, clean air and good food, the things anyone may know. Among the greatest I count the village hetman's expression when he saw his daughter's arm. Such a mixture of wonder, fear, and delight it was that I would have shaved his face for him in order to see it better. Herena, I think, enjoyed it as much as I; but when she had feasted upon it to the full, she hugged him and told him she had promised us refreshment and ducked through the doorway to embrace her mother.

As soon as we were inside too, the villagers' fear turned to curiosity. A few of the boldest men pushed their way in and squatted silently behind us as we sat on mattings around the little table where the hetman's wife—weeping and biting her lips all the while—spread our feast. The rest merely peered through the doorway and peeped through chinks in the windowless walls.

There were fried cakes of pounded maize, apples somewhat damaged by frost, water, and (as a great delicacy, and one at which some of the silent onlookers slavered openly) the haunches of two hares, boiled, pickled, salted, and served cold. The hetman and his family did not partake of these. I have called it a feast, for so these people thought it; but the simple sailor's dinner we had eaten on the tender a few watches before had been a banquet compared with it.

I found I was not hungry, though I felt tired and very

thirsty. I ate one of the cakes and picked at the meat while drinking copious draughts of water, then decided that the higher courtesy might consist in leaving the hetman's family some of their food, since they plainly had so little, and began to crack nuts.

This, it appeared, was the signal that my host might speak. He said, "I am Bregwyn. Our village is called Vici. My wife is Cinnia. Our daughter is Herena. This woman" —he nodded to indicate Burgundofara—"says that you are a good man."

"My name is Severian. This woman is Burgundofara. I am a bad man trying to be a good one."

"We of Vici hear little of the far world. Perhaps you will tell us what chance has brought you to our village."

He said this with an expression of polite interest and no more, yet it gave me pause. It would have been easy enough to put off these villagers with some tale of trade or pilgrimage; and indeed, if I had told him we hoped to return Burgundofara to her home beside the Ocean, it would not have been wholly a lie. But had I the right to say such things? I had told Burgundofara earlier that these were the people I had gone to the end of the universe to rescue. I glanced at the hetman's toil-worn, tearful wife and at the men, with their grizzled beards and hard hands. What right did I have to treat them like children?

"This woman," I said, "is from Liti. Perhaps you know of it?"

The hetman shook his head.

"The people there are fishers. She hopes to find her way back." I drew a deep breath. "I . . ." The hetman leaned forward ever so slightly as I groped for words. "I have been able to help Herena. To make her more whole. You know that."

"We are grateful," he said.

Burgundofara touched my arm. When I looked at her, her eyes told me that what I was doing might be perilous. I knew it already.

"Urth herself is not whole."

The hetman, and all the other men who squatted with their backs to the walls of the hut, edged closer. I saw a few nod.

"I have come to make her whole."

As though the words were forced from him, one of the men said, "It snowed before the corn was ripe. This is the second year." Several others nodded, and the man who sat behind the hetman, and thus facing me, said, "The sky people are angry with us."

I tried to explain. "The sky people—the Hierodules and Hierarchs—do not hate us. It is only that they are remote from us, and they fear us because of things we did before, long ago when our race was young. I have gone to them." I watched the villagers' expressionless faces, wondering whether any of them would believe me. "I have effected a conciliation—brought them nearer us and us nearer them, I think. They've sent me back."

That night while Burgundofara and I lay in the hetman's hut (which he and his wife and daughter had insisted on vacating for us), she had said, "They'll kill us eventually, you know."

I had promised her, "We'll leave here tomorrow."

"They won't let us," she had replied; and morning showed that we had both been correct, in some fashion. We left indeed; but the villagers told us of another village, called Gurgustii, a few leagues away, and accompanied us there. When we arrived, Herena's arm was exhibited and aroused much wonder, and we (not only Burgundofara and I, but Herena, Bregwyn, and the rest) were treated to a feast much like the last, save that fresh fish were substituted for the hares.

Afterward I was informed of a certain man who was a very good man and very valuable to Gurgustii, but who was now very ill. I told his fellow villagers that I could not guarantee anything, but that I would examine him and help him if I could.

The hut in which he lay seemed as old as the man himself, reeking of disease and death. I ordered the villagers who had crowded into it after me to get out. When they were gone, I rummaged about until I found a piece of ragged matting large enough to block the doorway.

With it in place, the hut was so dark I could scarcely see the sick man. As I bent over him, it seemed to me at first that my eyes were growing accustomed to the darkness. After a moment I realized it was no longer quite so dark as it had been. A faint light played across him, moving with the movements of my eyes. My first thought was that it came from the thorn I kept in the little leather sack Dorcas had sewn for the Claw, though it seemed impossible that it could shine through the leather and my shirt in such a way. I took it out. It was as dark as it had been when I had tried to light the corridor outside my cabin with it, and I put it away again.

The sick man opened his eyes. I nodded to him and tried to smile.

"Have you come to take me?" he asked. It was no more than a whisper.

"I'm not Death," I told him, "though I've been mistaken for him often enough."

"I thought you were, sieur. You look so kind."

"Do you want to die? I can manage that in a moment if you wish it."

"Yes, if I can't be well." His eyes closed again.

I pulled down the homespuns that had covered him and found he was naked beneath them. His right side was swollen, the lump the size of a child's head. I smoothed it away, thrilling to the power that surged out of Urth, through my legs and out my fingers.

Suddenly the hut was dark again, and I was sitting on its pounded earthen floor listening spell-caught to the sick man's breathing. It seemed that a long time had passed. I stood, tired and feeling I might soon be ill—it was just the way I had felt after I had executed Agilus. I took down the matting and stepped out into the sunshine.

Burgundofara embraced me. "Are you all right?"

I told her I was, and asked whether we could not sit down somewhere. A big man with a loud voice—I suppose he was one of the sick man's relations—elbowed his way through the crowd demanding to know whether "Declan" would recover. I said I did not know, all the while trying to force my way through the press in the direction Burgundofara indicated. It was after nones, and the autumn day had grown warm, as such days sometimes do. If I had felt better, I would have found the milling, sweating peons comic; they were just such an assembly as we had terrified when we had performed Dr. Talos's play at Ctesiphon's Cross. Now I was suffocated by them.

"Tell me!" the big man shouted in my face. "Will he be well?"

I turned on him. "My friend, you think that because your village has fed me, I'm obligated to answer your questions. You are mistaken!"

Others pulled him away, and I think knocked him down. At least, I heard the sound of a blow.

Herena took my hand. The crowd opened before us, and she led me to a spreading tree, where we sat on smooth, bare ground, no doubt where the village elders met.

Someone came bowing up to ask whether I required anything. I wanted water; a woman brought it, cold from the stream, in a dew-drenched stone jar capped with a cup. Herena had seated herself on my right, Burgundofara on my left, and we passed the cup among us.

The hetman of Gurgustii approached. Bowing, he indicated Bregwyn and said, "My brother has told me how you came to his village in a ship that sailed the clouds, and that you have come to reconcile us with the powers in the sky. All our lives we have gone to the high places and sent the smoke of offerings to them, yet the sky people are angry and send frost. Men in Nessus say the sun grows cold—"

Burgundofara interrupted. "How far is it?"

"The next village is Os, my lady. From there one may take a boat to Nessus in a day."

"And from Nessus we can get passage to Liti," Burgundofara hissed to me.

The hetman continued, "Yet the monarch taxes us as before, taking our children when we cannot give him grain.

We have gone to the high places as our fathers did. We of Gurgustii burned our best ram before the frost came. What is it we should do instead?"

I tried to tell them how the Hierodules feared us because we had spread through the worlds in the ancient times of Urth's glory, extinguishing many other races and bringing our cruelty and our wars everywhere. "We must be one," I said. "We must tell only the truth, that our promises may be relied upon. We must care for Urth as you care for your fields."

He and some of the rest nodded as though they understood, and perhaps they did. Or perhaps they at least understood some part of what I had said.

There was a disturbance at the back of the crowd, shouts and the sounds of rejoicing and weeping. Those who had sat leaped up, though I was too tired to do so. After more yelling and confused talk, the sick man was led forward, still naked except for a cloth (a length of homespun I recognized as one of his coverings) knotted around his waist.

"This is Declan," someone announced. "Declan, explain to the sieur how you came to be well."

He tried to speak, but I could not hear him. I gestured to the rest to be quiet.

"While I lay in my bed, my lord, a seraph appeared, clothed all in light." There were chuckles from the peons, who nudged one another as he spoke. "He asked me whether I desired to die. I told him I wished to live, and I slept; and when I woke again I was as you see me now."

The peons laughed, and several said, "It was the sieur here who cured you," and the like.

I shouted at them. "This man was there, and you were not! You make yourselves fools when you claim to know more than a witness!" It was the fruit of the long days I had spent in Thrax listening to the proceedings of the archon's court, and still more of those spent sitting in judgment as Autarch, I fear.

Though Burgundofara wanted to continue to Os, I was too fatigued to go farther that day, and I had no desire to

sleep in a stuffy hut again. I told the villagers of Gurgustii
that Burgundofara and I would sleep under their council
tree, and that they should find places in their homes for
those who had come with me from Vici. They did so; but
when I woke in the watches of the night, it was to find that
Herena lay with us.

CHAPTER XXX

Ceryx

WHEN WE LEFT GURGUSTII MANY OF ITS PEONS WOULD have come with us, as would a few of those who had brought us from Vici. I forbade them, not wanting to be carted about like a relic.

They objected at first; but when they saw I was adamant, contented themselves with lengthy (often repetitious) speeches of thanks and the presentation of gifts: a tangled staff for me, the frantic work of the two best wood-carvers in the place; a shawl embroidered with colored wool for Burgundofara that must have been the richest item of feminine apparel there; and a basket of food for us both. We ate the food on the road and threw the basket into the stream; but we kept the other things, I liking the staff for walking and she delighted with her shawl, which relieved the masculine severity of her slop-chest clothes. At twilight, just before the gates were shut, we entered the little town of Os.

It was here that the stream we had followed emptied into Gyoll, and here there were xebecs, carracks, and feluccas tied up along the riverfront. We asked for their captains, but all had gone ashore on missions of business or pleasure, and the sullen watchmen left to guard their vessels assured us we would have to return in the morning. One recommended the Chowder Pot; we were on our way there when we happened upon a man robed in tyrian and green, who stood upon an inverted tub addressing an audience of a hundred or so:

"—buried treasure! Everything hidden revealed! If there are three birds in a bush, the third may not know of the first, but I know. There is a ring—even as I speak —beneath the pillow of our ruler, the wise, the transcendent— Thank you, my good woman. What is it you wish to know? I know it, to be sure, but allow these good folk to hear it. Then I shall reveal it."

A fat townswoman had handed him a few aes. Burgundofara said, "Come on. I'd like to sit down and get something to eat."

"Wait," I told her.

I stayed in part because the mountebank's patter reminded me of Dr. Talos, and in larger part because something in his eyes recalled Abundantius. Yet there was another thing more fundamental than either, though I am not certain I can explain it. I sensed that this stranger had traveled as I had, that we had gone far and returned in a way that even Burgundofara had not; and that though we had not gone to the same place or returned with the same gain, we had both known strange roads.

The fat woman muttered something; the mountebank announced, "She begs to be informed as to whether her husband will find a new site for his stew, and whether the venture will succeed."

He threw his arms above his head, clasping a long wand with both hands. His eyes remained open, rolling upward until the whites showed like the skins of two boiled eggs. I smiled, expecting the crowd to laugh; yet there was something terrible about his blind, invocatory figure, and no one did. We heard the lapping of the river and the sigh of the evening breeze, though it blew too gently to stir my hair.

Abruptly his arms fell and his snapping black eyes were back in place. "The answers are: *Yes!* And *yes!* The new bathhouse will stand not half a league from where we are now."

"Easy enough," Burgundofara whispered. "The whole town can't be a league across."

"And you shall have more from it than you ever had

from the old," the mountebank promised. "But now, my dear friends, before the next question I wish to tell you something more. You think I prophesied for the money this good woman gave me." He had retained the aes in his hand. Now he tossed them up in a dark little column against the darkening sky. "Well, you're wrong, my friends! Here!"

He flung them to the crowd, a good deal more than he had received from the woman, I think. There was a wild scramble.

I said, "All right, let's go."

Burgundofara shook her head. "I want to listen to this."

"These are bad times, friends! You are hungry for wonders. For thaumaturgical cures and apples from pine trees! Why, only this afternoon I learned that some quack-salver has been touring the villages up the Fluminis, and was headed our way." His gaze locked with mine. "I know that he is here now. I dare him to step forward. We shall hold a competition for you, friends—a trial of magic! Come, fellow. Come to Ceryx!"

The crowd stirred and murmured. I smiled and shook my head.

"You, my good man." He leveled a finger at me. "Do you know what it is to train your will until it's like a bar of iron? To drive your spirit before you like a slave? To toil ceaselessly for an end that may never come, a prize so remote that it seems it *will* never come?"

I shook my head.

"Answer! Let them hear you!"

"No," I said. "I haven't done those things."

"Yet they are what must be done, if you would seize the scepter of the Increate!"

I said, "I know nothing of seizing that scepter. To tell the truth, I'm certain it could not be done. If you wish to be as the Increate is, I question whether you can do it by acting as the Increate does not."

I took Burgundofara by the arm and drew her away. We had passed one narrow side street when the staff I had been given in Gurgustii snapped with a loud report. I tossed the half that had remained in my hand into the gutter, and we continued up the steep slope that led from the embankment to the Chowder Pot.

It seemed a decent enough inn; I noticed that those who had gathered in its public room seemed to be eating almost as much as drinking, which was ever a favorable sign. When the host leaned across his bar to speak to us, I asked whether he could provide us with supper and a quiet room.

"Indeed I can, sieur. Not equal to your station, sieur, but as good as you'll find in Os."

I got out one of Idas's chrisos. He took it, stared at it for a moment as though surprised, and said, "Of course, sieur. Yes, of course. See me in the morning, sieur, and I'll have your change for you. Perhaps you'd like your supper served in your room?"

I shook my head.

"A table, then. You'll want to be far from the door, the bar, and the kitchen. I understand. Over there, sieur—the table with the cloth. Would that suit you?"

I told him it would.

"We've all manner of freshwater fish, sieur. Freshly caught, too. Our chowder's quite famous. Sole and salmon, smoked or salted. Game, beef, veal, lamb, fowl . . . ?"

I said, "I've heard food's hard to come by in this part of the world."

He looked troubled. "Crop failures. Yes, sieur. This is the third in a row. Bread's very dear—not for you, sieur, but for the poor. Many a poor child will go to bed hungry tonight, so let's give thanks that we don't have to."

Burgundofara asked, "You've no fresh salmon?"

"Only in the spring, I'm afraid. That's when they run, my lady. Otherwise they're sea caught, and they won't stand the trip so far up the river."

"Salt salmon, then."

"You'll like it, my lady—put down in our own kitchen not three months ago. You needn't trouble about bread, fruit, and so on now. We'll bring everything, and you may choose when you see it. We've bananas from the north, though the rebellion makes them dear. Red wine or white?"

"Red, I think. Do you recommend it?"

"I recommend all our wines, my lady. I won't have a cask in my cellar I can't recommend."

"Red, then."

"Very good, my lady. And for you, sieur?"

A moment before, I would have said I was not hungry. Now I found I salivated at the mere mention of food; it was impossible to decide what I wanted most.

"Pheasant, sieur? We've a fine one in the spring house."

"All right. No wine, though. Maté. Do you have it?"

"Of course, sieur."

"Then I'll drink that. It's been a long time since I've tasted it."

"It should be ready at once, sieur. Will there be anything more for you?"

"Only an early breakfast tomorrow; we'll be going to the quay to arrange passage to Nessus. I'll expect my change then."

"I'll have it for you, sieur, and a good, hot breakfast in the morning, too. Sausages, sieur. Ham, and . . ."

I nodded and waved him away.

When he was gone, Burgundofara asked, "Why didn't you want to eat in our room? It would have been much nicer."

"Because I have hopes of learning something. And because I don't want to be by myself, to have to think."

"I'd be there."

"Yes, but it's better when there are more people."

"What—"

I motioned her to silence. A middle-aged man who had been eating alone had stood and tossed a last bone on his trencher. Now he was carrying his glass to our table. "Name's Hadelin," he said. "Skipper of *Alcyone*."

I nodded. "Sit down, Captain Hadelin. What can we do for you?"

"Heard you talking to Kyrin. Said you wanted passage

down the river. Some others are cheaper and some can give you better quarters. I mean bigger and more ornaments; there's none cleaner. But there's nothing faster than my *Alcyone* 'cept the patrols, and we sail tomorrow morning."

I asked how long it would take him to reach Nessus, and Burgundofara added, "And to the sea?"

"We should make Nessus day after, though it depends on wind and weather. Wind's generally light and favorable this time of year, but if we get an early storm, we'll have to tie up."

I nodded. "Certainly."

"Otherwise it should be day after tomorrow, about vespers or a bit before. I'll land you anywhere you want, this side of the khan. We'll tie up there two days to load and unload, then go on down. Nessus to the delta generally takes a fortnight or a bit less."

"We'll have to see your ship before we take passage."

"You won't find anything I'm ashamed of, sieur. Reason I came over to talk is we'll be leaving early, and if it's speed you want, we've got it. In the run of things we'd have sailed before you got to the water. But if you and her will meet me here soon as you can see the sun, we'll eat a bite and go down together."

"You're staying in this inn tonight, Captain?"

"Yes, sieur. I stay on shore when I can. Most of us do. We'll tie up somewhere tomorrow night too, if that be the will of the Pancreator."

A waiter came with our dinners, and the innkeeper caught Hadelin's eye from across the room. "'Scuse me, sieur," he said. "Kyrin wants something, and you and her'll want to eat. I'll see you right here in the morning."

"We'll be here," I promised.

"This is wonderful salmon," Burgundofara told me as she ate. "We carry salt fish on the boats for the times when we don't catch anything, but this is better. I didn't know how much I'd missed it."

I said I was glad she was enjoying it.

"And now I'll be on a ship again. Think he's a good captain? I bet he's a demon to his crew."

By a gesture, I warned her to be quiet. Hadelin was coming back.

When he had pulled out his chair again, she said, "Would you like some of my wine, Captain? They brought a whole bottle."

"Half a glass, for sociability's sake." He glanced over his shoulder, then turned back to us, a corner of his mouth up by the width of three hairs. "Kyrin's just warned me against you. Said you gave him a chrisos like none he'd seen."

"He may return it, if he wishes. Do you want to see one of our coins?"

"I'm a sailor; we see coins from extern lands. Then too, there's some from tombs, sometimes. Plenty of tombs up in the mountains, I suppose?"

"I have no idea." I passed a chrisos across the table.

He examined it, bit it, and gave it back to me. "Gold all right. Looks a trifle like you, 'cept he seems to have got himself cut up. Don't suppose you noticed."

"No," I said. "I never thought of it."

Hadelin nodded and pushed back his chair. "A man doesn't shave himself sidewise. See you in the morning, sieur, madame."

Upstairs, when I had hung my cloak and shirt on pegs and was washing my face and hands in the warm water the inn servants had brought, Burgundofara said, "He broke it, didn't he?"

I knew what she meant and nodded.

"You should have contended with him."

"I'm no magus," I told her, "but I was in a duel of magic once. I was nearly killed."

"You made that girl's arm look right."

"That wasn't magic. I—"

A conch blared outside, followed by the confused clamor of many voices. I went to the window and looked out. Ours was an upper room, and our elevation gave me a good view over the heads of the crowd to its center, where the mountebank stood beside a bier supported on the shoulders of eight men. I could not help thinking for a moment that by speaking of him Burgundofara had summoned him.

Seeing me at the window, he blew his conch a second time, pointed to draw attention to me, and when everyone was staring called, "Raise up this man, fellow! If you cannot, I will. The mighty Ceryx shall make the dead walk Urth once more!" The body he indicated lay sprawled in the grotesque attitude of a statue overthrown, still in the grip of rigor.

I called, "You think me your competitor, mighty Ceryx, but I've no such ambition. We're merely passing through Os on our way to the sea. We're leaving tomorrow." I closed the shutters and bolted them.

"It was him," Burgundofara said. She had stripped and was crouched beside the basin.

"Yes," I said.

I expected her to reproach me again, but she only said, "We'll be rid of him as soon as we cast off. Would you like me tonight?"

"Later, perhaps. I want to think." I dried myself and got into our bed.

"You'll have to wake me, then," she said. "All that wine's made me sleepy." The voice of Ceryx came through the shutters, lifted in an eerie chant.

"I will," I told her as she slipped beneath the blankets with me.

Sleep was just closing my eyes when the dead man's ax burst open the door, and he stalked into the room.

CHAPTER XXXI

Zama

I DID NOT KNOW IT WAS THE DEAD MAN AT FIRST. THE ROOM was dark, the cramped little hall outside nearly as dark. I had been half asleep; I opened my eyes at the first blow of the ax, only to see the dim flash of steel when its edge broke through with the second.

Burgundofara screamed, and I rolled out of bed fumbling for weapons I no longer possessed. At the third blow, the door gave way. For an instant the dead man was silhouetted in the doorway. His ax struck the empty bed. Its frame broke, and the whole affair collapsed with a crash.

It seemed the poor volunteer I had killed so long ago in our necropolis had returned, and I was paralyzed with terror and guilt. Cutting the air, the dead man's ax mimicked the hiss of Hildegrin's spade as it swung past my head, then struck the plaster wall with a thud like the kick of a giant's boot. The faint light from the doorway was extinguished for a moment as Burgundofara fled.

The ax struck the wall again, I think not a cubit from my ear. The dead man's arm, as cold as a serpent and scented with decay, brushed my own. I grappled with him, moved by instinct, not thought.

Candles appeared, and a lantern. A pair of nearly naked men wrestled the dead man's ax away, and Burgundofara held her knife to his throat. Hadelin stood beside her with a cutlass in one hand and a candlestick in the other. The

217

innkeeper held his lantern up to the dead man's face, and dropped it.

"He's dead," I said. "Surely you've seen such men before. So will you and I be in time." I kicked the dead man's legs from under him as Master Gurloes had once taught us, and he fell to the floor beside the extinguished lantern.

Burgundofara gasped, "I stabbed him, Severian. But he didn't—" Her mouth snapped shut with the effort not to weep. The hand that held her bloodied knife shook.

As I put my arm about her, someone shouted, *"Look out!"*

Slowly, the dead man was getting to his feet. His eyes, which had been closed while he lay on the floor, opened, though they still held the unfocused stare of a corpse, and one lid drooped. A narrow wound in his side oozed dark blood.

Hadelin stepped forward, his cutlass raised.

"Wait," I said, and held him back.

The dead man's hands reached for my throat. I took them in my own, no longer afraid of him or even horrified by him. I felt instead a terrible pity for him and for us all, knowing that we are all dead to some degree, half sleeping as he was wholly asleep, deaf to the singing of life in us and around us.

His arms dropped to his sides. I stroked his ribs with my right hand, and life flowed through it, so that it seemed each finger was to unfold petals and bloom like a flower. My heart was a mighty engine that would run forever and shake the world with every beat. I have never felt so alive as I did then, when I was bringing life to him.

And I saw it—we all saw it. His eyes were no longer dead things, but the human organs by which a man beheld us. The cold blood of death, the bitter stuff that stains the sides of a butcher's block, stirred again in him and gushed from the wound Burgundofara had made. That closed and healed in an instant, leaving only a crimson stain upon the floor and a white line on his skin. Blood rose in his cheeks until they were no longer sallow but brown and held the look of life.

Before that moment, I would have said a man of middle age had died; the youth who stood blinking before me was no more than twenty. Recalling Miles, I put my arm about his shoulders and told him that we welcomed him once more to the land of the living, speaking softly and slowly as I would have to a dog.

Hadelin and the others who had come to aid us backed away, their faces filled with fear and wonder; and I thought then (as I think now) how strange it was that they should have been so brave when they faced a horror, but such cowards when confronted by the palinode of fate.

Perhaps it is only that when we contend with evil, we are engaged against our brothers. For my own part I understood then something that had puzzled me from childhood —the legend that in the final battle whole armies of demons will fly from the mere sight of a soldier of the Increate.

Captain Hadelin was last out the door. He paused there, mouth agape, seeking the courage to speak or perhaps merely seeking the words, then spun about and bolted, leaving us in darkness.

"There's a candle here someplace," Burgundofara muttered. I heard her searching for it.

A moment later I saw her as well, wrapped in a blanket, stooped over the little table that stood beside the ruined bed. The light that had come to the sick man's hut had come again, and she, seeing her own shadow traced black by it before her, turned and saw it and ran shrieking after the rest.

There seemed little to be gained by running after her. I blocked the doorway as well as I could with chairs and the wreck of the door, and by the light that played wherever I directed my eyes dragged the torn mattress to the floor, so the man who had been dead and I might rest.

I said rest and not sleep, because I do not think either of us slept, though I dozed once or twice, waking to hear him moving about the room on journeys not confined by our four walls. It seemed to me that whenever I shut my eyes they flew open to watch my star burning above the ceiling. The ceiling had become as transparent as tissue, and I could see my star hurling itself toward us, yet infinitely remote; and at last I rose and opened the shutters, and leaned out of the window to look at the sky.

It was a clear night, and chill; each star in heaven seemed a gem. I found I knew where my own star hung, just as the gray salt geese never fail of their landing, though we hear their cry through a league of fog. Or rather, I knew where my star should be; but when I looked, I saw only the endless dark. Rich-strewn stars lay in every other corner of the sky like so many diamonds cast upon a master's cloak; and perhaps belonged, every star, to some foolish messenger as forlorn and perplexed as I. Yet none were mine. Mine was there (somewhere), I knew, though it could not be seen.

In writing such a chronicle as this, one wishes always to describe process; but some events have no process, taking place at once: they are not—then are. So it was now. Imagine a man who stands before a mirror; a stone strikes it, and it falls to ruin all in an instant.

And the man learns that he is himself, and not the mirrored man he had believed himself to be.

So it was with me. I knew myself the star, a beacon at the frontier of Yesod and Briah, coursing through the night. Then the certainty had vanished, and I was a mere man again, my hands upon a windowsill, a man chilled and soaked with sweat, shaking as I listened to the man who had been dead move about the room.

The town of Os lay in darkness, green Lune just vanishing behind the dark hills beyond black Gyoll. I looked at the spot where Ceryx had stood with his audience, and in the dim light it seemed I could make out some traces of them still. Moved by an impulse I could not have explained, I stepped back into the room and dressed myself, then sprang over the sill and down onto the muddy street below.

The jolt was so severe that for a moment I feared I had broken an ankle. On the ship, I had been as light as lanugo, and my new leg had given me, perhaps, more confidence than it could support. Now I learned that I would have to learn to jump on Urth again.

Clouds had come to veil the stars, so that I had to grope for the objects I had seen from above; but I found that I had been correct. A brass candlepan held the guttered remains of a candle no bee would have acknowledged. The bodies of a kitten and a small bird lay together in the gutter.

As I was examining them, the man who had been dead leaped down beside me, managing his jump better than I had mine. I spoke to him, but he did not reply; as an experiment I walked a short distance down the street. He followed me docilely.

I was in no mood for sleep by then, and the fatigue I had felt after I restored him to life had been sponged away by a sensation I am not tempted to call unreality—the exultation of knowing that my being no longer resided in the marionette of flesh people were accustomed to call *Severian*, but in a distant star shining with energy enough to bring ten thousand worlds to flower. Watching the man who had been dead, I recalled how far Miles and I had walked when neither of us should have walked at all, and I knew that things were now otherwise.

"Come," I said. "We'll have a look at the town, and I'll stand you a drink as soon as the first dramshop unbars its door."

He answered nothing. When I led him to a patch of starlight, his face was the face of one who wanders amid strange dreams.

If I were to describe all our ramblings in detail, reader, you would be bored indeed; but it was not boring for me. We walked along the hilltops, north until we were halted by the town wall, a tumbledown affair that seemed to have been built as much from pride as fear. Turning back, we made our way down cozy, crooked lanes lined with half-timbered houses, to reach the river just as the first light of the new day peeped over the roofs behind us.

As we strolled along admiring the many-masted vessels, an old man, an early riser and doubtless a poor sleeper (as so many old people are) stopped us.

"Why, Zama!" he exclaimed. "Zama, boy, they said you was dead."

I laughed, and at the sound of my laughter the man who had been dead smiled.

The old man cackled. "Why, you never looked better in your life!"

I asked, "How did they say he'd died?"

"Drowned! Pinian's boat foundered up by Baiulo Island, that's what I heard."

"Does he have a wife?" When I saw the old man's curious glance, I added, "I only met him last night when we were out drinking, and I'd like to drop him off someplace. He's stowed a little more than's good for him, I'm afraid."

"No family. He's boardin' with Pinian. Pinian's old woman takes it out of his pay." He told me how to get there and how to recognize the house, which sounded squalid enough. "Not that I'd bring him to 'em so early, with him shippin' water. Pinian'll beat the cake out of him, sure as scullin'." He shook his head in wonder. "Why, everybody heard they'd fished out Zama's remains and brought 'em back with 'em!"

Not knowing what else to say I told him, "You never know what to believe," and then, moved by this wretched old man's clear delight at finding a strong young man still alive, I put my hand upon his head and mumbled some set phrases about wishing him well in this life and the next. It was a blessing I had occasionally given as Autarch.

I had intended to do nothing at all, and yet the effect was extraordinary. When I took away my hand, it seemed that the years had covered him like dust, and unseen walls had fallen to let in the wind; his eyes opened so that they looked as big as dishes, and he fell to his knees.

When we were some distance away, I glanced back at him. He was kneeling there still and staring after us, but no longer an old man. Nor was he a young one, but simply a man in essence, a man freed of the gyre of time.

Though Zama did not speak, he put his arm about my shoulders. I put mine over his, and in that fashion we strolled up the street Burgundofara and I had taken the evening before and found her at breakfast with Hadelin in the public room of the Chowder Pot.

CHAPTER XXXII

To the Alcyone

THEY HAD EXPECTED NEITHER OF US—THERE WERE NO extra places set at the table. I pulled up a chair for myself, and then (when he only stood and stared) another for Zama.

"We thought you were gone, sieur," Hadelin said. His face, and hers, told plainly enough where Burgundofara had spent the night.

"I was," I said, speaking to her and not to him. "But I see you got into our room all right to get your clothes."

"I thought you were dead," Burgundofara said.

When I did not reply, she added, "I thought this man had killed you. The doorway was blocked up with stuff I had to push over, but the shutters had been broken open."

"Anyway, sieur, you're back." Hadelin tried to sound cheerful and failed. "Still going downriver with us?"

"Perhaps," I said. "When I've seen your craft."

"Then you will be, sieur, I think."

The innkeeper appeared, bowing and forcing himself to smile. I noticed he had a butcher knife thrust through his belt behind his leather apron.

"Fruit for me," I told him. "Last night you said you had some. Bring some for this man too; we'll see whether he eats it. Maté for both of us."

"Immediately, sieur."

"After I've eaten, you and I can go up to my room. It's been damaged, and we'll have to decide by how much."

"That won't be necessary, sieur. A trifle! Perhaps we can

224

agree upon an orichalk as a token payment?" He tried to rub his hands in the way such people often do, but their tremors made the gesture ridiculous.

"Five, I should think, or ten. A broken door, a damaged wall, and a broken bed—you and I shall go up and make a reckoning."

His lips were trembling too, and suddenly it was no longer pleasant to terrify this little man who had come with his lantern and his stick when he heard one of his guests attacked. I said, "You shouldn't drink so much," and touched his hands.

He smiled, chirped, "Thank you, sieur! Fruit, yes, sieur!" and trotted away.

It was all tropical, as I had half expected: plantains, oranges, mangoes, and bananas brought overland to the upper river by trains of sumpters and shipped south. There were no apples and no grapes. I borrowed the knife that had stabbed Zama to peel a mango, and we ate in silence. After a time Zama ate too, which I thought a good sign.

"Something more, sieur?" the innkeeper asked at my elbow. "We've plenty."

I shook my head.

"Then perhaps . . . ?" He nodded toward the stair, and I rose, motioning for the others to remain where they were.

Burgundofara said, "You should have kept him frightened. It would have been cheaper." The innkeeper shot her a glance of raw hatred.

His inn, which had looked small enough the night before when I had been tired and it was wrapped in darkness, I saw to be tiny now, four rooms on our floor, and four more, I suppose, on the floor above. The room itself, which had seemed capacious enough when I lay upon the torn mattress listening to Zama move about, was hardly larger than the cabin Burgundofara and I had shared on the tender. Zama's ax, old and worn and intended for wood, stood in one corner.

"I didn't want you to come so I could get money from you, sieur," the innkeeper told me. "Not for this or anything. Not any time."

I looked about at the destruction. "But you'll have it."

"Then I'll give it away. There's many a poor man in Os these days."

"I imagine so." I was not really listening to what he said or to what I said myself, but examining the shutters; it was to see them that I had insisted on coming upstairs. Burgundofara had mentioned that they had been broken, and she was right. The wood had split away from the screws that had held the bolt. I recalled bolting them and later opening them. When I retraced my actions in memory, I found that I had merely touched them and they had flown open.

"It would be wrong, sieur, for me to take anything after what you've brought me. Why, the Chowder Pot will be famous forever all up and down the river." His eyes stared off into some heaven of notoriety invisible to me. "Not that we're not known already—the best inn in Os. But some'll come and stay here just to see this." Inspiration seized him. "I won't have it fixed, not nothing! I'll leave it just like it is!"

I said, "Charge them to come in."

"Yes, sieur, you have it. Not patrons, to be sure. But I'll charge the others, yes indeed!"

I was about to order him to do no such thing, to have the damage repaired instead; but when I had opened my mouth to speak, I shut it again. Was it to snatch away this man's good fortune—if good fortune it was—that I had returned to Urth? He loved me now as a father loves a son he admires without understanding. What right had I to harm him?

"My patrons were talking last night. I don't suppose, sieur, you know what happened after you brought poor Zama back?"

"Tell me," I said.

When we were downstairs again, I insisted on paying him, though he did not want to accept the money. "Dinner last night for the woman and me. Lodging for Zama and me. Two orichalks for the door, two for the wall, two for the bed, two for the shutters. Breakfast for Zama and me this morning. Put the woman's lodging and breakfast to

Captain Hadelin's score and see what mine comes to."

He did, writing out a full list on a scrap of brown paper with a sputtering and much chewed quill, then counting out neat stacks of silver, copper, and brass for me. I asked whether he was sure I had so much due.

"It's the same prices for everybody here, sieur. We don't charge by what a man has, but by what he's had—though I don't like charging *you* at all."

Hadelin's bill was settled with much less calculation, and the four of us left. Of all the inns at which I have stayed, I think I most regret leaving the Chowder Pot, with its good food and drink, and its company of honest rivermen. Often I have dreamed of going back, and perhaps sometime I shall. Certainly more guests came to our aid when Zama broke our door than there was any reason to expect, and I would like to think that one or even several of them were myself. Indeed it sometimes seems to me that I caught a glimpse of my own face in the candlelight that night.

However that may be, I had no thought of it as we stepped out into the morning-fresh street. The first hush of dawn was past, and carts rumbled along its ruts; women with their heads wrapped in kerchiefs paused on their way to market to stare at us. A flier like a great locust thrummed overhead; I watched it until it was out of sight, feeling the ghost of the strange wind blown from the pentadactyls that had attacked our cavalry at Orithyia.

"You don't see many anymore, sieur," Hadelin remarked with a gruffness I had not yet learned to recognize as deference. "Most won't fly now."

I confessed I had never seen any like that at all.

We turned a corner and had a fine view down the hill: the dark stone quay and the ships and boats moored there, and broad Gyoll beyond, its water glittering in the sun and its farther bank lost behind shining mist. "We must be well below Thrax," I said to Burgundofara, confusing her for a moment with Gunnie, to whom I had told something of Thrax.

She turned, smiling, and attempted to take my arm.

Hadelin said, "A good week, unless the wind's with you all
the way. Safe here. Surprised you know of a country place
like that."

By the time we reached the quay, a crowd trailed after
us, keeping well back for the most part but whispering and
pointing at Zama and me. Burgundofara tried to drive
them off, and when she failed appealed to me to do it.

"Why?" I said. "We'll sail soon enough."

An old woman cried out to Zama and rushed up to
embrace him. He smiled, and it was clear she meant no
harm. A moment later I saw him nod when she begged to
know if he was all right, and I asked whether she was his
grandmother.

She made a countrified curtsy. "Oh, no, sieur. But I
knew her and all the children in the old days. When I heard
Zama was dead, I felt like a piece of me'd died with him."

"So it had," I told her.

Sailors came to take our sarcins, and I realized I had
been watching Zama and the old woman so intently I had
never spared a glance for Hadelin's vessel. She was a xebec
and looked handy enough—I have always been lucky in
my ships. Already aboard, Hadelin motioned to us.

The old woman clung to Zama, tears rolling down her
cheeks. As I watched, he wiped one away and said, "Don't
cry, Mafalda." It was the only time he spoke.

The autochthons say that their cattle can speak but do
not, knowing that to speak is to call up demons, all our
words being only curses in the tongue of the empyrean.
Zama's seemed so in fact. The crowd parted as waves
separate for the terrible jaws of a kronosaur, and Ceryx
advanced through it.

His iron-shod staff was topped with a rotting human
head, his lean frame draped in raw manskin; but when I
saw his eyes I wondered that he bothered with such
trumpery, as one wonders to see a lovely woman decked
with glass beads and gowned in false silk. I had not known
him so great a mage.

Impelled by the training of my boyhood, I took the knife
Burgundofara put into my hand and saluted him before the

Increate should judge between us, the flat of the blade before my face.

No doubt he thought I meant to kill him, as Burgundofara was demanding. He spoke into his left hand and made ready to cast the poisoned spell.

Zama changed. Not slowly, as such things occur in tales, but with a suddenness more frightful he was again the dead man who had burst into our room. There was a cry from the crowd, like the shriek of a troop of apes.

Ceryx would have fled, but they closed before him like a wall. Perhaps someone held him, or obstructed him intentionally; I do not know. In an instant Zama was upon him, and I heard his neck break as a bone snaps in the jaws of a dog.

For a breath the two lay together, the dead man on the dead man; then Zama rose, living once more and now alive fully, or so it appeared. I watched him recognize the old woman and me, and his lips parted. Half a dozen blades pierced him before he could speak.

By the time I reached him, he was less a man than a gobbet of bleeding flesh. Blood spurted in weakening streams from his throat; no doubt his heart still beat under its welter of blood, though his chest had been opened with a billhook. I stood over him and tried to call him to life yet again. The eyes of the head on Ceryx's fallen staff rolled in their putrid sockets to stare at me; sickened, I turned away, wondering to find myself, a torturer, grown so cruel. Someone took my hand and led me toward the ship. As we went up the shaky gangplank, I discovered it was Burgundofara.

Hadelin received us among hurrying sailors. "They got him that time, sieur. Last night we were all afraid to strike first. Daylight makes a difference."

I shook my head. "They killed him because he was no longer dangerous to them, Captain."

Burgundofara whispered, "He ought to lie down. It takes a great deal out of him."

Hadelin pointed to a door under the sun deck. "If you'll go below, sieur. I'll show you the cabin. It's not big, but—"

I shook my head again. There were benches on either side of the door, and I asked to rest there. Burgundofara went to look at the cabin while I sat trying to wipe the image of Zama's face from my eyes and watching the crew make ready to cast off. One of the sun-browned rivermen seemed familiar; but I, who can forget nothing, sometimes have difficulty in bringing the quarry to bay in a memory that grows ever more vast.

CHAPTER XXXIII

Aboard the Alcyone

SHE WAS A XEBEC, LOW IN THE WATER AND NARROW AT THE waist. Her foremast carried an immense lateen sail, her pole mainmast three square sails that could be dropped to the main deck for reefing, and her mizzen a gaffsail, with a square topsail above it. Her gaffsail boom was lengthened by a flagstaff, so that on festive occasions (and such it appeared Hadelin considered our departure to be) an overwrought banner could be hung over the water. Flags of like design, representing no nation on Urth so far as I knew, flapped from the tops.

In truth, there is something irresistibly festive about a sailing, provided it takes place in daylight and good weather. At every moment it seemed to me that we were about to depart, and at every moment my heart grew lighter. I felt it was wrong to be happy, that I should be miserable and exhausted, as indeed I had been when I looked down at poor Zama's body and for some time after. Yet I could not continue so. I pulled up the hood of my cloak as I had once drawn up the hood of my guild cloak when I strode smiling down the Water Way to exile, and although this cloak (which I had taken from my stateroom on Tzadkiel's ship upon a morning that now seemed as remote as the first dawn of Urth) was fuligin purely by chance, I smiled once more at the realization that the Water Way stretched along this very river and the water lapping our sides must soon wash its dark curbs.

Afraid Burgundofara might return or that some sailor

would glimpse my face, I climbed the few steps to the quarterdeck and discovered we had put out while I sat alone with my thoughts. Os was already far behind us, and would have been out of sight had not the atmosphere been as clear as hyalite. Its wretched lanes and vicious people I knew well enough; but the sparkling morning air made its staggering wall and tumbledown towers seem those of just such an enchanted town as I had seen in Thecla's brown book. I remembered the story, of course, as I remember everything; and I began to tell it to myself, leaning over the railing and whispering the words as I watched the fading town, lulled by the easy rocking of our vessel, which heeled scarcely at all under the slightest of breezes.

THE TALE OF THE TOWN THAT FORGOT FAUNA

Long ago, when the plow was new, nine men journeyed up a river in search of a site upon which to establish a new city. After many a day of weary rowing through mere wilderness, they came upon a place where an old woman had built a hut of sticks and planted a garden.

There they beached their boat, for the supplies they had carried with them were gone, and for many days they had eaten only such fish as they could catch in the river and drunk only river water. The old woman, whose name was Fauna, gave them mead and ripe melons, beans white, black, and red; carrots and turnips; cucumbers as thick as your arm; and apples, cherries, and apricots.

That night they slept before her fire; and in the morning, as they walked over the land eating its grapes and strawberries, they saw that everything needed to build a great city was there, where stone could be floated down from the mountains upon rafts of logs, where there was good water in abundance and the rich soil engendered a green birth from every seed.

Then they held a council. Some urged that they should kill the old woman. Others, more merciful, that they should only drive her away. Still others proposed that they should trick her by this means or that.

But their leader was a pious man who said, "If we do any of these evil things, you may be sure the Increate will not permit it to pass without notice, for she has welcomed us and given us of all she possesses except her land. Let us offer our money for that. It may be she will accept it, not knowing the value of what she has."

So they polished each brass or copper bit, put them into a bag, and offered it to the old woman. But she refused, for she loved her home.

"Let her be tied, and laid into one of her own tubs," some said. "Then we will only have to push the tub into the current, and we will be rid of her; and which of us will have her blood upon his hands?"

Their leader shook his head. "Surely her ghost would haunt our new town," he told them. And so they added their silver to the money in the sack and offered it again; but the old woman refused as before.

"She is old," one said, "and in the course of nature she must die soon. I will remain here to care for her while you return to your families. When she is dead I will return also, bearing the news."

At this the leader shook his head, for he saw murder in the speaker's eyes; and at last they added their gold (which was not much) to the money already in the bag and offered that to the old woman as well. But she, who loved her home, refused just as before.

Then their leader said, "Tell us what you will take for this place. For I warn you we will have it by one means or another, and I cannot much longer restrain the rest."

At that the old woman thought long and hard; and at last she said, "When you build your town, you must put a garden in the midst of it, with trees that blossom and fruit, and humble plants likewise. And in the center of this garden you must erect a statue of me made of precious stuffs."

To this they readily agreed, and when they returned to the place with their wives and children, the old woman was no more to be seen. Her hut, her dovecotes, and her rabbit hutches they used for firewood, and they feasted on her produce while they built their town. But in the center of it, as they had sworn, they made a garden; and though it was not a large garden, they promised to make it bigger by and by. In the middle of this garden, they erected a statue of painted wood.

Years passed; the paint peeled away, and the wood cracked. Weeds sprang up in the flower beds, though there were always a few old women who pulled them out and planted marigolds and hollyhocks, and scattered crumbs for the doves that perched on the shoulders of the wooden figure.

The town gave itself a grand name and grew walls and towers, though its walls were but little walls to keep out beggars, and owls nested in the empty guardrooms of its towers. Its grand name was not used by travelers or farmers, the former calling the place Pestis and the latter Urbis. Yet many merchants and many outlanders settled there, and it grew until it reached the heels of the mountains, and the farmers sold their fields and meadows and were rich.

At last a certain merchant purchased the weedy little garden in the center of the Old Quarter and built godowns and shops upon its flower beds. He burned the gnarled old apples and mulberries in his own fireplaces, for wood was dear; and when he burned the wooden woman, ants fled from her to explode among the coals.

When the harvest was poor, the town fathers took what corn there was and shared it out at the price paid the year before; but a year came when the harvest failed. The merchants demanded to know by what right the fathers of the town did this, for they desired to sell what corn there was for the price it would bring.

Prompted by the merchants, the town's many poor asked too, demanding bread at public cost. Then the town fathers recalled that their own fathers had taught them the name by which they governed the town, but none could lay tongue to it. There was fighting and many fires—but no bread—and before the last fire had smoldered out, many had left the town to search for berries and hunt rabbits.

That town lies in ruins now, all its towers cast down; yet it is said that one old woman remains, who has made a garden at its center among the tumbled walls.

When I murmured the words I have just written here, Os had nearly vanished; but I remained where I was, leaning on the rail of the little quarterdeck near the sternpost, looking back along the upper river that lay gleaming to the north and east.

This part of Gyoll, below Thrax but above Nessus, is as different from that below Nessus as can be imagined. Though it carries already its burden of silt from the mountains, it flows too swiftly to foul its channel; and because it does not, and is hemmed by rocky hills on either side, it runs as straight as a spar for a hundred leagues.

Our sails had brought us to the center of the flood, where the current will bear a vessel three leagues in a watch; close-hauled, they gave us just enough way for the rudder to bite the swirling water. The upper world was fair and smiling and full of sunshine, though in the farthest east there was a patch of black no bigger than my thumb. From time to time the breeze that filled our sails died away, and the strange, stiff flags ceased their uneasy stirring and fell lifelessly to the masts.

I had been aware of two sailors crouched nearby but had assumed they were on watch, waiting to trim the mizzen (our mizzenmast extended through the sun deck) if the need arose. When I turned at last, thinking to go to the bow, they were looking up at me; and I recognized both.

"We've disobeyed you, sieur," Declan muttered. "But we did it because we love you for our lives. We beg you to forgive us." He could not meet my eyes.

Herena nodded. "My arm ached to follow you, sieur. It will cook and wash and sweep for you—do whatever you order it to do."

When I said nothing, she added, "It's only my feet that rebel. They won't stand idle when you go away."

Declan said, "We heard the doom you laid on Os. I can't write, sieur, but I remember it all, and I'll find someone who can. Your curse upon that evil city won't be forgotten."

I sat on the deck before them. "It isn't always good to leave your native place."

Herena held out her cupped hand—the hand I had shaped for her—then turned it upside down. "How can it be good to find the master of Urth and lose him again? Besides, I'd have been taken if I'd stayed with Mother. But I'd follow you anywhere, though an optimate waited to wed me."

"Did your father follow me too? Or any others? You can't remain with me unless you'll tell me the truth."

"I'd never lie to you, sieur. No, no others. I would have known them."

"Did you really follow me, Herena? Or did you and Declan run ahead of us, just as you ran ahead of us after you'd seen us land from the flying ship?"

Declan said, "She didn't mean to lie, sieur. She's a good girl. It was just a manner of speaking."

"I know that. But did you go ahead of me?"

Declan nodded. "Yes, sieur, we did. She told me the woman had been talking about going to Os the day before. So when you wouldn't let any of us go with you yesterday . . . " He paused, rubbing his grizzled chin and ruminating on the decision that had caused him to leave his native village.

"We went first, sieur," Herena finished simply. "You said nobody but the woman was to come with you and nobody could follow you. But you didn't say we couldn't go to Os at all. We left while Anian and Ceallach were making a staff for you."

"So you arrived before we did. And you talked to people, didn't you? You told them what had happened in your villages."

"We didn't mean any harm, sieur," Herena said.

Declan nodded. "I didn't. That's what she should say. It wasn't really her that talked, not until they asked her. It was me, though I've always been so slow with my words. Only I'm not, sieur, when I'm talking about you." He drew in breath, then burst out, "I've been beaten before, sieur. Twice by the tax gatherers, once by the law. The second time I was the only man in Gurgustii that fought, and they left me for dead. But if you want to punish me, all you have to do is tell me. I'll jump into the water right now if you tell me to, though I can't swim."

I shook my head. "You meant no harm, Declan. Thanks to you, Ceryx learned about me, and poor Zama had to die a second death, and a third. But whether all that came to good or evil, I don't know. Until we reach the end of time, we don't know whether something's been good or bad; we can only judge the intentions of those who acted. How did you learn that I was going to take this ship?"

The wind was rising; Herena drew her stola more closely around her. "We'd gone to sleep, sieur—"

"In an inn?"

Declan cleared his throat. "No, sieur, it was in a tun. We thought it would keep the rain off if it rained. Then too I could sleep at the open end and her in the butt, so there couldn't anyone get at her without passing me. There was some people that didn't want us to, but when I had explained how it was to them, they let us."

"He knocked two of them down," Herena said, "but I don't think he hurt them, sicur. They got back up and ran away."

"Then, sieur, when we'd been asleep for a while, a boy came and woke me. He was a potboy, sieur, at the inn where you were, and he wanted to tell me about how you were staying there and he'd served you and you'd brought back a dead man. So then she and I went up to see. There was a lot of people in the taproom, all talking about what had gone on, and some that knew us because we'd told them about you before. Like the potboy, sieur. They stood us ale because we didn't have any money, and we got boiled eggs and salt that was free to drinkers there. And she heard a man say you and the woman was going on the *Alcyone* tomorrow."

Herena nodded. "So this morning we came. Our tun wasn't far from the dock, sieur, and I got Declan up as soon as it was light. The captain wasn't there yet, but there was a man he'd left in charge, and when we said we'd work if they'd take us, he said all right, and we helped carry things. We saw you come, sieur, and what happened on the bank, and we've tried to stay close to you ever since."

I nodded, but I was looking toward the bow. Hadelin and Burgundofara had come up and were standing on the forecastle deck. The wind pressed her ragged sailor clothes against her, and I wondered to see how slender she was, remembering Gunnie's heavy, muscular body.

Declan whispered hoarsely, "That woman— Down under this floor here, sieur, with the captain—"

"I know," I told him. "They lay together last night too, at the inn. I have no claim on her. She's free to do as she wishes."

Burgundofara turned for a moment, glancing up at the sails (which were full now as though big with child) and laughing at something Hadelin had said to her.

CHAPTER XXXIV

Saltus Again

BEFORE NOON WE WERE RACING ALONG LIKE A YACHT. THE wind sang in the rigging, and the first big drops of rain spattered the ship like paint flung at her canvas. From my position by the quarterdeck rail, I watched the mizzentop and main topgallant struck and the remainder of our hamper reefed again and again. When Hadelin came to me, excessively polite, to suggest I go below, I asked him if it would not be wise to tie up.

"Can't, sieur. There's no harbor between here and Saltus, sieur. Wind'd beach us if I tied to the bank, sieur. A blow's coming, sieur, it is indeed. We've rode out worse, sieur." He dashed away to belabor the mizzen gang and shout obscenities at the helmsman.

I went forward. I knew there was a chance I would soon be drowned, but I was enjoying the wind and found I did not greatly care. Whether my life had come to its end or not, I had both succeeded and failed. I had brought a New Sun that could not possibly cross the gulf of space in my lifetime—nor in that of any infant born in mine. If we reached Nessus, I would reclaim the Phoenix Throne, scrutinize the acts of the suzerain who had replaced Father Inire (for I felt sure the "monarch" mentioned by the villagers could not be Inire), and reward or punish him as his conduct deserved. I would then live out the remainder of my life amid the sterile pomp of the House Absolute or the horrors of battlefields; and if I ever wrote an account of it, as I had the account of my rise whose final disposal began this narrative, there would be little of interest in it once I had described the termination of this voyage.

The wind snapped my cloak like a banner and made our lateen foresail flap like the wings of some monstrous bird as the tapered yard bent again and again to spill the blasts. The foresail had been reefed to the last point, and with every gust *Alcyone* shied toward Gyoll's rocky shore like a skittish steed. The mate stood with one hand on the backstay, watching the sail and cursing as monotonously as a barrel organ. When he caught sight of me, he stopped abruptly and mouthed, *"May I speak with you, sieur?"*

He looked absurd doffing his cap in that wind; I smiled as I nodded. "I suppose you can't furl the foresail without making her harder to steer?"

It was just at that moment that the full fury of the storm descended on us. Though so much of her hamper had been struck or reefed, *Alcyone* was laid on her beam ends. When she righted herself (and to the glory of her builders, she did right herself) the water all around us was boiling with hail, and the drumming of the hailstones on her decks was deafening. The mate sprinted for the overhang of the sundeck. I followed him and was startled to see him fall to his knees as soon as he had gained its shelter.

"Sieur, don't let her sink! I don't want it for me, sieur, I got a wife—two babies—only married last year, sieur. We—"

I asked, "What makes you think I can save your ship?"

"It's the captain, ain't it, sieur? I'll see to him, soon as it gets dark." He fingered the hilt of the long dirk at his side. "I got a couple hands that's sure to stand by me, sieur. I'll do it—I swear it to you, sieur."

"You're talking mutiny," I said. "And nonsense." The ship rolled again until one end of the main yard was under water. "I can no more raise storms—"

I was addressing no one. He had bolted from beneath the overhanging deck and vanished into the hail and pouring rain. I seated myself once more on the narrow bench from which I had watched the ship loaded. Or rather, I rushed through the void as I had been rushing through the void since Burgundofara and I had leaped into the black emptiness under that strange dome on Yesod; and as I did, I made the lay figure I moved with strings that might have strangled half Briah sit upon the bench.

In the space of a dozen breaths, or a hundred, the mate returned with Herena and Declan. He knelt again, while they crouched at my feet.

"Stop the storm, sieur," Herena pleaded. "You were kind to us before. You won't die, but we will—Declan and me. I know we've offended you, but we meant well and we beg you to forgive us."

Declan nodded mutely.

I told them all, "Violent thunderstorms are common in autumn. This one will soon pass, like other storms."

Declan began, "Sieur . . ."

"What is it?" I asked him. "There's no reason you shouldn't speak."

"We saw you. She and I did. We were up there where you left us when the rain came. The mate here, he ran. You walked, sieur. You walked, and the hail didn't hit you. Look at my clothes, sieur, or hers."

"What do you mean, Declan?"

The mate mumbled, "They're soaked, sieur. So'm I. But feel your cloak, sieur, feel your cheeks."

I did, and they were dry.

When it is confronted with the incredible, the mind flies to the commonplace; the only explanation I could think of was that the fabric was of some extern weave that could not be wet, and that my face had been shielded by the hood. I pushed it back and stepped out into the waist.

With my face turned to the wind, I could see rain streaming toward my eyes and hear the whizzing hail as it passed my ears; but no hailstone ever struck me, and my face and hands and cloak remained dry. It was as though the words—the foolish words, as I had always believed —of the munis had become truth, and all I saw and heard was mere illusion.

Almost against my will, I whispered to the storm. I had thought to speak as men speak to men, but I found that my lips produced the sounds of soft wind, of distant thunder rolling among the hills, and of the gentle tympanation of the rain of Yesod.

A moment passed, then another. The thunder rumbled away, and the wind fell. A few hailstones, like pebbles flung by a child, plopped into the river. I knew that with those few words I had called the storm back into myself, and the feeling was indescribable. Earlier I had somehow sent forth my feelings, and they had become a monster as wild as I was then, a monster with the strength of ten thousand giants. Now they were only feelings again, and I was angry again as I had been angry before, and not least angry because I was no longer certain where the line ran between this strange, sordid world of Urth and myself. Was the wind my breath? Or was my breath the wind? Was it the rush of my blood or the song of Gyoll that sounded in my ears? I would have cursed, but I feared what my curse might do.

"Thank you, sieur. Thank you!"

It was the mate, kneeling again and ready to kiss my boot if I had been ready to permit it. I made him rise instead and told him that there was to be no murder of Captain Hadelin. In the end I was forced to make him swear it, because I could see that he—like Declan or Herena—would cheerfully have acted in what he felt to be my cause in direct disobedience to my orders. I had become a miracle monger whether I liked it or not, and miracle mongers are not obeyed as are Autarchs.

Of the remainder of that day, as long as the light lasted, there is little to say. I thought much, but I did nothing but wander once or twice from the quarterdeck to the forecastle deck and back, and watch the riverbanks slide by. Herena and Declan, and indeed all the crew, left me strictly alone; but when Urth seemed about to touch the red sun, I called Declan to me and pointed toward the eastern shore, now brilliantly illuminated.

"Do you see those trees?" I asked. "Some are in ranks and files like soldiers, some in clusters, and some in triangles interlaced. Are those orchards?"

He shook his head sadly. "I'd my own trees, sieur. Nothing from them this year but green apples for cooking."

"But those *are* orchards?"

He nodded.

"And on the west bank too? Are those orchards as well?"

"The banks are too steep for fields, sieur. If you plow them, the rain washes everything away. But they do well enough in fruit trees."

Half to myself I said, "Once I stopped at a village called Saltus. There were a few fields and a few cattle, but it wasn't until I got farther north that I saw much fruit."

Hadelin's voice surprised me. "Strange you should mention that. Dock at Saltus in half a watch, sieur."

He looked like a boy who knows he is to be beaten. I sent Declan away and told Hadelin he had nothing to fear, that I had indeed been angry with him and with Burgundofara too, but that I was angry no longer.

"Thank you, sieur. Thank you." He turned aside for a moment, then looked back, meeting my eyes, and said something that required as much moral courage as anything I have ever heard. "You must think we were laughing at you, sieur. We weren't. In the Chowder Pot, we thought you'd been killed. Then down in your cabin, we couldn't help it. We were pulled together. She looked at me and me at her. It happened before we knew. Thought we were going to die, after, and I s'pose we nearly did."

I told him, "You have nothing more to worry about."

"I'd best go below and talk to her, then."

I went forward, but soon discovered that close-hauled as we were the view was actually better from the quarterdeck, which was higher. I was standing there, studying the northwestern bank, when Hadelin came back, this time bringing Burgundofara. When she saw me, she released his hand and went to the farther side of the deck.

"If you're looking for the spot where we're going to dock, sieur, it's just coming into sight. Can you see it? Look for the smoke, sieur. Not the houses."

"I see it now."

"They'll be fixing dinner for us in Saltus, sieur. A good inn's there."

I answered, "I know," thinking as I did how Jonas and I had walked there through the forest after the uhlans had scattered our party at the Piteous Gate, of finding the wine in our ewer, and many other things. The village itself seemed larger than I remembered. I had thought most of the houses stone; these were wood.

I looked for the stake to which Morwenna had been chained when I had first spoken with her. As the crew struck our sails and we glided into the little bay, I found the patch of waste ground where it had stood, but there were no stake and no chain.

I searched my memory, which is perfect, except perhaps for a few slight lapses and distortions. I recalled the stake and the soft clinking of the chain when Morwenna raised her hands in supplication, the way the midges buzzed and bit, and Barnoch's house, all built of mine stone.

"It's been a long time," I told Hadelin.

Sailors loosed the halyards, sail after sail dropped to the deck, and with the way remaining to her, the *Alcyone* slid toward her berth; hands with boat hooks stood on the grating decks that extended behind the sundeck and beyond the forecastle, ready to fend us from the wharf or draw us to it.

They were hardly needed. Half a dozen loungers scurried out to catch our lines and make them fast, and the helmsman laid us alongside so smoothly that the fenders of old cordage hanging from *Alcyone*'s quarter merely kissed the timbers.

"Terrible storm today, Cap'n," one of the loungers called. "Just cleared away a bit ago. Water up over the street here. You're lucky you missed it."

"We didn't," Hadelin said.

I went ashore half-convinced that there were two villages with the same name—perhaps Saltus and New Saltus, or something of the sort.

When I reached the inn it was not as I recalled it; yet it was not so very different, either. The courtyard and its well were much the same; so were the wide gates that let in riders and carts. I took a seat in the public room and ordered supper from an innkeeper I did not recognize, wondering all the while whether Burgundofara and Hadelin would sit with me.

Neither did; but after a time Herena and Declan came to my table, bringing with them the brawny sailor who had manned the aft boat hook and a greasy, close-faced woman they said was the ship's cook. I invited them to sit down, which they did only reluctantly and after making it quite ·clear that they would not permit me to buy them food or wine. I asked the sailor (who I assumed must have stopped here often) if there were no mines in the area. He told me a shaft had been driven into a hillside about a year ago upon the advice of a hatif that had whispered in the ears of several of the principal citizens of the village, and that a few interesting and valuable items had been brought to the surface.

From the street outside we heard the tramp of booted feet, halted by a sharp command. They reminded me of the kelau who had marched singing from the river through that Saltus to which I had come as an exiled journeyman, and I was about to mention them in the hope of leading the conversation to the war with Ascia when the door burst open and a gaudily uniformed officer stalked in, followed by a squad of fusiliers.

The room had been abuzz with talk; it fell deathly still.

The officer shouted to the innkeeper, "Show me the man you call the Conciliator!"

Burgundofara, who had been sitting with Hadelin at another table, rose and pointed to me.

CHAPTER XXXV

Nessus Again

WHEN I LIVED AMONG THE TORTURERS, I OFTEN SAW clients beaten. Not by us, for we inflicted only such punishments as had been decreed, but by the soldiers who conveyed them to us and took them from us. The more experienced shielded their heads and faces with their arms, and their bellies with their shins; it leaves the spine exposed, but little can be done to protect the spine in any case.

Outside the inn I tried to fight at first, and it seems probable that the worst of my beating took place after I lost consciousness. (Or rather, when the marionette I manipulated from afar had.) When I became aware of Urth again, the blows still rained down, and I tried to do as those unlucky clients had.

The fusiliers used their boots and, what were much more dangerous, the iron-shod butts of their fusils. The flashes of pain I felt seemed remote; I was aware mostly of the blows, each sudden, jolting, and unnatural.

At last it was over, and the officer ordered me to rise; I floundered and fell, was kicked, tried again, and fell again; a rawhide noose was slipped around my neck, and I was lifted with that. It strangled me, yet helped me balance too. My mouth was full of blood; I spit it out again and again, wondering whether a rib had punctured my lungs.

Four fusiliers lay in the street, and I recalled that I had wrested his weapon from one, but had been unable to release the catch that would have allowed it to fire—on such small matters do our lives turn. Some comrades of the four examined them and found that three were dead.

"You killed them!" the officer shouted at me.

I spat blood in his face.

It was not a rational act, and I expected another beating for it. Perhaps I would have received one, but there were a hundred people or more around us, watching by the light that streamed from the windows of the inn. They muttered and stirred, and it seemed to me that a few of the soldiers felt as they did, reminding me of the guardsmen in Dr. Talos's play who had sought to protect Meschiane, who was Dorcas and the mother of us all.

A litter was contrived for the injured fusilier, and two village men pressed into service to carry it. A cart filled with straw sufficed for the dead. The officer, the remaining fusiliers, and I walked ahead of them to the wharf, a distance of a few hundred paces.

Once, when I fell, two men dashed out of the crowd to help me up. Until I was again on my feet, I supposed that they were Declan and the sailor, or perhaps Declan and Hadelin; but when I gasped my thanks to them, I found that they were strangers. The incident seemed to enrage the officer, who fired his pistol into the ground at their feet to warn them away when I fell a second time, and kicked me until I rose again with the aid of the noose and the fusilier who held it.

The *Alcyone* lay at the wharf, just as we had left her; but alongside her was such a craft as I had never seen before, with a mast that looked too slight to carry sail, and a swivel gun on her foredeck far smaller than the *Samru*'s.

Seeing the gun and the sailors manning it seemed to put new heart into the officer. He made me stop and face the crowd, and ordered me to point out my followers. I told him I had none and that I knew none of the people before me. He struck me with his pistol then. When I got up once more, I saw Burgundofara near enough to have touched me. The officer repeated his demand, and she vanished into the darkness.

Perhaps he struck me again when I refused again, but I

do not recall it; I rode above the horizon, futilely directing my vitality toward the broken figure sprawled so far away. The void put it at naught, and I channeled Urth's energies instead. His bones knit, and his wounds healed; but I noted with dismay that the cheek torn by the pistol sight was that which Agia's iron claw had once torn too. It was as if the old injury had reasserted itself, only slightly weakened.

It was still night. Smooth wood supported me, but leaped and pounded as though lashed to the back of the most graceless destrier that ever galloped. I sat up and found I was aboard a ship, and that I had lain in a puddle of my own blood and spew; my ankle was chained to a staple. A fusilier stood nearby with one hand on a stanchion, keeping his balance with difficulty on that wild deck. I asked him for water. As I had learned when I marched through the jungle with Vodalus, when one is a captive it does no harm to ask favors—they are not often granted, but when they are refused nothing is lost.

This principle was confirmed when (to my surprise) my guard lurched off toward the stern and returned with a bucket of river water. I stood, cleaned myself and my clothing as thoroughly as I could, and began to take an interest in my surroundings, which were in fact novel enough.

The storm had cleared the sky, and the stars shone on Gyoll as though the New Sun had been flourished across the empyrean like a torch, leaving a trail of sparks. Green Lune peered from behind towers and domes silhouetted on the western bank.

Without sails or oars, we skipped like a thrown stone down the river. Feluccas and caravels with all sail set appeared to ride at anchor in midchannel; we darted among them as a swallow flits between megaliths. Aft, two gleaming plumes of spray rose as high as the barren mast, silver walls erected and demolished in a moment.

Not far away I heard guttural, half-formed sounds that might almost have been words. It was as if some suffering beast sought to speak, and then to whisper. Another man lay on the deck near where I had lain, and a third crouched over him. My chain would not let me reach them; I knelt to add the length of my calf to it, and thus got close enough to see them as well as they could be seen in the darkness.

Both were fusiliers. The first lay on his back, unmoving yet twisted as if in agony, his expression a hideous grimace. When he noticed me he tried to speak again, and the other man murmured, "It's right, Eskil. Doesn't matter now."

I said, "Your friend's neck has been broken."

He answered, "You should know, vates."

"I broke it, then. I thought so."

Eskil made some strangled sound, and his comrade bent over him to listen. "He wants me to kill him," he told me when he straightened up again. "He's been asking for the last watch—ever since we put out."

"Do you intend to do it?"

"I don't know." His fusil had been across his chest; as he spoke, he laid it on the deck, holding it there with one hand. I saw light glint on the oiled barrel.

"He'll die soon no matter what you do. You'll feel better afterward if you let him die naturally."

I would have said more, perhaps, but Eskil's left hand was moving, and I fell silent to watch it. Like a crippled spider it crept toward the fusil, and at last closed on it and drew it toward him. His comrade could have taken it back easily; but he did not, and seemed as fascinated as I.

Slowly, with an infinity of pain and labor, Eskil lifted and turned it until its barrel was directed toward me. Dimly by starlight, I watched his stiff fingers, fumbling, fumbling.

As the striker, so the stricken. Earlier I might have saved myself, if only I could have discovered the catch that would have permitted the weapon to fire. He who knew so well where it was and how it operated would have killed me, could only he have made his numb fingers release it. Impotent both, we stared at each other.

At last his strength could no longer support the weight of the fusil. It fell clattering to the deck, and I felt that my heart would burst for pity. In that moment I would have pulled the trigger myself. My lips moved—but I scarcely knew what it was I said.

Eskil sat up and stared.

As he did, our vessel slowed. The deck sank until it was nearly level, and the plumes of water behind us vanished as a wave does that breaks on the beach. I stood up to see where we were; Eskil stood too, and soon the friend who had nursed him and my guard joined us.

The embankment of Gyoll rose to our left, cutting off the night sky like the blade of a sword. We drifted along it almost in silence, the roaring of whatever engines they had been that had propelled us with such speed muffled now. Steps descended to the water, but there were no friendly hands to tie us up. A sailor leaped from the bow to do it, and another threw him our mooring line. A moment more and a gangplank stretched from ship to stair.

The officer appeared at the stern, flanked by fusiliers with torches. He halted to stare at Eskil, then called all three soldiers to him. They held a long conference in tones too faint for me to hear.

At last the officer and my guard approached me, followed by the men with torches. After a breath or two the officer said, "Take off his shirt."

Eskil and his friend came to stand beside us. Eskil said, "You must remove your shirt, sieur. If you don't we'll have to tear it off."

To test him I asked, "Would you do that?"

He shrugged, and I unfastened the fine cloak I had taken from the ship of Tzadkiel and let it fall to the deck, then pulled the shirt over my head and dropped it on the cloak.

The officer came nearer and made me turn so that he could examine my ribs on both sides. "You should be nearly dead," he muttered. And then, "It's true, what they tell of you."

"Since I don't know what's been said, I can neither confirm nor deny it."

"I'm not asking you to. Dress yourself again. I advise it."

I looked around for my cloak and shirt, but they were gone.

The officer sighed. "Somebody's filched them—one of the sailors, I suppose." He glanced toward Eskil's friend. "You must have seen it, Tanco."

"I was looking at his face, sieur, not at his clothes. But I'll try to find them."

The officer nodded. "Take Eskil with you." At a gesture from him, one of the torchbearers handed his torch to the other and bent to free my leg.

"They won't find them," the officer told me. "There are a thousand hiding holes on a boat like this, and the crew will know them all."

I told him I was not cold.

The officer slipped off his uniform cape. "The man who took them will cut them up and sell the pieces, I imagine. He should make something from them. Wear this—I've got another one in my cabin."

I disliked taking his cape, but it would have been foolish to refuse his generosity.

"I must fetter your hands. Regulations." The manacles gleamed like silver in the torchlight; still, they bit into my wrists like others.

The four of us crossed the gangplank to water stairs that seemed nearly new, mounted them, and marched in single file up a narrow street bordered with little gardens and rambling houses mostly of a single story: a torchbearer first, I following him, the officer behind me with his drawn pistol hanging at his side, and the second torchbearer bringing up the rear. A laborer on his way home stopped to stare at us; other than he, there was no one about.

I looked over my shoulder to ask the officer where he was taking me.

"To the old port. One of the hulks there has been fitted up to hold prisoners."

"And then?"

I could not see him, but I could visualize his shrug. "I don't know. My orders were to arrest you and bring you here."

So far as I could see, "here" was a public garden. Before we walked into the darkness beneath the trees, I looked up and beheld myself through their frost-blighted leaves.

CHAPTER XXXVI

The Citadel Again

IT WAS MY HOPE TO SEE THE OLD SUN RISE BEFORE I WAS locked away. That was not to be. For a long time, or at least for what felt like a long time, we climbed a gentle hill. More than once our torches set fire to raddled leaves overhead that ignited a few others, releasing the pungent smoke that is the very breath of autumn before they smoldered out. More leaves strewed the path we trod, but they were sodden with rain.

At last we came to a brooding wall so lofty that the light of our torches failed to reveal its summit, so that for a moment I took it for the Wall of Nessus. A man in half armor leaned on the shaft of his vouge before the dark and narrow archway of a sally port in the wall. When he caught sight of us, he did not straighten his stance, or show any other sign of respect for the officer; but when we had traced the path almost to his feet, he pounded the iron door with the steel-shod butt of his weapon.

The door was opened from within. As we passed through the thickness of the wall—which was great, but not nearly so great as that of the Wall of Nessus—I stopped so suddenly that the officer behind me collided with me. The guard within was armed with a long, double-edged sword, whose squared tip he permitted to rest upon the paving stones.

"Where am I?" I asked the officer. "What is this place?"

"Where I told you I would bring you," he answered. "There is the hulk."

I looked and saw a mighty tower, all of gleaming metal.

The guard drawled, "He's afraid of my blade. She has a good edge, fellow—you'll never feel it."

The officer snapped, "You will address this prisoner as *sieur*."

"While you're here, sieur, perhaps."

What the officer might have said or done to him then, I do not know; while they spoke a woman had come out of the tower, followed by a serving boy with a lantern. The officer saluted this woman, who by the richness of her uniform was of superior rank, in the most negligent fashion and said, "You find sleep difficult, I see."

"Not at all. Your message said you would come, and I know you for a man of your word. I prefer to inspect our new clients personally. Turn about, fellow, and let me see you."

I did as she bid.

"A fine specimen, and you haven't marked him at all. He didn't resist?"

The officer said, "We present you with a tabula rasa."

When he added nothing further, one of the soldiers with torches whispered, "He fought like a devil, Madame Prefect." The officer shot him a glance that indicated he would pay for the remark.

"With such a docile client," the woman continued, "I'll hardly need you and your men to get him to a cell, I suppose?"

The officer said, "We'll lock him up for you, if you wish."

"But if you don't, you'll have to have his irons now."

He shrugged. "I've signed for them."

"Take them, then." She turned to her serving boy. "He may try to escape us, Reechy. If he does, give me your lantern and retake him."

The officer murmured, *"Don't,"* as he freed my hands, then stepped away and made me a quick salute. The man with the sword grinned and swung back the narrow sally port door, the officer and his torchbearers filed out, and the door shut with a crash. I felt I had lost my only friend.

"That way, a Hundred and Two," the woman said, and pointed toward the doorway through which she had come.

I had been looking about, at first with the hope of escape, then with a numb astonishment I cannot possibly describe. Words burst from me; I could no more have held them back than I could have silenced my heart. *That's our Matachin Tower! That one's the Witches' Keep—but it's straight now! And there's the Bear Tower!*

"You're called a holy man," she said. "I see you're wholly deranged." As she spoke, she held out her hands so I could see she was not armed, and gave me a twisted smile that would have been enough warning if the officer had not warned me already. It was plain the ragged boy had no weapon and posed no threat; she, I imagined, had a pistol or something worse under her rich uniform.

Most do not know it, but it is difficult to learn to strike another human being with all one's force; some ancient instinct makes even the most brutal soften the blow. Among the torturers I had been taught not to do so. I struck her, the heel of my hand against her chin, as hard as I have ever struck anyone in my life, and she crumpled like a doll. I kicked the lantern, which went out as it flew from the boy's hand.

The guard at the sally port raised his sword, but only to bar the way. I whirled and made off toward the Broken Court.

The pain that struck me at that moment was like the pain of the Revolutionary, the only pain I have ever felt that could be compared with it. I was being torn apart, and the separation of each limb was prolonged and prolonged until being quartered with the sword would have been nothing to it. The ground seemed to leap and reel under me, even when that hideous flash of pain was gone and I lay in the dark. All the great guns of the Battle of Orithyia were thundering together.

Then I had returned to the World of Yesod. Its pure air filled my lungs, and the music of its breezes soothed my ears. I sat up and found that it was only Urth as she seemed to one who had suffered Abaddon. As I rose I thought of all the aid I had sent this ruined body; yet my arms and legs were stiff and cold, and pain lingered in every joint.

I had lain upon a cot in a room that seemed oddly familiar. The door, which I felt sure had been of solid metal when I had last seen it, was a lattice of bars; it looked out into a narrow hall whose twistings I had known from childhood. I turned back to study the odd shape of the room.

It was the bedchamber Roche had occupied as a journeyman, and it was to this very room that I had come to don lay clothing on the evening of our excursion to the House Azure. I stared at it in astonishment. Roche's bed, a trifle wider, had stood just where my cot was now. The position of the port (I recalled how surprised I had been to find Roche had a port, and that I myself had later been given a room without one) and the angles of the bulkheads were unmistakable.

I went to the port. It was open, admitting the breeze that had awakened me. No bars crossed it; but of course no one could have climbed down the smooth walls of the tower, and only a very small man could have squeezed his shoulders through the port. I thrust out my head.

Below me lay the Old Yard just as I recalled it, basking in the late summer sunshine; its cracked flagstones looked a trifle newer, perhaps, but otherwise they were the same. The Witches' Keep now leaned awry, precisely as it had always leaned in the recesses of my memory. The wall lay in ruins, exactly as in my day, its unsmeltable metal slabs half in the Old Yard and half in the necropolis. A lone journeyman (so I already thought him) lounged at the Corpse Door, and though he wore a strange uniform and clasped a sword, as Brother Porter had not, he stood at the spot where Brother Porter used to stand.

Soon a boy, just such a ragged apprentice as I myself had been, crossed the Old Yard on some errand. I waved and shouted to him, and when he looked up I recognized him and called his name: *"Reechy! Reechy!"*

He waved in return and went on about his business, clearly afraid to be seen speaking to a client of his guild. *His guild*, I write, but I was sure by then that it had been mine too.

Long shadows told me it was still early morning; they were confirmed a few moments later by the slamming of doors and the footsteps of the journeyman bringing my atole. My door lacked the slot it ought to have had, so that he was forced to stand aside holding his stack of trays while another journeyman with a vouge, looking almost like a soldier, unlocked for him.

"You seem well enough," he said as he put my tray on the floor inside the doorway.

I told him that at times I had felt better.

He edged closer. "You killed her."

"The woman called Madame Prefect?"

He nodded, as did the other journeyman. "Broke her neck."

"If you'll take me to her," I told them, "I may be able to restore her."

They exchanged a glance and went away, slamming the barred door behind them.

So she was dead, and from the looks I had seen she had been hated. Once Cyriaca had asked me whether my offer to free her was not a final torment. (The latticed summerhouse floated from the depths of memory to stand, complete with twining vines and green moonlight, in my morning-bright cell.)

I had told her that no client would believe us; but I had believed Madame Prefect—believed at least that I could escape from her, though I had known she did not. And all the while some weapon had been trained upon me from the Matachin Tower, perhaps from this very port, though more likely from the gun room near the top.

My reverie was interrupted by the arrival of still another journeyman, this time accompanied by a physician. My door was thrown open once again; the physician stepped inside, and the journeyman locked it behind him and stood back, ready to fire through the bars.

The physician sat on my cot and opened a leather case. "How do you feel?"

"Hungry." I tossed aside my bowl and spoon. "They brought me this, but it's mostly water."

"Meat is for the monarch's defenders, not for subversives. You were hit by the convulsor?"

"If you tell me so. I know nothing about it."

"You were not, in my opinion. Stand up."

I stood, then moved my arms and legs as he ordered, let my head roll back and to each side, and so forth.

"You weren't hit. You're wearing an officer's cape. Were you an officer?"

"If you like. I was a general, at least by courtesy. Not recently."

"And you don't tell the truth. That's a junior officer's, for your information. These idiots think they hit you. I hear the man who fired at you swears it."

"Then question him."

"To listen to him denying what I know already? I'm not such a fool. Shall I explain what happened?"

I told him I wished someone would.

"Very well. The earthquake came as you fled from Madame Prefect Prisca, at the instant this idiot on the gun deck fired. He missed as anyone would; but you fell and struck your head, and he thought he'd hit you. I've seen a good many of these supposedly wonderful happenings. They're always quite simple, once you realize that the witnesses are confusing cause and effect."

I nodded. "There was an earthquake?"

"Certainly, and a big one—we're fortunate to have got off as lightly as we did. Haven't you looked outside yet? You must be able to see the wall from here." He stepped over to the port and looked out himself, then pointed (as people do) as if I had. "A big section fell next to the zoetic transport there. Lucky the ship didn't fall too. You don't think you knocked that down yourself, do you?"

I told him I had never had any notion of why it had fallen.

"This coast is quake prone, as the old records indicate clearly enough—praise to our monarch, by the way, for having them brought here—but there hasn't been one since the river changed its course, so most of these fools think there'll never be another." He chuckled. "Though after last night a few have changed their minds, I imagine."

He was already on his way out as he spoke. The journeyman banged my door closed and locked it again.

I thought of Dr. Talos's play, in which the ground shakes and Jahi says: "The end of Urth, you fool. Go ahead and spear her. It's the end for you anyway."

How little I had talked with him upon the World of Yesod.

CHAPTER XXXVII

The Book of the New Sun

AS IN MY TIME, WE PRISONERS WERE FED TWICE A DAY AND our water carafes replenished at the evening meal. The apprentice carried my tray, gave me a wink, and returned when the journeyman was no longer about, with cheese and a loaf of fresh bread.

The evening meal had been as scanty as the morning one; I began to eat what he had brought me, while I thanked him for it.

He squatted in front of my cell door. "May I talk to you?"

I said I did not govern his acts, and he was likely to know the rules of the place better than I.

He flushed, his dark cheeks growing darker still. "I mean, will you talk with me?"

"If it won't get you a beating."

"I don't think there'll be any trouble, at least not now. But we ought to keep our voices down. Some of the others are probably spies."

"How do you know I'm not?"

"Because you killed her, of course. The whole place is turned upside down. Everybody's glad she's dead, but there's sure to be an investigation and no telling who'll be sent to take her place." He paused, seeming to think deeply about what he would say next. "The guards say you said you might be able to bring her back."

"And you don't want me to."

He waved that away. "Could you have? Really?"

"I don't know—I'd have to try. I'm surprised they told you."

"I wait around and listen to them talk, shine boots or run errands for money."

"I have none to give you. Mine was taken from me by the soldiers who arrested me."

"I wasn't after any." He stood up and dug in one of the pockets of his ragged trousers. "Here, you better take these."

He held them out; they were worn brass tokens of a design unfamiliar to me.

"Sometimes you can get people to bring you extra food or whatever."

"You brought me more food, and I gave you nothing."

"Take them," he said. "I want to give them to you. You might need them." When I would not extend my hand, he tossed them through the bars and disappeared down the corridor.

I picked up his coins and dropped them into one of my own pockets, as puzzled as I have ever been in my life.

Outside, afternoon had become chill evening with the port still open. I pushed the heavy lens shut and dogged it down. Its broad, smooth flanges, of a shape I had never considered, had clearly been intended to hold the void at bay.

As I finished my bread and cheese, I thought of our passage back to Urth on the tender and my exultation aboard Tzadkiel's ship. How marvelous it would be to send this old Matachin Tower hurtling among the stars! And yet there was something sinister about it, as about all things perverted from a noble purpose to a shameful one. I had grown to manhood here feeling nothing of that.

The bread and cheese gone, I wrapped myself in the cape the officer had given me, shut out the light with one arm, and tried to sleep.

Morning brought more visitors. Burgundofara and Hadelin arrived, escorted by a tall journeyman who saluted them with his weapon and left them outside my door. My surprise was no doubt written on my face.

"Money can do wonders," Hadelin said; his twisted mouth showed how painful the amount had been, and I wondered whether Burgundofara had concealed the wages she had brought from the ship, or if he considered that money his own now.

Burgundofara told me, "I needed to see you one last time, and Hadelin arranged it for me." She wanted to say more, but the words caught in her throat.

Hadelin said, "She wants you to forgive her."

"For leaving me for him, Burgundofara? There's nothing to forgive; I had no right to you."

"For pointing you out when the soldiers came. You saw me. I know you saw me."

"Yes," I said, remembering.

"I didn't think—I was afraid—"

"Afraid of me."

She nodded.

Hadelin said, "They'd have got you just the same. Somebody else would have pointed you out."

I asked him, "You?"

He shook his head and stepped back from the bars.

When I had been Autarch, supplicants had often knelt before me; now Burgundofara knelt, and it seemed hideously inappropriate. "I had to talk to you, Severian. One last time. That was why I followed the soldiers to the wharf that night. Won't you forgive me? I wouldn't have done it, but I was so afraid."

I asked whether she remembered Gunnie.

"Oh, yes, and the ship. Except that it seems like a dream now."

"She was you, and I owe her a great deal. For her sake—your sake—I forgive you. Now and at every other time. Do you understand?"

"I think so," she said; and instantly she was happy, as if a light had been kindled in her. "Severian, we're going down the river to Liti. Hadelin goes there often, and we'll buy a house where I'll live when I'm not with him on

Alcyone. We want to have children. When they come, can I tell them about you?"

Although I believed at the time that it was only because I could see Hadelin's face as well as hers, a strange thing took place as she spoke: I grew conscious of her future, as I might have been of the future of some blossom that Valeria had plucked in the gardens.

I told her, "It may be, Burgundofara, that you will have children as you wish; if you do, you may tell them anything you like about me. It may also be that in a time to come you'll want to find me again. If you look, you may. Or you may not. But if you look, remember you aren't looking because I've told you to, or because I've promised you'll find me."

When they had gone, I thought for a moment about her and about Gunnie, who had once been Burgundofara. We say that a man is as brave as an atrox, or that a woman is as lovely as a red roe, as Burgundofara was. But we lack any such term for loyalty, because nothing we know is truly loyal—or rather, because true loyalty is found only in the individual and not in the type. A son may be loyal to his father or a dog to its master, but most are not. As Thecla I had been false to my Autarch, as Severian to my guild. Gunnie had been loyal to me and to Urth, not to her comrades; and perhaps we are unable to advance some paragon of loyalty to an apothegm only because loyalty (in the final analysis) is choice.

Yet how strange that Gunnie should sail the empty seas of time to become Burgundofara again. A poet would sing that she searched for love, I suppose; but it seemed to me she searched for the illusion that love is more than it is, though I would like to believe that it was for some higher love which has no name.

Another visitor soon came—but was no visitor at all, since I could not see his face. A whisper that seemed to originate in the empty corridor asked, "Are you the theurgist?"

"If you say it," I answered. "But who are you, and where are you?"

"Canog, the student. I'm in the cell next to you. I heard the boy talking to you, and the woman and the captain just now."

I asked, "How long have you been here, Canog?" hoping he might advise me upon certain matters.

"Nearly three months. I'm under sentence of death, but I don't think it'll be carried out. Usually they're not, after such a long time. Probably the old phrontiserion has interceded for her erring child, eh? At least, I hope so."

I had heard much such talk in my own day; it was strange to find it unchanged. I said, "You must know the ways of the place by now."

"Oh, it's just as the boy told you, meaning not so bad if you've a little money. I got them to give me paper and ink, so now I write letters for the guards. Then too, a friend brought a few of my books; I'll be a famous scholar if they keep me here long enough."

Having always asked the question when I toured the dungeons and oubliettes of the Commonwealth, I asked why he was imprisoned.

He was silent for a time. I had opened the port again, but even with a breath of wind coming through it I was conscious of the reek from the slop jar under my cot as well as the general stench of the place. The cawing of rooks rode upon the breeze; through my barred door came the endless tramping of boots upon metal.

At last he said, "We don't pry into those matters here."

"I'm sorry I've offended you, but you asked such a question of me. You asked if I was the theurgist, and it's as a theurgist that I've been imprisoned."

Another long pause.

"I killed a fool of a shopkeeper. He'd been asleep behind his counter, I knocked over a brass candlestick, and up he came roaring, with the pillow sword in his hand. What else could I do? A man has a right to save his own life, doesn't he?"

"Not under every circumstance," I said. I had not known the thought was in me until I had expressed it.

* * *

That evening the boy brought my food, and with it Herena, Declan, the mate, and the cook I had seen briefly in the inn of Saltus.

"I got them inside, sieur," the boy said. He tossed back his wild black hair with a gesture fit for any courtier. "The guard owes me a few favors."

Herena was weeping, and I pushed my arm between the bars to stroke her shoulder. "You're all in danger," I told them. "You may be arrested because of me. You mustn't stay here long."

The mate said, "Let them come for me with their sweet-arsed soldier boys. They'll find no virgin."

Declan nodded and cleared his throat, and I realized with some astonishment that he was their leader. "Sieur," he began in his deep, slow voice, "it's you who are in danger. They kill people in this place as we do pigs at home."

"Worse," the boy put in.

"We mean to speak to the magistrate on your behalf, sieur. We waited there this afternoon, but we weren't admitted. Poor people wait for days, they say, before they get to speak with him; but we'll wait as long as we have to. Meantime, we mean to do what we can in other ways."

Alcyone's cook looked at him with a significance I did not understand.

Herena said, "But now we want you to tell all of us about the New Sun's coming. I've heard more than the others, and I've tried to tell them what you told me, but that was only a little. Will you tell us everything now?"

"I don't know whether I can explain so you'll understand it," I said. "I don't know that I understand it myself."

"Please," the cook said. It was the only word I was ever to hear from her.

"Very well, then. You know what's happened to the Old Sun: it is dying. I don't mean that it's about to go out like a lamp at midnight. That would take a very long time. The wick—if you can think of it so—has been trimmed by only the width of a hair, and the corn has rotted in the fields. You don't know it, but the ice in the south is already gathering new strength. To the ice of ten chiliads will be added the ice of the winter now almost upon us, and the two will embrace like brothers and begin their march upon these northern lands. Great Erebus, who has established his kingdom there, will soon be driven before them, with all his fierce, pale warriors. He will unite his strength with Abaia's, whose kingdom is in the warm waters. With others, less in might but equal in cunning, they will offer allegiance to the rulers of the lands beyond Urth's waist, which you call Ascia; and once united with them will devour them utterly."

But everything that I said to them is much too long to be written here, each word a word. I told them all I knew of the history of the Old Sun's dying, and what that would do to Urth, and I promised them that at last someone would bring a New Sun.

Then Herena asked, "Aren't you the New Sun yourself, sieur? The woman who was with you when you came to our village said you were."

I told her I would not speak of that, fearing that if they knew it—yet saw me imprisoned—they would despair.

Declan wished to know how Urth would fare when the New Sun came; and I, understanding little more than he did himself, drew upon Dr. Talos's play, never thinking that in a time yet to come Dr. Talos's play would be drawn from my words.

When they had gone at last, I realized I had not so much as touched the food the boy had brought me. I was very hungry, but when I reached for the bowl, my fingers brushed something else—a long and narrow bundle of rags so placed that it lay in shadow.

The voice of my neighbor floated through the bars. "That was a fine tale. I took notes as fast as I could, and it should make a capital little book whenever I'm released."

I was unwinding the rags and scarcely heard him. It was a knife—the long dirk the mate had worn aboard the *Alcyone.*

CHAPTER XXXVIII

To the Tomb of the Monarch

FOR THE REMAINDER OF THE EVENING, I GAZED AT THE knife. Not in fact, of course; I had rewrapped it in its rags and hidden it under the mattress of my cot. But as I lay upon that mattress staring up at the metal ceiling that was so like the one I had known in the apprentices' dormitory as a child, I felt the knife below my knees.

Later it revolved before my closed eyes, luminant in the darkness and distinct from hilt of bone to needle point. When I slept at last, I found it among my dreams as well.

Perhaps for that reason, I slept badly. Again and again I woke and blinked at the cell light glowing above my head, rose and stretched, and crossed to the port to search for the white star that was another self. At those times I would gladly have surrendered my imprisoned body to death, if I could have done it with honor, and fled, streaming through the midnight sky to unite my being. In those moments I knew my power, that could draw whole worlds to me and incremate them as an artist burns his earths for pigments. In the brown book, now lost, that I carried and read so long that at last I had committed to memory its whole contents (though they had once seemed inexhaustible) there is this passage: *"Behold, I have dreamed a dream more; the sun and the moon and eleven stars made obeisance to me."* Its words show plainly how much wiser the peoples of ages long past were than we are now; not for nothing is that book titled *The Book of the Wonders of Urth and Sky.*

267

I too dreamed a dream. I dreamed that I called the power of my star down upon myself, and rising, crossed (Thecla as well as Severian) to our barred door, and grasping its bars, bent them until we could easily have passed between them. But when we bent them it seemed we parted a curtain, and beyond it beheld a second curtain and Tzadkiel, neither larger than ourselves nor smaller, with the dirk afire.

When the new day like a flood of tarnished gold poured at last through the open port and I waited for my bowl and spoon, I examined those bars; and though most were as they ought to have been, those at the center were not quite so straight as the rest.

The boy carried in my food, saying, "Even if I only heard you once, I learned a lot from you, Severian. I'll be sorry to see you go."

I asked whether I was to be executed.

As he set down my tray, he glanced over his shoulder at the journeyman guard leaning against the wall. "No, it's not that. They're just going to take you somewhere else. A flier's coming for you today, with Praetorians."

"A flier?"

"Because it can fly over the rebel army, I suppose. Have you ever ridden in one? I've only watched them taking off and landing. It must be terrific."

"It is. The first time I flew in one, we were shot down. I've ridden in them often since, and even learned to operate them myself; but the truth is that I've always been terrified."

The boy nodded. "I would be too, but I'd like to try it." Awkwardly, he offered his hand. "Good luck, Severian, wherever they take you."

I clasped it; it was dirty but dry, and seemed very small. "Reechy," I said. "That's not your real name, is it?"

He grinned. "No. It means I stink."

"Not to my nose."

"It's not cold yet," he explained, "so I can go swimming.

In the winter I don't have much chance to wash, and they work me pretty hard."

"Yes, I remember. But your real name is . . ."

"Ymar." He withdrew his hand. "Why are you looking at me like that?"

"Because when I touched you, I saw the flash of gems about your head. Ymar, I think I'm beginning to spread out. To spread through time—or rather, to be aware that I am spread through time, since all of us are. How strange that you and I should meet like this."

I hesitated for a moment, my voice bewildered among so many swirling thoughts. "Or perhaps it isn't really strange at all. Something governs our destinies, surely. Something higher even than the Hierogrammates."

"What are you talking about?"

"Ymar, someday you will become the ruler. You'll be the monarch, although I don't think you'll call yourself that. Try to rule for Urth, and not just in Urth's name as so many have. Rule justly, or at least as justly as circumstances permit."

He said, "You're teasing me, aren't you?"

"No," I told him. "Even though I know no more than that you will rule, and someday sit disguised beneath a plane tree. But those things I *do* know."

When he and the journeyman were gone, I thrust the knife into the top of my boot and covered it with my trouser leg. As I did, and afterward while I sat waiting on my cot, I speculated upon our conversation.

Was it not possible Ymar had reached the Phoenix Throne only because some epopt—myself—had prophesied he would? So far as I am aware, history holds no record of it; and perhaps I have created my own truth. Or perhaps Ymar, now feeling he rides his destiny, will fail to make the cardinal effort that would have won him a signal victory.

Who can say? Does not Tzadkiel's curtain of uncertainty veil the future even from those who have emerged from its mists? The present, when we leave it before us, becomes the future once more. I had left it, I knew, and waited deep in a past that was in my own day scarcely more than myth.

Watch followed weary watch, as ants creep through autumn to winter. When at last I had concluded beyond question that Ymar's information had been mistaken, that the Praetorians would come not that day but the next—or not at all—I glanced out the port hoping to amuse myself with the errands of those few persons who chanced to cross the Old Yard.

A flier rode at anchor there, as sleek as a silver dart. I had no sooner seen it than I heard the measured tread of marching men—broken as they mounted the stair, resumed when they reached the level at which I waited. I rushed to the door.

A bustling journeyman led the way. A bemedaled chiliarch sauntered after him; thrust well into his sword belt, his thumbs proclaimed him not a subordinate, but one infinitely superior. Behind them, in a single file maintained with the disciplined precision of hand-colored troops commanded by a child (though they were less visible than smoke), tramped a squad of guardsmen in the charge of a vingtner.

As I watched, the journeyman waved in the direction of my cell with his keys, the chiliarch nodded tolerantly and strolled nearer to inspect me, the vingtner bellowed some order, and the boots of the squad halted with a crash, succeeded at once by a second bellow and a second crash, as the ten phantom guardsmen grounded their weapons.

The flier differed scarcely at all from the one in which I had once inspected the armies of the Third Battle of Orithyia; and indeed it may have been the same device, such machines being maintained by generation after generation. The vingtner ordered me to lie on the floor. I obeyed, but asked the chiliarch (a hatchet-faced man of forty or so) whether I might not look over the side as we flew. This permission was refused, he doubtless fearing I was a spy—as in some sense I was; I had to content myself with imagining Ymar's farewell wave.

The eleven guardsmen who lined the seat astern, fading like so many ghosts into its pointillé upholstery, owed their near invisibility to the catoptric armor of my own Praetorians; and I soon realized they were my own Praetorians in fact, their armor, and what was more important, their traditions having been handed down from this unimaginably early day to my own. My guards had become my guards: my jailers.

Because our flier hurtled through the sky and I sometimes glimpsed streaking clouds, I expected our journey to be short; but a watch at least elapsed, and perhaps another, before I felt the flier drop and saw the landing line cast. Dismal walls of living rock rose upon our left, reeled, and were lost to sight.

When our pilot retracted the dome, the wind that lashed my face was so chill that I supposed we had flown south to the ice-fields. I stepped out—and looked up to see instead a towering ruin of snow and blasted stone. All around us ragged, faceless peaks loomed through pent clouds. We were among mountains, but mountains that had not yet put on the carven likenesses of men and women—such unshaped mountains, then, as are to be seen in the oldest pictures. I would have stood staring at them until dusk, but a cuff on the ear knocked me sprawling.

I rose consumed with impotent rage; I had suffered such abuse after I had been taken at Saltus and had succeeded in making that officer my friend. Now I felt I had accomplished nothing, that the cycle had begun again, that it was fated to persist, and perhaps to continue to my death. I resolved it would not. Before the day was over, the knife thrust into the top of my boot would end a life.

Meanwhile my own streamed from my clangorous ear, hot as though from the kettle where it drenched my chilled flesh.

I was driven into a stream far greater, of vast, hurrying wains burdened with yet more shattered rock, wains that rolled forward without oxen or slaves to draw them, no

matter how steep the gradient, launching dense clouds of
dust and smoke into the shining air and bellowing like
bulls when we crossed their path. Far up the mountain, a
giant in armor dug stone with his iron hands, looking
smaller than a mouse.

The hurrying wains gave way to hurrying men as we
went among plain and even ugly sheds whose open doorways revealed curious tools and machines. I asked the
chiliarch I intended to kill where he had brought me. He
motioned to the vingtner, and I got another blow from the
vingtner's gauntlet.

In a round structure larger than the rest, I was driven
down aisles lined with cabinets and seats until we reached
a circular curtain, like the wall of an indoor tent or
pavilion, at its center. I had recognized the building by
then.

"You are to wait here," the chiliarch instructed me.
"The monarch will speak to you. When you leave, you
will—"

A voice from the other side of the curtain, thick with
wine and yet familiar still, called, *"Loose him."*

"Obedience and obeisance!" The chiliarch jerked erect,
and he and his guardsmen saluted. For a moment all of us
stood like so many images.

When that voice was not heard again, the vingtner freed
my hands. The chiliarch whispered, "When you leave this
place you will say nothing of what you may have heard or
seen. Otherwise you will die."

"You are mistaken," I told him. "It is you that will die."

There was sudden fear in his eyes. I had been reasonably
sure he would not dare signal the vingtner to strike me
there, under the unseen gaze of his monarch. Nor was I
wrong; for the space of a heartbeat we stared at each other,
slayer and slain by both accounts.

The vingtner barked a command, and his squad turned
their backs to the curtain. When the chiliarch had assured
himself that none of the guardsmen would be able to see
what lay beyond the curtain when it parted, he told me,
"Go through."

I nodded and advanced to it; it was of crimson triple silk, luxurious to the touch. As I pushed it aside, I saw the faces I had expected. Seeing them, I bowed to their owner.

CHAPTER XXXIX

The Claw of the Conciliator Again

THE TWO-HEADED MAN LOUNGING UPON THE DIVAN BEYOND the crimson curtain raised his cup to acknowledge my bow. "I see you know to whom you come." It was the head on the left that spoke.

"You're Typhon," I said. "The monarch—the sole ruler, or so you think—of this ill-starred world, and of others as well. But it wasn't to you I bowed, but to my benefactor, Piaton."

With a mighty arm that was not his, Typhon brought the cup to his lips. His stare across its golden rim was the poisoned regard of the yellowbeard. "You have known Piaton in the past?"

I shook my head. "I'll know him in the future."

Typhon drank and set his cup upon a small table. "What is said of you is true, then. You maintain that you are a prophet."

"I hadn't thought of myself in that way. But yes, if you like. I know that you'll die on that couch. Does that interest you? That body will lie among the straps you no longer need to restrain Piaton and the implements you no longer need to force him to eat. The mountain winds will dry his stolen body until it is like the leaves that now die too young, and whole ages of the world will stride across it before my coming reawakens you to life."

Typhon laughed, just as I had heard him laugh when I bared *Terminus Est.* "You're a poor prophet, I fear; but I find that a poor prophet is more amusing than a true one.

If you had merely told me that I would lie—should my death ever occur, which I've begun to doubt—among the funeral breads in the skull cavity of this monument, you would only have told me what any child could. I prefer your fantasies, and it may be that I can make use of you. You're reported to have performed amazing cures. Have you true power?"

"That's for you to say."

He sat up, the muscular torso that was not his swaying. "I am accustomed to having my questions answered. A call from me, and a hundred men of my own division would be here to cast you"—he paused and smiled to himself —"from my sleeve. Would you enjoy it? That's how we treat workmen who won't work. Answer me, Conciliator! Can you fly?"

"I can't say, having never tried."

"You may have an opportunity soon. I will ask twice." He laughed again. "It suits my present condition, after all. But not thrice. Do you have power? Prove it, or die."

I allowed my shoulders to rise a finger's width, and fall again. My hands were still numb from the gyves; I rubbed my wrists as I spoke. "Would you allow that I have power if I could kill a certain man who had injured me just by striking this table before us?"

The unfortunate Piaton stared at me, and Typhon smiled. "Yes, that would be a satisfactory demonstration."

"Upon your word?"

The smile grew broader. "If you like," he said. "Prove it!"

I drew the dirk and drove it into the tabletop.

I doubt that there were provisions for the confinement of prisoners on the mountain; and as I considered those made for me, it occurred to me that my cell in the vessel that would soon be our Matachin Tower must have been a makeshift as well, and a shift made not very long ago. If Typhon had merely wished to confine me, he might easily have done it by emptying one of the solidly built sheds and locking me inside. It was clear he wished to do more—to terrify and suborn me, and thus win me to his cause.

My prison was a spur of rock not yet cut from the robe of the giant figure that already bore his face. A little shelter of stones and canvas was set up for me on that windswept spot, and to it were brought meat and a rare wine that must have been stored for Typhon himself. As I watched, a timber nearly as thick as the *Alcyone*'s mizzenmast, though not so high, was set into the rock where the spur left the mountain, and a smilodon chained to its base. The chiliarch hung from the top of this timber on a hook passed between his hands, which were manacled as my own had been.

For as long as the light lasted I watched them, though I soon realized that a battle raged at the foot of the mountain. The smilodon appeared to have been starved. From time to time it sprang up and sought to grasp the chiliarch's legs. Always he lifted them so it fell a cubit short; and its great claws, though they grooved the wood like chisels, would not support it. In that one afternoon I had as much vengeance as I wish ever to have. When night came I carried food to the smilodon.

Once on my journey to Thrax with Dorcas and Jolenta, I had freed a beast bound much as the chiliarch was now; it had not attacked me, perhaps because I bore the gem called the Claw of the Conciliator, perhaps only because it had been too weak to do so. Now this smilodon ate from my hands and licked them with its broad, rough tongue. I touched its curving tusks, like the ivory of the mammoths; and I scratched its ears as I would have Triskele's, saying, "We have borne swords. We know, do we not?"

I do not believe the beasts can comprehend more than the simplest and most familiar phrases, yet I felt the massive head nod.

The chain was fastened to a collar with two buckles as wide as my hand. I loosed it and set the poor creature free, but it remained at my side.

The chiliarch was not so readily released. I was able to climb the timber easily enough, locking my knees around it as I once had locked them around the pines in the necropolis as a boy. By then the horizon had dropped far below my star, and I could easily have lifted him free from his hook and flung him into the gulf below; but I dared not drop him for fear he would fall into it, or that the smilodon would attack him. Although the light was too faint for me to see it, its eyes gleamed as it stared up at us.

In the end I looped his hands about my neck and clambered down as well as I could, nearly slipping and half choking, but reaching the safety of the rock at last. When I carried him to the shelter, the smilodon followed and lay at our feet.

By morning, when seven guardsmen arrived with food, water, and wine for me and torches lashed to poles with which to drive back the smilodon, their chiliarch was fully conscious and had eaten and drunk. The consternation on the soldiers' faces when they saw that he and the smilodon were gone entertained us; but it was nothing compared to their expressions when they discovered both in my shelter.

"Come ahead," I told them. "The beast won't harm you, and your chiliarch will discipline you only if you have been false to your duty, I feel sure."

They advanced, though hesitantly, eyeing me with almost as much fear as the smilodon.

I said, "You saw what your monarch did to your chiliarch because he permitted me to retain a weapon. What will he do to you when he learns you've permitted your chiliarch to escape?"

The vingtner answered, "We'll all die, sieur. There'll be a couple more stakes, and three or four of us hung from each." The smilodon snarled as he spoke, and all seven stepped back.

The chiliarch nodded. "He's right. I'd order it myself, if I retained my office."

I said, "Sometimes a man is broken by losing such an office."

"Nothing's ever broken me," he replied. "This won't, either."

I think that was the first time I looked at him as a human being. His face was hard and cold, but full of intelligence and resolution. "You're right," I told him. "Sometimes indeed—but not this time. You must flee and take these men with you. I put them under your orders."

He nodded again. "Can you release my hands, Conciliator?"

The vingtner said, "I can, sieur." He stepped forward with the key, and the smilodon voiced no protest. When the manacles fell to the rock upon which we sat, the chiliarch picked them up and tossed them over the edge.

"Keep your hands clasped behind you," I told him. "Cover them with your cape. Have these men march you to the flier. Everyone will think you're being taken elsewhere for further punishment. You'll know where you can land with safety better than I."

"We'll join the rebels. They should be glad to get us." He rose and saluted, and I rose too and returned his salute, having been habituated to it during my time as Autarch.

The vingtner asked, "Conciliator, can't you free Urth from Typhon?"

"I could, but I won't unless I must. It's easy—very easy—to slay a ruler. But it's very difficult to prevent a worse one from coming to his place."

"Rule us yourself!"

I shook my head. "If I say I have a mission of greater importance, you'll think I'm joking. Yet it's the truth."

They nodded, clearly without comprehension.

"I'll tell you this. This morning I've been studying this mountain and the speed with which the work here is going forward. From those things, I know Typhon has only a short time to live. He'll die on the red couch where he lies now; and without his word, no one will dare to draw aside the curtain. One after another will creep away. The machines that dig like men will return for fresh instructions, but they won't receive them, and in time the curtain itself will fall to dust."

They were staring at me openmouthed. I said, "There will never be another ruler like Typhon—a monarch over many worlds. But the lesser ones who will follow him, of whom the best and greatest will be named Ymar, will imitate him until every peak you see around us wears a crown. That's all I'll tell you now, and all I *can* tell you. You must go."

The chiliarch said, "We'll stay here and die with you, Conciliator, if you desire it."

"I don't," I told them. "And I won't die." I tried to reveal the workings of Time to them, though I do not understand them myself. "Everyone who has lived is still alive, somewhen. But you are in great danger. Go!"

The guardsmen backed away. Their chiliarch said, "Won't you give us some token, Conciliator, some proof that we once encountered you? I know my hands are profaned with your blood, and so are Gaudentius's; but these men never harmed you."

The word he had used suggested the token he received. I took off the thong and the little sack of manskin Dorcas had sewn for the Claw, which now held the thorn I had plucked from my arm beside unresting Ocean, the thorn upon which my fingers had closed aboard Tzadkiel's ship. "This has been drenched in my blood," I told them.

With one hand on the smilodon's head, I watched them walk the promontory that held my shelter, their shadows still long in the morning light. When they reached the mass of rock that was fast becoming Typhon's sleeve, the chiliarch concealed his wrists under his cape as I had suggested. The vingtner drew his pistol, and two soldiers aimed their weapons at the chiliarch's back.

Thus disposed, prisoner and guard, they descended the stair on the farther side and were lost to me in the bustling roadways of that place I had not yet named the Accursed Town. I had sent them away lightly enough; but now that they were gone, I knew once more what it was to lose a friend—for the chiliarch too had become my friend—and my heart, though it may be (as some have said) as hard as metal, felt ready to crack at last.

"And now I must lose you too," I told the smilodon. "In fact, I should have sent you away while it was still dark."

It made a deep rumbling that must have been its purr, surely a sound seldom heard by man and woman. That thunderous purr was echoed faintly from the sky.

Far across the lap of the colossal statue, a flier lifted into the air, rising slowly at first (as those vessels always do when they rely upon the repulsion of Urth alone), then streaking away. I recalled the flier I had seen when I had parted from Vodalus, after the occurrence I placed at the very beginning of the manuscript I cast into the ever-changing universes. And I resolved then that if ever leisure should come to me again, I would pen a new account, beginning as I have with the casting away of the old.

Whence comes this unslakable thirst to leave behind me a wandering trail of ink, I cannot say; but once I referred to a certain incident in the life of Ymar. Now I have spoken with Ymar himself, yet that incident remains as inexplicable as the desire. I would prefer that similar incidents in my own life not suffer a similar obscurity.

The thunder that had been so distant sounded again, nearer now, the voice of a column of night-black cloud that outreached even the arm of Typhon's colossal figure. The Praetorians had laid down the food and drink they had brought at some distance from my little shelter. (Such service is the price of undying loyalty; those who profess it seldom labor quite so diligently as a common servant whose loyalty is to his task.) I went out, the smilodon with me, to carry it back to whatever protection we could give it. The wind had already begun her storm song, and a few raindrops splattered the rock before us, as big as plums and icy cold.

"This is as good a chance as you'll ever have," I told the smilodon. "They're running for shelter already. Go now!"

It leaped away as though it had been awaiting my consent, clearing ten cubits at every bound. In a moment it had vanished over the edge of the arm. In a moment more it reappeared, a tawny streak darkening to rain-wet brown from which workers and soldiers fled like coneys. I was glad to see that, for all the weapons of beasts, no matter how terrible they seem, are merely toys compared to the weapons of men.

Whether it returned safely to its hunting grounds, I am

unable to say, though I trust it did. As for myself, I sat under my shelter for a time listening to the storm and munching bread and fruit, until at last the wild wind snatched the canvas from over my head.

I rose; when I looked through the curtains of the downpour, I saw a party of soldiers cresting the arm.

Astonishingly I also saw places without rain or soldiers. I do not mean that these newly seen places now spread themselves where the abyss had stretched. Its aching emptiness remained, rock dropping a league at least like a cataract, with the dark green of the high jungle far below —the jungle that would hold the village of sorcerers through which the boy Severian and I would pass.

Rather it seemed to me that the familiar directions of up and down, forward and back, left and right, had opened like a blossom, revealing petals unguessed, new Sefiroth whose existence had been hidden from me until now.

One of the soldiers fired. The bolt struck the rock at my feet, splitting it like a chisel. Then I knew they had been sent to kill me, I suppose because one of the men who had gone with the chiliarch had rebelled against his fate and reported what had transpired, though too late to prevent the departure of the rest.

Another leveled his weapon. To escape it, I stepped from the rain-swept rock into a new place.

CHAPTER XL

The Brook Beyond Briah

I STOOD IN FLOWER-SPANGLED GRASS, SWEET-SMELLING AND softer than any other I have known; overhead the sky was azure, racked with clouds that hid the sun and barred the upper air with indigo and gold. Faintly, very faintly, I could still hear the roar of the storm that swept across Mount Typhon. Once there came a flash—or rather the shadow of a flash, if such a thing can be imagined—as if lightning had struck the rock, or one of the Praetorians had fired again.

When I had taken two steps, these things were no longer to be discerned; yet it seemed not so much that they were gone as that I had lost the ability (or perhaps only the will) to detect them, as when grown we no longer see things that interested us as children. Surely, I thought, this cannot be what the green man called the Corridors of Time. There are no corridors here, but only hills and waving grass and a sweet wind.

As I went farther, it seemed to me that everything I saw was familiar, that I walked in a place where I had been before, though I could not recall what it was. Not our necropolis with its mausoleums and cypresses. Not the unfenced fields where I had once walked with Dorcas and so come upon Dr. Talos's stage—those fields had cowered beneath the Wall of Nessus, and there were no walls here. Not the gardens of the House Absolute, full of rhododendrons, grottos, and fountains. Closest, I thought, to the pampas in spring, but for the color of the sky.

Then I heard the song of rushing water, and a moment later I saw its silver gleam. I ran to it, remembering as I ran how once I had been lame, and how I had drunk from a certain stream in Orithyia, then seen the pug marks of a smilodon; I smiled to myself between draughts to think that they would not frighten me now.

When I lifted my head, it was not a smilodon I saw, but a minute woman with brightly colored wings who was wading upon the water-washed stones some distance upstream as though to cool her legs. *"Tzadkiel!"* I shouted. Then I fell mute with confusion, having recalled the place at last.

She waved and smiled; and, most astonishingly, leaped from the water and flew, her gay wings rippling like dyed faille.

I knelt.

Still smiling, she dropped to the bank beside me. "I don't think you've seen me do that before."

"Once I saw you—a vision of you—hanging with wide wings in the vacancy between the stars."

"Yes, I can fly there because there's no attraction. Here I must be quite small. Do you know what a gravity field is?"

She waved an arm no longer than my hand at the meadow, and I said, "I see this one, mighty Hierogrammate."

She laughed at that, a music like the tintinnabulation of tiny bells. "But it seems we have met?"

"Mighty Hierogrammate, I am the least of your slaves."

"You must be uncomfortable there on your knees, and you've met another self of mine since I parted from her. Sit down and tell me about it."

And so I did. And it was pleasant indeed to sit upon that bank, occasionally refreshing my laboring tongue with the cold, clean water of the brook, and recount to Tzadkiel how I had seen her first between the pages of Father Inire's book, and how I had helped to capture her aboard her own ship, and how she had been male and called herself Zak, and how she had cared for me when I was injured. But you, who are my reader, know all these things (if indeed you exist), because I have written them here, omitting nothing, or at least very little.

When I spoke to Tzadkiel beside the brook, I strove to be as brief as I could; but she would not allow it, urging me down this byway and that one until I had told her of the small angel (of whom I had read in my brown book) who had met Gabriel, and of my childhoods in the Citadel, at my father's villa, and in the village called Famulorum near the House Absolute.

And at last, when I had paused for breath for perhaps the thousandth time, Tzadkiel said, "No wonder I accepted you; in all those words there was not one lie."

"I've told lies when I thought there was need of them, and even when there was none."

She smiled and made no answer.

I said, "And I'd lie to you now, mighty Hierogrammate, if I thought my lies would save Urth."

"You've saved her already; you began aboard my ship and you completed your task in our sphere, upon and within the world you call Yesod too. It must have appeared to Agilus and Typhon, and to many of the others who struggled against you, that the fight was an unequal one. If they had been wise, they would have known the fight was over already, some where and some time; but if they had been wise, they would have known you for our servant and not fought against you at all."

"Then I cannot fail?"

"No, you *have* not failed. You could have on the ship and later; but you couldn't die before the test, nor can you now, until your task is accomplished. If it weren't so, the beating would have killed you, and the weapon in the tower, and much else. But your task will be accomplished soon. Your power is from your star, as you know. When it enters your old sun and brings the birth of the new . . ."

I said, "I've boasted too often of not fearing death to tremble at the thought today."

She nodded. "That's well. Briah's no enduring house."

"But this place is Briah, or part of it. It's a passage in

your ship, the one you showed me when you led me to my
stateroom."

"If that is so, you were near Yesod when you were with
me on our ship. This is the Brook Madregot, and it runs
from Yesod to Briah."

"Between the universes?" I asked. "How can that be?"

"How could it not be? Energy gropes for some lower
state, always; which is merely to say that the Increate tosses
all the universes between his hands."

"But it's a stream," I protested. "Like the streams of
Urth."

Tzadkiel nodded. "Those too are of energy seeking a
lower state, and what is perceived is dictated by the
instrument. If you had other eyes, or another mind, you
would see all things otherwise."

I thought about that for a time, and at last I said, "And
how would I see you, Tzadkiel?"

She had been sitting upon the bank beside me; now she
lay down in the grass, her chin in her hands and her bright
wings rising above her back like fans with painted eyes.
"You called these fields of gravity, and so they are, among
other things. Do you know the fields of Urth, Severian?"

"I've never followed the plow, but I know them as well
as a city man can."

"Just so. And what is found at the edges of your fields?"

"Fences of split wood or hedges, to keep out cattle. In the
mountains, walls of dry-laid stones to discourage deer."

"And nothing else?"

"I can think of nothing," I said. "Though perhaps I saw
our fields with the wrong instrument."

"The instruments you have are the right instruments for
you, because you've been shaped by them. That's another
law. Nothing else?"

I recalled the hedgerows, and a sparrow's nest I had once
seen in one. "Weeds and wild things."

"Here too. I myself am such a wild thing, Severian. You
may think I've been stationed here to help you. I only wish
it were so, and because I do I'll help you if I can; but I'm a
part of myself that was banished long ago, long before the

first time you met me. Perhaps someday the giantess you call Tzadkiel—although that's my name too—will want me to be a part of her again. Until then I will remain here, between the attractions of Yesod and Briah.

"To answer what you asked, if you had some other instrument, you might see me as she does; then you could tell me why I've been exiled. But until you can see such things, I know no more than you. Do you wish, now, to return to your world of Urth?"

"I do," I replied. "But not to the time I left. As I told you, when I got back to Urth I thought it must freeze before the New Sun came; no matter how fast I drew my star to me, it was so distant that whole ages of the world would pass before it reached us. Then I realized I was in no age I knew, and I thought I'd have to wait in weariness. Now I see—"

"Your whole face brightens when you talk of it," the small Tzadkiel interrupted me. "I understand how they knew you for a miracle. You will bring the New Sun before you sleep."

"If I can, yes."

"And you want my help." She paused to stare at me with as serious a face as ever I was to see her wear. "I've many times been called a liar, Severian, but I would help you if I could."

"Yet you cannot?"

"I can tell you this: Madregot flows from the glory of Yesod"—she pointed upstream—"to the destruction of Briah, down that way." She pointed again. "Follow the water, and you'll be at a time nearer the coming of your star."

"If I'm not there to guide—but I'm the star too. Or at least I was. I can't . . . it's as if that part of myself is numb."

"You're not in Briah now, remember? You'll know your New Sun again when you return there—if he still exists."

"He must!" I said. "He—I—will need me, need my eyes and ears to tell him what passes on Urth."

"Then it would be best," the small Tzadkiel remarked,

"not to go too far downstream. A few steps, perhaps."

"When I came here, I wasn't in sight of it. I may not have walked straight toward it."

Her little shoulders moved up and down, carrying her tiny, perfect breasts with them. "Then there's no telling, is there? So this is as good a place as any."

I stood, recalling the brook as I had first seen it. "It went straight across my path," I told her. "No, I think I'll take a few steps with the water, as you suggested."

She rose too, leaping into the air. "No one can say just how far a step will take him."

"Once I heard a fable about a cock," I said. "The man who told it said it was only a foolish tale for children, but there was some wisdom in it, I think. Seven, it said, was a fortunate number. Eight carried the little cock too far." I took seven strides.

"Do you see anything?" the small Tzadkiel asked.

"Only you, the brook, and the grass."

"Then you must walk away from it. Don't jump across it, though, or you'll end in another place. Go slowly."

I turned my back to the water and took a step.

"What do you see now? Look down the stems of the grass to the roots."

"Darkness."

"Then take another step."

"Fire—a sea of sparks."

"Another!" She fluttered beside me like a painted kite.

"Only stems, as of common grass."

"Good! A half step now."

I edged forward cautiously. During the whole time we had talked in that meadow, we had been in shadow; now it seemed some blacker cloud obscured the face of the sun, so that a band of darkness stood before me, no wider than my outspread arms, yet deep.

"What now?"

"Twilight before me," I said. And then, though I sensed rather than saw it, "A shadowy door. Must I go through?"

"That's for you to decide."

I leaned closer, and it seemed to me that the meadow

was strangely tilted, just as I had seen it from my shelter on the mountain. Though it was only three steps behind me, the music of the Madregot sounded far away.

Dim letters floated in the darkness; it was a moment before I realized they were reversed and that the largest spelled my name.

I stepped into the shadow, and the meadow vanished; I was lost in night. My groping hands felt stone. I pushed at it, and it moved—reluctantly at first, then smoothly, yet with the resistance of great weight.

As though at my ear, I heard the crystal chiming of the small Tzadkiel's laughter.

CHAPTER XLI

Severian from His Cenotaph

A COCK CROWED; AND AS THE STONE SWUNG BACK, I SAW the starry sky and the single bright star (blue now with its velocity) that was myself. I was whole once more. And near! Fair Skuld, rising with the dawn, was not so brilliant and did not show so broad a disk.

For a long time—or at least, for a time that seemed long to me—I studied my other self, still far beyond the circle of Dis. Once or twice I heard the murmur of voices, but I did not trouble to see whose they were; and when at last I looked around me, I was alone.

Or nearly so. An antlered buck watched me from the crest of a little hill to my right, his eyes faintly gleaming, his body lost in the deeper dark beneath the trees that crowned the hill. On my left, a statue stared with sightless eyes. A last cricket chirped, but the grass was jeweled with frost.

As I had in the meadow about Madregot, I had the feeling of being in a familiar place without being able to identify it. I was standing upon stone, and the door I had pushed back was of stone also. Three narrow steps led to a clipped lawn. I went down them, and the door swung silently behind me, changing its nature, or so it seemed, as it moved; so that when it had shut it appeared no door at all.

I stood in the slightest of dells, a thousand paces or more from lip to lip, set among gentle hills. There were doors in these, some no wider than those of private rooms, some greater than the stone doorway in the obelisk behind me. The doors and the flagged paths that led from them told me I stood upon the grounds of the House Absolute. The long shadow of the obelisk was not born of the plenilune moon, but of the first crescent of the sun, and that shadow pointed to me like an arrow. I was in the west—in a watch or less the horizon would rise to conceal me.

For a moment I regretted that I had given the Claw to the chiliarch; I wanted to read the inscription on the stone door. Then I remembered how I had examined Declan in the darkness of his hut, and I stepped nearer it and used my eyes.

To the Honor of
SEVERIAN THE GREAT
Autarch of Our Commonwealth
by Right the First Man of Urth
Memorabilus

It was a lofty shaft of blue chalcedony, and something of a shock. I was thought dead, so much was clear; and this pleasant vale had been appointed my proxy resting place. I would have preferred the necropolis beside the Citadel —the place where I must indeed repose at last, or at least be thought to—or the stone town, to which the first remark would apply with greater force.

That led me to wonder just where on the grounds I was, as well as to speculate on whether Father Inire or some other had been the erector of my monument. I shut my eyes, allowing my memory to rove at will, and to my astonishment found the little stage that Dorcas, Baldanders, and I had cobbled together for Dr. Talos. Here was the very spot, and my absurd memorial stood where at another time I had feigned to think the giant Nod a statue. Recalling the moment, I glanced at the one I had seen upon stepping back into Briah, and found it was, just as I had supposed, one of those harmless half-living creatures. It was moving slowly toward me now, its lips curved in an archaic smile.

For a breath I admired the play of my own light on its pale limbs, but it seemed to me it had been only two watches or three since daylight had come to the slopes of Mount Typhon, and the vitality I felt now put me in no mood to contemplate statues or seek rest in one of the secluded arbors scattered throughout the gardens. A hidden archway not far from where the buck had stood gave access to the Secret House. I ran to it, murmured the word that mastered it, and went in.

How strange and yet how good it was to thread those narrow passages once more! Their suffocating constriction and padded, ladderlike steps summoned up a thousand memories of gambades and trysts: coursing the white wolves, scourging the prisoners of the antechamber, reencountering Oringa.

Had it been true, as Father Inire had originally intended, that these tortuous passageways and cramped chambers were known only to himself and the reigning Autarch, they would have been fully as dull as any dungeon and, if anything, less pleasant. But the Autarchs had revealed them to their paramours, and those paramours to their own gallants, so that they soon held at least a round dozen intrigues on any fine spring evening, and perhaps at times a hundred. The provincial administrator who brought to the House Absolute certain dreams of adventure or romance seldom realized that they stole past on slippered feet within an ell of his sleeping head. Entertaining myself with such reflections as these, I had walked perhaps half a league (halting from time to time to spy out both public halls and private apartments through the oillets the place provided) when I stumbled over the body of an assassin.

He lay, as he had surely lain for a year at least, upon his back; the sere flesh of his face had begun to fall away from his skull, so that he grinned as though at discovering death was but a jest in the end. His outstretched hand had lost its grip upon the venom-daubed batardeau lying across its palm. As I bent to inspect it and him, I wondered whether he had contrived to nick himself; far stranger things have taken place within the Secret House. More probably, I decided, he had fallen victim to some defense of his intended victim's—waylaid, perhaps, when his mission was betrayed, or felled by some wound before he could reach safety. For a moment I considered taking his batardeau to replace the knife I had lost so many chiliads ago, but the thought of wielding a poisoned blade was repugnant.

A fly buzzed about my face.

I waved it away, then watched in amazement as it burrowed into the dry flesh, followed by a score of others.

I stepped back; before I could turn away, all the hideous stages of putrefaction presented themselves in order reversed, like urchins at an almshouse who thrust the youngest of their company to the front: the wrinkled flesh swelled and seethed with maggots, retreated to the lividity of death, and finally resumed the coloration and almost the appearance of life; the flaccid hand closed on the corroded steel hilt of the batardeau until it gripped it like a vise.

Recalling Zama, I was ready to run when the dead man sat up—or to wrest his weapon from him and kill him with it. Perhaps these impulses canceled each other; in the event I did neither, merely stood aside to watch him.

He rose slowly and stared at me with empty eyes. I said, "You had better put that away before you hurt someone." Such weapons are usually sheathed with the sword, but there was a scabbard for his at his belt, and he did as I suggested.

"You are confused," I told him. "It would be wise for you to stay here until you come to yourself. Don't follow me."

He made no reply, nor did I expect any. I slipped by him and walked away as quickly as I could. When I had gone fifty strides or so, I heard his faltering steps; I began to run, making as little noise as possible and dodging down this turning and that.

How far it was, I cannot say. My star was still ascendant, and it seemed to me I might have dashed around the whole circuit of Urth without tiring. I ran by many strange doors without opening any, knowing that all would lead from the

Secret House to the House Absolute by one means or another. At last I came to an aperture closed by no door; a strong draft from it carried the sound of a woman's weeping, and I halted and stepped through.

I found myself in a loggia, with arches on three sides. The woman's sobs seemed to come from my left; I went to one of the arches and peered out. It overlooked that wide and windy gallery we called the Path of Air—the loggia was one of those constructions that appear merely ornamental though they serve the needs of the Secret House.

Shadows on the marble floor far below me showed that the woman was ringed by half a dozen scarcely visible Praetorians, one of whom supported her by the elbow. At first I could not see her eyes, which were bent toward the floor and lost in her raven-dark hair.

Then (I cannot tell by what chance) she glanced up at me. Hers was a lovely face of that complexion called olive and as smoothly oval as an olive, too, with something in it that tore my heart; and though it was strange to me, I had the sensation of return once again. I felt that in some lost life I had stood just where I was standing then; and that in that life I had seen her beneath me in just that way.

She and the shadows of the Praetorians were soon almost out of sight. I shifted from one arch to the next to keep them in view; and she stared back at me, until she was looking over the shoulder of her pale gown when I last glimpsed her.

She was as lovely and as unknown at that final glimpse as at the first. Her beauty was reason enough for any man to stare at her, but why did she stare at me? If I had understood her expression at all, it had been one of mingled hope and fear, and perhaps she too had some sense of a drama being played upon a second occasion.

A hundred times I reviewed my scrapes and escapes in this Secret House, whether as Thecla alone, or as Severian and Thecla united, or as the old Autarch. I could not find the moment—yet it existed; and I began, as I walked on, to search those veiled lives that lie behind the last, memories that I have scarcely mentioned in this narrative, that dim as they grow stranger and stretch backward, perhaps, to Ymar, and behind Ymar to the Age of Myth.

Yet overwhelming all these shadowy lives—and incomparably more vivid, as a mountain may be seen to the very expression in its eyes when the forest about its base has sunk into a green haze—hurtled the white star that was myself. I was there also; and I saw before me, seemingly still very distant (though I knew it was much nearer than it appeared) the crimson sun that was to be, after so many centuries, simultaneously my destruction and my apotheosis. To its left and right, brave Skuld and sullen Verthandi seemed inconsequential moons. The night-dark dot of Urth crept across its face, nearly lost among its mottlings; and in the dying moments of that night I wandered, bewildered and wondering, underground.

CHAPTER XLII

Ding, Dong, Ding!

WHEN I HAD ENTERED THE SECRET HOUSE, I HAD SCARCELY known where I was bound. Or rather, I had scarcely been conscious of it; unconsciously, I had been directing my steps toward the Hypogeum Amaranthine, as I at length realized. I intended to learn who it was who sat the Phoenix Throne, and to reclaim it if I could. When the New Sun arrived, our Commonwealth would require a ruler who understood what had taken place; so I thought.

A certain door of the Secret House opened behind the velvet arras that hung behind the throne. I had sealed it with my word in the initial year of my reign; and I had hung the narrow space between the arras and the wall with bells, so that no one could walk there without making some sound that would be overheard by the occupant of the throne.

Now the door opened smoothly and silently at my command. I stepped out and closed it after me. The little bells, suspended upon silk threads, tinkled softly; above them larger bells, from whose tongues the threads hung, whispered with brazen voices and let fall a shower of dust.

I stood motionless, listening. At last the bells ceased their jingling, though not before I had heard the laughter of the small Tzadkiel in it.

"What is that ringing?" It was an old woman who spoke, her tones thin and cracked.

Another spoke in a man's deep voice. I could not make out his words.

"Bells!" the old woman exclaimed. "We heard bells. Are you grown so deaf, chiliarch, that you didn't hear them too?"

Now I wished indeed for the batardeau, with which I might have slit the arras and so peered out; as the deep voice spoke again, it struck me that others who had stood where I stood must have had the same thought, and sharp knives to boot. I searched the arras with my fingertips.

"They rang, we tell you. Send someone to inquire."

Perhaps there were many such rents, for I found one in a breath, made by some watcher only a trifle below my own height. Applying my eye to it, I saw that I stood three strides to the right of the throne. Only the hand of the occupant was visible to me where it lay upon the arm, as thin as that of an anatomy, a hand webbed with blue veins and spangled with gems.

Before the throne, head bent, crouched a form so vast that for a moment I thought it was that Tzadkiel who had commanded the ship. Its disordered hair was caked with blood.

Behind it stood a cluster of shadowy guardsmen, and beside it a helmetless officer whose insignia and virtually invisible armor marked him as the chiliarch of the Praetorians, though he was not, of course, the chiliarch who had held the post during my reign, nor the one whom I had carried down from the upright timber in an epoch now unimaginably distant.

Before the throne and thus almost out of my field of view, a ragged woman leaned upon a carven staff. She spoke just as I realized that she was there, saying, "They ring to welcome the New Sun, Autarch. The whole of Urth prepares for his coming."

"In our childhood," the old woman on the throne muttered, "we had little to do but read history. Thus we know that there have been a thousand prophets such as you, my poor sister—no, say a hundred thousand. A hundred thousand crazed paupers who fancied themselves great rhetors and sought to make themselves great rulers as well."

"Autarch," answered the ragged woman, "won't you hear me? You speak of thousands and hundreds of thousands. A thousand times at least I have heard objections such as you bring, but you have not yet heard what I will say."

"Go on," the woman on the throne told her. "You may speak as long as you amuse us."

"I haven't come to amuse you, but to tell you that the New Sun has come often before, seen perhaps by only a single person, or a few. You must recall the Claw of the Conciliator, for it vanished in our time."

"It was stolen," muttered the old woman who sat the throne. "We never saw it."

"But I did," the ragged woman with the staff said. "I saw it in the hands of an angel, when I was just a girl and very ill. Tonight as I was coming here I saw it again, in the sky. So did your soldiers, although they are afraid to tell you. So did this giant who has come as I have to warn you and has been savaged for it. So would you see it, Autarch, if you would quit this tomb."

"There have been such portents before. They have portended nothing. It would take more than the sight of a bearded star to change our mind."

I thought of stepping onto the stage then to end the play, if I could; and yet I remained where I was, wondering for whose entertainment such plays are staged. For it *was* a play, and in fact a play I had seen before, though never from the audience. It was Dr. Talos's play, with the old woman on the throne in a role the doctor had taken for himself, and the woman with the staff in one of the roles that had been mine.

I have just written that I chose not to step forth, and it is true. But in the very act of making my decision, I must have moved a trifle. The little bells laughed again, and the larger bell from whose tongue they depended struck once, though ever so softly.

"Bells!" the old woman exclaimed again. "You, sister, you witch or whatever you call yourself. Go out! There's a guard at our door. Tell their lochage we wish to know why the bells ring."

"I will not leave this place at your command," the woman said. "I have answered your question already."

The giant looked up at that, parting his lank hair with blood-smeared hands. "If bells ring, they're ringing because a New Sun is coming," he rumbled in a voice almost too deep to be understood. "I do not hear them, but I do not need to hear them." Though I doubted my eyes, it was Baldanders himself.

"Are you saying we are mad?"

"My hearing is not acute. Once I studied sound, and the more one learns of that, the less one hears it. Then too, my tympanic membranes have grown too wide and thick. But I have heard the currents that scour the black trenches and the crash of the waves upon your shore."

"Silence!" the old woman commanded.

"You can't order the waves to be silent, madame," Baldanders told her. "They are coming, and they are bitter with salt."

One of the Praetorians struck the side of his head with the butt of his fusil; it was like the blow of a mallet.

Baldanders seemed unaffected. "The armies of Erebus follow the waves," he said, "and all the defeats they suffered at your husband's hands will be avenged."

From those words I knew the identity of the Autarch, and the shock of seeing Baldanders once more was as nothing to that. I must have started, because the small bells rang loudly, and a larger one spoke twice.

"Listen!" Valeria exclaimed in her cracked voice.

The chiliarch looked stricken. "I heard them, Autarch."

Baldanders rumbled, "I can explain them. Will you hear also what I say?"

"And I," the woman with the staff told Valeria. "They ring for the New Sun, as the giant has already announced to you."

Valeria muttered, "Speak, giant."

"What I am about to say is not important. But I will say it in order that you will listen to what is important afterward. Our universe is neither the highest nor the lowest. Let matter become overdense here, and it bursts into the higher. We see nothing of that because everything runs from us. Then we talk of a black hole. When matter grows overdense in the universe below us, it explodes into ours. We see a burst of motion and energy, and we speak of a white fountain. What this prophetess calls the New Sun is such a fountain."

Valeria murmured, "We have a fountain in our garden that foretells, and I heard someone call it the White Fountain many years ago. But what has any of this to do with the bells?"

"Be patient," the giant told her. "You learn in a breath what I learned in a lifetime."

The woman with the staff said, "That's well. Only breaths remain to us. A thousand or so, it may be."

The giant glared at her before he spoke again to Valeria. "Things opposite unite and appear to disappear. The potential for both remains. That is one of the greatest principles of the causes of things. Our sun has such a black hole as I described to you at its core. To fill it, a white fountain has been drawn across the void for millennia. It spins as it flies, and in its motion emits waves of gravitation."

Valeria exclaimed, "What! Waves of dignity? You're mad, just as this chiliarch has told us."

The giant ignored her interruption. "These waves are too slight to render us giddy. Yet Ocean feels them and breeds new tides and fresh currents. I heard them, as I have already told you. They brought me here."

The chiliarch snarled, "And if the Autarch orders it, we'll toss you back."

"Bells feel them in the same way. Like Ocean, their mass is delicately poised. Thus they ring, just as this woman says, pealing the coming of the New Sun."

I was about to step out, but I saw that Baldanders was not yet finished.

"If you know anything of science, madame, you must know that water is but ice given energy."

I could not see her head from my vantage point, but Valeria must have nodded.

"The legend of the mountains of fire is more than a legend. In ages when men were only higher beasts, there were indeed such mountains. Their spew of fire was rock rendered incandescent by energy, as water is ice made fluid. A world below this, charged with too much energy, flared into our own—as with universes, so with worlds. In those ages, the young Urth was little more than a falling drop of that watery rock; men and women lived upon its floating scum and thought themselves secure."

I heard Valeria sigh. "When we were ourselves young, we nodded over such prosy stuff for endless days, having nothing better to do. But when our Autarch came for us and we woke to life, we found no agnation in all that we had studied."

"It has arrived at last, madame. The force that made your bells sound has warmed the cold heart of Urth once more. Now they toll the death of continents."

"Is that the news you have come to tell us, giant? If the continents die, who will live?"

"Those on ships, possibly. Those whose ships are in the air or in the void, certainly. Those who live under the sea already, as I have now for fifty years. But it matters nothing. What—"

Baldanders's solemn voice was interrupted by the banging of a door some distance down the Hypogeum Amaranthine and the tatoo of running feet. A junior officer sprinted up to the chiliarch, saluting while Baldanders and the woman with the staff turned to stare.

"Sieur . . ." The man faced his commander but could not keep his frightened eyes from wandering toward Valeria.

"What is it?"

"Sieur, another giant—"

"Another giant?" Valeria must have leaned forward at that. I saw a flash of gems and a wisp of gray hair beneath it.

"A woman, Autarch! A naked woman!"

Although I could not see her face, I knew Valeria must be addressing Baldanders when she asked, "And what can you tell us about this? Is it your wife, perhaps?"

He shook his head; and I, recalling the crimson chamber in his castle, speculated upon his living arrangements in thalassic caverns I could scarcely conceive.

"The lochage is bringing the giant woman for questioning," the young officer said.

His chiliarch added, "Do you wish to behold her, Autarch? If not, I can conduct the interrogation."

"We are tired. We will retire now. In the morning, tell us what you have learned."

"Sh-she s-says," the young officer stammered, "that certain cacogens have landed a man and a woman from one of their ships."

For a moment, I imagined it was to Burgundofara and myself that this referred; but Abaia and his undines were not likely to be in error by whole ages.

"And what else?" Valeria demanded.

"Nothing else, Autarch. Nothing!"

"It is in your eyes. If it is not soon upon your tongue, it will be buried with you."

"It's only a groundless rumor, Autarch. None of our men have reported anything."

"Out with it!"

The young officer looked stricken. "They say Severian the Lame has been seen again, Autarch. In the gardens, Autarch."

It was then or never. I lifted the arras and stepped from under it, as all the little bells laughed and above them a great bell pealed three times.

CHAPTER XLIII

The Evening Tide

"YOU ARE NO MORE SURPRISED TO SEE ME THAN I AM TO SEE you," I told them. And for three, at least, it was true.

Baldanders (whom I had never expected to see again when he had dived into the lake, and yet whom I *had* seen again looking just as I recalled him, when he fought for me before Tzadkiel's Seat of Justice) was grown too large for me to think him human ever again, his face heavier still and more misshapen, his skin as white as that of the water woman who had once saved me from drowning.

The girl whose brother had begged for a coin outside their jacal had become a woman of sixty or more, and the gray of age overlay the leanness and brownness of long roads. Earlier she had propped herself with her staff in a way that showed it was more than her badge of office; now she stood with shining eyes, as straight as a young willow.

Of Valeria I will not write—save to say that I should have known her instantly anywhere. Her eyes had not aged. They were still the bright eyes of the girl who had come to me wrapped in furs across the Atrium of Time; and Time had no power over them.

The chiliarch saluted and knelt to me as the castellan of the Citadel once had, and after a pause that grew embarrassingly long, his men and the young officer knelt too. I motioned for them to stand, and to give Valeria time to recover herself (for I feared for a moment that she might faint or worse), I asked the chiliarch whether he had been a junior officer when I sat the Phoenix Throne.

"No, Autarch. I was only a boy."

"Yet clearly you recall me."

"It's my duty to know the House Absolute, Autarch. There are pictures and busts of you in some parts of it."

"They . . ."

The voice was so weak I scarcely heard it. I turned to make sure it was indeed Valeria who spoke.

"They don't really look as you did. They look the way I thought—"

I waited, wondering.

She waved a hand. It was a weak old woman's gesture. "As I thought you might when you came back to me, back to our family tower in the Old Citadel. They look the way you do now." She laughed, and began to sob.

Following hers, the giant's words sounded like the rumbling of cart wheels. "You look as you always have," he said. "I do not remember many faces, Severian; but I remember yours."

"You're saying that we have a quarrel to settle. I would rather leave it unsettled and give you my hand."

Baldanders rose to take it, and I saw that he had grown to fully twice my height.

The chiliarch inquired, "Autarch, has he the freedom of the House Absolute now?"

"He does. He is indeed a creature of evil; but so are you, and so am I."

Baldanders rumbled, "I will do no evil to you, Severian. I never have. When I flung away your jewel, I did so because you believed in it. That did harm, or so I believed."

"And good, but that is all behind us. Let's forget those things if we can."

The prophetess said, "He has done harm too by saying here that you would bring destruction. I have told them the truth—that you would bring a rebirth, but they would not credit me."

I told her, "He has told the truth, as well as you. If the new is to be born, the old must be swept aside. One who plants wheat kills grass. You are both prophets, although of different kinds; and each of you has prophesied as the Increate instructed you."

Then the great doors of lapis lazuli and silver at the most distant end of the Hypogeum Amaranthine—doors used in my reign only for solemn processions and the ceremonial presentations of extern ambassadors—were flung wide; and this time it was not a lone officer who burst into the hypogeum but two score troopers, each brandishing a fusil or a blazing spear. Their backs were turned even toward the Phoenix Throne.

For a moment they occupied my attention so completely that I forgot how many years had passed since Valeria had last seen me—for me the time had not been years, but fewer perhaps than a hundred days all told. And so from the side of my mouth in the old way I had often used when we stood together at some lengthy ritual, the stealthy way of talking that I had learned as a boy whispering behind Master Malrubius's back, I murmured, "This will be something worth seeing."

Hearing her gasp, I glanced at her and saw her tear-stained cheeks and all the damage time had wrought. We love most when we understand that the object of our love has nothing else; and I do not think I have ever loved Valeria more than I did then.

I put my hand upon her shoulder, and though that was not a time or place for intimate scenes, I have been glad since that I did, for there was time for nothing more. The giantess crawled through the doorway, her hand first, like some five-legged beast, then her arm. It was larger than the trunks of many trees that are counted as old, and as white as sea foam; but disfigured by a crusted burn that cracked and bled even as it appeared.

I heard the prophetess mumble some prayer that ended with mention of the Conciliator and the New Sun. It is strange to hear yourself prayed to; and stranger still to realize that the supplicant has forgotten you are present.

A gasp then, and not just from Valeria but from us all, I believe, save Baldanders. The undine's face appeared with her other hand, and although they did not in reality fill all that wide door, so large were they, and the mass of brilliant green hair, that they appeared to. I have sometimes heard it said in hyperbole that eyes are as big as platters. Of her eyes it was so; they wept tears of blood, and more blood trickled from her nostrils.

I knew she must have followed Gyoll from the sea, and from Gyoll traced its tributary, which wandered through the gardens where Jolenta and I had once floated upon it. I called to her, "How were you caught and driven from your element?"

Perhaps because she was a woman, her voice was not so deep as I anticipated, though it was deeper even than Baldander's. Yet there was a lilt to it, as though she who struggled to pass the doorway even as she spoke and was so clearly dying had yet some vast joy that owed nothing to her own life or the sun's. She said, "Because I would save you . . ."

With those words her mouth filled with blood; she spat it out, and it seemed some drain had opened from an abattoir.

I asked, "From the storms and fires that the New Sun will bring? We thank you, but we have been warned already. Are you not a creature of Abaia's?"

"Even so." She had dragged herself through the doorway to the waist. Now her flesh seemed so heavy it must be torn from her bones by its own weight; her breasts hung like the haycocks a child sees, who stands upon his head. I understood that it would never be possible to return her to her water—that she would die here in the Hypogeum Amaranthine, and a hundred men would be needed to dismember her corpse, and a hundred more to bury it.

The chiliarch demanded, "Then why shouldn't we kill you? You're an enemy of our Commonwealth."

"Because I came to warn you." She had allowed her head to sink to the terrazzo, where it lay at so unnatural an angle that her neck might have been broken; yet she still spoke.

"I can give you a more forcible reason, chiliarch," I said. "Because I forbid it. She saved me once when I was a boy, and I remember her face as I remember everything. I would save her now if I could." Looking at her face, a face of supernal beauty made hideous by its own weight, I asked, "Do you remember that?"

"No. It hasn't yet occurred. It will, because you spoke."

"What's your name? I've never known it."

"Juturna. I want to save you . . . not earlier. Save all of you."

Valeria hissed, "When has Abaia sought our good?"

"Always. He might have destroyed you . . ."

For the space of six breaths she could not continue, but I motioned Valeria and the rest to silence.

"Ask your husband. In a day, or a few days. He's tried to tame you instead. Catch Catodon . . . cast out his conation. What good? Abaia would make of us a great people."

I was reminded then of what Famulimus had asked me when I met her first: "Is all the world a war of good and bad? Have you not thought it might be something more?" And I felt myself upon the marches of a nobler world, where I should know what it might be. Master Malrubius had led me from the jungles of the north to Ocean speaking of hammer and anvil, and it seemed to me also that I sensed an anvil here. He had been an aquastor, like those who had fought for me in Yesod, created from my mind; thus he had believed, as I had, that the undine had saved me because I would be a torturer and an Autarch. It might be that neither he nor the undine were wholly wrong.

While I hesitated, lost among such thoughts, Valeria, the prophetess, and the chiliarch had whispered among themselves; but soon the undine spoke again. "Your day fades. A New Sun . . . and you are shadows."

"Yes!" The prophetess seemed ready to leap for joy. "We are the shadows cast by his coming. What more can we be?"

"Another comes," I said, for I thought I heard the patter of hurrying feet. Even the undine lifted her head to listen.

The sound, whatever it was, grew louder and louder still. A strange wind whistled down that long chamber, fluttering its antique hangings so that they strewed the floor with dust and pearls. Roaring like the thunder it flung back the double doors that had been propped open by the undine's waist, and it carried that perfume—wild and saline, as fetid and fecund as a woman's groin, that once met can never be forgotten; so that at that instant I would not have been surprised to hear the crash of surf or the mewing of gulls.

"It's the sea!" I called to the others. Then, as I tried to adjust my mind with what must surely have occurred, "Nessus must be under water."

Valeria gasped, "Nessus drowned two days ago."

As she spoke, I snatched her up; her frail body seemed lighter than a child's.

The waves came then, the uncountable white-maned destriers of Ocean, foaming across the undine's shoulders so that for a breath I saw her as though I saw two worlds together, at once a woman and a rock. She lifted her heavy head higher at their coming and cried out in triumph and despair. It was the wail a storm gives as it sweeps over the sea, and a cry I hope never to hear again.

The Praetorians were clattering up the steps of the dais to escape the water, the young officer who had seemed so frightened and feeble before taking Jader's sister (a prophetess no longer, for she had no more to prophesy) by the hand and drawing her up with him.

"I will not drown," Baldanders rumbled. "And the rest do not matter. Save yourself if you can."

I nodded without thinking and with my free arm jerked aside the arras. The Praetorians crowded forward, so that the bells that had pealed three times for me jangled madly and broke their cracked, dry straps, falling clangorously.

Not whispering but shouting, for the word would never be of use again, I commanded the sealed door through which I had come. It flew open, and through it came the assassin, mute still, half-unknowing, numbed by the memory of the ashen plains of death. I called to him to halt, but he had caught sight of the crown and Valeria's poor, ravaged face beneath it.

He must have been a swordsman of renown; no master-at-arms could have struck more quickly. I saw the flash of the poisoned blade, then felt the fiery pain of its thrust through my wife's poor, raddled body into my own, where it reopened the wound that Agilus's avern leaf had made so many years before.

CHAPTER XLIV

The Morning Tide

THERE WAS A SHIMMERING AZURE LIGHT. THE CLAW HAD returned—not the Claw destroyed by Ascian artillery, nor even the Claw I had given the chiliarch of Typhon's Praetorians, but the Claw of the Conciliator, the gem I had found in my sabretache as Dorcas and I walked down a dark road beside the Wall of Nessus. I tried to tell someone; but my mouth was sealed, and I could not find the word. Perhaps I was too distant from myself, from the Severian of bone and flesh borne by Catherine in a cell of the oubliette under the Matachin Tower. The Claw endured, shining and swaying against the dark void.

No, it was not the Claw that swayed but I, swaying gently, gently while the sun caressed my back.

The sunlight must have brought me to myself, as it would have raised me from my deathbed. The New Sun must come; and I was the New Sun. I lifted my head, opened my eyes, and spat a stream of crystal fluid like no water of Urth's; it seemed not water at all, but a richer atmosphere, corroborant as the winds of Yesod.

Then I laughed with joy to find myself in paradise, and in laughing felt that I had never laughed before, that all the joy I had ever known had been but a vague intuition of this, sickly and misguided. More than life, I had wished a New Sun for Urth; and Urth's New Sun was here, dancing about me like ten thousand sparkling spirits and tipping each wave with purest gold. Not even on Yesod had I seen such a sun! Its glory eclipsed every star and was like the eye

309

of the Increate, not to be looked upon lest the pyrolater go blind.

Turning from that glory, I cried out as the undine had, in triumph and despair. Around me floated the wrack of Urth: trees uprooted, loose shingles, broken beams, and the bloated corpses of beasts and men. Here spread what the sailors who had fought against me on Yesod must have seen; and I, seeing it now as they had, no longer hated them for drawing work-worn knives against the coming of the New Sun, but felt a fresh surprise that Gunnie had defended me. (Not for the first time, I wondered too if she had tipped the balance; had she fought against me, she would have fought me, and not the eidolons. Such was her nature; and if I had died, Urth would have perished with me.)

Far off I heard, or thought I heard, an answering cry over the murmur of the many-tongued waves. I started toward it but soon halted, hampered by my cloak and boots; I kicked off the boots (though they were good ones and nearly new) and let them sink. The junior officer's cloak soon followed, something I was later to regret. Swimming, running, and walking great distances have always made me conscious of my body, and it felt strong and well; the assassin's poisoned wound had healed like the poisoned wound Agilus had made.

Yet it was merely well and strong. The inhuman power that it had drawn from my star was gone, though it must surely have healed me while it remained. When I tried to reach the part of myself that had once been there, it was as though one who had lost a leg sought to move it.

The cry came again. I answered, and dissatisfied with my progress (as well as I could judge, each wave I breasted drove me back as far as I had swum forward), I took a deep breath and swam some distance underwater.

I opened my eyes almost at once, for it seemed to me that the water held no sting of salt; and as a boy I had swum with open eyes in the wide cistern beneath the Bell Keep, and even in the stagnant shallows of Gyoll. This water appeared as clear as air, though blue-green at its depths. Vaguely, as we may see a tree above us mirrored in some quiet pool, I beheld the bottom, where something white moved in so slow and errant a fashion that I could not be sure whether it swam or merely drifted. The very purity and warmth of the water alarmed me; I grew fearful that I might somehow forget it was not air in fact and lose myself as I had once been lost among the dark and twining roots of the pale blue nenuphars.

I breached then, shooting free of the waves by two cubits, and saw, still some way off, a ragged raft to which two women clung, and on which a man stood shading his eyes with his hand while he scanned the tossing surface.

A dozen strokes carried me to them. The raft had been built of whatever floating stuff they could find, and bound together in any way that would serve. Its core was a large table such as an exultant might have spread for an intimate supper in his suite; and the table's eight sturdy legs, now pawing the air by pairs, seemed parodies of masts.

When I had clambered onto the back of a cabinet (somewhat cumbered by the well-meant help I got), I saw that the survivors comprised a fat, bald man and the two women, both fairly young, one short and blessed with the merry, round face of a cheerful doll, the other tall, dark, and hollow-cheeked.

"You see," the fat man said, "not all's lost. There'll be more, mark my word."

The dark woman muttered, "And no water."

"We'll get something, never fear. Meantime, none to share amongst four's but a bit worse than none to share amongst three, provided it's doled out fairly."

I said, "This must be fresh water all around us."

The fat man shook his head. "I fear it's the sea, sieur. High tides because of the Day Star, sieur, and they've swallowed up the countryside at present. Gyoll's mixed in with them, to be sure, so the water's not quite so salt as they say old Ocean is, sieur."

"Don't I know you? You seem familiar."

He bowed as skillfully as any legate, all the while keeping a hand braced on one of the table legs. "Odilo, sieur.

Master steward, sieur, and charged by our benign Autarch, whose smiles are the hopes of her humble servants, sieur, with the regulation of the whole of the Hypogeum Apotropaic in its entirety, sieur. Doubtless you saw me there, sieur, upon some visit you made to our House Absolute, though I did not have occasion to wait upon you there, sieur, I'm sure, as I would have recollected such an honor to the very day of my demise, sieur."

The dark woman said, "Which may be this."

I hesitated. I did not want to feign to be the exultant Odilo plainly took me for; but to announce myself the Autarch Severian would be awkward even if I were believed.

The doll-faced woman rescued me. "I'm Pega, and I was the armagette Pelagia's soubrette."

Odilo frowned. "Hardly well mannered for you to introduce yourself in such a way, Pega. You were her ancilla." And then to me. "She was a good servant, sieur, I have no question. A trifle giddy, perhaps."

The doll-faced woman looked chastened, though I suspected the expression was entirely assumed. "I did madame's hair and took care of her things, but she really kept me to tell her all the latest jokes and gossip, and to train Picopicaro. That was what she said, and she always called me her soubrette." A fat tear rolled down her cheek, gleaming in the sun; but whether it was for her dead mistress or the dead bird, I could not be sure.

"And this, ah, female will not introduce herself to Pega and me. That is, beyond her name, which is—"

"Thais."

"I am enriched by this introduction," I said. By then I had remembered that I held honorary commissions in half a dozen legions and epitagms, all of which I could employ as incognitos without a lie. "Hipparch Severian, of the Black Tarentines."

Pega's mouth shaped a tiny circle. "Ooh! I must've seen you in the procession!" She turned to the woman who had called herself Thais. "His men wore lacquered *cuir-bouilli* with white plumes, and you never saw such destriers!"

Odilo murmured, "You went with your mistress, I take it?"

Pega made some response, but I gave it no heed. A corpse bobbing a chain from the raft had caught my eye, and I thought how absurd it was that I should squat on a dead man's furniture and dissemble to servants with Valeria rotting underwater. How she would have mocked me! At a pause in the talk, I asked Odilo whether his father had not been steward before him in the same place.

He beamed with pleasure. "He was indeed, sieur, and gave the most complete satisfaction all his life. That was in the great days of Father Inire, sieur, when, if I may say so, sieur, our Hypogeum Apotropaic was famous all across the Commonwealth. May I ask why you inquire, sieur?"

"I merely wondered. It's more or less the usual thing, I believe."

"It is, sieur. The son's given an opportunity to show his mettle if he can; and if he does, he retains the office. You may not believe it, sieur, but my father once encountered your namesake before he had become Autarch. Do you know of his life and deeds, sieur?"

"Not as much as I'd like to, Odilo."

"Graciously spoken, sieur. Most graciously spoken indeed." The fat steward nodded and beamed at the two women to make sure they appreciated the exquisite courtesy of my reply.

Pega was studying the sky. "It's going to rain, I believe. Maybe we won't die of thirst after all."

Thais said, "Another storm. We'll drown instead."

I told them I hoped not, and began to examine my emotional state before I remembered it could no longer be the power of my star that had summoned the clouds gathering in the east.

Odilo was not to be deprived of his anecdote. "It was late one night, sieur, and my father was making his final rounds when he saw someone attired in the fuligin habiliments of a carnifex, though without the customary sword of execution. As was to be expected, his first thought was that the man was arrayed for a masque, of which there are always several in one part or another of the House Absolute on any given night. Yet he knew none was to take place in our Hypogeum Apotropaic, neither Father Inire nor the then Autarch having much fondness for those diversions."

I smiled, recalling the House Azure. The dark woman shot me a significant glance and ostentatiously covered her lips with her hand, but I had no desire to cut Odilo's recital short; now that I would no longer wander through the Corridors of Time, all that concerned the past or the future seemed infinitely precious to me.

"His next thought—which had better been his first, sieur, as he often owned to my mother and me as we sat by the fireside—was that this carnifex had set out upon some sinister mission, supposing himself apt to pass unobserved. It was vital, sieur, as my father understood at once, to learn if his errand served Father Inire or some other. My father therefore approached him as boldly as if he'd a cohort of hastarii at his back and asked his business straight out."

Thais murmured, "If he had been set upon some evil errand, he would have owned it, no doubt."

Odilo said, "My dear lady, I don't know whom you may be, as you have refrained from informing us even when our exalted guest obligingly made us privy to his own patrician identity. But you obviously know nothing of artifice, nor of the intrigues carried out daily—and nightly!—among the myriad hallways of our House Absolute. My father was well aware that no agent entrusted with an irrevealable commission would disclose it, however abrupt the demand. He hazarded that some involuntary gesture or fleeting expression might betray treachery, were such intended."

"Wasn't that Severian masked?" I asked. "You said he was dressed as a torturer."

"I'm quite certain he wasn't, sieur, as my father described him often—a most savage countenance, sieur, severely scarred on one cheek."

"I know!" Pega broke in. "I've seen his portrait and his bust. They're in the Hypogeum Abscititious, where the

Autarch put them when she married again. He looked like he'd cut your throat whistling."

I felt that someone had cut my own.

"Quite apropos!" Odilo approved. "My father said much the same, though he never put it so succinctly that I can recall."

Pega was examining me. "He never had children, did he?"

Odilo smiled. "One would have heard of *that*, I imagine."

"Legitimate children. But he could have covered any woman in the House Absolute, just by cocking an eyebrow. Exultants, all of them."

Odilo told her to hold her tongue and said, "I do hope you will forgive Pega, sieur. After all, it's rather a compliment."

"To be told I look like a cutthroat? Yes, it's the kind I'm always getting." I spoke without reflection and continued in the same way, seeking at once to turn the talk to Valeria's remarriage and to conceal the grief I felt. "But wouldn't the cutthroat have to be my grandfather? Severian the Great would be eighty or more if he were alive, surely. Whom should I ask about him, Pega? My mother or my father? And don't you think there must have been something about him after all, for him to command so many fine chatelaines when he'd been a torturer in his youth, even if the Autarch took a new husband?"

To fill the silence that followed my little speech, Odilo said, "That guild is abolished, sieur, I believe."

"Of course you do. That's what people always believe."

The whole of the east was black already, and the motion of our improvised raft had grown perceptibly more lively.

Pega whispered, "I didn't mean to offend, Hipparch. It's just that . . ." Whatever it was, was lost in the breaking of a wave.

"No," I told her. "You're right. He was a hard man from all I know of him; and a cruel one too, at least by reputation, though perhaps he wouldn't have owned to that. Quite possibly Valeria wed him for his throne, though

I believe she's sometimes said otherwise. Her second husband made her happy, at least."

Odilo chortled. "Well put, sieur. A distinct hit. You must take care, Pega, when you cross swords with a soldier."

Thais stood, grasping a table leg with one hand and pointing with the other. *"Look!"*

CHAPTER XLV

The Boat

IT WAS A SAIL, LIFTED AT TIMES SO HIGH THAT WE COULD glimpse the dark hull under it—at others nearly lost, dipping and spinning down the trenches of the flood. We shouted till we were hoarse, all of us, and capered and waved our arms, and at last I lifted Pega onto my shoulder, balancing as precariously as I had in the tossing howdah of Vodalus's baluchither.

The wind spilled from the gaff-rigged sail. Pega groaned. "They're sinking!"

"No," I told her, "they're coming about."

The little jib emptied and flapped in its turn, then filled again. I cannot say just how many breaths or how many beatings of my heart passed before we saw the sharp jibboom stabbing the sky like a flagstaff set on a green hill. Time has seldom gone more slowly for me, and I feel they might have numbered several thousands.

A moment more, and the boat lay within long bowshot of us, with a rope trailing in the water. I plunged in, not sure that the others would follow me, but feeling I would be better able to help them on board than on the raft.

At once it seemed I had plunged into another world, more outlandish than the Brook Madregot. The unresting waves and clouded sky vanished as if they had never existed. I sensed a mighty current, yet I could not have said by what means I knew of it; for although the drowned pastures of my drowned nation slipped under me and its trees gestured to me with supplicating limbs, the water

317

itself seemed at rest. It was as if I watched the slow rolling of Urth across the void.

At length I saw a cottage with its walls and stone chimney still standing; its open door appeared to beckon me. I felt a sudden terror and swam upward toward the light as desperately as when I had been drowning in Gyoll.

My head broke the surface; water streamed from my nostrils. For a moment it seemed that both raft and boat were gone, but a wave lifted the boat so that I glimpsed its weather-stained sail. I knew I had been underwater a long time, even though it had not seemed so. I swam as fast as I could, but I was careful to keep my face in air as much as possible, and I closed my eyes when it was not.

Odilo stood in the stern with a hand on the tiller; when he saw me, he waved and shouted some encouragement I could not hear. In a moment or two, Pega's round face appeared above the gunnel, then another face, one I did not know, brown and wrinkled.

A wave picked me up as a cat does her kittens, and I dove headfirst down its farther side and found the floating rope in the trough. Odilo abandoned the tiller (which was held with a loop of cordage in any case, as I saw when I got on board) and joined in hauling me in. The little boat had only a couple of cubits of freeboard, and it was not difficult to brace my foot on the rudder and vault over the stern.

Although Pega had first seen me less than a watch before, she hugged me like a stuffed toy.

Odilo bowed as though we were being presented to each other in the Hypogeum Amaranthine. "Sieur, I feared that you had lost your life among these raging seas!" Odilo bowed again. "Sieur, it is exceeding pleasant as well as quite astonishing, sieur, if I may say so, sieur, to see you once again, sieur!"

Pega was more straightforward. "All of us thought you were dead, Severian!"

I asked him where the other woman was, then caught sight of her as a bucketful of water flew over the side and back into the flood. Like a sensible woman, she was bailing; and like a woman of sense, bailing downwind.

"She's here, sieur. We are all here, all here now, sieur. I myself was the first to reach this craft." Odilo inflated his chest with pardonable pride. "I was able to assist the females a bit, sieur. But no one had seen you at all, sieur, not since we cast our lots with the waves, if I may phrase it thus, sieur. We are most happy, sieur, indeed we are quite delighted—" He recollected himself. "Not that a young officer of your physique and undoubted prowess could be in much danger, sieur, where such humble persons as we had come safely through, sieur. Though but narrowly, sieur. Very narrowly, sieur. And yet the young women were concerned for you, sieur, for which I hope and trust you'll forgive them."

"There's nothing to forgive," I told him. "I thank all of you for your help."

The old sailor whose boat it was made some complex gesture (half-concealed by his thick coat) that I was unable to follow, then spit to windward.

"Our rescuer," Odilo continued, beaming, "is—"

"Don't matter," the sailor snapped. "You get down there and trim that mains'l. Jib's fouled, too. You stamp now and stutter, or she'll capsize."

It had been ten years and more since I had sailed on the *Samru*, but I had learned then how a fore-and-aft rig operates, and I do not forget. I had trimmed the gaff mainsail before Odilo and Pega had fathomed the mysteries of its simple rigging, and with a little help from the stay I freed the jib and payed out the sheet.

For the remainder of the day we lived in fear of the storm, flying before the strong winds that preceded it, always escaping but never completely sure we had. By night the danger seemed to have lessened, and we hove to. The sailor gave each of us a cup of water, a round of hard bread, and a scrap of smoked meat. I had known I was hungry, but I discovered that I was ravenous, as was everyone else.

"We've got to keep both eyes open for something to eat," he directed Odilo and the women solemnly. "Sometimes, when there's a wreck, you can find biscuit boxes or barrels of water. This's about the biggest wreck there ever was, I suppose." He paused, squinting at his vessel and the surrounding flood, still lit by the lingering incandescence of Urth's new sun. "There's islands—or there was—but we might not find them, and we've not got food enough nor water neither to reach the Xanthic Lands."

"I have observed," Odilo said, "that in the course of life events attain some nadir from which they are afterward elevated. The destruction of the House Absolute, the death of our beloved Autarch—if she has not, by the mercy of the Increate, somewhere survived—"

"She has," I told him. "Believe me." When he stared at me with his eyes filled with hope, I could only add weakly, "I feel it."

"I trust so, sieur. Your feelings do you credit. But as I was saying, circumstances then reached their worst for us all." He looked about, and even Thais and the old sailor nodded.

"And yet we lived. I discovered a floating table and thus was able to proffer my assistance to these poor women. Together we discovered still more furniture and constructed our raft, on which we were soon joined by our exalted guest; and at last you, Captain, rescued us, for which we are extremely grateful. That I should call a tendency. Our circumstances will incline toward the better for some time to come, I believe."

Pega touched his arm. "You must have lost your wife, and your family too, Odilo. It's admirable of you not to mention them, but we know how you must feel."

He shook his head. "I never married. I'm glad of it now, though I've often regretted it. To be the steward of an entire hypogeum, and particularly, as I was in my youth, to be steward of my Hypogeum Apotropaic in the time of Father Inire, requires the most unremitting effort; one has hardly a watch in which to sleep. Previous to my own father's lamented demise, there was a certain young person, the confidential servitrix of a chatelaine, if I may say so, to whom I hoped—but the chatelaine retired to her estates. For a time, the young person and I corresponded."

He sighed. "Doubtless she found another, for a woman will always find another if she wishes. I hope and trust that he was worthy of her."

I would have spoken then to relieve the tension if I could; but torn between amusement and sympathy as I was, I could think of nothing innocuous to say. Odilo's inflated manner rendered him ridiculous, and yet I was conscious it was a manner that had evolved over many years, through the reigns of many Autarchs, as a means of preserving such people as Odilo had lately been from dismissal and death; and I was conscious too that I myself had been one of those Autarchs.

Pega had begun to talk to him in a low tone that was nearly a whisper, and although I could hear her voice above the slap of the waves against our side, I could not tell what was said. Nor was I sure I wished to hear it.

The old sailor had been rummaging under the little poopdeck that covered the last couple of ells of the stern. "Haven't but four blankets," he announced.

Odilo interrupted Pega to say, "Then I must do without. My clothing is dry now, and I should not be uncomfortable."

The sailor tossed a blanket to each of the women, and one to me, keeping the last for himself.

I put mine in Odilo's lap. "I'm not going to sleep for a while; I have some things to think about. Why don't you use it until I'm ready for it? When I get sleepy, I'll try to take it without waking you."

Thais began, "I—" and though I was not meant to, I saw Pega elbow her so sharply she had to catch her breath.

Odilo hesitated; I could hardly make out his drawn face in the fading light, but I knew he must be very tired. At last he said, "That is most kind, sieur. Thank you, sieur."

I had finished my bread and smoked meat long before. Not wishing to give him time to repent his decision, I went to the bow and stared out over the water. The waves still retained a twilight gleam from the sun, and I knew that their light was mine. I understood at that moment how the Increate must feel about his creation, and I knew the sorrow he knows because the things he creates pass away. I think it may be a law binding even him—that is to say, a logical necessity—that nothing can be eternal in the future that is not rooted in eternity in the past, as he himself is. And as I contemplated him in his joys and sorrows, it came to me that I was much like him, though so much smaller; thus an herb, perhaps, might think concerning a great cedar, or one of these innumerable drops of water about Ocean.

Night fell, and all the stars came out, so much the brighter for having hidden like frightened children under the gaze of the New Sun. I searched them—not for my own star, which I knew I would never see again, but for the End of the Universe. I did not find it, not upon that night nor any night since; yet surely it is there, lost among the myriad constellations.

Virescent radiance peeped across my shoulder like a ghost, and I, remembering the colored and many-faceted lanterns at the stern of the *Samru,* imagined we had hoisted a similar light; I turned to look, and it was the bright face of Lune, from which the eastern horizon had fallen like a veil. No man since the first had seen it as brilliant as I did that night. How strange to think that it was the same poor, faint thing I had seen only the night before beside the cenotaph! I knew then that our old world of Urth had perished, even as Dr. Talos had foretold, and that our boat floated not there, but upon the waters of the Urth of the New Sun, which is called Ushas.

CHAPTER XLVI

The Runaway

FOR A LONG WHILE I STOOD THERE IN THE BOW, SIFTING THE sentinels of the night as Ushas's swift motion revealed them. Our ancient Commonwealth had drowned; but the starlight that touched my eyes was more ancient still, had been old when the first woman nursed the first child. I wondered if the stars would weep, when Ushas herself was old, to learn of the death of our Commonwealth.

Certainly I, who had once been such a star, wept then.

From this I was taken by a touch at my elbow. It was the old sailor, the captain of our boat; he who had seemed so aloof before now stood with his shoulder next to mine, staring across the floodwaters as I did. It struck me that I had never learned his name.

I was about to ask it when he said, "Think I don't know you?"

"Possibly you do," I told him. "But if so, you have the advantage of me."

"The cacogens, they can call up a man's thought and show it to him. I know that."

"You think I'm an eidolon. I've met them, but I'm not one of them; I'm a man like you."

He might not have heard me. "All day I been watching you. I been lying awake watching you ever since we laid down. They say they can't cry, but it's not true, and I saw you crying and remembered what they said and how it's wrong. Then I thought, how bad can they be? But it's bad luck to have them on a ship, bad luck to think too much."

"I'm sure that's true. But those who think too much cannot help it."

He nodded. "That's so, I suppose."

The tongues of men are older than our drowned land; and it seems strange that in so great a time no words have been found for the pauses in speech, which have each their own quality, as well as a certain length. Our silence endured while a hundred waves slapped the hull, and it held the rocking of the boat, the sigh of the night wind in the rigging, and pensive expectation.

"I wanted to say there's nothing you can do to her that'll hurt me. Sink her or run her aground, I don't care."

I told him I supposed I might do both, but that I would not do them intentionally.

"You never did me much harm when you were real," the sailor said after another long pause. "I wouldn't have met Maxellindis if it hadn't been for you—maybe that was bad. Maybe it wasn't. We'd some good years together, Maxellindis and me."

I examined him from a corner of my eye as he stared blindly over the restless waves. His nose had been broken, perhaps more than once. In my mind I straightened it again and filled in his lined cheeks.

"There was that time you pounded me. Remember, Severian? They'd just made you the captain. When it came my turn I did the same to Timon."

"Eata!" Before I knew what I was doing, I had grabbed him and picked him up just as I used to when we had been apprentices together. "Eata, you little snot-nose, I thought I'd never see you again!" I spoke so loudly that Odilo moaned and stirred in his sleep.

Eata looked startled. His hand went toward the knife at his belt, then drew away.

I put him down. "When I reformed the guild you were gone. They said you'd run away."

"I did." He tried to swallow, or perhaps only to catch his breath. "It's good to hear you, Severian, even if you're just a bad dream. What did you call them?"

"Eidolons."

"A eidolon. If the cacogens are going to show me somebody out of my head, I might have had worse company."

"Eata, do you remember the time we were locked out of the necropolis?"

He nodded. "And Drotte made me try to squeeze through the bars, but I couldn't do it. Then when the volunteers opened it, I ran off and left you and him and Roche to the crows. None of you seemed much afraid of Master Gurloes, but I was, back then."

"We were too, but we didn't want to show it in front of you."

"I suppose." He was grinning; I could see his teeth flash in the green moonlight, and the black smudge where one had been knocked out. "That's what boys are like, like the skipper said when he showed his daughter."

Wildly and momentarily it occurred to me that if Eata had not run, it might have been he who saved Vodalus, he who did and saw all the things that I had seen and done. It may be that in some other sphere it happened so. Pushing away the thought, I asked, "But what have you been doing all this time? Tell me."

"Not much to tell. When I was captain of apprentices it was easy enough to slip away and see Maxellindis whenever her uncle's boat was docked somewhere around the Algedonic Quarter. I had talked to the sailors and learned to sail a bit myself; and so when it came feast time, I couldn't go through with it, couldn't put on fuligin."

I said, "I did it only because I couldn't imagine living in any place except the Matachin Tower."

Eata nodded. "But I could, see? I'd thought all that year about living on the boat and helping Maxellindis and her uncle. He was getting stiff, and they needed somebody spry and stronger than her. I didn't wait for the masters to call me in to choose. I just ran off."

"And after that?"

"Forgot the torturers as fast as I could and as much as I could. Only lately I've started trying to remember what it was like, living in the Matachin Tower when I was young.

You won't believe this, Severian, but for years I couldn't look at Citadel Hill when we went up or down that reach. I used to keep my eyes turned away."

"I do believe you," I told him.

"Maxellindis's uncle died. There was a tap he used to go to, way down south in the delta in a place called Liti. You've probably never heard of it. Maxellindis and me came to get him one night, and he was sitting there with his bottle and glass, with one arm on the table and his head down on his arm; but when I tried to shake his shoulder he fell out of the chair, and he was cold already."

"'Men to whom wine had brought death long before lay by springs of wine and drank still, too stupefied to know their lives were past.'"

"What's that?" Eata asked.

"Just an old story," I said. "Never mind, go on."

"After that, just her and me worked the boat. The two of us could do it about as well as the three of us had before. We never really got married. When we both wanted to we never had the money, somehow. And when we had the money, there was always some kind of quarrel. After a couple of years everybody thought we were married anyway." He blew his nose, flinging the mucus over the side.

"Go on," I said again.

"We did some smuggling, and one night we got stopped by a cutter. Eight or ten leagues south of Citadel Hill, that was. Maxellindis jumped—I heard the splash—and I would have too, but one of the taxmen threw a *achico* at my feet and tripped me up. You know what they are, I suppose."

I nodded. "Was I Autarch still? You might have appealed to me."

"No. I thought about it, but I was sure you'd send me back to the guild."

"I wouldn't have," I told him, "but would that have been worse than what the law did to you?"

"It would have been for the rest of my life. That's what I kept thinking about. Anyway, they took me upriver with our boat in tow. I was held till the assize, and then the judge ordered me flogged and made me sign on a carrack. They kept me in irons till we were out of sight of the coast, and they worked me like a slave, but I got to see the Xanthic Lands, and I went over the side there and stayed for two years. It's not such a bad place if you've got some money."

I said, "But you came back."

"There was a riot, and this girl that I'd been living with got killed in it. They have them there every couple years over the price of food in the market. The soldiers break heads, and I guess they broke hers. There was a caravel anchored off Blue Flower Island right then, and I went to see the captain and he gave me a berth. A man can be a terrible fool when he's young, and I thought maybe Maxellindis had got us another boat. But when I came back she wasn't on the river. I've never seen her again. She died, I guess, the night the cutter got its grapple on us."

He paused, chin in hand. "Maxellindis was almost as good a swimmer as I ever was. You remember I could swim almost as well as you and Drotte, but maybe a nixie pulled her down. That used to happen, sometimes, specially on the lower reaches."

I said, "I know," remembering Juturna's huge face as I had glimpsed it as a boy, when I had almost drowned in Gyoll.

"Not much more to tell. I'd brought back a bit of money in a silk cestus I'd had a man make for me over there, and I got a little more when the caravel paid off. I bought this boat here on shares, and here I am. But I can still speak a little of the Xanthic tongue, and more will come to my mouth when I hear it in another one. Or it would if we had more water and a little more food."

I told him, "There are many isles in that sea. I saw them on a chart in the Hypotherm Classis once."

He nodded. "I guess a couple hundred, and a lot more that don't show on any chart I've seen. You'd think a ship couldn't miss them all, but it can. Unless you're pretty lucky, you can pass right between them without ever knowing they're there. A lot depends on when it's night

and when it's day, and a lot more on how high up your
lookout stands—if he's in the maintop of a carrack or the
bow of my little boat."

I shrugged. "We can only hope."

"That's like the frog said when he seen the stork. But his
mouth was dry, and he couldn't quite get the word out."

Eata paused for a moment, studying me instead of the
waves. "Severian, do you know what's happened to you?
Even if you're just a dream from the cacogens?"

"Yes," I said. "But I'm not a phantom. Or if I am, it's
Tzadkiel the Hierogrammate you should blame for me."

"Then tell me what happened to you, just like I told you
everything that's happened to me."

"All right, but I want to ask you something first. What
took place here on Urth after I left?"

Eata sat down on a locker from which he could look up
at me without turning his head. "That's right," he said.
"You sailed off to bring the New Sun, didn't you? Did you
ever find him?"

"Yes and no. I'll tell you all about that as soon as you tell
me what happened on Urth."

"I don't know much about what you'd probably like to
hear." He rubbed his jaw. "Anyway, I'm not so sure I can
remember just what went on or just when it was. All the
while Maxellindis and me were together you were Autarch,
but mostly they said you were off fighting the Ascians.
Then, when I got back from the Xanthic Lands, you were
gone."

I said, "If you stayed two years, you must have been
eight with Maxellindis."

"That would be about right. Four or five with her and
her uncle, and two or three after, just us two on the boat.
Anyway, your autarchia, she was Autarch. People talked
about it because of her being a woman, and they said she
didn't have the words.

"So when I traded my extern gold for chrisos, some had
your face on them and some hers, or anyway some woman's. She married Dux Caesidius. They had a big celebration all up and down Iubar Street, meat and wine for

everybody. I got drunk, and I didn't get back to my boat
for three days. People said their marrying was good—she
could stay in the House Absolute and take care of the
Commonwealth while he took care of the Ascians."

"I remember him," I said. "He was a fine commander."
It was strange to summon up that hawk face and imagine
its fierce, surly owner lying with Valeria.

"Some said she did it because he looked like you," Eata
told me. "But he was handsomer, I think, and maybe a
little taller."

I tried to remember. Handsomer, certainly, than I had
been with my scarred face. It seemed to me that Caesidius
had been a bit below me in height, though every man is
taller when everyone kneels to him, to be sure.

"And then he died," Eata continued. "That was last
year."

"I see," I said.

For a long while I stood with my back against the
gunwale, thinking. The rising moon, now almost overhead,
cast the shadow of the mast like a black bar between us.
From its farther side, Eata sounded strangely youthful.
"Now what about the New Sun, Severian? You promised
you'd tell me all about him."

I began, but while I spoke of stabbing Idas I saw that
Eata was asleep.

CHAPTER XLVII

The Sunken City

I TOO SHOULD HAVE SLEPT, BUT I DID NOT. FOR A WATCH OR more I remained standing in the bow, looking sometimes at the sleepers and sometimes at the water. Thais lay as I have so often lain, face down, her head cradled in her folded arms. Pega had curled her plump body into a ball, so that I might have believed her a kitten turned into a woman; her spine was pushed against Odilo's side. He lay upon his back with his belly rising into the air, his arms above his head.

Eata sprawled, still more than half sitting, his cheek to the gunwale; I thought he must be exhausted. As I studied him, I wondered whether he would still believe me an eidolon when he woke.

Yet who was I to call him mistaken? The true Severian —and I felt sure there had once been a true Severian—had disappeared among the stars long ago. I stared up at them, trying to find him.

At length I realized I could not, not because he was not there (for he was), but because Ushas had turned away from him, hiding him, with many others, behind her horizon. For our New Sun is only one star among myriads, though perhaps now, when none but he can be seen by day, men will forget that.

No doubt our sun is as fair as all the rest from the deck of Tzadkiel's ship. I winnowed them still, even when I knew I would never discover that Severian who was no dream of Eata's; and at last I understood that I searched for the ship.

I did not find it, but the stars were so lovely I did not grudge the effort.

The brown book that I no longer carry with me, a book that has no doubt been destroyed with a thousand millions of others in what was the library of Master Ultan, had spun a tale of a great sanctuary, a place veiled by a diamond-sprinkled curtain lest men see the face of the Increate and die. After ages of Urth, a bold man forced his way into that temple, slew all its guardians, and tore down the curtain for the sake of the many diamonds sewn into it. The small chamber he found beyond the curtain was empty, or so the tale says; but when he walked out and into the night, he looked at the sky and was consumed by flames. How terrible it is that we know our stories only when we have lived them!

Perhaps it was the memory of this tale. Perhaps it was no more than the thought of the drowned library, of which Cyby, I feel sure, had been the final master—and in which Cyby, I feel certain, must have died. However it may be, the knowledge that Urth had been destroyed came to me with a clarity and horror it had not had before, not even when I had seen the ruined cottage with its chimney still standing, though that had filled me with so much dread. The forests where I had hunted were gone, every tree and every stick. The million little freeholdings that had nourished a million Melitos and sent them north armed with so much ingenuity and humble courage, the broad pampas from which Foila had ridden at the gallop with her lance and her high heart—all were gone, every turnip and every blade of grass.

A dead child, rocked by the waves, seemed to gesture to me. When I saw him, I understood that there was but one way in which I might expiate what I had done. A wave beckoned, the dead boy beckoned, and even as I told myself I lacked the will to take my own life, I felt the gunwale slipping from my hands.

Water closed over me, yet I did not drown. I felt I might breathe that water, yet I did not breathe. Illuminated by

Lune, which flamed now like an emerald, the flood spread
about me like green glass. Slowly I sank through an abyss
that seemed clearer than air.

Far off, great shapes loomed—things a hundred times
larger than a man. Some seemed ships and some clouds;
one was a living head without a body; another had a
hundred heads. In time they were lost in the green haze,
and I saw below me a plain of muck and silt, where stood a
palace greater than our House Absolute, though it lay in
ruins.

I knew then that I was dead, and that for me death held
no release. A moment later I knew also that I was dreaming, that with the crowing of the cock (whose bright black
eyes would not again be pierced by the magicians) I would
wake to find myself sharing the bed with Baldanders. Dr.
Talos would beat him, and we would go forth in search of
Agia and Jolenta. I gave myself to the dream; but almost, I
think, I had rent the Veil of Maya, that glorious spinning of
appearances hiding the last reality.

Then it was whole once more, though fluttering still in
the icy winds that blow from Reality to Dream and carry
us with them like so many leaves. The "palace" that had
suggested the House Absolute was my city of Nessus. Vast
as it had been, it seemed larger than ever now; many
sections of the Wall had fallen like our Citadel wall,
making it truly an infinite city. Many towers had fallen too,
their walls of brick and stone crumbled like the rinds of so
many rotten melons. Mackerel schooled where yearly the
Curators had paced in solemn procession to the cathedral.

I tried to swim and discovered that I was swimming
already, my arms and legs stroking rhythmically without
my willing it. I stopped, but I did not (as I had expected)
float to the surface. Drifting torpidly in an unseen current,
I discovered the channel of Gyoll stretched below me,
crossed by its proud bridges still, but robbed of its river
now that water was everywhere. Drowned things waited
there, decayed and decked with green and streaming
weeds: wrecked vessels and tumbled columns. I tried to
expel the final breath from my lungs, that I might drown as

well. Air indeed bubbled forth; but the chill water that rushed in did not bring with it the chill of death.

Still I sank, ever so slowly, until I stood where I had never thought to stand, in the mud and filth at the bottom of the river. It was like standing upon the deck of Tzadkiel's ship, for there was scarcely pressure enough on the soles of my bare feet to hold me down. The current urged me to go with it, and I felt myself a ghost who might be dispersed with a puff of breath if only the breath muttered words of exorcism.

I walked—or rather, say that I half swam and feigned to walk. Each step raised a cloud of silt that drifted beside me like a living creature. When I paused and looked up, I beheld green Lune, a shapeless blur above the unseen waves.

When I looked down again, a yellowed skull lay at my feet, half-buried in the mud. I picked it up; the lower jaw was gone, but otherwise it was whole and showed no injury. From its size and unworn teeth, I guessed it to have been a boy's or a young man's. Some other, then, had drowned in Gyoll long ago, perhaps some apprentice who had died too long before my time for me to hear his short, sad tale, perhaps only a boy from the tenements that had crowded the filthy waters.

Or perhaps it was the skull of some poor woman, strangled and thrown into the river; so women and children, and men as well, had perished in Nessus every night. It came to me that when the Increate had chosen me his instrument to destroy the land, only babes and beasts had died in innocence.

And yet I felt that the skull had been a boy's, and the boy had somehow died for me, the victim of Gyoll when Gyoll had been cheated of his due sacrifice. I took it by the eyes, shook out the mud, and carried it with me.

Long stairs of stone descended deep into the channel, mute testimony to the number of times its levees had been raised and its landings extended from above. I climbed them all, though I might have floated up nearly as readily.

The tenements had fallen, every one. I saw a mass of tiny

fish, several hundred at least, clustered in the wreckage; they scattered in sparks of argent fire at my approach, revealing a bleached corpse partly devoured. After that I did not dismiss their schools again.

Doubtless there were many such dead in the city, which had once been so large as to excite the admiration of all the world; but what of me? Was I not another drifting corpse? My arm was cold to my own touch, and the weight of water burdened my lungs; even to myself, I seemed to walk in sleep. Yet I still moved or believed I moved against all currents, and my cold eyes saw.

The locked and rusted gate of the necropolis stood before me, wisps of mazed kelp threading its spikes like the mountain paths, the unchanged symbol of my old exile. I launched myself upward, swimming several strokes and thus flourishing the skull without intending it. Suddenly ashamed, I released it; but it appeared to follow me, propelled by the motion of my hand.

Before I had embarked upon the ship of the Hierodules that was to carry me to the ship of Tzadkiel, I had crouched in air, surrounded by circling, singing skulls. Here spread the reality this ceremony had foretold. I knew that; I understood it, and I was certain in my knowledge —the New Sun must do what I now did, going weightless through his drowned world, ringed by her dead. The loss of her ancient continents was the price Urth had paid; this journey was the price I had to pay, and I was paying it at this moment.

The skull settled softly upon the sodden earth in which the paupers of Nessus had been laid, generation after generation. I picked it up again. What words had the lochage addressed to me in the bartizan?

The exultant Talarican, whose madness manifested itself as a consuming interest in the lowest aspects of human existence, claimed that the persons who live by devouring the garbage of others number two gross thousands—that if a pauper were to leap from the parapet of this bridge each time we draw breath, we should live forever, because Nessus breeds and breaks men faster than we respire.

They leap no longer, the water having leaped for them. Their misery, at least, is ended; and perhaps some survived.

When I reached the mausoleum where I had played as a boy, I found its long-jammed door shut, the force of the onrushing sea having completed a motion begun perhaps a century ago. I laid the skull on its threshold and swam hard for the surface, a surface that danced with golden light.

CHAPTER XLVIII

Old Lands and New

EATA'S BOAT WAS NOWHERE IN SIGHT. TO WRITE, AS I MUST write, that I swam all that day and most of the following night seems preposterous, yet it was so. The water the others had called salt did not seem salt to me; I drank when I thirsted and was refreshed by it. I was seldom tired; when I was, I rested on the waves, floating.

I had already discarded all my clothes except my trousers, and now I slipped those off. From an old habit of prudence, I examined the pockets before I abandoned them; there were three small brass coins there, the gift of Ymar. Their legends, like their faces, had worn away; and they were dark with verdigris—in appearance precisely the ancient things they were. I let them slip from my fingers, with all Urth.

Twice I saw great fish, which were perhaps dangerous; but they appeared to pose no threat to me. Of the water women, of whom Idas had been, perhaps, the smallest, I saw nothing. Nor did I see Abaia, their master. Nor Erebus, nor any other such monstrous thing.

Night came with teeming stars in her train, and I floated on my back and gazed at them, rocked by the warm arms of Ocean. How many rich worlds flew above me then! Once when I had fled from Abdiesus, I had huddled in the lea of a boulder and stared at these same stars, trying to imagine their companions and how men might live upon them and lift cities that knew less of evil than ours. Now I knew how foolish all such dreams must be, for I had seen another world and found it stranger than anything I might have imagined. Nor could I have dreamed the heteroclite crewmen I had met aboard Tzadkiel's ship, nor the jibers; and yet both had come from Briah, even as I; and Tzadkiel had not scrupled to take them into his service.

But though I rejected all such dreams, I found that they came unbidden. About certain stars, though they appeared but embers wafted through the night, I seemed to see stars smaller still; and as I watched them, dim vistas took shape in my mind, lovely and terrifying. At last clouds came to blot the stars, and for a time I slept.

When morning came, I watched the night of Ushas fall from the face of the New Sun. No world of Briah could hold a sight more wonderful, nor had I seen a thing more marvelous on Yesod. The young king, bright with such gold as is not found in any mine, strode across the waves; and the glory of him was such that he who looked on it should never look upon another.

Waves danced for him and cast ten thousand drops to honor his feet, and he turned each to diamond. A great wave came—for the wind was rising—and I rode it as a swallow rides the spring air. At its crest I could stay for less than a breath, but from that summit I glimpsed his face; and I was not blinded, but knew his face for my own. It is a thing that has not happened since, and perhaps never will. Between us, five leagues or more away, an undine rose from the sea, lifting her hand to him in salute.

Then the wave subsided, and I with it. If I had waited, a second wave would have come, I think, raising me a second time; but for many things (of which that moment was for me the chief) there can be no second time. So that no inferior memory should obscure it, I sounded the sunbright water, pushing ever deeper, eager to test the powers I had discovered only the night before.

They remained, although I no longer swam half in dream, and the urge to end my life had vanished. My world was now a place of palest, purest blue, floored with ocher and canopied in gold. The sun and I floated in space and smiled down upon our spheres.

When I had swum a while—how many breaths I cannot say, for I did not draw breath—I recalled the undine and set out to find her. I feared her still, but I had learned at last that such as she were not always to be feared; and though Abaia had conspired to prevent the coming of our New Sun, the age in which my death might have prevented it was past. Deeper I swam and deeper, for I soon learned how much easier it was to see a thing that moved against the bright surface.

Then all thoughts of the undine evaporated. Under me lay another city, one I did not know, a city that was never Nessus. Its towers sprawled along the floor of Ocean, where the stumps of a few yet stood; and ancient wrecks lay among them, who had been ancient already when the wrecks had been fair young ships launched to shouts of joy, with banners in their rigging and dancing on their forecastles.

Searching among the fallen towers I discovered treasures so noble they had withstood the passing of aeons —splendid gems and bright metals. But I did not find the things I sought—the name of the city and the name of the forgotten nation that had raised it, and had lost it to Ocean just as we had lost Nessus. With shards and shells, I scraped lintels and pedestals; there were many words written there, but in a character I could not read.

For several watches, I swam and searched among those ruins and never raised my eyes; but at last a huge shadow glided down the sand-strewn avenue before me, and I looked up to behold the undine, kraken-tressed and ship-bellied, pass swiftly overhead and vanish in a dazzle of sunfire.

At once I forgot the ruins. When I reached the air again, I blew out water and foggy breath like a manatee and threw back my head to toss my hair away from my eyes. For as I shot up, I had seen the shore: a low, brown coast from which I was barred by less water than had once divided the Botanic Gardens from the bank of Gyoll.

In hardly more time than I take to dip my pen, there was land beneath my feet. I waded out of the sea while loving it still, even as I had earlier dropped from the stars while loving them; and in truth there is no place in Briah that is not lovely when it no longer holds the threat of death, save for the places men have made so. But it was the land that I loved best, for it was to the land that I was born.

 Yet what a terrible land it was! Not a blade of grass grew anywhere. Sand, a few stones, many shells, and thick, black mud that baked and cracked in the sun made up the whole of it. Some lines of Dr. Talos's play returned to torment me:

The continents themselves are old as raddled women, long since stripped of beauty and fertility. The New Sun comes, and he will send them crashing into the sea like foundered ships. And from the sea lift new—glittering with gold, silver, iron, and copper. With diamonds, rubies, turquoises, lands wallowing in the soil of a million millennia, so long ago washed down to the sea.

I, who boast of forgetting nothing, had forgotten that it was the demons who had spoken so.

A thousand times I was tempted and worse than tempted to return to Ocean; but I did not, trudging north along a strand that appeared to continue infinitely, unchanged, to north and south. Wreckage littered the beach, splintered building timbers and uprooted trees, all tossed there by the waves like so many jackstraws, with sometimes a rag or a stick of smashed furniture among them. Occasionally I found a broken branch so fresh that it still carried unwithered leaves, as if unaware that its very world had passed away. "Lift, oh, lift me to the fallen wood!" So Dorcas had sung to me when we had camped beside the ford, and so she had written upon the silvered glass in our chamber in the Vincula of Thrax. As ever, Dorcas had been wiser than either of us knew.

At length the shore bent inward to make a great bay, a bay so large that its innermost recesses were lost in the distance. Across a league of sparkling water I could see the bay's farther lip. It would have been easy enough for me to swim to the other side, but I was reluctant to plunge in.

The New Sun had nearly vanished behind the rising

shoulder of the world, and although it had been pleasant enough to sleep cradled by the waves, I had no desire to do it again, nor did I want to sleep wet ashore. I decided to camp where I was, build a fire if I could, and eat if I could find food; for the first time that day it occurred to me that I had not tasted food since the meager meal we had shared on the boat.

There was firewood enough for an army, but though I sifted it for the kegs and boxes Eata had hoped to find, they were not there; after two watches, a stoppered bottle half-full of rough red wine was the sole discovery I could boast, the wrack of some low tavern like that in which Maxellindis's uncle had died. By striking stone upon stone and discarding those that seemed least promising, I eventually produced an occasional feeble spark; but nothing that would ignite the still-damp tinder I had collected. When the New Sun was hidden and my futile efforts were mocked by the silent fires of stars, I gave up and settled down to sleep, somewhat warmed by the wine.

I had thought never to behold Apheta again. In that I had been mistaken, for I saw her that night, looking down from the sky just as she had looked down at me when I had left Yesod with Burgundofara. I blinked and stared, but soon saw only the green disk of Lune.

It did not seem to me that I slept, but Valeria sat beside me weeping for drowned Urth; her sweet, warm tears pattered on my face. I woke and found I was hot and flushed, and that Lune was concealed behind clouds from which fell a gentle rain. Not far down the beach, a door without a doorway offered the shelter of a crude roof. I crept beneath it, buried my face in my arm, and slept once more, wishing never to wake.

Again green light drenched the beach. One of the flapping horrors that had snatched me from the wreck of the old Autarch's flier fluttered mothlike between my eyes and Lune, waxing ever larger; for the first time I knew that notules were its wings. It landed clumsily among white wolves on the cracked mud.

Without memory of mounting, I was upon its back and

slipping off. Moonlit waves closed about me, and I saw the
Citadel below me. Fish as large as ships swam between the
towers, which I had been wrong to think fallen; save for the
water and their wreaths of weed, all stood as they had
before. For a moment I trembled to think I might be
impaled on their spires. The great gun that had fired at me
when I had been taken to the Prefect Prisca now boomed
again, its bolt cleaving Ocean with a roar of steam.

The bolt struck me, but it was not I who died—this
drowned Citadel vanished like the dream it was, and I
found that I was swimming through the gap in the curtain
wall and into the real Citadel itself. The tops of its towers
thrust above the waves; and Juturna sat among them,
submerged to the neck, eating fish.

"You lived," I called, and felt that this too was merely a
dream.

She nodded. "You did not."

I was weak with hunger and fear, but I asked, "Then am
I dead? And have I come to a place of the dead?"

She shook her head. "You live."

"I'm asleep."

"No. You have . . ." She paused, chewing, her enormous
face without expression.

When she spoke again, fish that were not the huge fish of
my dream but silvery creatures no bigger than perch
leaped from the water before her chin to snap at the
fragments that dropped from her lips. "You have resigned
your life, or endeavored to do so. To some extent you have
succeeded."

"I'm dreaming."

"No. You no longer dream. Thus would you die, if you
could."

"It was because I couldn't watch Thecla in torment,
wasn't it? Now I've seen Urth die like that, and I was
Urth's killer."

"Who were you," she asked me, "when you stood before
the Hierogrammate's Seat of Justice?"

"A man who had not yet destroyed everything he ever
loved."

"You were Urth, and thus Urth lives."

I shouted, "This is Ushas!"

"If you say it. But Urth lives in Ushas and in you."

"I must think," I told her. "Go away and think." I had not meant to plead, but when I heard my voice I knew it for a beggar's.

"Then do so."

I looked without hope at the half-submerged Citadel.

Juturna pointed like a village woman directing some lost traveler, her hands and arms extending in directions I had not seen until she indicated them. "That way the future, this way the past. There is the margin of the world, and beyond that, your sun's other worlds and the worlds of other suns. Here is the stream that rises in Yesod and rushes to Briah."

I did not hesitate.

CHAPTER XLIX

Apu-Punchau

THE WATERS WERE NO LONGER BLACK WITH NIGHT, BUT darkly green; in them it seemed I glimpsed innumerable strands of weed, standing upright and swaying in the current. Hunger filled my mind with the memory of Juturna's fish; yet I watched Ocean wane, becoming thinner and lighter, each minute droplet separating itself from its fellows until what remained was merely mist.

I drew breath, and it was of air and not water. I stamped, and I stood upon solid ground.

What had been the flood was a pampa of waist-high grass, a sea of grass whose shore was lost in swirling white, as though a rout of ghosts danced there swiftly, silently, and somberly. The caress of the mist failed to horrify me, but it was as mucid as that of any specter in a midnight tale. Hoping to find food and to warm myself, I began to walk.

It is said that they who wander in darkness, and still more they who do so in a mist, merely scribe circles across the plain. Perhaps it was so for me, but I do not believe it. A faint wind stirred the mist, and I kept that wind ever at my back.

Once I had strode grinning along the Water Way and imagined myself unlucky, and I had been ecstatic in my misfortune. Now I knew that I had then begun the journey that was to make me Urth's executioner; and although my task was done, I felt I could never be happy again —although after a watch or two I would have been happy

343

enough, I suppose, if only my warm journeyman's cloak
had been returned to me.

At last Urth's old sun rose behind me, and rose in glory
crowned with gold. The specters fled before it; I beheld the
spreading pampa, an endless, whisperous green Ocean,
across which raced a thousand waves. Endless, that is,
except in the east, where mountains lifted haughty fast-
nesses not yet stamped with the human form.

I continued westward, and it came to me as I walked that
I, who had been the New Sun, would hide myself behind
the horizon if I could. Perhaps he who had been the Old
Sun had felt the same. There had been such an Old Sun,
after all, in Dr. Talos's *Eschatology and Genesis,* and
although our performance remained forever incomplete,
Dr. Talos, who had himself become a wanderer in western
lands, had once intended to take the part.

Long-legged birds stalked the pampa but fled when I
drew too near. Once, just after the sun appeared, I saw a
spotted cat; but it was full fed and slunk away. Condors
and eagles wheeled overhead, black specks against the
brilliant blue sky. I was as famished as they; and though
there could be none in such a place, from time to time I
imagined the odor of frying fish, misled no doubt by the
memory of the shabby inn where I had first encountered
Baldanders and Dr. Talos.

A client in a cell can endure three days or more without
water, so Master Palaemon had taught us; but for one who
must labor under the sun, the time is much less. I would
have died that day, I believe, if I had not found it—as I did
when my shadow stretched long behind me. It was only a
narrow stream, scarcely broader than the brook beyond
Briah had seemed in my sight, and so deeply sunk into the
pampa that it was invisible until I had nearly tumbled into
its ravine.

I scrambled down the rocky sides as readily as any
monkey and sated my thirst with sun-warmed water that
tasted of mud to one who had drunk of the clean sea. Had
you been with me then, reader, and insisted I walk farther
with you, I think I would have taken your life. I sank down

among the stones, too weary to go another step, and slept before I closed my eyes.

But not, I think, for long. Nearby a big cat coughed, and I woke shaking with a fear older than the first human dwelling. When I was a boy sleeping beside the other apprentices in the Matachin Tower, I had often heard that cough from the Bear Tower and had not been frightened. It is the presence or absence of walls that makes the difference, I think. I had known then that walls enclosed me, and that others imprisoned the smilodons and atroxes. I knew now that there were none, and I gathered stones by starlight, stacking them, as I told myself, for missiles—but in fact (as I now believe) to build a wall.

How strange it was! When I had swum and walked far beneath the flood, I had fancied myself a godling, or at least something more than a man; now I felt myself something less. Yet it seems to me upon reflection to be not so strange after all. In this place I was, perhaps, at a time far earlier than that at which Zak had done whatever he had done aboard the ship of Tzadkiel. Here the Old Sun had not yet dimmed, and even those influences that cast shadows behind them as long as mine when I walked to the ravine might fail to reach me.

Dawn came at last. The sun of the preceding day had left me reddened and tender; I stayed in the ravine, where there was at times a little shade, and made my way through the stream or beside it, finding the body of a peccary killed when it had come to drink. I tore a bit of meat away, chewed it, and washed it down with muddy water.

It was about nones when I came in sight of the first pump. The ravine was nearly seven ells deep, but the autochthons had built a series of little dams like the steps of a stair, piling up the river stones. A wheel hung with leathern buckets reached thirstily down for the water, turned by two squat, mummy-colored men who grunted with satisfaction each time a bucketful splashed into their clay trough.

They shouted to me in a tongue I did not know, but did

not try to stop me. I waved to them and walked on, wondering to see them watering their fields, for among the constellations of the previous night had been the crotali, the winter stars that bring the rattle of ice-sheathed branches.

I passed a score of similar wheels before I reached the town, where a stone stair led up from the water. Women came there to wash clothes and fill jugs, and remained to gossip. They stared at me; and I displayed my hands so they could see I was unarmed, though my nakedness must have made that clear enough without the gesture.

The women talked among themselves in some lilting language. I pointed to my mouth to show I was hungry, and a gaunt woman a trifle taller than the rest gave me a strip of old, coarse cloth to tie around my waist, women being much the same in every place.

Like the men I had seen, these women had small eyes, narrow mouths, and broad, flat cheeks. It was a month or more before I understood why these seemed so different from the autochthons I had seen at Saltus Fair, in the market of Thrax, and elsewhere, though it was only that these people had pride and were far less inclined to violence.

The ravine was wide at the stair and gave no shade. When I saw that none of the women meant to feed me, I climbed the steps and sat on the ground in the shadow of one of the stone houses. I am tempted to insert here all sorts of musings, things that I actually thought of later in my stay in the stone town; but the truth is that I thought then of nothing. I was very tired and very hungry, and in some pain. It was a relief to get out of the sun, and not to walk, and that was all.

Later the tall woman brought me a flat cake and a jar of water, setting them three cubits beyond my reach and hurrying off. I ate the cake and drank the water, and slept that night in the dust of the street.

Next morning I wandered about the town. Its houses were built of river stones laid with a mortar of mud. Their roofs were nearly flat, of meager logs covered with more mud mixed with straw, husks, and stalks. At one door, a woman gave me half a blackened meal cake. The men I saw ignored me. Later, when I had come to know the people better, I understood that this was because they had to be able to explain anything they saw; because they had no notion who I was or where I had come from, they pretended they had not seen me.

That evening I sat in the same place as before, but when the tall woman came again, putting my cake and jar a bit nearer this time, I picked them up and followed her back to her house, one of the oldest and smallest. She was afraid when I pushed aside the tattered matting that formed her door, but I sat in a corner while I ate and drank, and tried to show her by my looks that I meant no harm. That night it was warmer beside her tiny fire than it had been outside.

I set to work repairing the house by taking down parts of the walls that seemed ready to fall and restacking them. The woman watched me for a time before she went into the town. She did not return until late afternoon.

The next day I followed her and discovered she went to a larger house where she ground maize in a quern, washed clothes, and swept. By then I had mastered the names of a few simple objects, and I helped her whenever I understood her work.

The master of that house was a shaman. He served a god whose frightful image was set up just beyond the town to the east. After I had labored for his family for a few days, I learned that his principal act of worship had been completed each morning before I arrived. After that I rose earlier and carried the sticks to the altar where he burned meal and oil, and at the midsummer feast slit the throat of a coypu to the slap of dancing feet and the thudding of little drums. Thus I lived among these people, sharing as much of their lives as I could.

Wood was very precious. Trees would not grow on the pampa, and they could give up only the edges of their fields to them. The tall woman's fire, like all the rest, was of stalks, cobs, and husks, mixed with sun-dried dung. At times stalks appeared even in the fire the shaman kindled new each day when, singing and chanting, he caught the Old Sun's rays in his sacred bowl.

Though I had rebuilt the walls of the tall woman's house, there seemed little I could do about the roof. The poles were small and old, and several were badly cracked. For a time, I considered erecting a stone column to shore it up, but such a column would have left the house very cramped.

After some thought, I tore down the whole sagging structure and replaced it with intersecting arches like those I remembered from the shepherd's bothy where I had once left a shawl of the Pelerines, all of loose-laid river stones, all meeting over the center of the house. I used more stonés, pounded earth, and the poles from the roof for the scaffolding needed until each arch was whole, and strengthened the walls to bear the outward thrust with yet more stones I carried from the river. The woman and I had to sleep outside while the construction was in progress; but she did so without complaint, and when everything was complete and I had plastered the beehive roof with mud and matted grass as before, she had a new dwelling, high and sturdy.

When I started to work, tearing away the old roof, no one paid much attention to me; but when that was done and I began to lay up my arches, men came from the fields to watch, and some helped me. While I was dismantling the last scaffolding, the shaman himself appeared, bringing the hetman of the town.

For some time, they walked around and around the house; but when it became clear that the scaffolding was no longer holding up the roof, they carried torches inside. And at last, when all my work was finished, they made me sit down and questioned me about it, using many gestures because I still knew so little of their tongue.

I told them all I could, piling chips of flat stone to show how it was done. Then they asked me about myself: where I had come from and why I lived among them. It had been so long since I had been able to talk with anyone other than the woman that as much of my tale came stumbling forth

as I could give form to. I did not expect them to believe me;
it was enough that they—that someone—had been told.

At last, when I stepped outside to point toward the sun, I
found that evening had come while I had stammered and
scratched my crude pictures in the dirt floor. The tall
woman sat beside the door, her black hair whipped by a
fresh, cold wind from the pampas. The shaman and the
hetman came out too, carrying their guttering torches, and
I saw that she was very frightened.

I asked what the trouble was, but the shaman began a
long speech before she could reply, a speech of which I
grasped no more than every tenth word. When he had
finished, the hetman spoke in the same way. What they
said drew men from the houses around us, some with
hunting spears (for these were not warlike people), some
with adzes or knives. I turned back to the woman and
asked what was happening.

She whispered furiously in return, telling me the shaman
and the hetman had said that I had said I brought the day
and walked through the sky. Now we would have to remain
where we were till day came without my bringing it; when
that happened, we would die. She wept. Perhaps tears
rolled down her gaunt cheeks; if so, I could not see them by
the flickering light of the torches. It struck me that I had
never seen one of these people cry, not even little children.
Her dry, rattling sobs moved me more than any tears I
have ever seen.

We waited before her house for a long while. Fresh
torches arrived, and fuel and live embers carried from the
houses nearby gave us several small fires. Despite them, my
legs became stiff from the cold that seeped from the earth.

Our only hope appeared to lie in outlasting these people,
in drawing taut their nerves. But when I studied their faces,
faces that might have been so many wooden masks
smeared with ocher clay, I felt that they would outwear the
year, far less a short summer's night.

If only I could speak their tongue fluently, I thought, I
might be able to wake fear enough in them, or at least
explain what I had actually meant. The words—words not,

alas, in their tongue but in my own—reechoed through my mind, so that I fell to speculating about them. Did I myself know what those words meant? Those or any others? Surely not.

Desperate, and driven by the same unquenchable impulse to sterile self-expression that has led me to write and revise the history I sent to molder and drown in Master Ultan's library and soon after flung into the void, I began to gesticulate, to tell my story once again, as well as I could, this time without the use of words. My own arms cradled the infant I had been, thrashed helplessly in Gyoll until the undine saved me. No one moved to stop me, and after some time I stood up so that I might use my legs as well as my arms, walking pantomime down the empty, cluttered corridors of the House Absolute, and galloping for the destrier that had died beneath me at the Third Battle of Orithyia.

It seemed I heard music; and some later time I heard it indeed, for many of the men who had come when they heard the speeches of the hetman and the shaman were humming, beating a solemn cadence upon the ground with the butts of stone-tipped spears and antler-headed adzes; one played a nose flute. Its piping notes swarmed about me like bees.

In time I saw that some of the men were looking toward the sky and nudging one another. Thinking they detected the first gray radiance of dawn, I looked too; but I saw rising only the cross and the unicorn, the stars of summer. Then the shaman and the hetman prostrated themselves before me. At that instant, by the most marvelous good fortune, Urth looked upon the sun. My shadow fell across them.

CHAPTER L

Darkness in the House of Day

THE TALL WOMAN AND I MOVED INTO THE SHAMAN'S HOUSE and took the best room. I was no longer permitted to work. The injured and the ill were brought to me for healing; some I cured as I had cured Declan, or as we of the guild had been taught to prolong the lives of our clients. Others died in my arms. Perhaps I could have revivified the dead as well, as I had recalled poor Zama; I never attempted to do so.

Twice we were attacked by nomads. The hetman fell in the first battle, I rallied his warriors, and we turned the nomads back. A new hetman was chosen, but he seemed to regard himself—and to be regarded by his own people—as little more than my subordinate. In the second battle, it was I who led the war party while he took the nomads from the rear with a small force of picked bowmen. Together we herded and slaughtered them like sheep, and we were not molested again.

Soon the people began work on a new structure much larger than anything they had built before. Although its walls were very thick and its arches strong, I feared that they might not support so great a weight as a roof of mud and straw would impose; I taught the women to fire clay tiles just as they fired their pots, and to lay them to make a roof. When the building was completed, I recognized the roof upon which Jolenta would die, and I knew I would be buried beneath it.

Though you may think it incredible, before that time I

351

had seldom thought of the undine or the directions she had indicated to me, preferring to revisit in memory the Urth of the Old Sun, as it was in the days of my childhood or under my autarchy. Now I explored fresher memories, for much as I feared them, I found I feared death more.

When I had sat upon a spur of rock thrust from the slope of Mount Typhon and watched Typhon's soldiers coming for me, I had seen the meadow that is beyond Briah as clearly as I now saw our fields of maize. But then I had been the New Sun, with all the power of my star to draw upon, though it was so far away. Now I was the New Sun no more, and the Old Sun still had long to rule. Once or twice when I was nearly asleep, it seemed to me that the Corridors of Time slanted from some corner of our room. Always, when I tried to flee down any, I woke; and there was only stone, and the roof poles above.

Once I descended again to the ravine and retraced my steps to the east from which I had come. At last I stumbled over the pitiful little wall I had reared at the coughing of the cat, but though I went farther still, I returned to the stone town the day after I had left it.

At last, when I had lost all count of years, it came to me that if I could not rediscover the entrance to the Corridors of Time—and I could not—I must find Juturna; and that to find her I must first find the sea.

At dawn the next day, I wrapped some meal cakes and dried meat in a cloth and left the stone town, walking westward. My legs had grown stiff; and when after seven or eight watches of steady walking I fell and twisted my knee, I felt I had almost become again that Severian who had boarded the ship of Tzadkiel. Like him, I did not turn again, but continued as I had set my face. I had become used to the heat of the Old Sun long before, and it was the waning of the year.

The young hetman and a party of men from the stone town overtook me while Urth looked upon the Old Sun from her left. After a time, they seized my arms and tried

to force me to go back; I refused, telling them I was bound
for Ocean and hoped never to return.

I sat up, but I saw nothing. For a moment, I felt sure I
had gone blind.

Ossipago appeared, shining with blue radiance. He said,
"We are here, Severian."

Knowing him for a mechanism, the servant and yet the
master of Barbatus and Famulimus, I answered, "With
light—the god from the machine. That was what Master
Malrubius said when he came."

Barbatus's pleasant baritone flouted the gloom. "You're
conscious. What do you remember?"

"Everything," I said. "I've always remembered everything." Dissolution was in the air, the fetor of rotting flesh.

Famulimus sang, "For that were you chosen, Severian.
You and you alone from many princes. You alone to save
your race from lethe."

"And then to abandon it," I said.

No one answered.

"I have thought about that," I told them. "I would have
tried to return sooner, if I had known how."

Ossipago's voice was so deep that one felt rather than
heard it. "Do you understand why you could not?"

I nodded, feeling foolish. "Because I'd used the power of
the New Sun to retrace time until the New Sun itself no
longer existed. Once I believed you three were gods, and
then that the Hierarchs were still greater gods. So the
autochthons believed me a god, and feared I would plunge
into the western sea leaving them in night with winter
always. But only the Increate is God, kindling reality and
blowing it out. All the rest of us, even Tzadkiel, can only
wield the forces he's created." I have never been clever at
thinking of analogies, and now I groped for one. "I was like
an army retreating so far that it's cut off from its base." I
could not bite back the next words. "An army defeated."

"In war no force may fail, Severian, until its trumpets
blow 'Surrender.' Till then, though it may die, it does not
know defeat."

Barbatus remarked, "And who can say that this was not for the best? We're all tools in his hands."

I told him, "I understand something more—something I had not really understood until this moment: why Master Malrubius spoke to me of loyalty to the Divine Entity, of loyalty to the person of the monarch. He meant that we must trust, that we must not refuse our destinies. You sent him, of course."

"The words were his, just the same—by now you should know that, too. Like the Hierogrammates, we summon personalities of the past from remembrance; and like the Hierogrammates, we do not falsify them."

"But there are so many things I don't know. When we met on Tzadkiel's ship, you hadn't known me before, and from that I knew it to be our final meeting. Yet you are here, all three."

Sweetly Famulimus sang, "Thus surprised are we, Severian, to find you here where men have scarce begun. Though we have traced the time line down so far, whole ages of the world have passed since we've seen you."

"And yet you knew I would be here?"

Stepping from the shadows, Barbatus said, "Because you told us so. Have you forgotten we were your councilors? You told us how the man Hildegrin was destroyed, so we've watched this place for you."

"And I. I died too. The autochthons—my people—"

I broke off, but no one else spoke. And at last I said, "Ossipago, bring your light, please, to where Barbatus stood."

The mechanism turned his sensors toward Barbatus, but did not move.

Famulimus sang softly, "Barbatus, you must guide him now, I fear. But truly our Severian should know. How can we ask that he should bear all loads, while yet by us not treated as a man?"

Barbatus nodded, and Ossipago moved nearer the place where Barbatus had been standing when I woke. I saw there what I had feared to see, the corpse of the man the autochthons had called Head of Day. Golden bands wreathed his arms, bracelets studded with orange jacinths and flashing green emeralds.

"Tell me how you did this," I demanded.

Barbatus stroked his beard and did not reply.

"You know who schooled you by the restless sea, and fought for you when Urth lay in the scales," Famulimus crooned.

I stared at her. Her face was as lovely and as inhuman as ever—not without expression, but bearing an expression that had little or nothing to do with mankind and its concerns.

"Am I an eidolon? A ghost?" I looked at my hands, hoping to be reassured by their solidity. They were shaking; to quiet them I had to jam them against my thighs.

Barbatus said, "What you call eidolons are not ghosts, but beings maintained in existence by some external source of energy. What you call matter is all, in actuality, merely bound energy. The only difference is that some is held in material form by its own energy."

At that moment I wanted to cry more than I have ever wanted anything in my life. "Actuality? You think there's really any actuality?" The release of tears would have been nirvana; harsh training yet held, and no tears came. For an instant I wondered wildly whether eidolons could weep at all.

"You speak of what is real, Severian; thus do you hold to what is real still. A moment since we spoke of him who makes. Among your folk the simple call him God, and you, the lettered, name him Increate. What were you ever but his eidolon?"

"Who maintains me in existence now? Ossipago? You may rest, Ossipago."

Ossipago rumbled, "I don't respond to commands from you, Severian. You learned that long ago."

"I suppose that even if I were to kill myself, Ossipago could still call me back to existence."

Barbatus shook his head, though not as a human being would have. "There would be no point—you could take your life again. If you truly want to die, go ahead. There are funeral offerings here, including a great many stone knives. Ossipago will bring you one."

I felt as real as I ever have; and when I searched among my memories, I found Valeria there still, and Thecla and old Autarch, and the boy Severian (who had been Severian only). "No," I said. "We will live."

"I thought so." Barbatus smiled. "We've known you half our lives now, Severian, and you're a weed that grows best when stepped upon."

Ossipago seemed to clear his throat. "If you wish to speak more, I will take us to a better time. I have a link to the pile on our craft."

Famulimus shook her noble head, and Barbatus looked at me.

"I'd rather we conferred here," I told them. "Barbatus, when we were on the ship, I fell down a shaft. One doesn't fall swiftly there, I know; but I fell a long way, I think nearly to the center. I was badly hurt, and Tzadkiel cared for me." I paused, trying to remember all the details I could.

"Proceed," Barbatus urged me. "We don't know what you're going to tell us."

"I found a dead man there, with a scarred cheek like mine. His leg had been injured years before, just like mine. He was hidden between two machines."

"Yet meant for you to find, Severian?" Famulimus asked.

"Perhaps. I knew Zak had done it. And Zak was Tzadkiel, or part of Tzadkiel; but I didn't understand that then."

"Yet you do now. It is the time for speech."

I did not know what else to say and finished weakly, "The dead man's face was bruised, but it looked very much like mine. I told myself that I couldn't have died there, that I wouldn't die there, because I felt sure I'd be laid in the mausoleum in our necropolis. I've told you about that."

Ossipago rumbled, "Many times."

"The funeral bronze is so like me, so much like the way I look now. Then there was Apu-Punchau. When he appeared . . . the Cumaean, she was a Hierodule, like you. Father Inire told me."

Famulimus and Barbatus nodded.

"When Apu-Punchau appeared, he was me. I knew it, but I didn't understand."

"Neither did we," Barbatus said, "when you told us about it. I think I may now."

"Then tell me!"

He gestured toward the corpse. "There is Apu-Punchau."

"Of course, I knew that long ago. They called me by that name, and I saw this place built. It was to be a temple, the Temple of Day, the Old Sun. But I'm Severian, and Apu-Punchau the Head of Day, too. How could my body rise from death? How could I die here at all? The Cumaean said it wasn't his tomb, but his house." I seemed to see her before me as I spoke, the old woman hiding the wise snake.

"She told you too that she knew not that age," Famulimus sang.

I nodded.

"How could the warm sun die that rose each day? And how could you then die, that were that sun? Your people left you here with many a chant. And sealed your door, that you might live forever."

Barbatus said, "We know that eventually you'll bring the New Sun, Severian. We've passed through the time, as through many others, to that meeting with you in the giant's castle—which we thought would be our last. But do you know when the New Sun was made? The sun you brought to this system to heal its old one?"

"When I was landed on Urth it was the age of Typhon, when the first great mountain was carved. But before that I was on Tzadkiel's ship."

"Which sometimes sails more swiftly than the winds that drive it," Barbatus grunted. "So you know nothing."

Famulimus sang, "If you would have our counsel now,

tell all. We cannot be good guides if we walk blind."

And so, beginning with the murder of my steward, I recounted everything that had happened to me from that time until the last moment I could recall before I woke in the House of Apu-Punchau. I have never been apt in winnowing needed details from the rest (as you, the reader of this, know too well), in part because it seems to me that all details are needed. Still less so was I then, when I could labor with my tongue and not my pen; I told them a great many things that I have not put into this record.

While I spoke, a sunbeam found its way through some chink; so I knew that I had returned to life in the night, and that a new day had begun.

And I was talking still when the potters' wheels began their whir, and we heard the chatter of women trooping to the river that would fail their town when the sun cooled.

At last I said, "So much for me, and now for you. Can you unravel the mystery of Apu-Punchau for me now that you've heard all this?"

Barbatus nodded. "I believe we can. You know already that when a ship sails swiftly between the stars, minutes and days on board may be years or centuries on Urth."

"It must be so," I admitted, "when time was first measured by the coming and going of the light."

"Therefore your star, the White Fountain, was born some while, and doubtless a long while, before the reign of Typhon. I'd guess that the time is not far distant now."

Famulimus appeared to smile, and perhaps it was in fact a smile. "Indeed it must be so, Barbatus, when by the star's own power he came here. Flying his time, he runs till he must halt; then halts he here because he cannot run."

If Barbatus was discomposed by this interruption, nothing indicated it. "It may be that your power will return when the light of your star is first seen on Urth. If that is so, when that time comes Apu-Punchau may waken, provided he chooses to leave the place where he has found himself."

"Wake to death in life?" I asked. "How horrible!"

Famulimus disagreed. "Say wonderful, Severian, instead. To life from death to aid the folk that loved him."

I considered that for a time while all three stood waiting patiently. At last I said, "Perhaps death is only horrible to us because it's a dividing of the terror of life from the wonder of it. We see only the terror, which is left behind."

Ossipago rumbled, "So we hope, Severian, as much as you."

"But if Apu-Punchau is myself, what was the body I found on Tzadkiel's ship?"

Nearly whispering, Famulimus sang, "The man whom you saw dead your mother bore. Or so it seems to me from what's been said. Now I would weep for her if I had tears, though not—perhaps—for you still living here. What we did here for you, Severian, the mighty Tzadkiel accomplished there, remembrance taking from your dead mind to build your mind and you anew."

"Do you mean that when I stood before Tzadkiel's Seat of Justice, I was an eidolon Tzadkiel himself had made?"

Ossipago muttered, "*Made's* too strong a term, if I have as much access to your tongue as I like to think. *Made tangible*, possibly."

I looked from him to Famulimus for enlightenment.

"You were reflected thought in your dead mind. He fixed the image, make it whole, mended the fatal wound you'd borne."

"Made me a walking, speaking picture of myself." Although I pronounced the words, I could scarcely bring myself to think about what they meant. "The fall killed me, just as my people killed me here."

I bent to look at the corpse of Apu-Punchau more closely. Barbatus muttered, "Strangled, I believe."

"Why couldn't Tzadkiel have called me back as I called back Zama? Healed me as I healed Herena? Why did I have to die?"

I have never been more startled than I was by what happened next: Famulimus knelt and kissed the floor before me.

Barbatus said, "What makes you think Tzadkiel wields

such power? Famulimus and Ossipago and I are nothing
before him, but we're not *his* slaves; and great though he is,
he's not the head of his race and its savior."

No doubt I should have felt ennobled. The fact is that I
was merely stunned and excruciatingly embarrassed. I
motioned urgently to Famulimus to rise again and blurted,
"But you walk the Corridors of Time!"

Barbatus prostrated himself in turn as Famulimus rose.

She sang, "For but a little way, Severian—that we may
speak with you, do common things. Our clocks run widder-
shins round both your suns."

From his knees Barbatus said, "If we'd let Ossipago take
us to a better place, as he wished, it would have been an
earlier one. That would not have been a better place for
you, I think."

"One further question, illustrious Hierodules, before
you return me to my own period. When I spoke with
Master Malrubius beside the sea, he dissolved into a
glittering dust. And yet—" I could not say it, but my eyes
sought out the corpse.

Barbatus nodded. "That eidolon, as you call them, had
been in existence only briefly. I don't know what energies
Tzadkiel called upon to support you on the ship; it may
even be that you yourself drew the support you needed
from whatever source was at hand, just as you took power
from the ship when you tried to raise your steward. But
even if it was a source you left behind when you came here,
you had lived a long time before that, on the ship, in Yesod,
on the ship again, in the tender, in Typhon's time, and so
on. During all that time you breathed, ate, and drank
matter that was not unstable, converting it to your body's
use. Thus it became a substantial body."

"But I'm dead—not even here, dead back there on
Tzadkiel's ship."

"Your twin lies dead there," Barbatus told me. "As
another lies dead here. I might say in passing that if he
weren't dead, we couldn't have done what we did, because
every living being is more than mere matter." He paused

and glanced toward Famulimus for help, but received none. "What do you know of the anima?"

I thought then of Ava, and what she had said to me: *"You're a materialist, like all ignorant people. But your materialism doesn't make materialism true."* Little Ava had died with Foila and the rest. "Nothing," I muttered. "I know nothing of the anima."

"In a way, it's like a line of verse. Famulimus, what was the one you quoted to me?"

His wife sang, "Awake! for Morning in the Bowl of Night, Has flung the Stone that puts the Stars to Flight."

"Yes," I said. "I understand."

Barbatus pointed. "Suppose I were to write those lines upon that wall—and then to write them again upon that other wall. Which would be the true lines?"

"Both," I said. "And neither. The true lines are not writing, nor speech either. I can't say what they are."

"That is the way of the anima, as I understand it. It was written there." He indicated the dead man. "Now it is written in you. When the light of the White Fountain touches Urth, it will be written there again. Yet the anima will not be erased in you by that writing. Unless—"

I waited for him to continue.

Ossipago said, "Unless you come too close. If you write a name in the dust and retrace it with your finger, there are not two names, but one. If two currents flow through a conductor, there is one current."

While I stared in disbelief, Famulimus sang, "You came too near your double once, you know; that was here, in this poor town of stones. Then he was gone, and only you remained. Our eidolons are always of the dead. Have you not wondered why? Be warned!"

Barbatus nodded. "But as for our returning you to your own time, we can't help you. Your green man knew more than we, perhaps; or at least he had more energy at his disposal. We'll leave you food, water, and a light; but you'll have to wait for the White Fountain. It shouldn't be long, as Famulimus said."

She had begun to fade into the past already, so that her song seemed to come from far away. "Do not destroy the corpse, Severian. However tempted you may be—be warned!"

Barbatus and Ossipago had faded while I watched Famulimus. When her voice was gone, there was no sound in the House of Apu-Punchau but his own faint breath.

CHAPTER LI

The Urth of the New Sun

FOR ALL THAT REMAINED OF THAT DAY I SAT IN THE DARK and cursed myself for a fool. The White Fountain would shine in the night sky, I knew, and everything the Hierodules had said implied it; yet I had failed to understand it until they had gone.

A hundred times I relived the rain-swept night when I had descended from the roof of this very structure to aid Hildegrin. How near had I come to Apu-Punchau before I had merged with him? Five cubits? Three ells? I could not be sure. But surely it was no mystery that Famulimus had told me not to try to destroy him; if I were to come near enough to strike, we would merge—and he, having deeper roots in this universe, would overwhelm me just as I would overwhelm him in the unimaginably distant future when I would journey to this place with Jolenta and Dorcas.

Yet if I had longed for the mysterious (as I certainly did not), there was riddle enough. The White Fountain shone already, that seemed certain, for without it I would not have been able to come to this ancient place or heal the sick. Why, then, had I been unable to travel the Corridors of Time as I had from Mount Typhon? Two explanations seemed likely.

The first was simply that on Mount Typhon my whole being had been spurred by fear. We are strongest in a crisis, and Typhon's soldiers had been coming for me, doubtless to kill me. Yet I faced another crisis now, for Apu-Punchau might rise and come toward me at any moment.

363

The second was that such power as I had received from the White Fountain was diminished by distance just as its light was. It must have been far nearer Urth in Typhon's time than in Apu-Paunchau's; but if it were indeed thus diminished, the passing of one day would scarcely make a difference, and a day at most was the longest for which I could hope, with my other self alive again and so near. I would have to escape as soon as I could, and wait elsewhere.

It was the longest day of my life. If I had been merely awaiting nightfall, I could have wandered in memory, recalling that marvelous evening when I had walked up the Water Way, the tales told in the Pelerines' lazaretto, or the brief holiday that Valeria and I had once enjoyed beside the sea. As it was, I dared not; and whenever I relaxed my guard, I found my mind turned of its own accord to dreadful things. Again I endured my imprisonment in the jungle ziggurat by Vodalus, the year I had spent among the Ascians, my flight from the white wolves in the Secret House, and a thousand similiar terrors, until at last it seemed to me that a demon desired that I surrender my miserable existence to Apu-Punchau, and that the demon was myself.

Slowly the noises of the stone town died away. The light, which earlier had come from the wall nearest me, now penetrated the wall beyond the altar on which Apu-Punchau lay, cutting the gloom with blades of hammered gold thrust between the crevices.

At last it faded. I rose, stiff in every joint, and began to probe the wall for weaknesses.

It had been built of cyclopean stones, with smaller stones driven between them by workmen swinging huge wooden mauls. The small stones were wedged so tightly that I tested fifty or more before finding one that could be pried loose; and I knew that I would have to remove one of the great stones to make an opening through which I could pass.

Even the small stone required a watch at least of tugging

and prying. I used a jasper-bladed knife to scrape away the mud around it, then broke that knife and three others trying to get it out. Once I abandoned the task in disgust and mounted the wall like a spider, hoping that the roof would supply an easier road to freedom, as the thatch had in the hall of the magicians. But the vaulted ceiling was as solid as the walls, and I dropped to the floor again to bloody my fingers on the loose stone.

Suddenly, when it seemed certain it could never be freed, it slipped clattering to the floor. For five long breaths I waited paralyzed, fearing that Apu-Punchau would wake. As far as I could judge, he never stirred.

Yet something else was stirring. The immense stone above tilted ever so gently to the left. Dried mud cracked, sounding as loud as the breaking of river ice in the stillness, and came rattling down around me.

I stepped back. There was a grinding, as of a mill, and a second shower of mud. I moved to one side and the great stone fell with a crash, leaving behind it a rough black circle full of stars.

I looked at one and knew myself, a pinprick of light nearly lost in the opaline haze of ten thousand more.

No doubt I should have waited—certainly it was possible that a dozen more great stones might follow the first. I did not. A leap carried me onto the fallen one, another into the aperture in the wall, and a third into the street. The noise had wakened the people, of course; I heard their angry voices, saw the faint red glow of their fires seep past their doors as wives puffed dying embers while husbands groped for spears and toothed warclubs.

I did not care. All about me stretched the Corridors of Time, waving meadows roofed with the lowering sky of Time and whisperous with the brooks that ripple from the most supernal universe of all to the least.

Bright-winged, the small Tzadkiel fluttered beside one. The green man raced beside another. I chose one that ran as lonely as I, and mounted to it. Behind me along a line that seldom exists, Apu-Punchau, the Head of Day, stepped from his house and squatted to eat the boiled maize and roast meat his people had left for him. I too hungered; I waved to him, then saw him no more.

When I returned to the world called Ushas, it was onto a sandy beach—the beach I had left when I dove into the sea in search of Juturna, and as near that place and time as I could make it.

A man carrying a wooden trencher heaped with smoking fish was walking the sea-wet sand fifty cubits or so in front of me. I followed him, and when we had gone twenty paces he reached a bower, dripping with sea spray yet draped in wildflowers. Here he set his trencher upon the sand, took two backward steps, and knelt.

Catching up, I asked in the speech of the Commonwealth who would eat his fish.

He looked around at me; I could see he was surprised to find me a stranger. "The Sleeper," he said. "He who sleeps here and hungers."

"Who is this Sleeper?" I asked.

"The lonely god. One feels him here, always sleeping, ever hungry. I bring the fish to show that we are his friends, so he will not devour us when he wakes."

"Do you feel him now?" I asked.

He shook his head. "Sometimes it is stronger—so strong we see him by moonlight lying here, though he vanishes when we come near. Today I did not feel him at all."

"Did not?"

"I do now," he said. "Since you have come."

I sat down on the sand and picked up a large piece of fish, motioning for him to join me. The fish was so hot it burned my fingers, so I knew it had been cooked close by. He sat too, but did not eat until I made a second gesture.

"Are you always the one?"

He nodded. "Each god has someone, a man for a man-god, a woman for a woman-god."

"A priest or a priestess."

He nodded again.

"There is no God but the Increate, all the rest being his

creatures." I was tempted to add, "Even Tzadkiel," but I did not.

"Yes," he said. And he turned his face away, not wishing, I think, to see my look if he offended me. "That is so for the gods, certainly. But for humble creatures like men, there are lesser gods, possibly. To poor, wretched men these lesser gods are very, very exalted. We strive to please them."

I smiled to show I was not angry. "And what do such lesser gods do to help men?"

"Four gods there are."

From his singsong, I knew he had recited the words many times, no doubt in the teaching of children.

"First and greatest is the Sleeper. He is a man-god. He is always hungry. Once he devoured the whole land, and he may do so again if he is not fed. Though the Sleeper has drowned, he cannot die—thus he sleeps here on the strand. Fish belong to the Sleeper—you must beg his leave before you fish. Silver fish I catch for him. Storms are his anger, calm his charity."

I had become the Oannes of these people!

"The other man-god is Odilo. His are the lands beneath the sea. He loves learning and right conduct. Odilo taught men to speak and women to write. He is the judge of gods and men, but punishes no one who has not sinned thrice. Once he bore the cup of the Increate. Red wine is his. Wine his man brings him."

It had taken a breath for me to recall just whom Odilo had been. Now I realized that the House Absolute and our court had become the frame for a vague picture of the Increate as Autarch. In retrospect, it seemed inevitable.

"There are two women-gods also. Pega is the day goddess. All beneath the sun is hers. Pega loves cleanness. She taught women to strike fire and to bake and weave. She mourns them in childbirth and comes to all at the moment of death. She is the comforter. Brown bread is the offering her woman brings her."

I nodded approvingly.

"Thais is the night goddess. All below the moon is hers.

She loves the words of lovers and lovers' embraces. All who couple must beg her leave, speaking the words as one in the darkness. If they do not, Thais kindles a flame in a third heart and finds a knife for the hand. Aflame, she comes to children, announcing that they are to be children no longer. She is the seducer. Golden honey is the offering her woman brings her."

I said, "It seems you have two good gods and two evil gods, and that the evil gods are Thais and the Sleeper."

"Oh, no! All gods are very good, particularly the Sleeper! Without the Sleeper, so many would starve. The Sleeper is very, very great! And when Thais does not come, her place is taken by a demon."

"So you have demons too."

"Everyone has demons."

"I suppose," I said.

The trencher was nearly bare, and I had eaten my fill. The priest—my priest, I should write—had taken only a single small piece. I rose, picked up what was left, and tossed it into the sea, not knowing what else to do with it. "For Juturna," I told him. "Do your people know Juturna?"

He had jumped to his feet as soon as I stood up. "No—" He hesitated, and I could see that he had almost spoken the name he had given me, but that he was afraid to do so.

"Then perhaps she is a demon to you. For most of my life I thought her a demon too; it may be that neither you nor I have made a great mistake."

He bowed, and although he was a bit taller and by no means plump, I saw Odilo in that bow as clearly as if the man himself stood before me.

"Now you must take me to Odilo," I said. "To the other man-god."

We walked the beach together in the direction from which he had come. The hills, which had been barren mud when I had left, were covered with soft, green grass. Wildflowers bloomed there, and there were young trees.

I tried to estimate the time I had been gone, and to count the years I had lived among the autochthons in their stone town; and though I could not be sure of either figure, it seemed to me they must have been much the same. I marveled then to think of the green man, and how he had come for me in the jungles of the north at the very moment I required him. We both had walked the Corridors of Time, yet he had been a master while I was only an apprentice.

I asked my priest when it had been that the Sleeper had devoured the lands.

He was deeply tanned; even so, I saw the blood drain from his face. "Long ago," he said. "Before men came to Ushas."

"Then how do men know of it?"

"The god Odilo taught us. Are you angry?"

Odilo had overheard my conversation with Eata, then. I had supposed him sleeping. "No," I said. "I only wish to hear what you know of it. Was it you who came to Ushas?"

He shook his head. "My father's father and my mother's mother. They fell from the sky, scattered like seeds by the hand of the God of all gods."

I said, "Not knowing fire or anything else," and as I spoke I recalled what the young officer had reported: that Hierodules had landed a man and woman on the grounds of the House Absolute. Remembering that, it was simple enough to guess who my priest's forebears had been—the sailors routed by my memories had paid for their defeat with their pasts, just as I would have lost the future of my descendants had my own past been defeated.

It was not much farther to the village. A few unreliable-looking boats were beached there, unpainted boats built largely of gray driftwood, or so it seemed to me. On the shore, an ell or more above the high-tide mark, stood a square of huts formed by four perfectly straight lines. The square was Odilo's doing, I felt sure; it exhibited the love of order for order's sake so characteristic of an upper servant. Then I reflected that the ramshackle boats had probably been inspired by him as well; it was he, after all, who had built our raft.

Two women and a gaggle of children emerged from the

square to watch us pass, and a man with a mallet stopped pounding dry grass into the seams of a boat to join them; my priest, walking half a step behind me, nodded toward me and made a gesture too swift for me to catch. The villagers fell to their knees.

Inspired by the sense of theater I have often been forced to cultivate, I raised my arms, spread my hands, and gave them my blessing, telling them to be kind to one another and as happy as they could. That is really all the blessing we godlings can ever give, though no doubt the Increate can do much more.

Ten strides put the village behind us, though not so far behind that I could not hear the boatwright begin his pounding again, or the children resume their play and their weeping. I asked how much farther it was to wherever Odilo lived.

"Not far," my priest said, and pointed.

We were walking inland now, climbing a grassy little hill. From the crest we could see the crest of the next, and upon it three bowers side by side, decked as my own had been with twined lupine, purple loosestrife, and white meadow rue.

"There," my priest told me. "There the other gods sleep."

Appendix

The Miracle of Apu-Punchau

NO SORT OF WONDER IS MORE CONVINCING TO THE PRIMI-
tive mind than one affecting the presumably immutable
workings of the heavens. Severian's prolongation of the
night, however, may leave less credulous minds puzzling
over the ways in which such a marvel might be achieved
without a cataclysm greater than that which accompanied
the arrival of the New Sun.

At least two plausible explanations could be put forward.
Mass hypnosis is invoked by historians to explain all
multiply attested wonders that cannot be degraded in any
other fashion; but it is something no actual hypnotist offers
to produce.

If mass hypnosis is discarded, the only alternative appears to be an eclipse in the broadest sense—that is, the
passage of some opaque body between the Old Sun and
Urth.

In this context, it should be noted that the stars seen in
the skies of the Commonwealth in winter rise in spring
over the stone town (presumably due to the precession of
the equinoxes); but that during his prolongation of the
night Severian sees his accustomed spring stars. This
would seem to favor the second explanation, as does the
immediate manifestion of the Old Sun, already higher
than the rooftops, after the capitulation of the autochthons. Nothing Severian writes indicates what the opaque
body may have been; but the thoughtful reader will find

little difficulty in advancing at least one plausible speculation.

—G.W.